Praise for Chuck Palahniuk

"Palahniuk doesn't write for tourists. He writes for hard-core devotees drawn to the wild, angry imagination on display and the taboo-busting humor."
—*The New York Times*

"One of the darkest and most singular minds in contemporary American lit."
—*Kirkus Reviews*

"Palahniuk displays a Swiftian gift for satire, as well as a knack for crafting mesmerizing sentences."
—*The San Francisco Examiner*

"Few authors have captured the pathologies of modern life quite like Palahniuk."
—*Rocky Mountain News*

"Chuck Palahniuk is one of the most intriguing writers of our time."
—*Tucson Citizen*

Chuck Palahniuk

Make Something Up

Chuck Palahniuk is the author of fourteen novels—
*Beautiful You, Doomed, Damned, Tell-All, Pygmy, Snuff,
Rant, Haunted, Diary, Lullaby, Choke, Invisible Monsters, Survivor,* and *Fight Club*—which altogether have
sold more than five million copies in the United States.
He is also the author of *Fugitives and Refugees,* published
as part of the Crown Journey Series, and the nonfiction
collection *Stranger Than Fiction.* He lives in the Pacific
Northwest.

chuckpalahniuk.net

Also by Chuck Palahniuk

Fight Club
Survivor
Invisible Monsters
Choke
Lullaby
Fugitives and Refugees
Diary
Stranger Than Fiction
Haunted
Rant
Snuff
Pygmy
Tell-All
Damned
Doomed
Beautiful You

Make Something Up

Chuck

Palahniuk

Make Something Up

STORIES YOU CAN'T UNREAD

ANCHOR BOOKS
A Division of Penguin Random House LLC
New York

FIRST ANCHOR BOOKS EDITION, APRIL 2016

Copyright © 2015 by Chuck Palahniuk

All rights reserved. Published in the United States by Anchor Books,
a division of Penguin Random House LLC, New York. Originally published in
hardcover in the United States by Doubleday, a division of
Penguin Random House LLC, New York, in 2015.

Anchor Books and colophon are registered trademarks of
Penguin Random House LLC.

The Library of Congress has cataloged the Doubleday edition as follows:
Palahniuk, Chuck.
[Short stories. Selections]
Make something up : stories you can't unread /
by Chuck Palahniuk. — First edition.
pages ; cm
I. Title.
PS3566.A4554A6 2015   813'.54—dc23   2014039591

Anchor Books Trade Paperback ISBN: 978-0-345-80712-0
eBook ISBN: 978-0-385-53806-0

Book design by Michael Collica

www.anchorbooks.com

Printed in the United States of America
20 19 18 17 16 15 14 13 12 11

Contents

Make Something Up

KNOCK-KNOCK

My old man, he makes everything into a Big Joke. What can I say? The old man loves to get a laugh. Growing up, half the time I didn't have a clue what his jokes were about, but I laughed anyways. Down at the barbershop, it didn't matter how many guys my father let take cuts ahead of him in line, he just wanted to sit there all Saturday and crack people up. Make folks bust a gut. Getting his hair cut was definitely a low priority.

He says, "Stop me if you've heard this one before . . ." The way my old man tells it, he walks into the oncologist's office and he says, "After the chemotherapy, will I be able to play the violin?"

In response, the oncologist says, "It's metastasized. You've got six months to live . . ."

And working his eyebrows like Groucho Marx, tapping the ash from an invisible cigar, my old man says, "Six months?" He says, "I want a second opinion."

So the oncologist, he says, "Okay, you've got cancer *and* your jokes stink."

So they do chemotherapy, and they give him some radiation like they do even if the shit burns him up so bad on the inside he tells me that taking a piss is like passing razor blades. He's

1

still every Saturday down by the barbershop telling jokes even if now he's bald as a cue ball. I mean, he's skinny as a bald skeleton, and he's getting to haul around one of those cylinders of oxygen under pressure, like some little version of a ball-and-chain. He walks into the barbershop dragging that pressurized cylinder of oxygen with the tube of it going up and looping around his nose, over his ears, and around his bald head, and he says, "Just a little off the top, please." And folks laugh. Understand me: My old man is no Uncle Milty. He's no Edgar Bergen. The man's skinny as a Halloween skeleton and bald and going to be dead by six weeks so it don't matter what he says, folks are going to hee-haw like donkeys just out of their genuine affection for him.

But, seriously, I'm not doing him justice. It's my fault if this doesn't come across, but my old man is funnier than he sounds. Maybe his sense of humor is a talent I didn't inherit. Back when I was his little Charlie McCarthy, the whole time I was growing up, he used to ask me, "Knock-knock?"

I'd say, "Who's there?"

He'd say, "Old Lady . . ."

I'd say, "Old Lady, who?"

And he'd say, "Wow, I didn't know you could yodel!"

Me, I didn't get it. I was so stupid, I was seven years old and still stuck in the first grade. I didn't know Switzerland from Shinola, but I want for my old man to love me so I learned to laugh. Whatever he says, I laugh. By "Old Lady" my guess is he means my mom who ran away and left us. All's my old man will say about her is how she was a "Real Looker" who just couldn't take a joke. She just was NOT a Good Sport.

He used to ask me, "When that Vinnie van Gogh cut off his ear and sent it to the whore he was so crazy about, how'd he send it?"

The punch line is "He sent it by 'ear mail,'" but being seven years old, I was still stuck back on not knowing who van Gogh is or what's a whore, and nothing kills a joke faster than asking my old man to explain himself. So when my old man says, "What do you get when you cross a pig with Count Dracula?" . . . I knew to never ask, "What's a 'Count Dracula'?" I'd just get a big laugh ready for when he tells me, "A 'Ham-pire'!"

And when he says, "Knock-knock . . ."

And I say, "Who's there?" And he says, "Radio."

And I say, "Radio who?" And he's ALREADY started to bust a gut when he says, "Radio not I'm going to cum in your mouth . . ." Then—what the hell—I just keep laughing. My whole growing up I figure I'm just too ignorant to appreciate a good joke. Me, my teachers still haven't covered long division and all the multiple-cation tables so it's not my old man's fault I don't know what's "cum."

My old lady, who abandoned us, he says she hated that joke so maybe I inherited her lack of humor. But love . . . I mean you have to love your old man. I mean, after you're born it's not like you get a choice. Nobody wants to see their old man breathing out of some tank and going into the hospital to die sky-high on morphine and he's not eating a bite of the red-flavored Jell-O they serve for dinner.

Stop me if I already told you this one: but my old man gets that prostrate cancer that's not even like cancer because it takes twenty, thirty years before we even know he's so sick, and the next thing I know is I'm trying to remember all the stuff he's taught me. Like, if you spray some WD-40 on the shovel blade before you dig a hole the digging will go a lot easier. And he taught me how to squeeze a trigger instead of pulling it and wrecking my aim. He taught me to remove bloodstains. And he taught me jokes . . . lots of jokes.

And, sure, he's no Robin Williams, but I watched this movie

3

one time about Robin Williams who gets dressed up with a red rubber ball on his nose and this big rainbow-colored afro wig and those big clown shoes with a fake carnation stuck in his buttonhole of his shirt that squirts water, and the guy's a hotshot doctor who makes these little kids with cancer laugh so hard they stop dying. Understand me: These bald kid skeletons—who look worse off than my old man—they get HEALTHY, and that whole movie is based on a True Story.

What I mean is, we all know that Laughter is the Best Medicine. All that time being stuck in the hospital Waiting Room, even I read the *Reader's Digest*. And we've all heard the true story about the guy with a brain cancer the size of a grapefruit inside his skull and he's about to croak—all the doctors and priests and experts say he's a goner—only he forces himself to watch nonstop movies about the Three Stooges. This Stage Four cancer guy forces himself to laugh nonstop at Abbott and Costello and Laurel and Hardy and those Marx brothers, and he gets healed by the end-orphans and oxy-generated blood.

So I figure, what've I got to lose? All I need to do is remember some of my old man's favorite gags and get him started back laughing on the road to recovery. I figure, what could it hurt?

So this grown-up son walks into his father's hospice room, pulls up a chair beside the bed, and sits down. The son looks into his old man's pale, dying face and says: "So this blond gal walks into a neighborhood bar where she's never been before, and she's got tits out to HERE and a tight little heinie and she asks the bartender for a Michelob, and he serves her a Michelob, except he sneaks a Mickey Finn into her bottle and this blonde goes unconscious, and every guy in the bar leans her over the edge of the pool table and hikes up her skirt and fucks her, and at closing time they slap her awake and tell her she's got to leave. And every few days this gal with the tits and the ass walks in and

4

asks for a Michelob and gets a Mickey Finn and gets fucked by the crowd until one day she walks in and asks the bartender, can he maybe give her a Budweiser instead?"

Granted—I have NOT landed this particular shaggy-dog story since I was in the first grade, but my old man used to love this next part . . .

The bartender smiles *so nice* and says, "What? You don't like Michelob no more?"

And this Real Looker, she leans over the bar, all confidential and she whispers, "Just between you and me . . ." she whispers, "Michelob makes my pussy hurt . . ."

The first time I learned that joke, when my old man taught it to me, I didn't know what was "pussy." I didn't know "Mickey Finn." I didn't know what folks meant when they talked about "fucking," but I knew all this talk made my old man laugh. And when he told me to stand up and tell that joke in the barbershop it made the barbers and every old man reading detective magazines laugh until half of them blew spit and snot and chewing tobacco out their noses.

Now the grown-up son tells his old dying father this joke, just the two of them alone in that hospital room, late-late at night, and—guess what—his old man doesn't laugh. So the son tries another old favorite, he tells the joke about the Traveling Salesman who gets a phone call from some Farmer's Daughter he met on the road a couple months before, and she says, "Remember me? We had some laughs, and I was a good sport?" and the man says, "How're you doing?" and she says, "I'm pregnant, and I'm going to kill myself." And the salesman, he says, "Damn . . . you ARE a good sport!"

At seven years old I could REALLY put that joke over—but, tonight the old man's still not laughing. How I learned to say "I Love You" was by laughing for my old man—even if I had to fake

5

it—and that's all I want in return. All I want from him is a laugh, just one laugh, and he's not coming across with even a giggle. Not a snicker. Not even a groan. And worse than not-laughing, the old man squints his eyes shut, tight, and opens them brimming with tears, and one fat tear floods out the bottom of each eye and washes down each cheek. The old man's gasping his big toothless mouth like he can't get enough air, crying big tears down the wrinkles of both cheeks, just soaking his pillow. So this kid—who's nobody's little kid, not anymore—but who can't seem to forget these jokes, he reaches into his pants pocket and gets out a fake carnation flower that just-for-laughs sprays water all over the old crybaby's face.

The kid tells about the Polack who's carrying a rifle through the woods when he comes across a naked gal laying back on a bed of soft green moss with her legs spread, and this gal is a Real Looker, and she looks at the Polack and his gun and says, "What're you doing?" And the Polack says, "I'm hunting for game." And this Real Looker, she gives him a big wink and she says, "I'm game."

So—POW!—the Polack shoots her. It used to be this joke constituted a gold-plated, bona fide, sure-thing laugh riot, but the old man just keeps dying. He's still crying and not even making an effort to laugh, and no matter what, the old man has got to meet me halfway. I can't save him if he doesn't want to live. I ask him, "What do you get when you cross a faggot with a kike?" I ask him, "What's the difference between dog shit and a nigger?"

And he's still not getting any better. I'm thinking maybe the cancer's got into his ears. With the morphine and what all, it could be he can't hear me. So just to test, can he hear me, I lean into his crybaby face and I ask, "How do you get a nun pregnant?" Then, more loud, maybe too loud for this being a mackerel-snapper hospital, I yell, "You FUCK her!"

In my desperation I try fag jokes and wetback jokes and kike jokes—really, every effective course of treatment known to medical science—and the old man's still slipping away. Lying here, in this bed, is the man who made EVERYTHING into a Big Joke. Just the fact he's not biting scares the shit out of me. I'm yelling, "Knock-knock!" and when he says nothing in response it's the same as him not having a pulse. I'm yelling, "Knock-knock!"

I'm yelling, "Why did the Existentialist cross the road?"

And he's STILL dying, the old man's leaving me not knowing the answer to anything. He's abandoning me while I'm still so fucking stupid. In my desperation I reach out to take the limp, blue fingers of his cold-cold dying hand and he doesn't flinch even when I grind a Joy Buzzer against the blue skin of his ice-cold palm. I'm yelling, "Knock-knock?"

I'm yelling, "Why'd the Old Lady walk out on her husband and her four-year-old kid?"

Nothing kills a joke like asking my old man to explain himself, and lying there in that bed, he stops breathing. No heartbeat. Totally flatlined.

So this kid who's sitting bedside in this hospital room, late-late at night he takes the joke equivalent of those electric paddles doctors use to stop your heart attack, the hee-haw equivalent of what a paramedic Robin Williams would use on you in some Clown Emergency Room—a kind of Three Stooges defibrillator—the kid takes a big, creamy, heaped-up custard pie topped with a thick-thick layer of whipped cream, the same as Charlie Chaplin would save your life with, and the kid reaches that pie up sky-high overhead, as high as the kid can reach, and brings it down, hard, lightning-fast, slam-dunking it hard as the blast from a Polack's shotgun—POW!—right in his old man's kisser.

And despite the miraculous, well-documented healing pow-ers of the Comedic Arts my old man dies taking a big bloody shit in his bed.

No, really, it's funnier than it sounds. Please, don't blame my old man. If you're not laughing at this point, it's my fault. I just didn't tell it right, you know, you mess up a punch line and you can totally botch even the best joke. For example, I went back to the barbershop and told them how he died and how I tried to save him, right up to and including the custard pie and how the hospital had their security goons escort me up to the crazy ward for a little seventy-two-hour observation. And even telling that part, I fucked it up—because those barbershop guys just looked at me. I told them about seeing—and smelling—my old man, dead and smeared all over with blood and shit and whipped cream, all that stink and sugar, and they looked and looked at me, the barbers and the old guys chewing tobacco, and nobody laughed. Standing in that same barbershop all these years later, I say, "Knock-knock."

The barbers stop cutting hair. The old goobers stop chewing on their tobacco.

I say, "Knock-knock?" Nobody takes a breath, and it's like I'm standing in a room full of dead men. And I tell them, "Death! DEATH is there! Don't you people never read Emily . . . Dickerson? You never heard of Jean-Paul . . . Stuart?" I wiggle my eyebrows and tap the ash from my invisible cigar and say, "Who's there?" I say, "I don't know who's there—I can't even play the violin!"

What I do know is I've got a brain filled with jokes I can't ever forget—like a tumor the size of a grapefruit inside of my skull. And I know that eventually even dog shit turns white and stops stinking, but I have this permanent head filled with crap I've been trained my whole life to think is funny. And for the first time since I was a Little Stooge standing in that barbershop saying *fag* and *cunt* and *nigger* and saying *kike,* I figure out that I wasn't *telling* a joke—*I was* the joke. I mean, I finally *Get It.* Understand me: A bona fide gold-plated joke is like a Michelob served ice-cold . . . with a Mickey Finn . . . by somebody smiling *so nice* you won't never know how bad you've been fucked. And a punch line is called a "punch line" for a VERY good reason, because punch lines are a sugarcoated fist with whipped cream hiding the brass knuckles that socks you right in the kisser, hitting you—POW!—right in your face and saying, *"I am smarter than you"* and *"I'm bigger than you"* and *"I call the shots, here, Buddy-BOY."*

And standing in that same old Saturday morning barbershop, I scream, "Knock-knock!"

I *demand,* "KNOCK-KNOCK!"

And finally one old barbershop codger, he says in barely a tobacco whisper, so soft you can hardly hear him, he asks, "Who's there?"

And I wait a beat, just for the tension—my old man, he taught me that timing is crucial, timing is EVERYTHING—until, finally, I smile *so nice* and I say, "Radio not . . ."

■

ELEANOR

Randy hate trees. He hate trees so passionate that when the Internet journalize about the wholesale defenestration of the Amazon rain jungle, Randy, he consider that to be a fine and noble term of events.

Mostly, pine trees. He hate the way a pine tree move: It move slow, then move fast. First so excoriating slow you forget it always be moving. That the method a tree get its tonnage of board feet up higher and higher until it be zeroed-in, right on top a person's head. After that, a pine tree move fast, like booby-trap fast. Too fast to perception.

Leastwise, Randy daddy never perception it coming. Postdating a lifetime of setting choke and pulling green chain, Randy daddy already be living on bothered time. One fast move, and all that raw lumber smatter the hairy dome of his thin skull to a billion bloody fractions.

Randy figure he got better things to do than set around, and maybe get landed on by a hundred tons of celluloid fiber. Randy hate Oregon.

Randy transpire to live someplace pink stucco where trees don't never enter into the picture. Randy, he pocket the life assurance money, and stow his pit bull in his car. He steer south, exacerbating faster and faster the whole way, like if a pack of vapid wolfhounds be perusing his Randy ass.

In California, the reality agent point her eyeballs at Randy ride: a Celica tricked out with twice the blue book worth in aftermarket chrome. And the regent, she take note of Randy pit bull. Such standard, confessional rebellions. The regent readily exhume Randy shave head, and his fresh-inked facial taboo be leaking blood still. The regent prop open her laptop and recede to source a pirate download. She tell Randy, "Dawg." She say, "Dawg, you go be so skinny on this crib."

The reality agent, she be name Gazelle.

And Gazelle laptop play a movie before Randy prolapsed eyeballs. It be explicit content burn from content burn from content burn from content burn from content, one thousand generation remove from anything paid good money for. The regent say, "Dawg." She say, "Dawg, this be entitle *Run and Hide Little White Girl, IV.*"

Said movie be starring Jennifer-Jason Morrell. She betray a blond sneak thief out to brutalize a fly crib where a dozen bro dawgs capitulate to respire. The bro dawgs be metastasizing in bed after a brash, all-nighter of Rémy Martin–fueled fecundity. The plot commence when Jennifer Jason, she allege to obfuscate the gold linkage off from around said dozing necks. It not until those big, hot-blooded bro dawgs wake up—understandably eviscerated—that said movie be hit it stride.

It be pink stucco on the outside, the house in the film. A swimming pool fill the backyard, with one edge where the carbonated waters appear to gently spill out into infamy. Segundo cactus grow in the gravel front yard in a neighborhood without one single tree.

On the walk-through, the reality agent, Gazelle, she point out the specialty features, including the two-story entryway failure with white-marble floorage. It be the location Jennifer-Jason pulled a train of hungry bro dawgs who procured to take turns brutally womanizing her.

Randy and the reality agent, they only stand and awe. Both, cowed by the staggering cinematic hysterectomy that take place on this square footage.

He be immolating deep, Randy, he say, "Sister dawg, I can smell the hypocrisy!"

And Gazelle, she say, "Dawg, when you take ownership. You be selling tickets and be gilding gilded tours."

Gazelle mentor that this white-marble floorage, right here, be an ideal placement to location a Christmas tree. Still, Randy, he hate trees, alive or dead.

The reality agent, she persist on promenading Randy through the futility room, the pouter room, a walled-in closet, the reckless nook, the tedium room, and the nifty home offense, when Randy already be sold. Randy only want to know if there be room for a dog run. Randy point his finger to eradicate his dog, an American Bull terrier. Her name be Eleanor.

Randy and Gazelle pace off the gravel yardage. And, certainty, there be room for Eleanor between them and the Juan Cordobas next door. So Randy, he esquire to perchance the house for an all-cash transition.

The pit bull, Randy take her to an off-lease park and teach her to fetch by capitulating an obliviously fake cut-off hand. It like a lacerated prop leftover from a Halloween blockbuster. Up close, the fake blood on the severed wrist look totally vicarious. The fingertips be blackened and garrulous. Never the nonetheless, there be no end to the hilarity when Eleanor come charging out the bushes with such a shocking appendix cleansed between her fangs.

Randy play fetch this way simply to agonize his neighbors,

those Juan Cordoba busybodies who perambulate the stereotype that pit bulls do nothing all day except utilize their razor-sharp mandibles to be masturbating tiny babies.

Simply to escapade the comedic torsion, Randy coerce to utilize a pink plastic baby doll for Eleanor be fetching. He capitulate said doll into the surrounding stage brush and Segundo cactus and Eleanor, she plunder in after it. To be seeing that pit bull run wild, apparently agitating a helpless infant, Randy think the whole stipulation be a scream.

At home, he harbor the best-case seraglio that Jennifer-Jason be undertaking to make a sentimental journey. Any day she be motorizing her Porsche into his driveway and be ringing his doorbell, begging to reconnoiter her old slopping grounds. When that happen, he dream he be seizing Jennifer-Jason in his firm-but-tender apprehension, and Randy be interjecting—like so manly others—to meticulously and thoroughly womanize her.

In the meanwhile, to relinquish his solitude, Randy flummox Gazelle. He display her some leftover life assurance money, saying, "Sister dawg, I be proffering cash terms for you to join with me in the holy state of acrimony." Randy, he romanticize her, grilling her steaks and spoiling her fine figure by serving her baked Nebraska for dessert. And, eventually, Gazelle, she subside to marry him.

Beyond that, Randy tell himself that living in California be an improvement. To live in that architecturally impotent house, Randy know, it impugn his tiresome life with a deep colorectal repugnance. Respiring there, he feel like a real somebody. Like a museum curtailer or the guard who guard an infernal flame.

Randy hate being a nobody. It be like some falling tree already berated him to fractions.

The secret truth be the death of Randy daddy, it leave Randy feeling deeply and justifiably defecated.

Never the nonetheless, any improvement in his lifestyle prove to be merely flatulent. His new soul mate, Gazelle, she always disappear, going to the Yearning Annex or the shelter for baffled wives. And when Randy attend to bring her home she imitate to the projective service caseworkers that Randy be responsible for her lambada being permeated when Gazelle, herself, be confounded in him that the actual traumatic perforation got taken place during some long-ago, late-night autofellatio incident.

Never the nonetheless, Randy scared. He certify that if Gazelle can make her approbations stick then he be the one comprehended by the courts and confectioned to serve hard time behind bars. Instead of Jennifer-Jason, he be trapped by circumcisions beyond his control. In prison, Randy be the one to get his tender propensity brutally womanized, night and day, by roving gangs of hungry bro dawgs. All of them bent on committing fruitless acts of prison cellular reproduction.

Adding insult to incendiary, the Internet journalize that Jennifer-Jason be contracting a severe case of kill herself. In salutation of her lifetime achievement, Randy erect a little shrine for display her photo in the front yard. He hope pilgrims pilgrimage, but those Juan Cordobas next door they say his shrine be nasty on account of the photo be showing Jennifer-Jason enjoying her three-day vocation.

Every explicit screen capture Randy mount in his shrine, it absconded.

Season-wise, in California, spring, summer, and Christmas all look pretty much identical except that his neighbors put up a Naiveté Scene next door. It don't help the stipulation when they complain about Eleanor making too much noise and Randy yell over the backyard fence how at least his dog know to bark English.

Christmas be also when, everywhere, there be fresh-cut Ore-

14

gon evergreens lurking around for new victims. One of those coniferous assassins, Randy deduct, be having his name on it.

The next-door neighbors put up a Naiveté Scene on account of them being Pope-kissing Juan Cordobas. It be complete with a plastic-shaped Joseph and Virgin Mary. The plastic baby be curdled face-up in an orange crate stultified with loads of yellow straw. That propane Jesus baby look rotted from exposure to so much solar reparation. With its cracked plastic face and faded paint, to Randy it look worse than offal.

Trouble be, to Eleanor, that Jesus, it look just like the doll she be acclimatize to fetch for so long. Eleanor always pucker her eyeballs at it. Now the pit bull be near to conniption, like some unscrupulous Jennifer-Jason Morrel, extenuating over that churchy kitsch.

Maybe just to respite him, Gazelle invest they go shopping. She fully attenuate to perchance a tree with a diagram wide enough to fill the two-story entryway failure. She completely dislodge his complaints, obliterating his warnings about how his own daddy be antedated by the impact of another such Oregon monster. No, Gazelle, she say, "Dawg." She say, "Dawg, we be decimate that tree with colorful glass Christmas desecrations."

To buy a tree, Randy calculate, be cheaper than pay an ex-wife antimony. So they procure said tree and decimate it with a thousand armaments of blown glass. To be doing this, they leave open the front door.

No surprise nobody, Eleanor the pit bull extrapolate herself from out the house.

Exacerbating faster than fast, she purloin the plastic Jesus doll and mitigate North by Northwest at an accelerating rate of escape.

Some people be driving past, maybe a Jew or a Jehovah's witless, but somebody who don't recognize that Jesus be the son of

God, they think Eleanor be jaw on a regular baby. They get this deputized look. Every pointed busybody eyeball be prolapsed. And they start to peruse Eleanor and be phoning video blasts until cotillions of scurrilous Juan Cordoba low-riders be also closely perusing Eleanor at dangerously high rates. All of them be smoldering illegal firearms.

Obfuscating the melee, Gazelle, she lectern Randy. The sister go on and on about some urinal be hanging on the wall of some France art mausoleum. She shout, "Marcel Duchamp, dawg!"

One minute she be copping his spunk; the next, Gazelle be regurgitating semesters of half-digested Yearning Annex lecterns. The sister dawg be nothing if not a corundum. She deride him, going, "Dawg, don't you never read no Lewis Hyde?"

And finale, Randy detect one word of what Gazelle be yelling.

Effervescing from his open front door, Randy shout, "Run and hide, Eleanor!"

And behind him, he hear Gazelle, heavily indoctrinated on Rémy Martin. She be snarling, "Dawg!" Gazelle hallow, "Dawg, this be for you permeating my lambada!" And utilizing all her inconsiderate strength, she be attesting to tipple over the Christmas tree!

And the next misfortunate occurrence be a cotillion tons of killer pine needles and fractal glass desecrations slam into Randy spine. Never the nonetheless, he not die before he witness a heart-warning naiveté debacle.

His pit bull, Eleanor, she be recompensing Jesus Christ return from the dead. Clutch in the context of a pit bull sharp fangs, this dead, faded cymbal be turning back into being a real Holy Child.

And relaxing out from his holey body, Randy, he see how life be like a tree.

First, life move slow. So excoriating slow you forget you life always be moving. You life always be moving. You life always be moving. Then, you life, it move faster than fast. By the end, you life move too fast to perception. Never the nonetheless, still sensitizing hot blood extrapolate from his body, exacerbating from the armament-inflected striations, Randy, he be Christmas singing, "Run and hide, Eleanor! Run and hide!"

And languaging on that threshold which divine between the leaving and the dead—already half a haunt—Randy be singing, "Rum imbibe, Jell-O mold!"

Lathering his strength, Randy be whisper-singing, "Hun abide! Come inside! Sweeten tide! Sugar fried! Kitten spied! Mitten dyed! Signified! Qualified! Genocide! Bonnie and Clyde!" All his words fall to pieces while Randy go to curdle happy never after in the bosom of his antedated daddy.

And meantime as for the pit bull . . .

As fast as her furry feet be carry her, Eleanor be reverberating back up North. And while those Juan Cordoba low-riders be fast, there be no denying that Eleanor the pit bull, lickety-split, she easy, always and forever, she be the fascist.

■

HOW MONKEY GOT MARRIED, BOUGHT A HOUSE, AND FOUND HAPPINESS IN ORLANDO

Many years ago, in a world before disillusionment, Monkey walked through the forest, her mouth overflowing with pride. After much effort and sacrifice, she had finished her lengthy schooling. To Raven, Monkey bragged, "Look at me! I have an undergraduate degree in Communications!" To Coyote, she boasted, "I have completed many valuable internships!" In a world before she'd feasted on shame and defeat, Monkey paraded her resume into the Human Resources department of Llewellyn Food Product Marketers, Inc.

Monkey demanded a face-to-face audience with Hamster, who was the Human Resources liaison, and Monkey boldly put forward her resume and bid, "Let me prove myself. Give me a knight's errand."

Thus came Monkey to stand behind a folding table. In grocery stores or department stores, Monkey offered cubes of sausage skewered with toothpicks. Monkey offered dollops of apple pie served in tiny paper cups, or paper napkins cradling sample bites of tofu. Monkey spritzed perfume and offered her own slender neck for lumbering Moose to sniff, and the Moose bought and bought. Blessed was Monkey with charm, and when she smiled at Stag or Panther or Eagle, they smiled in return and sought to buy whatever product Monkey was shilling. She sold cigarettes to Badger, who did not smoke. And Monkey sold beef jerky to Ram, who did not eat meat. So clever was Monkey that she sold hand lotion to Snake, who had no hands!

Back at Llewellyn Foods, Hamster said, "I have an opening in Vegas," and Vegas became but the first in a long chain of triumphs. For now was Monkey part of a team and proved herself to be a team player, and when Hamster bid Monkey relocate—to Philly, to the Twin Cities, to San Fran—Monkey was always eager to flog a new sandwich spread or pimp a new sports drink. And seeing herself a small success, Monkey went again before Hamster at Human Resources and bid, "You have been my advocate, Hamster, and I have served Llewellyn Foods. Test me further."

And Hamster replied, "You want a challenge?" Hamster said, "We have a cheese that's not moving."

And so arrogant was Monkey that she bade, "Give me your problematic cheese." Without so much as a glance at the product in question, Monkey promised to deliver a minimum 14 percent share in the highly competitive mid-level imported dairy solids market, and Monkey further promised that such success would last at least seven weeks, positioning this new cheese before the forthcoming holiday entertainment season. In exchange, Hamster granted that Llewellyn Foods would reward Monkey with the position of Northwest Regional Supervisor so that Monkey might settle in Seattle and buy a condo and find a mate and finally begin a family to balance her career. Most importantly, Monkey would never again be compelled to offer her neck to another stupid sniffing Moose. Or to smile winningly at the Jackal in Safeway who circled back, again and again, to gobble up her cookies.

In this long-ago time, before she knew the bitter taste of failure, Monkey stood behind yet another folding table, this one in a supermarket in Orlando. Monkey smiled above a vast forest of toothpicks, like a king-sized bed of wooden nails, each pointed stick stuck in a small cube of something shiny and white. Monkey smiled and smiled, and caught the eye of Grizzly Bear. At this, Monkey told herself, "Seattle, here I come!" But as Grizzly Bear crossed the supermarket, he stopped. Sniffing the air, Grizzly Bear lifted one knee, then the other, and checked the soles of his feet for spoor. He surreptitiously ducked his head and sniffed at his own armpits. Only then did Grizzly Bear's gaze come back to Monkey; but his smile was gone, and he would venture no closer. A look of disgust seemed to ripple his lips, and Grizzly Bear fled the scene. With the trap of her smile, Monkey tried next to snare Wolf, but Wolf would only venture so close before his nostrils flared. Widening his gray eyes in horror, Wolf dashed away. Likewise, Eagle seemed drawn by Monkey's charm, but would only swoop so low before Eagle gave a strangled squawk and his golden wings beat a retreat through the supermarket air.

Monkey hadn't noticed at first, perhaps her nose had been blunted by selling perfume and cigarettes, but the cheese smelled disgusting. It smelled like feces and burning hair, and it sweated tiny, clear drops of stinking oil. The way the cheese stank, Monkey asked herself, how could anyone tell it wasn't spoiled? The way this cheese reeked it might be loaded with salmonella. To test her theory, Monkey smiled to lure Pig, but not even Pig would partake of her smelly wares. The smile still frozen on her face, Monkey caught the eye of Gorilla. Standing at a safe distance, Gorilla wore a bright red vest, for he was the manager of the supermarket. His arms folded across his huge chest, Gorilla shook his mighty head at Monkey and said, "No one but a lunatic would put that cheese inside his mouth!"

That night in her Orlando motel room, Monkey telephoned Hamster and said, "I think my cheese is poison."

And over the phone Hamster replied, "Relax, your cheese is fine."

"It doesn't smell fine," Monkey insisted.

"We're counting on you," Hamster said. "If anybody can open a market niche for this cheese, you can." Hamster explained that Llewellyn Foods had contracted to introduce the cheese, nationwide, at a price point so low it represented a twelve-cent loss per unit. Hamster let slip that Monkey's archrival, Coyote, was launching the same cheese in Raleigh-Durham and wasn't reporting any consumer resistance. Over the telephone, Hamster gave forth with a great sigh of exasperation and said that perhaps Coyote would make a better Northwest Regional Supervisor. That maybe Coyote just wanted Seattle more.

After hanging up, Monkey told herself, "I will not lose this promotion to Coyote." She told herself, "Hamster is lying. Coyote couldn't sell nuts to Squirrel." Yet all night Monkey lay awake in bed, listening to Rabbit doing it with Mink in the next motel room, and fretting that, despite her advanced degree in Communications, she'd be stuck below a glass ceiling, getting sniffed by Moose for the rest of her career. For comfort, she wanted to telephone her mother and father, but told herself, "You are grown now, Monkey. Your problems are your own." Instead, she sat in bed, hearing the grunting and rutting through the motel wall and pretending to read *The Wapshot Chronicle*. As the sun rose on Orlando, Monkey got dressed and put on her makeup, worried that no one would ever love her. She'd never have a real home.

The following day, behind her bristling forest of toothpicks, Monkey waited for one animal in particular. Monkey beamed her smile at Owl; calling across the supermarket to Possum and Walrus and Cougar, she said, "Come taste my cheese! It's made in Switzerland from organic free-range milk with no bovine growth hormones or artificial ingredients." Still, Monkey's every word was a hopeful lie. She didn't know anything about the cheese. She didn't even know how it tasted. No one but a crazy person would place her lips around that nasty cheese.

That night, from her motel room, Monkey broke the chain of command. She telephoned Bison, who was the Director of National Operations, four levels above Hamster's head. Worse yet, Monkey telephoned Bison on his personal cell phone number. She introduced herself, but Bison said only, "Do you report to me?"

Monkey explained that she was part of the roving product demo team, assigned to penetrate the Florida market with a test cheese. She was pitching in the Orlando area, but she thought the cheese might be spoiled. Monkey called Bison "sir," something she'd promised herself she'd never call anyone—something she'd never even called her own father.

"Spoiled?" asked Bison. It was early evening in Chicago, but Bison's words sounded slurred. Monkey could hear liquid splash and glug as if someone were guzzling gin from a bottle. She could hear pills rattle. His voice boomed and echoed as if his home were cavernous, and Monkey pictured him speaking on a gold-encrusted telephone, seated in a great hall with a marble floor and frescoes painted on the ceiling.

"Sir," Monkey said, and winced, "even Mouse wouldn't touch it."

Bison asked, "Have you gone through Hamster?"

Said Monkey, "Sir, somebody's kid is going to taste this cheese and be poisoned, and I'll be brought up on charges of reckless homicide." She said, "Honestly, even *Skunk* told me it smelled awful."

In response, Bison declared that life wasn't a swimming pool. Over the phone, he rambled on about *stamina*. In turns, he sounded angry and weepy, but always soused. Apropos of nothing, he asked her, "What? Are you afraid of getting some shit in your ass?"

So on the third day Monkey was back at her folding table, behind her stockade of toothpicks, like pikes, like a fence of sharpened spikes. From beyond this barrier the other animals, the Panther and the Porcupine, they looked at her with faces of open contempt or deep pity. An invisible cloud of cheese stink held everyone at bay, and from the center of everyone's unhappy looks Monkey pleaded and cajoled for someone brave enough to try this new, marvelous product. Monkey railed that they were cowards. She dared them. She bribed them with double-their-money-back guarantees if they sampled the cheese and didn't love it. She coaxed them, saying, "Who's going to be first in line to discover sheer joy?"

From a safe distance Raven shouted, "You'd have to be suicidal to bite down on that!" Other animals nodded and snickered. Gorilla watched, impatiently tapping the toes of one foot, weaving his fingers together and cracking his huge knuckles, ready to throw Monkey out onto the sidewalk.

"If your stuff is so great, lady," challenged Ferret, "why don't *you* eat it?"

Monkey looked at the table spread with tiny cubes of white poison. She told herself, "Everyone thinks this terrible smell is me." Her arrogance was gone. Monkey hadn't slept in two days, and her pride was gone. She told herself, "I'd rather be dead than stand here for another moment with everyone despising me or feeling sorry for me." She imagined herself dying in terrible pain on the concrete floor of this Orlando supermarket. She imagined the charges of wrongful death, and her parents winning a landmark civil settlement against Llewellyn Foods. Monkey pinched a toothpick between two fingers and held it up between herself and the crowd. She held the cube of cheese high, like a torch. She imagined her own funeral and saw herself dead in a casket with these same fingers folded across her cold chest. Monkey saw her name and today's date chiseled on a tombstone. This cheese smelled the way death smelled. It smelled the way she would soon smell.

"Give me a knight's errand," Monkey told herself, holding the cheese on-high. "Test me further."

The crowd watched, dumbfounded. Slack jawed. Turkey wept quietly.

Monkey closed her eyes and brought the cheese to her mouth. Her lips plucked it from the toothpick, and she began to chew. Her eyes still closed, she heard Gorilla shout, his voice high-pitched with panic, "Someone call 9-1-1!"

Monkey ate the cheese yet she did not die. She ate and ate it. She never wanted to swallow, only to chew it, to grind the cheese between her teeth forever and to always savor it. She wanted to live forever so that she could eat nothing else. Worse than killing her, the cheese tasted—incredible. What had been the worst smell in the world, it became the best, and even after Monkey had gulped it down she sucked the wooden toothpick for the last hint of flavor. The cheese was inside her; it was part of her, and she loved it.

Smiling, Monkey opened her eyes to find everyone staring, their faces knotted in horror. Their eyes bulged as if they'd caught her eating her own scat. As repugnant as she'd seemed before, now she seemed even more repulsive to them, but Monkey didn't care. With all the animals watching she ate another cube of cheese, and another. She wanted to be filled with this glorious taste and smell until her belly ached.

That night in her motel room the telephone rang. It was Hamster calling. Hamster said, "Hold on while I get Bison on the other line." Monkey waited, and after a few clicks a voice said, "Bison, here."

Bison said, "On the advice of Legal, we're pulling the cheese from outlets." He said, "We can't risk the liability."

Monkey knew her job hung in the balance. She told herself to stay quiet and just let events run their course, but instead she said, "Wait."

Hamster said, "Nobody's blaming you."

Monkey said, "I was wrong." She said, "You can fire me, but that cheese is delicious." She said, "Please." She said, "Sir."

With a shrug in his voice, Bison said, "This matter is out of our hands." Over the phone he said, "Tomorrow, you dispose of your stock samples."

"Ask Coyote," Monkey pleaded. "Coyote's pitching it."

"Coyote's in Seattle," said Bison. "We've promoted him to the Northwest Regional Supervisor slot."

Caught in an obvious lie, Hamster said, "Take this one for the team, princess. Or you're fired."

After all of this time pitching perfume and beef jerky and hand lotion, Monkey finally had a product she actually believed in. Until now Monkey had wanted the world to love her, and now she was willing to take a backseat to a cheese. She didn't care how much the other animals glared at her in undisguised disgust, she'd debase herself completely in the eyes of a million animals out of the slim chance that one would taste what she tasted and affirm her faith. If that were to happen, that brave animal would also love the cheese and Monkey would no longer be alone in the world. She would martyr her dignity for the glory of this cheese.

According to a text message from Iguana the entire wholesale stock had already been auctioned to a liquidator. The following day, Monkey deliberately missed her flight to Cleveland. For point-of-sale pitch sessions Monkey always wore a pink polo shirt from Brooks Brothers, always a two-button polo with only the upper button open. Pink read as gamine, sporty, preppy, and Monkey never popped the collar. However, with everything at stake today she pulled out her heavy artillery: a chemise top with floss shoulder straps and a hem so short it fluttered above a wide margin of her exposed stomach. She wedged her breasts into a padded bra. To put this cheese across, Monkey would play the temple whore and pimp herself worse than Llewellyn Foods had ever dared. Brazenly, she took her folding table and toothpicks and white cubes of mouthwatering, soul-filling nirvana and went back to the Orlando supermarket. Behind her altar of samples, Monkey was a zealot. A fanatic. She was an evangelical, railing and haranguing everyone within the crowded market. She was a lunatic in their eyes—someone who would eat this cheese was capable of anything—and this seemed to protect her for the moment. If she could only communicate her passion and be understood by one other animal, that would be enough.

"Satisfaction is here for the taking," said Monkey. "Absolute bliss can be yours for free!" Only the smell of the cheese kept Duck and Ox from seizing her, from grabbing Monkey and tossing her bodily from the building, but Grizzly Bear shouted obscenities at her through cupped paws, and Parrot pelted her with stinging pennies.

No one stood on Monkey's side. She stood alone, armed only with her faith.

Monkey was still a team player, but now she was the only one on her team.

Chaos broke out. The herd rushed her table, overturning it, and her samples tumbled to the dirty floor. On the dusty concrete, where Monkey had envisioned herself dead only the day before, her sacred cheese was being trod upon. This cheese which she loved more than her own life, now it was ground under the hooves of Reindeer and smeared beneath the paws of Tiger. A huge hand closed around Monkey's arm and wrenched her toward the door. It was Gorilla, dragging her in the direction of the rest of her Llewellyn Foods career, where she could sleep every night. Sleepwalk through every day. A future where she need never fully awaken.

The only cube that was left was the cheese stabbed on the toothpick in Monkey's hand. It was her sword and her grail, and Monkey thrust it at Gorilla's eyes. She thrust the toothpick deep into the back of Gorilla's mouth, and he choked and gagged and spat out the cheese, but Monkey caught the wet, white cube as it fell. She lifted the slimy cheese cradled in the palm of one hand and slapped it between Gorilla's lips. With the stampede of animals lifting them both and carrying them toward the exit, Monkey kept her hand muzzled across Gorilla's mouth, her eyes meeting his eyes until Gorilla chewed and swallowed. Until she felt the huge muscles of his struggling arms relax and go slack with understanding.

■

ZOMBIES

It was Griffin Wilson who proposed the Theory of De-Evolution. He sat two rows behind me in Organic Chem, the very definition of an evil genius. He was the first to take the Great Leap Backward.

Everybody knows because Tricia Gedding was in the nurse's office with him when he took the leap. She was on the other cot, behind a paper curtain faking her period to get out of a pop quiz in Perspectives on Eastern Civ. She said she heard the loud "Beep!" but didn't think anything of it. When Tricia Gedding and the school nurse found him on his own cot, they thought Griffin Wilson was the resuscitation doll everybody uses to practice CPR. He was hardly breathing, barely moving a muscle. They thought it was a joke because his wallet was still clenched between his teeth and he still had the electrical wires pasted to either side of his forehead.

His hands were still holding a dictionary-sized box, still paralyzed, pressing a big red button. Everyone's seen this box so often that they hardly recognized it, but it had been hanging on the office wall: the cardiac defibrillator. That emergency heart shocker. He must've taken it down and read the instructions. He simply took the waxed paper off the gluey parts and pasted the electrodes on either side of his temporal lobes. It's basically a peel-and-stick lobotomy. It's so easy a sixteen-year-old can do it.

In Miss Chen's English class, we learned, "To be or not to be . . ." but there's a big gray area in between. Maybe in Shakespeare times people only had two options. Griffin Wilson, he knew that the SATs were just the gateway to a big lifetime of bullshit. To getting married and college. To paying taxes and trying to raise a kid who's not a school shooter. And Griffin Wilson knew drugs are only a patch. After drugs, you're always going to need *more* drugs.

The problem with being Talented And Gifted is sometimes you get *too smart.* My uncle Henry says the importance of eating a good breakfast is because your brain is still growing. But nobody talks about how, sometimes, your brain can get just *too big.*

We're basically big animals, evolved to break open shells and eat raw oysters, but now we're expected to keep track of all three hundred Kardashian sisters and eight hundred Baldwin brothers. Seriously, at the rate they reproduce the Kardashians and the Baldwins are going to wipe out all other species of humans. The rest of us, you and me, we're just evolutionary dead ends waiting to wink out.

You could ask Griffin Wilson anything. Ask him who signed the Treaty of Ghent. He'd be like that cartoon magician on TV who says, "Watch me pull a rabbit out of my ass." Abracadabra, and he'd know the answer. In Organic Chem, he could talk String Theory until he was anoxic, but what he really wanted to be was happy. Not just not sad, he wanted to be happy the way a dog is happy. Not constantly jerked this way and that by flaming Instant Messages and changes in the federal tax code. He didn't want to die, either. He wanted to be—and not to be—but at the same time. That's what a pioneering genius he was.

The Principal of Student Affairs made Tricia Gedding swear to not tell a living soul, but you know how that goes. The school district was afraid of copycats. Those defibrillators are everywhere these days.

Since that day in the nurse's office, Griffin Wilson has never seemed happier. He's always giggling too loud and wiping spit off his chin with his sleeve. The Special Ed teachers clap their hands and heap him with praise just for using the toilet. Talk about a double standard. The rest of us are fighting tooth and nail for whatever garbage career we can get, while Griffin Wilson is going to be thrilled with penny candy and reruns of *Fraggle Rock* for the rest of his life. How he was before, he was miserable unless he won every chess tournament. The way he is now, just yesterday, he took out his dick and started to jerk off during morning roll call. Before Mrs. Ramirez could hurry us through the S's and the T's—people are answering "here" and they're answering "present," too slow, snickering and staring—before Mrs. Ramirez can rush down the aisle and stop him, Griffin Wilson shouts, "Watch me pull a rabbit out of my pants," and he sprayed hot baby gravy all over a bookcase full of nothing except a hundred *To Kill a Mockingbird*s. He was laughing the whole time.

Lobotomized or not, he still knows the value of a signature catchphrase. Instead of being just another grade grubber, now he's the life of the party.

The voltage even cleared up his acne.

It's hard to argue with results like that.

It wasn't a week after he'd turned zombie that Tricia Gedding went to the gym where she does Zumba and got the defibrillator off the wall in the girls locker room. After her self-administered peel-and-stick procedure in a bathroom stall, she doesn't care where she gets her period. Her best friend, Brie Phillips, got to the defibrillator they keep next to the bathrooms at the Home

Depot, and now she walks down the street, rain or shine, with no pants on. We're not talking about the scum of the school. We're talking about the class president and the head cheerleader. The best and the brightest. Everybody who played first string on all the sports teams. It took every defibrillator between here and Canada, but, since then, when they play football nobody plays by the rules. And even when they get skunked, they're always grinning and slapping high fives.

They continue to be young and hot, but they no longer worry about the day when they won't be.

It's suicide, but it's not. The newspaper won't report the actual numbers. Newspapers flatter themselves. Anymore, Tricia Gedding's Facebook page has a larger readership than our daily paper. Mass media, my foot. They cover the front page with unemployment and war, and they don't think *that* has a negative effect? My uncle Henry reads me an article about a proposed change in state law. Officials want a ten-day waiting period on the sale of all heart defibrillators. They're talking about mandatory background checks and mental health screenings, but it's not the law, nor yet.

My uncle Henry looks up from the newspaper article and eyes me across breakfast. He levels me this stern look and asks, "If all your friends jumped off a cliff, would you?"

My uncle's what I have instead of a mom and dad. He won't acknowledge it, but there's a good life over the edge of that cliff. There's a lifetime supply of handicapped-parking permits. Uncle Henry doesn't understand that all my friends have already jumped.

They may be "differently abled" but my friends are still hooking up. More than ever, these days. They have smoking-hot bodies and the brains of infants. They have the best of both worlds. LeQuisha Jefferson stuck her tongue inside Hannah Finerman

31

during Beginning Carpentry Arts, made her squeal and squirm right there, leaned up against the drill press. And Laura Lynn Marshall? She sucked off Frank Randall in the back of International Cuisine Lab with everybody watching. All their falafels got scorched, and nobody made a federal case out of it.

After pushing the red defibrillator button, yeah, a person suffers some consequences, but he doesn't know he's suffering. Once he undergoes a Push-Button Lobotomy a kid can get away with murder.

During Study Hall, I asked Boris Declan if it hurt. He was sitting there in the lunchroom with the red burn marks still fresh on either side of his forehead. He had his pants down around his knees. I asked if the shock was painful, and he didn't answer, not right away. He just took his fingers out of his ass and sniffed them, thoughtfully. He was last year's Junior Prom King.

In a lot of ways he's more chill now than he ever was. With his ass hanging out in the middle of the cafeteria, he offers me a finger to sniff and I tell him, "No, thank you."

He says he doesn't remember anything. Boris Declan grins this sloppy, dopey smile. He taps a dirty fingertip to the burn mark on one side of his face. He points this same butt-stained finger to make me look across the way. On the wall where he's pointing is this guidance counselor poster that shows white birds flapping their wings against a blue sky. Under that are the words "Actual Happiness Only Happens by Accident" printed in dreamy writing. The school hung that poster to hide the shadow of where another defibrillator used to hang.

It's clear that wherever Boris Declan ends up in life it's going to be the right place. He's already living in Brain Trauma Nirvana. The school district was right about copycats.

No offense to Jesus, but the meek won't inherit the earth. To judge from reality TV the loudmouths will get their hands on everything. And I say, Let Them. The Kardashians and the Baldwins are like some invasive species. Like kudzu or zebra mussels. Let them battle over the control of the crappy real world.

For a long time I listened to my uncle and didn't jump. Anymore, I don't know. The newspaper warns us about terrorist anthrax bombs and virulent new strains of meningitis, and the only comfort newspapers can offer is a coupon for twenty cents off on underarm deodorant.

To have no worries, no regrets, it's pretty appealing. So many of the cool kids at my school have elected to self-fry that, anymore, only the losers are left. The losers and the naturally occurring pinheads. The situation is so dire that I'm a shoo-in to be valedictorian. That's how come my uncle Henry is shipping me off. He thinks that by relocating me to Twin Falls he can postpone the inevitable.

So we're sitting at the airport, waiting by the gate for our flight to board, and I ask to go to the bathroom. In the men's room I pretend to wash my hands so I can look in the mirror. My uncle asked me, one time, why I looked in mirrors so much, and I told him it wasn't vanity so much as it was nostalgia. Every mirror shows me what little is left of my parents.

I'm practicing my mom's smile. People don't practice their smiles nearly enough so when they most need to look happy they're not fooling anyone. I'm rehearsing my smile when—there it is: my ticket to a gloriously happy future working in fast food. That's opposed to a miserable life as a world-famous architect or heart surgeon.

Hovering over my shoulder and a smidgen behind me, it's reflected in the mirror. Like the bubble containing my thoughts in a comic strip panel, there's a cardiac defibrillator. It's mounted on the wall in back of me, shut inside a metal case with a glass door you could open to set off alarm bells and a red strobe light. A sign above the box says "AED" and shows a lightning bolt striking a Valentine's heart. The metal case is like the hands-off showcase holding some crown jewels in a Hollywood heist movie.

Opening the case, automatically I set off the alarm and flashing red light. Quick, before any heroes come running, I dash into a handicapped stall with the defibrillator. Sitting on the toilet, I pry it open. The instructions are printed on the lid in English, Spanish, French, and comic book pictures. Making it foolproof, more or less. If I wait too long I won't have this option. Defibrillators will be under lock and key, soon, and once defibrillators are illegal only paramedics will have defibrillators.

In my grasp, here's my permanent childhood. My very own Bliss Machine.

My hands are smarter than the rest of me. My fingers know to just peel the electrodes and paste them to my temples. My ears know to listen for the loud beep that means the thing is fully charged.

My thumbs know what's best. They hover over the big red button. Like this is a video game. Like the button the president gets to press to trigger the launch of nuclear war. One push and the world as I know it comes to an end. A new reality begins.

To be or not to be. God's greatest gift to animals is they don't get a choice.

Every time I open the newspaper I want to throw up. In another ten seconds I won't know how to read. Better yet, I won't have to. I won't know about global climate change. I won't know about cancer or genocide or SARS or environmental degradation or religious conflict.

The public address system is paging my name. I won't even know my name.

Before I can blast off, I picture my uncle Henry at the gate, holding his boarding pass. He deserves better than this. He needs to know this is not his fault.

With the electrodes stuck to my forehead, I carry the defibrillator out of the bathroom and walk down the concourse toward the gate. The coiling electric wires trail down the sides of my face like thin, white pigtails. My hands carry the battery pack in front of me like a suicide bomber who's only going to blow up all my IQ points.

When they catch sight of me, businesspeople abandon their roller bags. People on family vacations, they flap their arms, wide, and herd their little kids in the other direction. Some guy thinks he's a hero. He shouts, "Everything is going to be all right." He tells me, "You have everything to live for."

We both know he's a liar.

My face is sweating so hard the electrodes might slip off. Here's my last chance to say everything that's on my mind so with everyone watching I'll confess: I don't know what's a happy ending. And I don't know how to fix anything. Doors open in the concourse and Homeland Security soldiers storm out, and I feel like one of those Buddha monks in Tibet or wherever who splash on gasoline before they check to make sure their cigarette lighter actually works. How embarrassing that would be, to be soaking in gasoline and have to bum a match off some stranger, especially since so few people smoke anymore. Me, in the middle of the airport concourse, I'm dripping with sweat instead of gasoline, but this is how out of control my thoughts are spinning.

From out of nowhere my uncle grabs my arm, and he says, "If you hurt yourself, Trevor, you hurt me."

He's gripping my arm, and I'm gripping the red button. I tell him this isn't so tragic. I say, "I'll keep loving you, Uncle Henry . . . I just won't know who you are."

Inside my head, my last thoughts are prayers. I'm praying that this battery is fully charged. There's got to be enough voltage to erase the fact that I've just said the word "love" in front of several hundred strangers. Even worse, I've said it to my own uncle. I'll never be able to live that down.

Most people, instead of saving me, they pull out their telephones and start shooting video. Everyone's jockeying for the best full-on angle. It reminds me of something. It reminds me of birthday parties and Christmas. A thousand memories crash over me for the last time, and that's something else I hadn't anticipated. I don't mind losing my education. I don't mind forgetting my name. But I will miss the little bit I can remember about my parents.

My mother's eyes and my father's nose and forehead, they're dead except for in my face. And the idea pains me to know that I won't recognize them anymore. Once I punch out, I'll think my reflection is nothing except me.

My uncle Henry repeats, "If you hurt yourself, you hurt me, too."

I say, "I'll still be your nephew, but I just won't know it."

For no reason, some lady steps up and grabs my uncle Henry's other arm. This new person, she says, "If you hurt yourself, you hurt me, as well . . ." Somebody else grabs that lady, and somebody grabs the last somebody, saying, "If you hurt yourself, you hurt me." Strangers reach out and grab hold of strangers in chains and branches, until we're all connected together. Like we're molecules crystallizing in solution in Organic Chem. Everyone's holding on to someone, and everyone's holding on to everyone, and their voices repeat the same sentence: "If you hurt yourself, you hurt me . . . if you hurt yourself, you hurt me . . ."

These words form a slow wave. Like a slow-motion echo, they move away from me, going up and down the concourse in both directions. Each person steps up to grab a person who's grabbing a person who's grabbing a person who's grabbing my uncle who's grabbing me. This really happens. It sounds trite, but only because words make everything true sound trite. Because words always screw up whatever you're trying to say.

Voices from other people in other places, total strangers say by telephone, watching by video cams, their long-distance voices say, "If you hurt yourself, you hurt me . . ." And some kid steps out from behind the cash register at Der Wiener Schnitzel, all the way down at the food court, he grabs hold of somebody and shouts, "If you hurt yourself, you hurt me." And the kids making Taco Bell and the kids frothing milk at the Starbucks, they stop, and they all hold hands with someone connected to me across this vast crowd, and they say it, too. And just when I think it's got to end and everyone's got to let go and fly away, because everything's stopped and people are holding hands even going through the metal detectors they're holding hands, even then the talking news anchor on CNN, on the televisions mounted up high by the ceiling, the announcer puts a finger to his ear, like to hear better, and even he says, "Breaking News." He looks confused, obviously reading something off cue cards, and he says, "If you hurt yourself, you hurt me." And overlapping his voice are the voices of political pundits on Fox News and color commentators on ESPN, and they're all saying it.

The televisions show people outside in parking lots and in tow-away zones, all holding hands. Bonds forming. Everyone's uploading video of everyone, people standing miles away but still connected back to me.

And crackling with static, voices come over the walkie-talkies of the Homeland Security guards, saying, "If you hurt yourself, you hurt me—do you copy?"

By that point there's not a big enough defibrillator in the universe to scramble all our brains. And, yeah, eventually we'll all have to let go, but for another moment everyone's holding tight, trying to make this connection last forever. And if this impossible thing can happen then who knows what else is possible? And a girl at Burger King shouts, "I'm scared, too." And a boy at Jack in the Box shouts, "I am scared *all the time.*" And everyone else is nodding, Me Too.

To top things off, a huge voice announces, "Attention!" From overhead it says, "May I have your attention, please?" It's a lady. It's the lady voice who pages people and tells them to pick up the white paging telephone. With everyone listening, the entire airport is reduced to silence.

"Whoever you are, you need to know . . . ," says the lady voice of the white paging telephone. Everyone listens because everything thinks she's only talking to them. From a thousand speakers she begins to sing. With that voice, she's singing the way a bird sings. Not like a parrot or an Edgar Allan Poe bird that speaks English. The sound is trills and scales the way a canary sings, notes too impossible for a mouth to conjugate into nouns and verbs. We can enjoy it without understanding it. And we can love it without knowing what it means. Connected by telephone and television, it's synchronizing everyone, worldwide. That voice so perfect, it's just singing down on us.

Best of all . . . her voice fills everywhere, leaving no room for being scared. Her song makes all our ears into one ear.

38

This isn't exactly the end. On every TV is me, sweating so hard an electrode slowly slides down one side of my face.

This certainly isn't the happy ending I had in mind, but compared to where this story began—with Griffin Wilson in the nurse's office putting his wallet between his teeth like a gun—well, maybe this is not such a bad place to start.

■

LOSER

The show still looks exactly like when you were sick with a really high fever and you stayed home to watch TV all day. It's not *Let's Make a Deal*. It's not *Wheel of Fortune*. It's not Monty Hall, or the show with Pat Sajak. It's that other show where the big, loud voice calls your name in the audience, says to "Come on down, you're the next contestant," and if you guess the cost of Rice-A-Roni then you fly round-trip to live for a week in Paris.

It's *that* show. The prize is never anything useful, like okay clothes or music or beer. The prize is always some vacuum cleaner or a washing machine, something you might maybe get excited to win if you were, like, somebody's wife.

It's Rush Week, and the tradition is everybody pledging Zeta Delt all take this big chartered school bus and need to go to some TV studio and watch them tape this game show. Rules say, all the Zeta Delts wear the same red T-shirt with printed on it the Greek Zeta Delta Omega deals, silk-screened in black. First, you need to take a little stamp of Hello Kitty, maybe half a stamp and wait for the flash. It's like this little paper stamp printed with Hello Kitty you suck on and swallow, except it's really blotter acid.

All you do is, the Zeta Delts sit together to make this red

40

patch in the middle of the studio audience and scream and yell to get on TV. These are not the Gamma Grab'a Thighs. They're not the Lambda Rape'a Dates. The Zeta Delts, they're who everybody wants to be.

How the acid will affect you—if you're going to freak out and kill yourself or eat somebody alive—they don't even tell you.

It's traditional.

Ever since you were a little kid with a fever, the contestants they call down to play this game show, the big voice always calls for one guy who's a United States Marine wearing some band uniform with brass buttons. There's always somebody's old grandma wearing a sweatshirt. There's an immigrant from some place where you can't understand half of what he says. There's always some rocket scientist with a big belly and his shirt pocket stuck full of pens.

It's just how you remember it, growing up, only now—all the Zeta Delts start yelling at you. Yelling so hard it scrunches their eyes shut. Everybody's just these red shirts and big-open mouths. All their hands are pushing you out from your seat, shoving you into the aisle. The big voice is saying your name, telling you to come on down. You're the next contestant.

In your mouth, the Hello Kitty tastes like pink bubblegum. It's the Hello Kitty, the popular kind, not the strawberry flavor or the chocolate flavor somebody's brother cooks at night in the General Sciences building where he works as a janitor. The paper stamp feels caught partway down your throat, except you don't want to gag on TV, not on recorded video with strangers watching, forever.

All the studio audience is turned around to see you stumble down the aisle in your red T-shirt. All the TV cameras, zoomed in. Everybody clapping exactly how you remember it. Those Las Vegas lights, flashing, outlining everything onstage. It's some-

41

thing new, but you've watched it done a million-zillion times before, and just by automatic you take the empty desk next to where the United States Marine is standing.

The game show host, who's not Alex Trebek, he waves one arm, and a whole part of the stage starts to move. It's not an earthquake, but one whole wall rolls on invisible wheels, all the lights everywhere flashing on and off, only fast, just blink, blink, blink, except faster than a human mouth could say. This whole big back wall of the stage slides to one side, and from behind it steps out a giant fashion model blazing with about a million-billion sparkles on her tight dress, waving one long, skinny arm to show you a table with eight chairs like you'd see in somebody's dining room on Thanksgiving with a big cooked turkey and yams and everything. Her fashion model waist, about as big around as somebody's neck. Each of her tits, the size of your head. Those flashing Las Vegas–kind of lights blinking all around. The big voice saying who made this table, out of what kind of wood. Saying the suggested retail price it's worth.

To win, the host lifts up this little box. Like a magician, he shows everybody what's underneath—Just this whole *thing* of bread in its naturally occurring state, the way bread comes before it's made into anything you can eat like a sandwich or French toast. Just this bread, the whole way your mom might find it at the farm or wherever bread grows.

The table and chairs are totally, easy yours, except you have to guess the price of this big bread.

Behind you, all the Zeta Delts crowd really close together in their T-shirts, making what looks like one giant, red pucker in the middle of the studio audience. Not even looking at you, all their haircuts are just huddled up, making a big, hairy center. It's like forever later when your phone rings, and a Zeta Delt voice says what to bid.

That bread just sitting there the whole time. Covered in a brown crust. The big voice says it's loaded with ten essential vitamins and minerals.

The old game show host, he's looking at you like maybe he's never, ever seen a telephone before. He goes, "And what do you bid?"

And you go, "Eight bucks?"

From the look on the old grandma's face, it's like maybe they should call some paramedics for her heart attack. Dangling out one sweatshirt cuff, this crumpled scrap of Kleenex looks like leaked-out stuffing, flapping white, like she's some trashed teddy bear somebody loved too hard.

To cut you off using some brilliant strategy, the United States Marine, the bastard, he says, "Nine dollars."

Then to cut him off, the rocket science guy says, "Ten. Ten dollars."

It must be some trick question, because the old grandma says, "One dollar and ninety-nine cents," and all the music starts, loud, and the lights flash on and off. The host hauls the granny up onto the stage, and she's crying and plays a game where she throws a tennis ball to win a sofa and a pool table. Her grandma face looks just as smashed and wrinkled as that Kleenex she pulls out from her sweatshirt cuff. The big voice calls another granny to take her place, and everything keeps rushing forward.

The next round, you need to guess the price of some potatoes, but like a whole big thing of real, alive potatoes, from before they become food, the way they come from the miners or whoever that dig potatoes in Ireland or Idaho or some other place starting with an "I." Not even made into potato chips or French fries.

If you guess right, you get some big clock inside a wood box like a Dracula coffin standing on one end, except with these church bells inside the box that ding-ding whatever time it is. Over your phone, your mom calls it a *grandfather clock*. You show it to her on video, and she says it looks cheap.

You onstage with the TV cameras and lights, all the Zeta Delts call-waiting you, you cup your phone to your chest and go, "My mom wants to know, do you have anything nicer I could maybe win?"

You show your mom those potatoes on video, and she asks: Did the old host guy buy them at A&P or the Safeway?

You speed-dial your dad, and he asks about the income tax liability.

Probably it's the Hello Kitty, but the face of this big Dracula clock just scowls at you. It's like the secret, hidden eyes, the eyelids open up, and the teeth start to show, and you can hear about a million-billion giant, alive cockroaches crawling around inside the wood box of it. The skin of all the supermodels goes all waxy, smiling with their faces not looking at anything.

You say the price your mom tells you. The United States Marine says one dollar more. The rocket science guy says a dollar higher than him. Only, this round—you win.

All those potatoes open their little eyes.

Except now, you need to guess the price of a whole cow-full of milk in a box, the way milk comes in the kitchen fridge. You have to guess the cost of a whole thing of breakfast cereal like you'd find in the kitchen cabinet. After that, a giant deal of pure salt the way it comes from the ocean only in a round box, but more salt than anybody could eat in an entire lifetime. Enough salt, you could rim approximately a million-billion margaritas.

All the Zeta Delts start texting you like crazy. Your in-box piling up.

Next come these eggs like you'd find at Easter only plain white and lined up inside some special kind of cardboard case.

A whole, complete set of twelve. These really minimalist eggs, pure white . . . so white you could just look at them forever, only right away you need to guess at a big bottle like a yellow shampoo, except it's something gross called cooking oil, you don't know what for, and the next thing is you need to choose the right price of something frozen.

You cup one hand over your eyes to see past the footlights, except all the Zeta Delts are lost in the glare. All you can hear is their screaming different prices of money. Fifty thousand dollars. A million. Ten thousand. Just loony people yelling just numbers.

Like the TV studio is just some dark jungle, and people are just some monkeys just screeching their monkey sounds.

The molars inside your mouth, they're grinding together so hard you can taste the hot metal of your fillings, that silver melting in your back teeth. Meantime, the sweat stains creep down from your armpit to your elbow, all black-red down both sides of your Zeta Delt T-shirt. The flavor of melted silver and pink bubblegum. It's sleep apnea only in the day, and you need to remind yourself to take the next breath . . . take another breath . . . while the supermodels walking on sparkle high heels try pimping the audience a microwave oven, pimping a treadmill while you keep staring to decide if they're really good-looking. They make you spin this doohickey so it rolls around. You have to match a bunch of different pictures so they go together perfect. Like you're some white rat in Principles of Behavioral Psychology 201, they make you guess what can of baked beans costs more than another. All that fuss to win something you sit on to mow your lawn.

Thanks to your mom telling you prices, you win a thing like you'd put in a room covered in easy-care, wipe-clean, stain-resistant vinyl. You win one of those deals people might ride on vacation for a lifetime of wholesome fun and family excitement. You win something hand-painted with the Old World charm inspired by the recent release of a blockbuster epic motion picture.

It's the same as when you felt sick with a high fever and your little-kid heart would pound and you couldn't catch your breath, just from the idea that somebody might take home an electric organ. No matter how sick you felt, you'd watch this show until your fever broke. All the flashing lights and patio furniture, it seemed to make you feel better. To heal you or to cure you in some way.

It's like forever later, but you win all the way to the Showcase Round.

There, it's just you and the old granny wearing the sweatshirt from before, just somebody's regular grandma, but she's lived through world wars and nuclear bombs, probably she's saw all the Kennedys get shot and Abraham Lincoln, and now she's bobbing up and down on her tennis shoe toes, clapping her granny hands and crowded by supermodels and flashing lights while the big voice makes her the promise of a sport-utility vehicle, a wide-screen television, a floor-length fur coat.

And probably it's the acid, but it's like nothing seems to add up.

It's like, if you live a boring-enough life, knowing the price of Rice-A-Roni and hot dog wieners, your big reward is you get to live for a week in some hotel in London? You get to ride on some airplane to Rome. Rome, like, in Italy. You fill your head full of enough ordinary junk, and your payoff is giant supermodels giving you a snowmobile?

If this game show wants to see how smart you really are, they need to ask you how much calories in a regular onion–cheddar cheese bagel. Go ahead, ask you the price of your cell phone minutes any hour of the day. Ask you about the cost of a ticket for going thirty miles over the speed limit. Ask the round-trip fare to Cabo for spring break. Down to the penny, you can tell them the price of decent seats for the Panic at the Disco! reunion tour.

They should ask you the price of a Long Island Iced Tea. The price of Marcia Sanders's abortion. Ask about your expensive herpes medication you have to take but don't want your folks to know you need. Ask the price of your History of European Art textbook which cost three hundred bucks—fuck you very much.

Ask what that stamp of Hello Kitty set you back.

The sweatshirt granny bids some regular amount of money for her showcase. Just like always, the numbers of her bid appear in tiny lights, glowing on the front of her contestant desk where she stands.

Here, all the Zeta Delts are yelling. Your phone keeps ringing and ringing.

For your showcase, a supermodel rolls out five hundred pounds of raw beefsteak. The steaks fit inside a barbecue. The barbecue fits onboard a speedboat that fits inside a trailer for towing it that fits a massive fifth-wheel pickup truck that fits inside the garage of a brand-new house in Austin. Austin, like, in Texas.

Meantime, all the Zeta Delts all stand up. They get to their feet and step up on their audience seats cheering and waving, not chanting your name, but chanting, "Zeta Delt!" Chanting, "Zeta Delt!" Chanting, "Zeta Delt!" loud enough so it records for the broadcast.

It's probably the acid, but—you're battling some old nobody you've never met, fighting over shit you don't even want.

Probably it's the acid, but—right here and now—fuck declaring a business major. Fuck General Principles of Accounting 301.

Stuck partway down your throat, something makes you gag.

And on purpose, by accident, you bid a million, trillion, gah-zillion dollars—and ninety-nine cents.

And everything shuts down to quiet. Maybe just the little clicking sounds of all those Las Vegas lights blinking on and off, on and off. On and off.

It's like forever later when the game show host gets up too close, standing at your elbow, and he hisses, "You can't do that." The host hisses, "You have to play this game to win . . ."

Up close, his host face looks cracked into a million-billion jagged fragments only glued back together with pink makeup. Like Humpty Dumpty or a jigsaw puzzle. His wrinkles, like the battle scars of playing his same TV game since forever started. All his gray hairs, always combed in the same direction.

The big voice asks—that big, deep voice booming out of nowhere, the voice of some gigantic giant man you can't see—he demands, can you please repeat your bid?

And maybe you don't know what you want out of your life, but you know it's *not* a grandfather clock.

A million, trillion . . . you say. A number too big to fit on the front of your contestant desk. More zeroes than all the bright lights in the game show world. And probably it's the Hello Kitty, but tears slop out both your eyes, and you're crying because for the first time since you were a little kid you don't know what comes next, tears wrecking the front of your red T-shirt, turning the red parts black so the Greek omega deals don't make any sense.

The voice of one Zeta Delt, alone in all that big quiet audience, somebody yells, "You suck!"

On the little screen of your phone, a text message says, "Asshole!"

The text? It's from your mom.

The sweatshirt grandma, she's crying because she won. You're sobbing because—you don't know why.

It turns out the granny wins the snowmobiles and the fur coat. She wins the speedboat and the beefsteaks The table and chairs and sofa. All the prizes of both the showcases, because your bid was way, way too high. She's jumping around, her bright-white false teeth throwing smiles in every direction. The game show host gets everybody started clapping their hands, except the Zeta Delts don't. The family of the old granny climbs up onstage—all the kids and grandkids and great-grandkids of her—and they wander over to touch the shiny sport-utility vehicle, touch the supermodels. The granny plants red lipstick kisses all over the fractured pink face of the game show host. She's saying, "Thank you." Saying, "Thank you." Saying, "Thank you," right up to when her granny eyes roll up backward inside her head, and her hand grabs at the sweatshirt where it covers her heart.

■

RED SULTAN'S BIG BOY

The horse looked huge, at least eighteen hands at the withers. A bigger issue was Lisa. She had her heart set on it: a purebred Arabian three-year-old the red-brown of polished mahogany. From its bloodlines, the horse had to be priced thousands out of their reach. Randall asked if it wasn't too much horse for a little girl.

"I'm thirteen, Daddy," his daughter stated indignantly.

Randall said, "But, a stallion?" That she'd called him "Daddy" wasn't lost on him.

"He's very gentle," she assured. She knew this from the Internet. She knew everything from the web. They were standing outside the rail that enclosed a paddock. As they watched, a trainer worked the Arabian, using a rope to guide him in circles and figure eights. Beside them, a livestock broker looked at his wristwatch, waiting for a decision.

The horse's name was Red Sultan's Big Boy. Sired of Red Sultan and the dame Misty Blue Spring Meadows. Lisa's own horse, a pinto gelding, had died the week before, and Lisa hadn't stopped crying until moments ago. She coaxed her father. "He's an investment."

"Six thousand," interjected the livestock broker. The man seemed to be sizing up Randall and Lisa as if they were a couple of hayseeds who wouldn't have two dimes to rub together. The broker said that since the housing boom had tanked, people were scuttling cabin cruisers or setting them adrift because they couldn't afford mooring costs. The price of hay was sky high, and boarding fees were making a horse something plain people could no longer afford.

Randall had never seen the ocean, but the broker's statement brought to mind a flotilla of yachts and cabin cruisers and speedboats. People's dreams and aspirations, all cast adrift. A Sargasso of abandoned pleasure craft, banding together in some empty expanse of open water.

"I've seen a lot of deals," the broker added, "but six grand is dirt cheap."

Randall was no expert in horse flesh, but he knew a deal. The stallion was so docile it ambled over and let Lisa stroke its muzzle. Using her thumb, she lifted its lips and inspected its gums and teeth—the horse equivalent of kicking the tires. Randall's common sense told him to keep looking. To check as far afield as Chickasaw County, visiting breeders and stables, and to keep looking at teeth. Compared to what he'd seen in his life, this horse ought to sell for thirty thousand dollars, even in a depressed market.

Lisa tested the smoothness of its coat against her cheek. "He's the one from the video."

If she meant the *Black Beauty* video or the *Black Stallion* or *National Velvet*, Randall couldn't decide. There were so many sappy stories about girls in love with horses. As of late, she'd acted so grown-up. It felt nice to see her excited, especially since her horse, Sour Kraut, had taken sick so fast. She'd been riding the pinto only the weekend before. Cherry leaves could poison a horse, too many of them, with their arsenic. Or eating nettles. Even wet, red clover. During the week Lisa lived with her

51

mother in town. Weekends, she came out to his place for visitation. The pinto had looked fine Sunday night. Monday morning, when Randall had gone to feed him, poor Sour Kraut had been collapsed, foam gushing from his mouth, dead.

Lisa didn't say as much, but her father suspected that she blamed him. She'd called Tuesday, a pleasant surprise. She almost never called midweek. He had to tell her the gelding was dead. She didn't cry, not at first. Probably on account of the shock. On the phone she'd sounded quiet and faraway, maybe angry. Already hating him. A teenager desperate to place blame. Her silence worried Randall more than sobbing would have.

The next Friday, he'd driven into town to collect her, and by then she was full-out bawling. Little girl wailing. Halfway back to his place, she'd dashed away her tears and brought out the phone from her overnight bag. She'd asked, "Tomorrow, can we go to the Conway Livestock Brokers? Please, Daddy?"

Lisa didn't waste anybody's time. Saturday morning, she made him hook up the trailer to his rig. Before they'd even seen a horse, she'd nagged him to drive faster, demanding, nonstop, "Do you have your checkbook? Are you sure? Let me see it, Daddy."

The Arabian didn't toss its head or paw the ground. In the paddock, it stood passively as Randall and the broker walked around it, lifting and inspecting each hoof. It seemed so even-tempered, Randall had to wonder if it was drugged. It seemed depressed. Almost defeated. To his way of thinking, they needed a vet to check out the animal. An Arabian this subdued had to be sick. Lisa didn't want to wait.

The divorce settlement had left him with the home place, which was only right because it had belonged to his family ever since the land had belonged to anyone. He'd gotten the acreage, the barn and corrals. He had Lisa on weekends. And until last week, he'd had Sour Kraut to look after. Randall would've paid thirty grand to see his child this giddy. Lisa glanced from the horse to him and back, back and forth, speechless. She was so clearly smitten.

Randall wrote the broker a check while Lisa was already leading the horse into their trailer. Red Sultan's Big Boy was theirs. Hers. The stallion followed her with the tame obedience of a loyal dog.

This was the first time in a long time Randall had felt like a good father.

If the stallion was drugged or sick, they'd find out soon enough.

That first weekend, Lisa was happier than he'd seen her since before the divorce. She'd signed up for dressage lessons at the Merriwethers' stable down the road. Randall's neighbors lived in houses barely visible to one another across vast, dark green fields of alfalfa. School was out, and cliques of teenage girls rode their horses together along the gravel shoulders of the quiet county roads. Meadowlarks sang atop fence posts. Dogs trotted along at the horses' heels, and the irrigation sprinklers tick-ticked long rainbows of water through the sunshine. When such a group arrived at his door, Randall stood on the porch and watched his daughter join up. Red Sultan was beautiful, and Lisa was obviously proud, preening. She'd braided the stallion's mane, and it had stood, patient and steady, while she'd threaded a blue-satin ribbon through the braids.

The girls clustered around the stallion, in hushed awe, lightly touching him as if to prove to themselves that he was for real. The scene reminded Randall of his own childhood. In those days, every couple of years a traveling sideshow outfit would roll into town towing an enclosed auto trailer. Painted down both sides of the trailer in old cowboy writing like twisted ropes were the words "See it! The Bonnie and Clyde Death Car!" They'd set up in the parking lot of Western Auto, or they'd off-load the car near the carnival midway at the county fair. It was a rusted two-door coupe riddled with little holes, streaked with rust, the windows busted out. The flat tires shot to shit. Headlights exploded. For the price of two bits, Randall would go shiver at the sight of bloodstains on the seats and stick his fingers in the bullet holes. That grim relic from the darkness of history. Somewhere, he still had a photograph of himself standing next to the car with Stu Gilcrest, both of them the age Lisa was now. Him and Stu, they'd argued over which caliber each of the little punched-in holes represented.

The car was evil. But it was okay because it was a piece of American history. That part of the big, real world had come into his life to prove the lessons he'd been taught were true. The wages of sin were death. Crime does not pay.

Today, the girls swarmed the horse just as Randall and his pals had swarmed the Death Car. One year had brought the James Dean Death Car or the Jayne Mansfield Death Car. Another time, it was the JFK Death Car. People flocked to touch them. To snap pictures. To prove to their friends they'd touched something terrible.

While the local girls came to crowd around her, Lisa pulled her phone from her back pocket, saying, "Of course it's him. I'll prove it." She keyed something. From the porch, Randall could hear a few tinny sounds from the phone. The girls watching with Lisa exploded in groans and laughter.

Whatever they'd just witnessed, now they were petting the red-brown muzzle and flanks. They sighed and cooed. They held their own telephones at arm's length and snapped selfies of their faces, their lips puckered, kissing the horse's cheeks.

The group wasn't gone two hours before his phone rang. He was in the kitchen checking email, watching the progress bar on his monitor not budge. Their service provider was a satellite company, but lousy Internet access wasn't tragic, not when a single keystroke could bring all the filth and degradation of the world into a person's peaceful, bright kitchen. These days it took real effort to keep purity in a child's life. High-speed connectivity wasn't worth Lisa's innocence. That was a fact her mother wouldn't accept. One of many.

On the phone was Stu Gilcrest from down the road. He said, "Your girl was just by here."

That's how good neighbors behaved. Theirs was a community where people kept tabs on one another's loved ones. Randall told him that, come July, Lisa would be around a lot more.

"All summer?" Stu marveled. "She's become a lovely little lady. You must be very proud." Something in his tone sounded subdued. He was keeping something back.

Randall thanked him. Sensing there was something else, he waited.

Over the phone, Stu said, "I see she's got herself a new horse."

Randall explained about Sour Kraut dying and bragged how he'd looked far and wide for a replacement. He waited for Stu to exclaim about the Arabian. Its beauty. The gentle manner of it.

When Stu spoke he'd lost his friendly, neighborly tone. "Nobody hopes I'm wrong more than I do." His words dropped to almost a growl. "But if I'm not mistaken, that's Red Sultan's Big Boy, isn't it?"

Randall was taken aback. A chill of dread embraced him. He ventured, "That there's a fine, fine horse."

Stu didn't respond, not that instant. He cleared his throat. He swallowed. "Randall," he began, "we've been neighbors since way back."

"Since three generations," Randall agreed. He asked what was the matter.

"All I'm saying," Stu spat the words, "is that you and Lisa will always be welcome on our place."

Randall asked, "Stu?"

"It's none of my business," his neighbor stammered, "but Glenda and I would much appreciate you not bringing that animal onto our property." This sounded as if it hurt to say.

Randall asked if he meant the horse. Had Lisa or the horse done anything to offend? The Gilcrests had a couple of girls near to Lisa's age. Girls could take offense and catfight and patch things up faster than a bolt of August heat lightning. They loved the drama.

The phone line clicked. A female voice joined the conversation. Stu's wife, Glenda. Randall pictured her on the extension, sitting on their bed. She said, "Randall, please understand. We can't have our girls anywhere near your place. Not until that horse is destroyed." Against Randall's protest, they both said good-bye and hung up.

Over the next four hours, almost all of the neighbors called. The Hawkins. The Ramirezes. The Coys and Shandys and Turners. It was clear that the group of riders was making a slow circuit of the district, taking County Road 17 to Boundary Lane, after that moving west along Sky Ridge Trail. They were paying calls at every girl's house or the home of a relative. It was this series of mothers, fathers, aunts, uncles, grandparents, and cousins who were telephoning in quick succession. After a few strained words of hello, each caller asked if Lisa wasn't in fact riding Red Sultan's Big Boy. And when Randall told them, yes, that was the case, to a person they informed him that the horse was unwelcome in the future. Furthermore, none of them would be calling at his place if the horse was on the property.

Lisa had been forced to ride the last leg of the circuit alone. By midafternoon, all her girlfriends had been forbidden to accompany her another step. Even as she trotted up to the house, abandoned by her friends, she didn't seem daunted. Her head held high, her back straight, if anything, she seemed smug. Triumphant, even.

The phone calls left Randall prepared for the worst. He expected to find the horse hostile and skittish, but the Arabian was gentle. As placid and sweet-natured as ever. As she ran a curry mitt over his flanks, Lisa said he was responsive to commands. His gait was smooth. Nothing, not passing cars or barking dogs or low-flying crop dusters, nothing spooked him. No one had said anything unkind. She seemed unfazed by everyone's reaction. They'd looked at the horse, but none of the girl's relatives had come forward to touch him. They'd simply ordered their girls to dismount and go no farther.

That night, after dinner, as Randall and his daughter washed dishes, a car stopped on the road, near the far end of their drive. The day's events had him nervous, and Randall listened for it to drive away. Instead, the living room front window burst. Footsteps retreated down the gravel to the car, and tires squealed into the distance. Amid the shards of glass on the carpet was a dark, curved shape. A horseshoe.

Lisa regarded the weapon, her lips bent into a little smile.

The next Saturday, they loaded Red Sultan's Big Boy into the trailer and set off for the Merriwether stables. Enid Merriwether had been teaching dressage to comers since Randall was a boy. The paddock parking lot was mobbed with females, mostly mothers and daughters and their horses. When Lisa swung open the gate of their trailer, the din of chatter fell to silence.

A girl giggled. The ladies glared the giggler into silence.

A voice said, "Well, if it isn't Red Satan's Bad Boy . . ." All heads turned to regard Enid Merriwether as the great horsewoman herself approached. The leather of her riding boots creaked. The sun glinted on the buttons of her tailcoat. In one hand swung a dressage whip. Her gaze took in the crowd of stewing, sullen women. Turning to Lisa, she said, not without sympathy, "I'm sorry, but we seem to be a little overenrolled for the season."

Randall stepped forward, saying, "I've seen more riders than this many." Not counting mothers, only counting girls and horses, it didn't appear to be more than an average turnout.

As if she hadn't heard, Lisa was leading the Arabian down the trailer ramp. Enid stepped back. Enid Merriwether, who'd never backed down from the most cantankerous beast, she eyed that Arabian and motioned for the crowd to give the horse more room. She brought the whip up, ready to use it. "I'll thank you to load that animal right back in your rig and remove him from these premises." The onlookers drew their breath.

Lisa, with a defiance that her father had never heard in her voice, his daughter shouted back, "Why?" Her face wasn't just flushed. She was the red a person sees when he looks at the sun with his eyes shut.

Miss Merriwether barked a laugh. "Why?" She looked at the crowd for agreement. "That horse is a killer!"

Lisa nonchalantly examined her manicure, saying, "He's not." She put her cheek against the horse's cheek and said, "Really. He's a lover boy."

The great horsewoman motioned to enroll the crowd. "He's worse than a killer. And everybody around these parts knows it."

Lisa looked at her father. Randall was dumbstruck. The stallion lifted his head, stretching his neck to sniff new air. The horse yawned.

Compassionately, even piteously, Enid Merriwether looked at the smirking girl. "Lisa Randall, you know darned well that horse is evil."

"He's not!" Lisa purred. She kissed him. The crowd of mothers flinched.

That night Randall banged together some boards to cover the busted front window. In the dusk he could see, out in the yard, where he'd mounded up some earth and planted a cross, two boards nailed crosswise, painted white and lettered with the name "Sour Kraut." He'd told Lisa her horse was buried there, but the truth was a flatbed had trucked the poor dead beast to a rendering plant across the state line in Harlow. As he watched, Lisa picked a bunch of daisies from a flower bed his mother's mother's ma had planted. She brought the bouquet to the fake grave and knelt. The evening breeze carried snatches of her prayer. She was talking about how much she loved her old horse, and how much she loved the new Arabian. Listening, it occurred to Randall that the love people feel for animals is the purest form of love. Loving an animal, a horse, cat, or dog, was always a romantic tragedy. It meant loving something that would die before you. Like that movie with Ali MacGraw. There was no future, just the affection of the present moment. You didn't expect a big payoff, someday.

The fading light made it harder to see her in the yard, but Lisa's words were clear. She said how much she was enjoying her summer. She said how beautiful Red Sultan's Big Boy was and how much everyone loved him. When she said, "I love you, Mom," Randall realized she'd been talking on her phone.

Before she came inside, he heard the phone ring in the kitchen. The Caller ID said, "Private Number." He picked up.

The voice was no one he'd ever spoken with in his life. No, he'd have remembered this voice. The wheezing quality. The breathless panting. In a voice he'd never forget, a stranger asked, "Am I correct in understanding that you currently possess the Arabian stallion known as Red Sultan's Big Boy?"

Randall braced himself for a stream of verbal abuse. He listened for Lisa walking up the porch steps.

Unbidden, the voice continued, "Please know that I am prepared to offer you the sum of five hundred thousand dollars for the animal in question."

A voice asked, "Who's on the phone, Dad?" It was Lisa, standing at his elbow.

"Nobody," Randall said and hung up.

That week, on a hunch he drove over the state line to the rendering plant in Harlow. It was no place folks went on a whim, the proverbial glue factory. The smell alone could knock a man down. He followed the road along a chain-link fence until he came to a locked gate. A travel trailer sat just inside, and Randall honked his horn and waited. A man came out of the trailer and asked his business, and Randall explained about shipping Sour Kraut's body a couple weeks back. Without unlocking the gate, the man brought forth a clipboard. Leafing through the pages, he stood with just the fence between them. "A pinto gelding, you say?"

Randall asked, "Do you have any record?"

A lot of pages deep, the man said, "Here we go. The hide was fine. The bones. The hooves." Clearly, they didn't waste a thing.

Randall asked, "Any sign of what killed him?"

The man said, "County makes us test for spongiform encephalitis."

Randall waited. Big in his head was the image of Sour Kraut collapsed on the stable floor. His neck stretched out, and his head fallen in a puddle of bloody foam.

The man turned the clipboard for him to see. His fingertip tapped a line where the word "atropine" was written. "Heart attack," the man said. "Chances are your horse got into some nightshade or a patch of potato vine."

Randall asked, "How long's it take?" Every muscle of him felt weak, as if he'd stepped out of a too-hot shower.

"Not long." The man shook his head. "That horse would've died where he ate it."

That same week, there came more of those strange telephone callers, each one offering to buy the horse. Among them was the broker who'd sold them the Arabian. Calling Thursday night, he wanted to buy back the horse. "Not for myself, mind you." The broker sounded defensive. "I'm acting strictly as the agent for a third party." He opened with a price of twelve thousand. Twice what Randall had paid. Flat out, Randall asked him what all the fuss was about. The broker asked, "You're saying you truly don't know?"

Wary, Randall shook his head. He remembered being on the phone and asked, "Know what?"

"You haven't seen the video?" The broker said, "Since it went viral, I'm getting inquiries from as far away as Kingdom Come."

Before Randall could hang up, he heard the broker say, "Your little girl's already called me and told me to field offers, but you're the fellah what holds the papers."

Up to then the worst Randall had ever seen was a classroom movie called *Signal 30*. Mr. O'Connor had made his class watch it in sixth grade, to make them more careful around railroad crossings and wearing seat belts. The memory was like bronzed baby shoes or the wad of cotton folks used to find in a bottle of aspirin: almost forgotten. The school movie showed black-and-white photos of wrecked cars and people speared through the chest by gory steering columns. Windshields were punched with cannonball holes made by blasting-out babies. The blood and motor oil had the same quality of inky black. That made it difficult to tell if a puddle on the pavement beside a crumbled sedan was from a cracked block or someone bleeding to death. A kid in class fainted, Logan Carlisle, maybe Eva Newsome fainted. An ominous storyteller's voice had stitched the nightmares together, asking, "The next time you think you can outrun a freight train, think again!" A train horn had blared, followed by sound effects of breaking glass and crashing metal, and the movie would flash the photo of dead teenagers strewn around a jalopy mashed to scrap by a Southern Pacific locomotive.

The booming voice asked, "Think it's safe to pass a stopped school bus? Well, think again!" Filling the movie screen would be some two-lane rural highway scattered with the mangled bodies of children.

The other worst thing Randall had seen was at a barbershop, where they used to keep a stack of true crime magazines under the *Playboy*s. Page after page of sex crime photos. Atrocities. Like a naked woman, pretty except for having her arms and legs hacked off with a meat cleaver, packed into an open suitcase with a black bar superimposed across her eyes to protect her dignity. One was a woman on the flowered rug in an olden-times hotel room, strangled by the cord of a rotary-dial telephone. On the coarse, yellowing pages was woman after woman, naked and dead in different ways, but all with black rectangles to keep their eyes secret.

Compared to *Signal 30* and the barbershop magazines, what Randall found on the Internet was worse. A person might as well eat poison as download this clip. He didn't have to watch more than a couple minutes to recognize his horse. What Red Sultan's Big Boy was doing to a naked, bent-over man was the ultimate abomination. An image Randall would be burdened to carry to his grave.

If nothing else, it felt comforting to know he was the last among his friends and neighbors to be stained by watching this strange, sad outrage. It was equally galling to imagine what others were imagining, him hosting the purebred under his roof. But where they saw sin, he recognized loneliness. A brand of loneliness that heretofore Randall hadn't known existed.

He hit Enter and watched the video clip play a second time.

It could be what occurred in the video wasn't about pleasure as much as it was about surviving the real version of what life did to you every day. Randall reasoned, it was about subjecting oneself to a greater power. Whether it was a pleasure or a physical test, it wasn't cluttered up with ideas of romantic love. More a religious love. Taking place was a penance or an act of contrition.

Randall conceded a longing to not be the master, to stop being in control. A want to please some brand of huge, weighty god. To feel its crushing approval.

He hit Enter to replay the experience.

It scared him to think the opposite. To consider that it might be a pleasure, a pleasure beyond anything most people would ever know, a pleasure worth dying for. A physical rapture.

From the recorded grunts and groans, the man under the horse thought he was having a grand old time. He must've known he was on videotape. None of that mattered, judging from how the man arched his back, and the eyes-closed smile on his face. It was strange to see someone that happy who wasn't pretending. On the computer screen, the man bent his knees deeper, thrusting his backside against the bucking hips of the stallion. Something dark, a shadow or blood, ran down his leg.

Randall hit Enter and the adventure began, anew. This time he watched the horse.

In retrospect, Randall recognized that the shadow running down the back of the man's leg had been semen. Too much to be human.

He hit Enter once more. He still had the front window to replace. He hit Enter all night. He muted the sound, but continued to watch when his phone rang. "As you might know," the caller began, "the horse has certain talents that make it extraordinarily valuable to a select group of buyers." It was the voice from a few nights back. "I feel duty-bound to warn you. Those people won't hesitate to use violence to their ends."

Randall watched the video until it was Friday night and time to pick up his daughter for the weekend.

They'd moved to the home place after Randall's father had died. The three of them, Lisa just a baby. Randall's pa had spent the last two years of his life in a care center, in town, where they'd go to see him almost every day. At the same time, the house had sat like a time capsule. The piano stood where it always had. There was a history attached to every plate or hammer. Nothing could be got rid of. Every throw pillow cued a long sermon to explain its every stain or the stitches where it had been mended. If Randall's wife had moved a carving fork from one drawer to another he'd moved it back. She bought green paint to redecorate the upstairs bedroom, and he'd made her return it. Randall's aunt had hung the wallpaper in that room. Every stitch in every quilt was sacrosanct. Every notch scratched in the kitchen door frame marked the growing up of someone now long dead. They'd become curators. Finally his wife had moved herself back into town. What all he saw as his legacy, Estelle took to be a curse.

Lisa came to visit, resentful and bored, until he'd bought her Sour Kraut. She'd cared for that horse with the same intensity that he'd cared for the house and farm. Neither of them could resist something helpless.

At Estelle's house, Lisa tossed her overnight bag into Randall's backseat. She was talking on her phone as she slid into the front seat beside him. She was saying, "Not my problem. If you think you can find another horse that will do the job don't waste my time." She snuck a glance at Randall and winked, telling the phone, "We've got other offers on the table."

Without looking at her, he asked, "Is it real?"

Lisa touch-screened her phone. "Is what real?" Then, with a laugh, asked, "Are you talking about the video?"

It was obscene. An atrocity.

Rolling her eyes, Lisa reasoned, "Paris Hilton. Kim Kardashian. Pam Anderson. Rob Lowe. Who hasn't made a sex tape?" She laughed. "Daddy, it's a scream."

Randall gripped the steering wheel tighter. "So you've seen it?"

It was an Internet classic, like a myth they'd read in school, she said. Leda and the Swan. Her friends had never seen anything more funny.

Randall said it wasn't funny. It was tragic.

Her thumbs twitching over her phone's tiny keys, summoning up facts, Lisa insisted, "Daddy, of course it's funny."

Randall asked, why?

She considered the question as if for the first time. "I don't know. Because he was white, I guess." She read details as they surfaced. The man was heterosexual, divorced with one child, and he died of a ruptured sigmoid colon. She grinned. "Isn't this just perfect?" She nodded smugly at the phone's screen. "He was a rich big shot for Hewlett-Packard or some other Fortune 500 member of the military-industrial complex."

Randall challenged, "What if it had been a girl your age?"

Lisa wagged a finger at him. "If it showed a girl, then anyone who even watched the video would go to jail."

Randall tested the waters, asking, "And if the man wasn't white?"

Lisa scrolled and tabbed, distracted in her search. "If it was a black guy, it would be racist. No one would post it on any site."

If the video had shown a woman with the horse, Lisa

explained that it would be misogynistic, promoting the abuse of women. Even a woman who had consented, she would be considered as coerced by her culture and acting out of internalized self-hatred. The same went for a homosexual. No, what made the video hilarious was the fact that the person acted upon was white, straight, a male, and an adult. Lisa said, "I wrote a whole paper on it for our unit on gender perspectives." She looked up from the phone, beaming. "I got an A."

Randall stammered, "But he died."

His daughter shrugged. "Not on the video. He died hours later in an emergency room."

Randall's phone rang. It was the livestock broker calling. He didn't pick up.

Lisa speculated lightly, "It's like watching Mother Nature get revenge for all the global warming the white patriarchy has inflicted on the environment." She sighed. "Don't take it so personally, Daddy. You just chose the wrong time in history to be a straight, white, Christian male."

It was the smugness in her voice. The supreme confidence. It made Randall feel sorry for her. Miles went by before he gathered the courage to ask, "Did you kill Sour Kraut?"

Scrolling through her text messages, his daughter replied, "The bidding is now at two-point-five million."

Those were the last words the two spoke to one another.

It was almost dusk when they got to the home place, but a group of teenage boys and girls were waiting to see Red Sultan's Big Boy. Going into the house, Randall could hear Lisa telling them that it would cost five dollars to see the horse. A selfie would cost ten.

Around dinnertime the broker texted to say the bidding was close to three million.

Randall texted back, "Cash?"

It was impossible to not start spending that money in his head. A top-notch education for Lisa. A new life someplace that would make Estelle happy. Freedom from the past. He typed, "What happens to the horse?"

The broker came back with, "LOL. I assure you that horse will not be pulling a carriage. The horse will live a life you and I can only dream of."

The horse in the video hadn't looked miserable. How could someone weigh the quality of that life against, say, pulling a plow? It seemed as if human beings could subject an animal to anything—crowded conditions, chemicals, mutilation, misery, and death—but not pleasure.

That weekend, Lisa paraded the horse around the district. Showing off.

Randall. Randall went hunting through scrapbooks. The family had never thrown anything away. He found the photograph of him and Stu Gilcrest in front of the Bonnie and Clyde Death Car. The two boys were grinning with glee. Each had a finger stuck into a bullet hole in the driver's door. Depending on who told their story, Parker and Barrow were villains or martyrs, but wherever their car was on display it was making more money than they'd ever robbed off banks.

Sunday evening, Lisa put flowers on Sour Kraut's fake grave, and Randall drove her home to her mother. Neither said goodbye.

Monday, he remembered what the broker had said about people cutting loose their cabin cruisers. Abandoning what they'd once treasured but could no longer support. He thought of the man in the video who believed he was having the time of his life when, in fact, his insides were already bleeding to death. Randall had written down a location the broker had told him to be at. It was nothing but sage land in the middle of a hundred square miles of nowhere. He loaded Red Sultan's Big Boy into the trailer.

Randall, he brought a .55-caliber big enough to blow a hole in Bonnie and Clyde.

He didn't go where they'd agreed to meet. Instead, he drove a hundred klicks north.

How he saw it, he was rescuing the horse in the best way possible. He opened the back of the trailer. Took off the Arabian's bridle. Unbraided the blue ribbons from its mane. With just a rope around its neck, he led it off a ways to where it was the only thing in sight. It continued to be the sweet-natured docile creature he'd first met. Not drugged, not sick, but damaged just the same. Randall took out the gun and set his mind to do what his own child had done to Sour Kraut. If she could, with malice and forethought, so could he be judge, jury, and executioner.

Whatever they heard next, the horse heard it first. His ears twitched toward a sound carried on the wind. Hooves, but not wild horses. Not mustangs, but horses gone wild.

Randall wasn't here first. Atop this vast windswept nowhere. Other plain people had been forced to this same desperate place, to commit the act he was about to commit. He wasn't alone, but everyone before him had found a better choice, and on the horizon grazed a herd of dreams they'd been driven to leave behind. All those seemingly impossible aspirations, they ran together in the distance, flourishing.

Randall looped the rope off the Arabian's neck. He clapped and stomped to spook the thing, but it wouldn't budge. Finally, he put the gun in the air and fired a few shots. That did the trick, and Red Sultan's Big Boy galloped away. Too late, Randall considered that he might've pried off the horse's shoes. He could've done a lot of things better.

To test if he'd done the right thing, Randall put the gun barrel to the side of his head and squeezed the trigger one last time. The hammer fell, but nothing more happened. The chamber was empty. He'd been forgiven.

Driving home he reminded himself that he was a member in good standing at the cooperative, and that meant they'd have to buy his crop. Randall's wasn't a good-sized operation, but he'd still manage to get by.

■

ROMANCE

You should congratulate me. My wife and I just had twins, and they seem okay. Ten fingers. Ten toes. Two little girls. But you know the feeling . . . I keep waiting for something to go wrong because that's how it is when things get too happy. I keep expecting to wake up from this beautiful dream.

I mean, back before I was married I had this one girlfriend who was fat. We were, both of us, fat together so we got along. That girlfriend, she was always testing us on new diets to lose weight, like eating nothing except pineapple and vinegar, or nothing but green algae from an envelope, and she was suggesting we take long walks together until she started to shed the pounds, her hips just melted away, and you never saw anybody so happy. Even then I knew something would wreck it. You know the feeling: When you love somebody, you're happy to see her happy, but I knew my girlfriend was going to dump me because now guys with careers and health insurance were getting her on their radar. I remember she was pretty and funny before, but now that she was getting so skinny it was obvious she possessed vast untapped reserves of self-control and self-discipline way out of my league, and my friends weren't any help because they were all circling, waiting for us to call it quits so they could

70

date her, and then it turned out it wasn't the pineapple or the self-discipline because she found out she really had cancer, but she slimmed down to wearing a bitch'n-hot Size Two before she died.

That's how I know happiness is like a ticking bomb. And how I met my wife is because I wasn't going to date anybody, not anymore, no way, so I was taking the Amtrak to Seattle. It was the year of Lollapalooza in Seattle, and I'd packed my tent and wrapped my sleeping bag to protect my bong so I could camp out all weekend like a Grizzly Adams, and I walked into the bar car on the train. You know how sometimes you just need to leave the friends and sobriety behind for a few days. I walked into the bar car, and there's this total stone-cold-fox pair of green eyes looking right directly at me. And I'm not a monster. I'm not some reality show blimp stuck in a hospital bed eating buckets of fried chicken all day, but I can understand why guys would want to work as guards in women's prisons or concentration camps where they could just date good-looking prisoners without those babes always saying, "Put a shirt on!" and asking, "Do you always have to sweat so much?" But on the train, here's this goddess wearing a Radiohead T-shirt cut off to show her bare middle, and her jeans sag down to where there ought to be bush showing, and she's wearing Mickey Mouse and Holly Hobbie rings around every finger, holding a beer to her beautiful lips and looking at me down the length of the brown bottle, just an ordinary MGD, not some pussy microbrew in a green bottle.

And guys like me, we know the score. Unless we're John Belushi or John Candy, no hottie is going to put you in that kind of an eye-lock so, right away, I know enough to look away from her in shame. The only reason why a girl like her would talk to me is to break the news that I'm a gross fat pig and I'm blocking her entire view of the ocean. Know your limits, I always say. Aim low and you won't be disappointed. Edging past her, I look without looking. I check her out, and she smells good, like some kind of dessert, like a baked pie, like a pumpkin pie with that red-brown spices on top. Better yet, the beer bottle in her mouth turns to follow me as I walk down the aisle to the bar and order a round, and it's not as if we're the last boy and girl in the whole world. A bunch of other people are drinking at the plastic tables, going to Lollapalooza from the look of their dreads and tie-dye. I walk all the way to the most faraway table from her, but this hottie watches me go all the way. You know the feeling, when somebody's watching, you can't take one step without stumbling, especially on a moving-around train. I go to take a drink as the train turns a corner, and I spill beer down my striped cowboy shirt. I'm pretending to watch the trees going by outside the window, but from a secret agent angle I'm watching her reflection in the glass, and she's still watching me. The only time she looks away is when she steps up to the bar and gives the bartender some money and he gives her another beer, and then her reflection is getting bigger and bigger until it's life-sized and she's standing next to my table and says, "Hi," and something else.

And I say, "What?"

And she points at my cowboy shirt, at the beer spilled there, and she says, "I like your buttons . . . shiny."

I tuck my chin and look down at the pearl-colored snaps. They're not buttons, they're snaps, but I don't want to scotch this moment. And right from the get-go I noticed she puts her fingers in her mouth sometimes—okay, she puts her fingers in her mouth a lot, and she uses a breathy, little-girl voice with some baby-talk words like *buh-sketti* instead of *spaghetti* and *skissors* in place of *scissors*—but for a regulation hottie that's just textbook being sexy.

She gives me a wink and licks the tip of her tongue around her lips, and with the wet still shining on them, she says, "I'm Britney Spears." She's such a tease. Sure, she's a little loaded. Impaired. By now we're both drinking those little bottles of tequila, and it's not as if we're driving this train. No, she's not Britney Spears, but she's the same caliber of hot. It's clear she's pulling my pud, but in a good way. And you just need to look at her to know all you need to know.

The only chance I have is to hold on and keep flirting back and buying the drinks. She asks me where I'm headed and I tell her Lollapalooza. She's walking her fingers up the front of my shirt, her fingertips stepping from snap to snap, from my belt up to my throat, then walking herself back down, and I'm hoping she can't feel how hard that makes my heart beat.

And she's such a flirt with her green eyes cutting from side to side or pecking up at me from under her long, fluttering eyelashes. And she must be beers and beers ahead of me because she keeps forgetting to end her sentences, and sometimes she points at something speeding by outside the window and she shouts, "A dog!" or one time she sees a car waiting at a rail crossing and Brit screams, "Slug Bug!" and clobbers my shoulder with her fistful of Hello Kitty and Mickey Mouse rings, and secretly I hope I have the bruise for the rest of my life. And we go to Lollapalooza and pitch my tent, and Brit's so drunk that when she wakes up the next morning she's still drunk. And no matter how much doobie I smoke I'm having trouble keeping up. And maybe it's because Brit's so skinny, but she seems to cop a buzz without drinking for hours, like maybe she's getting a contact high from my secondhand smoke. Our whole Lollapalooza is like the kind of beautiful classic romance you'd pay to jerk off to on the Internet, but it's happening to me. And we're dating for six months, all the way through Christmas, through Brit moving her stuff into my apartment, and I keep expecting Brit to wake up sober one morning, and she still hasn't.

We go to eat Thanksgiving at my mom's place, and I have to explain. It's not that Brit is a finicky eater, but the reason she's so skinny is she only likes to eat a zucchini squash cut in half lengthwise and hollowed down the middle to make a miniature Iroquois dugout canoe with knife scratches on the outside to look like Indian writing and a whole tribe of little braves carved out of raw carrot but with green peas for their heads, lined up and rowing the war canoe across a dinner plate covered with a thick layer of chocolate syrup, and you'd be surprised how many restaurants don't have that particular item on their regular menus. So most times Brit has to make it herself, and that takes half a day, and then she has to play with it on the living room carpet for another hour, and that's why she never seems to gain an ounce. And my mom, she's just stoked to see me dating, again.

And nothing you can smoke or shoot will ever get you as high as you'll feel walking down the street holding hands with a supermodel total stone-cold fox like my Brit. Guys driving down the street in their Ferrari Testarossas, guys with the six-pack abs and steroid pecs, for the first time in my life they have nothing over me. I'm walking down the street with Britney, and she's the prize every guy's trying so hard to win.

And the only buzz kill is how every Romeo comes to sniff a circle around her, trying to grab her in an eye-lock and giving her tits his best Pepsodent toothpaste smile. And this one time, riding on the bus, a pack of Romeos stand themselves around where Brit and I are sitting in the back of the bus. Brit likes to sit on the aisle right over the back wheels so she can see to punch me first when there's a Volkswagen, and this one big Romeo comes to stand with his crotch situated at her eye level, and when the bus hits a pothole maybe his hip brushes against her shoulder until Brit looks up at him, and talking around her fingers in her mouth Britney says, "Hello, Big Boy." And that's just how Brit can be: friendly. And she winks and waves her wet fingers for the Romeo to lean down, and he looks around to make sure his competition is clocking his good luck, and this Romeo squats down to Brit's eye level, his face all bedroom smirk. And maybe because she's trying to make me jealous, Brit says to this Romeo, her smok'n-hot green eyes look at him and she asks, "You want to see a magic trick?" And all the other Romeos perk up with looks that prove they're all listening, and Brit takes her fingers out of her mouth and slides them down inside the front of her pants, grinding her fingers around inside the skintight crotch of her jeans, and the back half of our bus gets so quiet with their watching her fingers wrestle behind her stone-washed denim zipper. And you can see these Romeos swallow, their Adam apples going up and down with all their extra spit and their eyes bulging like horny boners.

And as fast as clobbering a Slug Bug Britney yanks something out of her pants and yells, "Magic trick!" She swings this thing, shouting, "Puppet show!" And swinging from her hand is something on a little string, like a tea bag only bigger. It's like a hot dog bun smeared with ketchup swinging on a little string, and Britney screams, "Puppet show! Magic trick!" and smacks it across the cheek of the Romeo still squatting down next to her seat. And Brit chases after him, yelling and slapping his leather jacket with streaks of red. And other Romeos not looking at her on purpose, fixing their faces to stare down at their shoes or look out a window, she's swinging her little string to smack them upside their heads with red smears, the whole time squealing, "Puppet show! Magic trick!" laughing ha, ha, ha, ha, ha, shouting, "Puppet show! Magic trick!" The bus is ding-ding-dinging for the next stop, and a hundred passengers get off at the 7-Eleven, pushing and stampeding off the bus like they all need to buy Slurpees and cash in their winning Powerball mega-jackpot tickets. And I'm yelling after them, "It's okay, everybody!" I'm yelling out the bus window, waving to get their attention, "She's a performance artist!" I'm yelling, "She doesn't mean anything by it; it's just some political gender politics statement deal."

Even as the bus pulls away with just the two of us left on board, I'm yelling, "She's just a Free Spirit." As Brit goes up the aisle and starts flogging the driver with her tea bag thing, I'm yelling, "That's just her zany sense of humor."

And one night I come home from work and Brit's naked and standing sideways to the bathroom mirror, holding her belly in both hands, and since we met on the train she's gained a little weight, but it's nothing that a couple weeks of pineapple and vinegar won't fix. And Britney takes my hand and holds my fingers spread against her belly and says, "Feel." She says, "I think I ate a baby." And she looks at me like a puppy dog with her green hottie eyes, and I ask if she wants me to go with her to the clinic and take care of it, and she nods her head, yes. So we go on my day off, and there's the usual Sunday school teachers blocking the sidewalk. They hold a garbage bag full of nothing but broken-apart plastic baby doll arms and heads mixed together with ketchup, and Brit doesn't hesitate. She reaches into their bag and takes a leg and licks it clean like a French fry, and that's how cool my beautiful girlfriend is. And I open a *National Geographic* magazine while the nurse asks her if she's eaten anything today and Brit says she ate a whole canoe full of Iroquois warriors the day before, but, no, she hasn't eaten anything yet today. And I haven't finished reading this one article about ancient Egyptian mummies before there's a scream and

Britney comes running out of the back still wearing a paper dress and bare feet, like this is a big deal, like maybe she never had an abortion before, because she runs barefoot all the way back to my apartment, and to make her stop shaking and throwing up I have to ask her to marry me.

And it's obvious my friends are insanely jealous because they throw me this bachelor party, and when Britney goes to the ladies room all bummed out because the chef won't carve her a war canoe, my so-called "friends" all look at me and say, "Dude, she is the total most-hot, best thing, ever, but we don't think she's stoned . . ." My best friends say, "You didn't marry her yet, did you?" And their faces don't say Brit being knocked up is good news. And you know the feeling: You want your best friends and your fiancée to mesh, but my friends grit their teeth and look at me with their eyebrows worried tight together in the middle, and they say, "Dude, did it ever cross your mind that maybe—just maybe—Britney is mentally retarded?"

And I tell them to relax. She's just an alcoholic. I'm pretty certain she's a heroin junkie, too. That, and she's a sexual compulsive, but it's nothing so bad some talk therapy wouldn't fix her. Look at me: I'm fat; nobody's perfect. And maybe instead of a wedding reception we could get our two families together in a hotel conference room to surprise her with an intervention, and instead of a honeymoon we could get Britney committed to a ninety-day inpatient recovery program. We'll work through this. But no way is she retarded. She just needs some rehab.

It's obvious they're only badmouthing Britney because they are actually totally, Romeo-boner, insanely jealous. The minute I looked the other way, they'd be so up in her business. They say, "Dude, don't look now, but you fucked a retard," and that's how unpopular I am, that I have to settle for these shitty friends. Brit, they insist, has the intellect of a six-year-old. They think they're doing me a favor when they tell me, "Dude, she can't love you because she doesn't have the *capacity.*"

Like the only way somebody would marry me is if she had irreparable brain damage. And I tell them, "She can't be retarded, for crying out loud, because she wears a *pink thong.*" And it has to be love because every time we're together I come so hard my stomach hurts. And it's like I told my mom's boyfriend at Thanksgiving, no, Britney is not a *high-functioning anything.* My best guess is she's an alcoholic, glue-sniffing, dope-shooting slut, but we're working on getting her into treatment after she has the babies. And, maybe she's a nymphomaniac, but what's important here is she's *my nymphomaniac,* and that drives my family crazy with envy. I tell them, "I'm in love with a beautiful sex-crazed slut so why can't you just be happy for me?"

And after all that fuss there's a lot less people at our wedding than you'd expect.

And it could be that love makes you prejudiced, but I always thought Brit was pretty smart. You know the feeling, when you can watch TV together for a whole year and you both never argue over what shows. Seriously, if you knew how much TV we watch every week, you'd call us a happy marriage.

And now I have two little babies who smell like Thanksgiving pies. And when they're old enough I'm going to tell my little girls that everybody looks a little crazy if you're looking close enough, and if you can't look that close then you don't really love them. All the while life goes around, and it goes around. And if you keep waiting for somebody perfect you'll never find love, because it's how much you love them is what makes them perfect. And maybe I'm the retarded one because I keep waking up expecting my happiness to run out when I should just enjoy it. Being this crazy, in-love happy simply cannot be so easy. And I can't expect such total happiness to last the rest of my life, and there's got to be something wrong with me if I love my wife so much, and for right now I'm driving my new family home from the hospital with my beautiful wife sitting next to me and our twin baby girls safe in the backseat, and I'm still worried how happiness this great can't last forever when Britney screams, "Slug Bug!" and her fist clobbers my shoulder so hard I almost crash us into a whole Dairy Queen.

■

CANNIBAL

This is him. This is how he goes, the captain of the Red Team. He's all, "Listen up." He's desperate because they're still choosing sides. Because all the good picks are already taken, the captain says, "We'll make you a deal."

He folds his arms across his chest and the captain of the Red Team yells, "We'll take the fag . . . the four-eyes . . . and the spic—if you'll take Cannibal."

Because Phys Ed is almost over, the Blue Team confers, squeaking the toes of their court shoes against the gym floor. Their captain yells back, "We'll take the fag and the four-eyes, the spic, the Jew, the cripple, the gimp, *and* the retard—if you'll take Cannibal."

Because when this school grades you on Participation they mean: Do you take your share of the social rejects? And when they grade you on Sportsmanship, they mean: Do you marginalize the differently abled? Because of that the captain of the Red Team shouts, "We'll spot you a hundred points."

Hearing that the captain of the Blue Team shouts back, "We'll spot you a million."

Cannibal, he thinks he's such a stud because he's just looking at his fingernails, smiling and just smelling his fingers, not even aware of how he's holding everyone hostage. How this is the opposite of a slave auction. And everybody knows what he's thinking. Because of what Marcia Sanders told everybody. Because Cannibal is thinking about a movie that's chopped up in his head, some black-and-white movie he saw on cable TV where hard-boiled waitresses in olden times slung hash in some roadside diner. Because Cannibal's thinking how they popped their chewing gum, these waitresses. They smacked their chewing gum while they yelled, "Gimme slaughter on the pan and let the blood follow the knife." They yelled, "Gimme an order of first lady with a side of nervous pudding."

You knew it was olden times because in diner talk two poached eggs were "Adam and Eve on a raft." And "first lady" meant an order of spare ribs because of something from the Bible. An order of just "Eve" meant apple pie because of the story about the snake. Because nowadays nobody except Pat Robertson knew anything about the Garden of Eden. Around here, when the captain of the baseball team talks about eating a fur burger he's talking about chowing down on a muff pie, and he's really bragging about his tongue lapping at a blue waffle.

Because girls have their own food, too, like when they talked about Marcia Sanders having a bun in the oven, what they meant was she'd missed her red letter day.

Otherwise most of what he knew about sex Cannibal learned from the Playboy Channel where ladies never rode the cotton pony so when kids whispered about gobbling a bearded clam or snacking on a meat muffin he knew it meant what the bunnies do to the playmates, the same way a rattlesnake flickers its tongue to smell something it plans to bite on Animal Planet.

Because Cannibal had seen those centerfolds. You know the ones, of an old Miss America drinking from the furry cup. Those dirty pictures of her being a confirmed clam digger, because it was just those two ladies without a single tube steak or bald-headed yoghurt slinger standing there to make it a real marriage. Because that's how girls do, sometimes, when their crotch cobbler needs gobbling.

Because nobody ever explained otherwise, he was ready to go neck-deep in Marcia Sanders's jelly hole. Because his dad, old Mr. Cannibal, only ever watched the Playboy Channel, and Mrs. Cannibal only liked the *700 Club*, so it wasn't lost on their boy how sex stuff and Christian stuff both looked the same. Because when you turn on cable TV, it never fails. When you tune in and see an almost-beautiful girl almost acting on a set that looks almost realistic, Cannibal knows that her story will end by her being touched by an angel. Either that or she'll get a heaping helping of hot baby gravy sliding down one side of her face.

Because of that, Cannibal was already sporting a Spam javelin when Marcia Sanders looked at him in American Civics one day. No matter how he tries to hide it, his skin is polka dot with goose bumps, because he'd been remembering that hard-boiled diner talk yelled through a little window. The same way Catholics lined up in church to talk dirty through their own little window.

Because no matter how they called it, dirty talk made Cannibal drool. Those words picturing a whisker biscuit like those lunch meat curtains kids talk about when what they really mean is a camel toe soufflé.

In middle school when they grade you on Community Spirit, they mean: Do you cheer at pep rallies and football games? And when kids joke about Cannibal, they're talking about the one time when Marcia Sanders was a senior about to graduate. Because she's got those kind-of big lips and caved-in cheeks that make it look like she's always deep-throating a baloney pony, because of that Marcia Sanders was the most-popular. And because this was such a small school people considered her a real dish. Because she had nothing in fourth period she was the TA in American Civics where she approached Cannibal, because he was still only in seventh grade, and because she knew he'd never say no because he was so stoned on puberty.

She's all, "You like my hair, don't you?" Her head rolls to swing her hair like a spaghetti cape, and she goes, "This is the longest my hair's ever been."

The way she says this sounds dirty, because everything sounds dirty when it comes out of a sexy girl's mouth. And because Cannibal doesn't know any better, Cannibal agrees to reconnoiter with Marcia Sanders at her house because Mr. and Mrs. Sanders are gone to the lake that weekend. She only asks him because she says her boyfriend, the team captain of every sport, won't put her on like a gas mask. This is her, here's her, she says this, Marcia Sanders, she says, "You really want to do me, kid?" And because Cannibal has no idea what she means, he says, "Yeah."

Because then she says to come by her house after dark on Saturday and come to the kitchen door because she has a reputation to uphold. And because Marcia Sanders says he can be her secret boyfriend, Cannibal doesn't think twice.

Because at Jefferson Middle School when they grade you on Good Citizenship, they mean: Do you wash your hands after launching a corn canoe? Because half the time Cannibal doesn't know what he's thinking, he goes on Saturday night and Marcia Sanders folds the bedspread back on the king-sized waterbed in her parents' bedroom. She spreads two layers of bath towels across the waterbed and says to make sure his head goes in the middle of them. She says not to take off his clothes, but Cannibal figures that comes later because she unzips her jeans and folds them over the back of a chair, and because he's looking at her panties so hard she says to shut his eyes. Because Cannibal only pretends not to peek he sees her kneel on the padded rail at the edge of the waterbed, and he can see why it's called a ham wallet. After that he can't see jack because she slings one leg over his face and squats down until the room is nothing but fish taco blotting out everything except the underwater sound of Marcia Sanders's voice telling him what to do next.

Cannibal finds himself sunk, head-deep into waterbed with sloppy waterbed mattress squeezed up around his ears, hearing the lap of ocean waves. His body rocking from head to toe, hearing his heartbeat, hearing somebody's heartbeat. Because Marcia Sanders, out of nowhere her voice tells him, "Suck, already, you stupid dummy," Cannibal sucks.

Because she says, "Let's get this over with," he sucks like giving her insides a big hickey. It doesn't help that Cannibal is no ladies' man, like the one time Mrs. Cannibal told him to pin a corsage on his homecoming date but didn't specifically say to pin it *on her dress*. And it didn't help that every night you could walk past their house and hear Mr. Cannibal yelling, "I can't drink fast enough to stay married to you!"

Cannibal can't put up a fight against Marcia Sanders because when kids say his legs are thick as tree trunks, they're talking about willow trees. And when the *700 Club* talks about delightful, inspiring life stories, this ain't that because the harder Cannibal sucks the harder it gets because the suction is sucking back. Because he's battling her wet insides in this tug-of-war over nothing.

Cannibal is wearing Marcia Sanders like a gas mask, sucking on her like she's a snake bite with her thighs so earmuffed tight to the sides of his head he can't hear why she's screaming. Because on the Playboy Network, screaming is what you strive for. Cannibal's freaked out because a blue waffle on cable only smells like whatever your mom's cooking upstairs. Because a ham wallet on television never fights back, Cannibal sucks the way a tornado on the Weather Channel will bust one window and turn your entire house inside out.

Because Cannibal's never eaten a muff pie, he thinks the waterbed's sprung a leak because he hears a pop inside his head. It's like your ears pop when you ride a too-fast elevator to the top of the Sears Tower. Like when you snap your chewing gum or bite down on a ripe cherry tomato.

He figures the mattress is popped because what happens next is he's coughing water that tastes like tears. Because it's gallons, like Tammy Faye Bakker's cried a hundred years inside his mouth, and because Cannibal's never chowed down on a blue waffle the next thing he knows is that he's killed her because it's her insides gushing down his throat. Because she's hollering like a truck stop diner. All this happens in not even two heartbeats, but because he's watched the Playboy Network the next thing Cannibal knows is that he's made her gusher buckets of lady soup straight into his gullet. Because he's seen those videos where ladies geyser from jerking off, big spumes like Animal Planet whales spouting or those fire boats hosing down the Statue of Liberty during a Bicentennial Moment. Because he's seen their big sprays of lady gravy soaking into the orange-cheese-colored shag carpeting they always have in Playboy movies, Cannibal knows enough about lady juice not to spit it out, because the worst way to insult somebody is not to swallow what she's serving up.

Because his only experience with lady sauce is from cable TV, Cannibal doesn't realize there's a chunk of something solid mixed in. Not right away. Because bumping between his tongue and the roof of his mouth, right now, is this salt-flavored jellybean. It's a kidney bean that tastes like the water in a jar of pickles. It's knocking around like the last green olive in a jar of boiling-hot olive water. And because it's so small Cannibal just gulps it down.

Because half the time Cannibal doesn't know what he's thinking, he says, "You did it."

Marcia Sanders is fishing a fresh cotton pony out from her purse and goes, "I swear to you I didn't know." She never even takes off her top, and already she's zipping up her jeans.

And Cannibal goes, "I made you come."

She opens her mouth but doesn't say anything because then the doorbell rings, and it's her real boyfriend.

Because Cannibal makes Marcia Sanders geyser so hard she has to take a Tylenol and strap on a pussy plug, Cannibal knows he's a stud. Because Marcia Sanders must brag to Linda Reynolds because Linda Reynolds sidles up next to him outside the Chemistry modules and asks if he can be her secret boyfriend, too. Because Cannibal gobbles meat muffin so good Patty Watson wants a piece of his action because he makes every fur burger spout heaping helpings of special sauce. Because the quickest way to a woman's heart is through a man's stomach.

Because how far would a high schooler go to get back the rest of her life? And because Cannibal is giving everybody another shot at being virgins. He's everybody's dirty little secret, except he's not so secret. He brags like his every word's wearing sunglasses. And because he's not so little, not anymore. Because Cannibal's getting fat on the mistakes high schoolers make, it's Marcia Sanders who says they have to shut him up. Linda Reynolds campaigns to meet Cannibal out behind the Vocational Training modules with a swift tire iron to the head some Friday night because Cannibal's strutting around, too smart for his own good but too dumb to know he's total evil. Because now when Cannibal belches, it's your poor choice he's tasting.

And when Cannibal farts that's the smell of your parents' dead grandbaby.

Because if you believe Pat Robertson, the *700 Club* says that Jesus, one time, bade a legion of unclean spirits leave an afflicted man, and those demons went into a herd of swine. Because then those swine had to throw themselves off a cliff into the Sea of Galilee, that's how come Cannibal has to die. It's the only decent path to take.

Because even the priests who eat sins through the kitchen window at Catholic church, when they're filled full even they need to be burned at the stake. That's why a scapegoat goes to slaughter. Because if you believe in evolution the world is just everybody prancing down a yellow-brick road in Technicolor singing, "Because, because, because, because, *because* . . ." When the real truth is in the Old Testament where the seven tribes wander around, lost, always saying, "Begat, begat, begat, begat, *begat* . . ."

Because the upside is that maybe Cannibal will go to Heaven since except for his mouth he's still a virgin.

Because at this school no matter who the team captains pick now it's always not Cannibal, who personifies that thing that eventually comes for us all so we say, "Give us seat belts and give us pap smears and we'll take poverty and we'll take old age, just don't let Cannibal come stand next to us. Don't let Cannibal's shadow fall over our house."

Choosing sides, the captain of the Red Team says, "We'll give you our best pitcher . . ."

And we'll take the kid who picks his nose and eats it. And we'll take the kid who smells like piss. We'll take the leper and the left-handed Satanist and the AIDS-infected hemophiliac and the hermaphrodite and the pedophile. We'll take drug addiction and we'll take JPEGs of the world instead of the world, MP3s instead of music, and we'll trade real life for sitting at a keyboard. We'll spot you happiness and we'll spot you humanity, and we'll sacrifice mercy just so long as you keep Cannibal at bay.

Because Marcia Sanders doesn't begat anything her real boyfriend graduates and gets to go to Michigan State for an Accounting degree, because of all this Patty Watson makes a date to meet Cannibal on Friday night behind the Vocational Building and Linda Reynolds says she'll get a crowbar. And they all agree to wear latex gloves.

Because maybe they can all go back to playing games once Cannibal's gone.

■

WHY COYOTE NEVER HAD
MONEY FOR PARKING

It came to pass that Coyote and his wife had a baby. This was never who Coyote had wanted to be: a daddy. His long-term plan had been to find steady work as a rock star—the front man to wailing guitar anthems in stadium concerts, smoking weed with Jackass and falling asleep every night with his face wedged between the skinny flanks of Hyena—but now Coyote had obligations. Instead of sexy groupies, Coyote had a wife who didn't believe in abortion.

He'd bought a two-bedroom house in the Rainier Valley where their new baby never seemed to stop crying. Coyote didn't need a paternity test to know the baby had inherited his set of pipes. His baby wasn't a year old, and Coyote worried that it was already addicted to driving in cars. That didn't bode well for the precious environment. The only way he could lull the baby to sleep was by strapping it into the backseat of his beater Dodge Dart and driving around Seattle at roughly the speed of a shopping cart pushed along a supermarket aisle. No faster than five miles per hour, tops. Like clockwork, the baby woke at midnight. Coyote's wife nursed it, and he would carry it to the car. In their neighborhood nobody slept. Nobody worked, and nobody slept. All night Ox and Llama tipped back malt liquor, sitting on the

89

front porch of the house next door. Mongoose and Chipmunk played endless games of pickup basketball under the streetlight at the corner. On some nights, gunshots spit through the dark. The sound track of the neighborhood was car stereos so loud they rattled the glass in house windows. Car alarms. Police sirens. None of that made Coyote feel any better about the prospect of someday sending his kid to the local schools.

Somebody had ripped the radio out of his dashboard, and now Coyote was forced to sing if he wanted any music. Every night throbbed with amplified crap, and Coyote's voice got so tired he couldn't hear himself. Worse than the noise was how every addiction was sold curbside. You didn't even need to leave your car. You didn't even have to park. Driving around at five miles per hour, adding his screaming kid to the neighborhood mash-up, Coyote saw it all: Fox selling smack . . . Flamingo selling herself . . . Elephant shouting his order in the fast-food drive-thru. Rival gangbangers shotgunned each other from their cars without slowing down. "For a neighborhood where nobody works a job," Coyote asked himself, "why is everybody in such a damned hurry?" Even lazy lowlife scum seemed pressured to multitask.

On some late nights, traffic was bumper-to-bumper, every car steered by somebody craning his neck. They were commuters without jobs who never arrived at any workplace.

Take Flamingo, for example. Wearing her minidress, swinging her pink-leather purse from a gold-metal chain leashed over one bony shoulder, Flamingo probably earned ten times more than Coyote, but she never paid tax on a cent of it. Coyote knew a thing or two about untamed animals. First, every animal wears a badge. This might be a bracelet braided by their kid or a neck tattoo, but it's a hint about something secret they treasure. If you identify the badge and praise it—open sesame—you pick the lock on someone's heart. You only needed to read the clues. You didn't need college to teach you that, Coyote told himself. Hawking samples of dessert topping in too many supermarkets taught you what was important. His job with Llewellyn Foods wasn't the kind that gave your brain a raging career hard-on.

The second thing Coyote knew was that the essence of sexual attraction was availability. That was the appeal of pornography; a centerfold of Stork with her mouth open in a big oral sex O, her butt stuck toward the camera and her thong underwear fallen down around her high heels, she wasn't going to reject you. If Flamingo slid her index finger deep into her mouth as perverts drove past, it was more than likely she'd love even a big loser like you. Flamingo's Lycra miniskirt riding up asshole high appeared as a comforting reassurance—sexual hand-holding—to the lonely and shy. Every night the cars cruised around and around the block, and there was Flamingo: a sure thing. A safe bet.

Not that Coyote wasn't tempted, but it was his dick that got him stuck here in the first place: a jungle neighborhood, driving a beater car through a gridlock of perverts and junkies with a squalling kid strapped into the backseat.

The only way Coyote ever cheated was by topping up his glass of wine, adding a little, drinking a little, and when his wife asked him how many glasses he'd drunk, Coyote would tell her, "Just this one." For her part, his wife would drink half a glass of wine before stretching plastic wrap across what remained and placing it in the fridge for another day. Crazy as it sounded, Coyote's wife actually did that.

Rolling his car down a dark street, inching along in a gridlock of exhaust fumes with his baby asleep in the shadowy backseat, Coyote heard someone shout. "Five dollars," the shout came from among the garbage cans on the sidewalk. It was Flamingo, she shouted, "I'll treat you. Whatever you want, it's free for five dollars!"

How can it be free, Coyote asked himself, if it's five dollars? He wished traffic would move. At the edge of his vision he could see Flamingo step to the curb. The neighborhood ran on this principle: Everything was free if you'd pay enough. Flamingo rapped her boney knuckles against the passenger-side window, leaning down and pointing a finger at the button of the lock. She rapped at the window with one hand while she yanked the door handle with her other. She shouted, "It's free!" from so close that her purple lipstick smudged the glass, her lips like something lurid, like a fleshy purple doughnut sucking the algae from the inside of an aquarium. As loud as the baby ever screamed, Flamingo's snaggletooth mouth screamed, "Daddy, I'm giving it away!"

Her knocking left greasy knuckle prints. Her shouting misted the glass with her spit; the contents of her mouth sprayed only inches from his snoozing kid. The streetlights threw her looming shadow into the car, across the tiny sleeping face. Flamingo's dirty breath fogged the glass and her purple fingernails wiped at the fog and smeared it into a mess with her fingerprints and lipstick. Coyote kept the car moving forward the whole time, streaking Flamingo's purple lipstick, greasy finger-painting ghost the length of the curbside windows. A long, purple skid mark.

Coyote shuddered to think what pestilence coated his car, and he drove home, telling himself how nothing but clear glass had saved his family from a monster. Coyote's wife was still asleep as he tucked the baby into bed with her. He took a Kleenex out to where the car was parked at the curb, Ox and Llama eyeballing him from under their porch light. The mess was hard to see in the dark, but every time Coyote wiped his tissue came off with more purple. He tiptoed back into the house to get another tissue. He spat on it and wiped, mixing Flamingo's DNA with his own, smearing his spit with hers. At dawn Coyote's wife came out on the porch wearing her bathrobe and holding a cup of coffee and asked what he was doing. From the porch next door, Ox and Llama ogled her as if she were prey.

"What does it look like I'm doing?" Coyote snapped, irritated, for he'd been working all night. Not looking away from his task, he said, "I'm washing the fucking car."

"With Kleenex?" asked his wife. The sidewalk was littered with crumpled tissues, and she crouched in her bathrobe and began to gather them. "And diapers?" she asked. Among the discarded Kleenex were disposable diapers, each touched with a little purple. The purple blotches looked like hickeys or the lesions of some incurable sexually transmitted blood cancer.

Coyote had spat and spat up gobs until his spitter felt bone-dry. His elbow hurt from his arm scrubbing back and forth, and his throat ached.

While Turtle and Walrus brought out their chairs to play dominoes in the morning sunshine, Coyote took a quick shower and had to leave for work. "It's not fair," Coyote told himself, "everything that my neighbors touch they ruin." And he began plotting his revenge.

The next midnight, Coyote drove until his baby fell asleep, after that he kept driving until he found Flamingo. Without stopping, he drove along the gutter and leaned over to roll down the passenger side window. Flamingo took the bait and strutted alongside his car, asking, "Are you a cop?"

Coyote smiled and asked, "Do I look like a cop?" He kept the car rolling forward, forcing Flamingo to dodge around parking meters and fire hydrants in order to keep abreast of him. At his age Coyote should've been racing through life at top speed, but here he was barely in motion. At work he was a wage slave who demoed test products in supermarkets—stain remover, deodorant soap, yoghurt—smiling and begging strangers to try a taste or take a sniff. But tonight he was the consumer. Coyote called the shots.

Flamingo said, "You want, I could teach you some techniques . . ." She said it like two words: *Tech Neeks.* She gave him a look that brought Coyote's eyes to where his wedding ring gripped his steering wheel. Flamingo said, "Ten bucks, and you'll make your lady squeal so loud folks will figure you're beating her."

"Five bucks," Coyote said.

"Daddy, teaching is ten bucks," Flamingo said, shaking her wig "No" and raking the strands with her purple nails. "What I learn you is going to save your marriage." The way she pitched it, screwing Flamingo wasn't adultery so much as it was a continuing education investment in pleasing his wife. Railing Flamingo wouldn't be infidelity, it would be an endless gift that brought the mother of his baby more pleasure than a wardrobe of fur coats or a suitcase heavy with diamond rings.

Tooling along, Coyote said, "Let me check the bank." Steering with his knees, he leaned across the front seat and popped open the glove compartment where he collected spare change to pay for parking. Still trawling his car along, baiting Flamingo, Coyote picked out nickels and dimes, piling them in short stacks on the seat beside his thigh. He counted aloud, occasionally losing track of the total and starting over, really drawing out the suspense and wasting Flamingo's time. He'd made her walk eight blocks in stiletto heels while he counted pennies, before he arrived at ten dollars.

Coyote asked himself, why shouldn't you be able to buy sex the way you'd buy a hamburger? Flamingo tried to charge him another three dollars for the condom, but she gave up when Coyote started counting pennies again.

Flamingo's face settled into his lap, her nylon wig bobbing between his belly and the steering wheel. Coyote wasn't sure how a blow job would make him a better lover, but it seemed like a good first step. He gloated over the fact that he'd deliberately miscounted in the dark and shorted her thirty-seven cents.

Coyote's nuts drew up, as tight as a hairy fist, against the base of his dick. His hips bucked and humped like a playground dog's. When it was too late for him to do anything except blow his load, his baby woke up and crapped her training pants. He came to the wail of her little screams and the smell of shit.

But Flamingo was right. Filling her mouth more or less rescued Coyote's marriage, but not because he learned anything. It was ironic. It was horrible, but Coyote never loved his little family more than he did the moment after he unloaded between Flamingo's purple lips. As his dick fell soft, that same blood rushed straight from his nuts to make his heart swell. Cheating on his wife gave his heart an instant rock-hard erection. Even before Coyote caught his breath, as he pinched the milky condom off his dick and rolled down the driver's window, he yearned to tell his wife how much he adored her. As he dropped the fat, dripping rubber into the street, his wife appeared to Coyote as the most beautiful, most noble wife in the world. Coyote told himself he didn't deserve such a perfect wife.

Coyote tried not to consider how the same spunk that had become his precious baby was what he now threw in the gutter.

He tried not to think how Flamingo had once been somebody's little Bundle of Joy. Flamingo was a sure thing, and Coyote didn't want to ruin a good thing by overthinking it. Above all Coyote tried not to look in the rearview mirror just in case his baby might be awake and looking back. He'd only driven around for a couple hours, but going home he felt like Odysseus returning to Penelope after a voyage of twenty years.

He'd never do this again, Coyote told himself. He seldom took a second bite of anything: a new flavor of peanut butter . . . a potato chip improved with a new texture for better mouth feel . . . the front seat of his car was littered with these one-bite samples individually packaged. It was the nature of his job.

Infidelity, Coyote told himself, makes the heart grow fonder.

At home, he took a hot shower. He gargled. When he slid into bed beside his wife he put his arms around her and whispered, "I love you so much."

She was awake, and she turned her head to kiss him. Coyote's wife slid her hand inside the waistband of his shorts and fondled him. When he didn't respond she kissed his chest. She kissed his belly. Their sex life hadn't been all about making babies. They'd enjoyed anal and oral and costumes and dildos. They'd lived a rock-and-roll lifestyle, but when his wife started to put him into her mouth, Coyote told her, "Don't."

"I just want to show how much I love you," she said.

Coyote said, "Not tonight, okay," and he turned away from her. He couldn't bear to see his wife doing for free what even Flamingo charged ten dollars for.

It wasn't fair, Coyote told himself. He lived more or less in harness, dragging his ass to Llewellyn Foods and drinking coffee to stay awake under fluorescent lights in strategy meetings with Rhinoceros and Aardvark. For that, he got the lofty privilege of paying half his salary in income taxes and property taxes. He forked out money for medical insurance while everyone else went to the emergency room and gave fake names. Their Seattle neighborhood was one big giveaway with free hypodermic needles, free dental clinics, free public housing. Food stamps. Government cheese. There wasn't anything Coyote could afford to buy that everyone else wasn't already getting for free. Free cell phones for the homeless. Free bus passes. When they weren't shooting hoops, Mongoose and Chipmunk faked spinal cord injuries to get free parking in handicapped spaces. Flamingo charged her customers three dollars extra for condoms that she got from a county program at no cost. Most important of all, everyone around Coyote had free time.

Coyote didn't have the time to wipe his ass, he was so busy paying everyone's bills. They had the leisure time to stage protest rallies and demand more entitlements. While Coyote ate a baloney sandwich at his desk, his whole neighborhood was appearing on the television news or being profiled by some bleeding-heart newspaper journalist. Seattle's poor were so hungry that their biggest health issue was obesity.

So Coyote carried his own weight plus everyone else's.

At Llewellyn Foods, in his office cubicle, one day the phone rang. It was Hamster from Human Resources. Without explanation, she asked, "How soon can you be in Orlando?" She said, "We have an incident taking shape." A plane ticket was already waiting for him at SeaTac. If he hauled ass Coyote could make the next flight.

Coyote rushed home early to pack, and he found his wife sitting on the neighbors' porch. Plain as day, she was drinking a can of malt liquor with Llama and Ox, laughing like she wasn't a wife and mother. After he got her around the wrist and dragged her home, Coyote asked, "What did those losers tell you?" He

97

asked, "Did they bad-mouth me?" In truth, Coyote had been around to see Flamingo a minimum of one night every week. Usually two or three. Hell, the gasoline cost more than the blow jobs. Even when his baby wasn't crying, he'd strap it into the backseat and go for a slow drive. Flamingo had no value to him beyond the purple on his dick. She had no face other than that lipstick, but the lazy bastards in this neighborhood had nothing better to do than spy on him and spread gossip, and Coyote worried that word would filter back to his wife and she wouldn't understand.

"Ox told me that I was pretty," she said. "Llama said that my husband is very lucky."

"Well," Coyote countered, "maybe you shouldn't believe everything you hear." He didn't know that he was shouting.

His wife looked wounded. She said, "Honey, they're not so bad. You should hear their stories."

"I don't need to hear anybody," Coyote said. "I've got eyes!"

Those animals were born liars, he said. They scammed Social Security and stole everybody's mail so they could commit fraud. Llama had served time in prison, and Ox was worse. Coyote said how, night after night, he'd seen Ox hooking up with Flamingo for five-dollar blow jobs. Flamingo looked like a walking bag of crabs, and whatever plague she was incubating, Ox had to be infected. Here, Coyote was on a roll. He claimed Ox served time for raping Springbok. Llama, he said, was convicted for peddling kiddie porn. Everybody knew, Coyote said, that Flamingo went for no-charge abortions on almost a monthly basis; Flamingo probably had a standing appointment to get scraped. Coyote demanded to know how a self-proclaimed "decent" Catholic could socialize with ex-cons who were responsible for Flamingo's long trail of dead babies? Coyote paused in his tirade, just a moment, to allow his wife to burst into tears and beg his forgiveness.

Instead, she laughed. "Abortions?" she was laughing. "Flamingo wishes!"

Coyote waited. He told himself not to slap her. He waited for her laughter to run out.

Finally his wife caught her breath and said, "Flamingo's not even a girl."

Coyote felt all his blood evaporate through his skin. His hands tingled.

His wife continued to laugh, saying, "Flamingo is a . . . what's the word?" She made a fist and knocked her knuckles lightly on her forehead. Finally, she snapped her fingers and said, "A transvestite!" Still laughing, her breath reeking of malt liquor, she said, "You should see your face right now!"

And Coyote slapped her.

His wife fell to the floor and sat there, pressing one hand to a corner of her mouth. When she took the hand away there was blood on her palm. It wasn't a lot of blood, but it was enough so Coyote could see it. Coyote's wife looked at this itty-bitty smidgen of bright-red blood like it was the end of her world.

Coyote took his keys off the hall table and walked back to where the car was parked. With his baby seat empty, he merged into the gridlock of troubled strangers slowly going nowhere. He knew that marriage was like one of those movies where the only exciting parts are all squeezed into the three-minute preview. Part of his marketing job included showing different previews to test audiences at shopping malls, then asking them if they'd pay to watch the whole film. Coyote knew even before he had his seat belt buckled that his wife would be on the telephone filing assault charges against him. This was one of those cold nights when it doesn't take too long to get dark, and Coyote found himself searching the streets for Flamingo.

"It's not enough that I've ruined my life," Coyote told himself. "I've also wrecked the lives of my wife and child. The only life I haven't destroyed is Flamingo's." He planned to put both hands around Flamingo's scrawny neck and squeeze hard. Nothing Flamingo had taught him could save his marriage. Coyote rolled down all his windows and let the night blow through his car. He sang along to the radio he no longer had, inventing the lyrics to sad songs he'd never planned to write. Without too much hunting he found her in her usual spot among the garbage bags. Flamingo leaned over and peered into his car.

"You have a good voice," Flamingo said. "You want, I could be your sexy backup singer." She swung the door open and climbed in beside him.

Coyote looked at her fright wig, her purple lips. The seat between them was strewn with sample packets each containing a single cough drop. They looked like sealed condoms. Among them were a couple nickels and pennies. Flamingo knew all his dirty secrets but she smiled to see him anyway.

She said, "Where's your baby?" She'd noticed but never said.

Coyote wanted to ask, *Where's your pussy?* but he kept his trap shut. His beater car drifted to a stop, and he said, "You know, I hit my wife, today." His mouth pumped out the truth in little spurts, a few words at a time. He said, "I only came out tonight to kill you." His impulse was to cry, but that felt like it would be overplaying the scene. His crying wouldn't convince anyone of anything. He waited, but Flamingo didn't jump out of his car.

Her purple fingernails reached toward him, and she said, "Daddy, I know you never pay me the whole ten dollars." Her hand caught him around the neck and pulled.

And Coyote let himself be pulled. He toppled, falling, tangled in his seat belt. When he came to a rest, he said, "Every day of my life, I'm dying," his face pressed sideways to the smell of Flamingo's miniskirt. And before he could stop himself, Coyote fell asleep.

■

PHOENIX

On Monday night, Rachel calls long distance from a motel in Orlando. Listening to the phone ring on the other end of the line, she picks up the remote control and clicks through television stations with the sound muted. She counts fifteen rings. Sixteen. Ted answers on the twenty-sixth ring, out of breath, and she asks him to pass the receiver to their daughter.

"I'll go get her," Ted says, "but I can't promise any miracles."

There's a clunk as he sets the phone on the kitchen counter, and over the line Rachel can hear his voice get louder and fainter as he roves around the house, shouting, "April, honey? Come talk to Mommy!" She hears the squeak of the spring on the screen door. Ted's footsteps appear and disappear as he moves from the wooden floor of the hallway to the carpeted stairs.

Rachel waits. She sits on the bed. The motel room's rug and drapes smell vaguely like a vintage clothing store: a lot of mildewed fabric, a little stale sweat, and cigarette smoke. It's rare that she has to travel with her job; this is the first such trip since April was born three years ago. She clicks through silent football games and music videos without music.

—

The house where they live now isn't their first. Where they'd lived before, it had burned to the ground, but the fire was nobody's fault. That much had been proven in a court of law. It was a fabulous freak accident, written up in the annals of homeowners insurance history. They'd lost everything they owned, and then their daughter had been born blind. April was blind, but things could've turned out worse. That first house had been Ted's before they'd even met. Glass block had filled a wall of the dining room, casting a grid like a net over the black-lacquered table and chairs. When you flipped a switch gas flames danced magically on a bed of crushed granite in the living room fireplace. The bathtubs, toilets, and sinks were black porcelain. Vertical blinds dangled in the windows. Nothing was earth-toned or wood grained.

But it'd suited Ted, the house had. He owned a cat he'd named Belinda Carlisle and let drink from the black bidets. It was a long-haired sable Burmese, like a bubble of black hair. Ted loved Belinda Carlisle, but he knew enough not to let her get too close. The cat looked clean until you touched her; after that you'd both be covered in greasy dander. To deal with Belinda's shedding, Ted had one of those robot vacuum cleaners that scoured the floors all day. At least that was the idea. More than once the two had joined forces: The cat had diarrhea, and the robot scooted through it, crossing and crisscrossing the puddle all day, smearing the mess until it spread to every square inch of the black carpet.

When they'd been married almost a year, Rachel had announced that they needed to move. She was pregnant and didn't want to bring a newborn into this world of filthy rugs and open flames. They'd have to sell the house and give up Belinda Carlisle. Even Ted had to admit the place stunk like a cat box, no matter how often they changed the litter, and you couldn't be pregnant around a cat box. Over dinner, she explained toxoplasmosis. It was caused by the protozoan parasite Toxoplasma gondii and lived in the intestines of cats. It spread by laying its eggs in cat feces and could kill or blind infants.

She was used to explaining the issues to Ted. She knew he'd never be brilliant. That was his chief charm. He was loyal and even-tempered, and Ted was a hard worker if you stayed on top of him every second and told him exactly what to do. She'd married him for all the reasons she might hire a long-term employee.

She'd spoken slowly, between bites of spaghetti. The only way to mask the smell of cat was to add cilantro to everything. After her speech, Ted sat across the table, the shadows from the glass blocks making a contour map of his face and white shirt. She could hear the bubbles in his mineral water. It didn't matter what Ted cooked; nothing looked appetizing against his black-glazed china. He blinked. He asked, "What are you saying?"

Slower this time, Rachel had said, "We have to find a new house."

"No," said Ted, drawing out the word as if playing for time. "Before that."

Rachel wasn't annoyed. She'd rehearsed this for days. She could've paced it better. It was a lot to spring on him all at once. "I said we need to list this house."

Ted closed his eyes and shook his head. His brow furrowed, he prompted, "Before *that*."

"The part about Belinda Carlisle?" Rachel asked.

"Before that," Ted coaxed.

It worried Rachel to think that Ted wasn't stupid; that, instead, he just never listened to anything she said. She rewound their conversation in her mind. "Do you mean the part about being pregnant?"

"You're pregnant?" Ted had asked. He'd put his black napkin to his lips. To wipe them or hide them, Rachel couldn't tell.

—

It's still Monday night in Orlando, Rachel is still waiting on the phone. She peels the bedspread down and stretches out to watch the Home Shopping Channel. What she loves most about HSC is that it doesn't have commercials. Diamond cocktail rings rotate in slow motion, glittering under halogen lights and magnified to one hundred times their actual size. The pitchman always speaks with a down-home drawl and always sounds so excited when he says, "You'd better hurry'n order, folks, we don't got more'n a couple thousand of these ruby tiaras left . . ." Emerald solitaires sell for the same price as a jar of cashews from the minibar.

With the TV on mute, over the phone she can hear the neighbor's dog barking. The barking disappears as if muffled by something. As if April's put the receiver to her ear. Holding her breath to hear better, Rachel says, "Sweetheart? Boo-Boo? How are you and Daddy getting along without Mommy?" She talks until she feels like an idiot babbling to herself in an empty motel room. She wonders what she's botched this time. Did she forget a kiss good-bye?

This silence, Rachel suspects, is retribution. The night before her flight she'd noticed her teeth were yellowed. Too much coffee would do that. After dinner she'd prepared the bleaching trays and let April examine them. Rachel had explained how tightly they fit: Mommy couldn't answer any questions for at least an hour once the trays were on her teeth. Mommy couldn't talk at all. If April needed something, she'd need to ask her father. No sooner than she'd squirted the expensive bleaching gel into each tray and snapped it into her mouth, but April's hand was already tugging at her bathrobe wanting a bedtime story.

Ted wasn't any help. April went to bed in tears. Rachel's teeth still looked like hell.

From the sounds that come through the wall, the guests in the next room are full-fledged screwing. Rachel cups one hand around the receiver and hopes her daughter won't overhear. She worries that the line has been disconnected, and keeps asking, "April? Sweetheart, can you hear Mommy?" Resigned, Rachel asks the girl to hand the telephone back to her father. Ted's voice comes on.

"Don't stew about it," he says. "She's just giving you the silent treatment." His voice muffled, his mouth pointed somewhere else, he says, "You're just upset that Mommy's gone, aren't you?" A measure of dead air follows. Rachel can hear the carnival music and silly voices of a cartoon playing in the living room. It's not lost on her that she mostly listens to television with no sound while her daughter watches without visuals.

Still directed elsewhere, Ted's voice asks, "You still love Mommy, don't you?"

Another beat of silence follows. Rachel hears nothing until Ted begins to placate, "No, Mommy doesn't love her job more than she loves you." He doesn't sound very convincing. After a pause, he scolds, "Don't say that, missy! Never say that!" From the tone of his voice, Rachel braces herself for the sound of a slap. She wants to hear a slap. It doesn't come. Clear, speaking directly into the receiver, Ted says, "What can I say? Our kid can really hold a grudge."

Rachel's thrilled. The last thing she wants her daughter to be is a sop like Ted, but she keeps those words in her mouth. That's Monday's phone call, done.

—

Belinda Carlisle had been Ted's cat since she was a kitten. She was an old cat when they'd listed her on various websites for adoption. Old and gassy. Only medical researchers might bother. When euthanasia had loomed as their best option, Ted called Rachel into the kitchen and showed her the cat's fifty-pound bag of kibble. It was still over half full. He said, "Just give me this long to find her a new family."

To Rachel this had seemed like a good compromise. Every day meant two scoops out of the kibble. The bag became an hourglass counting down their final days with Belinda. After two weeks, Rachel was no longer so sure. The food bag was still half full. In fact, it seemed a little heavier than it had been when she'd first made her bargain. She suspected Ted was smuggling kibble from another source. Perhaps he kept a secret bag stashed in his car or somewhere in the garage, and he was using scoops of that to replenish the kitchen bag. To test her theory, she began to dole out double helpings for the cat's meals. Rachel told herself she was giving the cat a treat, indulging it instead of hurrying it toward its grave.

The increased rations had barely fit in the cat's bowl, but Belinda ate it all. She was getting fat, but she wasn't getting any closer to being gone. Like the parable of the loaves and fishes or that lamp in the Temple of David, the big bag of kibble was always half full.

———

Tuesday's call from Orlando doesn't go any better. Each night, she and Ted make small accountings to one another. He's raked the first fall of leaves. She's implemented the initial on-site catalysts for satellite microwave transmission. He's found a grocery that carries the cheese she likes so much. Rachel reports that she's resequenced the protocol script for the pre-systems recharge matrix. She says Orlando is a terrible place to find oneself without children.

When she stops speaking there's a stretch of silence, as if Ted's paying attention to something else. She listens for the sound of him keyboarding, doing emails while she talks. Finally Ted speaks. He says, "What's going on there?"

He means the sounds. The guests in the next room are screwing, again. Actually, they've never stopped, and their constant moaning and shrill cries have disappeared to Rachel's ears. The sounds have droned on so long they must be a pornographic film. No one was ever that much in love. It makes her furious to imagine Ted has been listening to strangers humping instead of the progress she's made.

While a sapphire hovers on television, Ted's voice says, "Take the phone, April. Tell Mommy 'good night.'"

To hear more, Rachel tries to subtract the sound of the freeway outside. She tunes out the hum of the minibar and the endearments grunted from beyond the wall. She hasn't taken a drink since some Christmas eggnog three years before, but now Rachel goes to the minibar and surveys the racks of little glass bottles, each priced higher than the diamond pendant on television. A dwindling countdown shows there are fewer than five thousand of these pendants left. For the price of pearl earrings Rachel mixes herself a gin-and-tonic and chugs it down.

Over the phone Rachel hears Ted's voice. Muffled in the background, he whines, begging, "Tell Mommy about the turtles you liked at the zoo." Nothing follows. Rachel feels a respect for her daughter that she's never felt for her husband. For dinner, she tears open a minibar bag of plain M&M's that costs more than a shopping channel engagement set. For every bag of potato chips or candy bar she eats, another will appear to replace it as if by magic.

Regarding the bag of cat food, Rachel had confronted Ted, but he'd denied any cheating. Rachel didn't cop to overfeeding, but she did point out that five weeks had gone by and Belinda Carlisle looked like a watermelon wearing a fur coat. Anymore, Rachel wasn't much of a skinny Minnie, either. "Are you saying," she'd asked, pointing to the food bag, "that this is a miracle?"

It didn't help that the realtor who'd listed the house told them the living room smelled bad. The realtor said their asking price was two hundred grand too high for the current market. Rachel's hormones didn't help, either.

Ted and Rachel had argued. Between Thanksgiving and Christmas they bickered almost every day. During that time the level in the food bag rose until kibble was spilling out on the kitchen floor. The cat was so bloated she could hardly drag herself around the living room carpet. That's when their overpriced house had caught fire.

—

On Wednesday evening, as usual, Rachel calls from Orlando. She half hopes April won't speak. That might prove that the girl's inherited some of Rachel's own gumption. As a test, Rachel asks, "Don't you love Mommy?" Under her breath she prays the girl won't take such obvious bait.

The world is a horrible place. The last thing Rachel wants to create is a kid who bruises like a ripe banana.

As if April needs further testing, Rachel says, "Let Mommy sing you a bedtime song," and she begins to croon a lullaby she knows will melt her daughter's resolve. Backing her up are the moans and groans from next door, those sounds without language that weak people make against their will. Rachel intends to sing all of the verses, but she loses her nerve when she hears

Ted's laugh. It sounds too clear. She guesses April has set down the receiver and walked away. That means Rachel has been singing to an empty kitchen. She ends by warning, "If you don't say 'good night' you'll make Mommy cry." If no one is listening it doesn't matter what she says. She pretends to cry. She escalates her pretend sobs to wailing. It's easier than she imagined, and when she finds she can't stop, Rachel hangs up.

—

Rachel hadn't invented the dangers of toxoplasmosis; she'd gone online and built an airtight case. This wasn't crazy talk. Neurobiologists had linked T. gondii to suicide and the onset of schizophrenia. All caused by exposure to cat poop. Some studies even suggested that the toxo brain parasites chemically coerced people to adopt more cats. Those crazy cat ladies were actually being controlled by an infection of single-cell invaders.

The problem with educating stupid people was that they didn't know they were stupid. The same went for curing crazy people. As far as the cat was concerned, Ted was both.

On the last night in their first house, as Rachel had later explained it to the police, they'd gone to a Christmas party in the neighborhood. The two of them were coming home. They'd been drinking eggnog, and as they'd trudged through the snow she'd explained to Ted that he didn't need to be such a softie. She spoke carefully, waiting for her words to stick. The footprints she left were splayed wide apart to balance her new weight.

Rachel was still working as a Level I Corporate Interface Consultant, but simply entering her second trimester felt like a full-time job. She worried that with a new baby the situation wouldn't get much better. You might be able to divide a man's love in half, but not in three ways.

The way Rachel told it to the police, she had walked into the darkened house, first. She hadn't even taken off her coat. She'd said, "It's freezing in here." The Christmas tree filled the living room's front window, blocking any streetlight. In fact everyone's first assumption was that the Christmas tree was the culprit. The usual suspects were always scented candles, faulty twinkle lights, an overloaded outlet. Ted pegged the roving robotic vacuum cleaner. His fingers were crossed that it had overheated. Some circuit had shorted out, and it had raced around filled with flammable cat hair and set fire to everything.

—

Thursday night in Orlando, it's the age-old paradox: The more Rachel tries to hurry the installation process the longer things take. She phones herself and leaves messages. "Memo to self: Finalize nomenclature for graphics inventory."

She takes her phone off the bedside table and begins to scroll through her photos. She has only one of April. Somehow it seems wrong to photograph a blind person. It's like stealing something valuable they don't even know they own. In this same spirit, Rachel self-edits to never say, "What a lovely sunset" or "Eyes this way, honey." Around April, to exclaim, "What a beautiful flower!" would seem like taunting.

She and Ted had met on a blind date, another phrase Rachel vigorously avoids.

Recently her daughter has begun to call out, "Look at me, Mom! Look at me! Are you watching?" April obviously had no idea what she was saying. That was simply the universal chorus of children, sighted or blind. The essence of being a parent was the shift from being the person who is watched to being the person who does the watching.

Again, Thursday, the girl refuses to utter a sound. Rachel scrutinizes with her ears. Rachel wheedles and promises until

Ted takes the phone and says, "Sorry." She can hear the helpless shrug in his voice as he says, "I can't make her talk."

To that Rachel says, "Try." Ted has a real talent for giving up. She suggests he poke April in the ribs to make her laugh. She asks, "Isn't she ticklish?"

In response Ted laughs, but mostly from disbelief. "You're asking if she's *ticklish*?" He snorts, "Where have you been the past three years?"

—

Following the night of the fire, all that Rachel would ever accept the blame for was throwing the switch. Before turning on the living room lights, Rachel said she'd gone to the thermostat and dialed up the heat. She'd switched on the gas fireplace at the same moment the screams had started. A wild banshee wail had filled the dark rooms. Like some wintery demon, an unearthly screeching sounded, and then the entire household seemed to catch fire. The Christmas tree flared. The black throw pillows flared. The black area rugs blazed. Ted rushed to embrace Rachel even as bedspreads and bath towels burst into raging orange flame. Through all of this echoed the screams of souls tortured in Hell. The air stank with smoke and scorched hair. The smoke detectors added to the head-splitting racket. They didn't have time to back their black car down the driveway and save it before flames were flapping like bright flags from every upstairs window. They were standing on the snowy front lawn when the fire trucks came sirening out of nowhere. The house was fully involved.

—

In Orlando Rachel has begun to speculate. It would be exactly like Ted to keep some awful truth from her, at least until she gets home. If April were in the hospital, if she'd been stung by a bee and had a severe reaction, or worse, Ted would think he was doing Rachel a kindness by not telling her over the phone. She goes online and searches for accidents in Seattle involving three-year-old girls in the past week. To her dismay she finds one. According to the news item a girl has been attacked by a neighbor's dog. Currently she was in the hospital in critical condition. Her name was being withheld pending notification of the victim's extended family.

That night, Rachel listens to her new messages. They are all from herself. "Memo to self: repercussions!" Just that one word, shrill and bullying. She has no idea to what she'd been referring at the time. She has to check the caller ID to even recognize herself. Was that how her voice really sounds?

All night the idea weighs on her: How many toddlers choke to death on rubber balls and never make the CNN scroll? She keeps hitting Refresh, hoping for updates on the *Seattle Times* story. What kind of mother is she if she can't sense whether her child is dead or alive?

—

The fire marshal hadn't thought it was arson, not at first. The episode had made them celebrities and not in a good way. They'd become living proof of something people didn't want to believe could really happen.

The fire marshal had picked through the charred rooms, charting the path of the blaze's ignition. It had started at the minimalist fireplace and traced a circle around the perimeter of the living room. Next, the perimeter of the dining room had kindled. He'd sketched a rough floor plan on a sheet of graph paper clipped to a clipboard. Using a mechanical pencil he drew a line from the dining room up the stairs and around the perimeter of the master bedroom and bathroom.

Tucked under his arm, he was carrying something wrapped

in a black-plastic garbage bag. "Damnedest thing I've ever seen," he told Ted and Rachel in the driveway. He'd held the bag open and let them peer inside. It smelled horrific, a combination of burnt hair and chemicals. Ted took one look and began to shake.

—

Friday night in Orlando, Rachel briefly entertains the idea of calling the police, but what could she say? She checks for an update about the three-year-old girl in critical condition. She calls a neighbor back home, JoAnne. They've had a passing acquaintance based on a mutual hatred of the local garbage collectors. JoAnne picks up on the nineteenth ring. Rachel asks if Ted has gotten their garbage can out to the curb that week. She doesn't want to tip her hand.

She listens, switching the phone from one ear to the other, but hears nothing. Most of what she doesn't hear is JoAnne's Rottweiler mix barking. It's always barking and clawing at their fence.

At last JoAnne says, "Garbage pickup is next week, Rachel." She sounds guarded. She says Rachel's name as if she's signaling to other people within earshot. She asks how Orlando is, and Rachel racks her brains trying to remember if she'd mentioned the trip beforehand. Testing, Rachel says, "I hope Ted's not spoiling April while I'm gone." The pause that follows lasts too long.

"April?" Rachel prods. "My daughter?"

JoAnne says, "I know who April is." Now she sounds irritated.

Rachel can't help herself. "Did Cesar bite my baby?"

The line goes dead.

—

At least the fire marshal had solved the mystery of why their old house stank every winter. Belinda Carlisle, the marshal con-

114

jectured, had been using the crushed granite of the fireplace as a litter box. Any time they'd switched on the gas jets, Ted and Rachel had been parboiling untold pounds of buried cat waste. The insurance adjuster told them that what had occurred was without precedent. Rachel noticed he could hardly contain his laughter as he explained how the cat must've been voiding her bowels at the same moment Rachel flipped the fireplace switch.

One moment, Belinda was taking a secret late-night crap in the dark little cave of the fire box. In the cold house maybe she savored the gentle warmth of the pilot light. She would've heard the cricket click-click-click of the electronic spark igniter. Instantly, jets of blue flame would've shot at her from every direction.

It had been this furry, flaming demon that had exploded, screaming, and raced around the house, setting fire to every cloth item before falling dead in an upstairs closet beneath Rachel's dry cleaning stored in flammable plastic.

———

Saturday, Rachel phones home three times and gets the voicemail. She pictures the house empty. It's too easy to picture Ted weeping beside a hospital bed. When he finally picks up, she asks for April. "If that's how you want it, young lady," she threatens, "no Christmas, no merry go round, no pizza, unless you speak up." She waits, not wanting to be hurtful. She blames her mood on a rum-and-cola, a double, that costs more than a turquoise belt buckle from TV. "I had a little girl who was blind," she taunts, trying to provoke a response. "What are you, now, Helen Keller?"

It's the rum talking. On television an enlarged topaz sparkles hypnotically, rotating slowly with the sound turned down.

In the depth of the quiet Rachel can hear breathing. It's not her imagination. April is breathing, sounding stubborn, huffing angry little snorts as if her chubby arms are crossed over her chest and her cherub cheeks are flushed red with anger.

Taking a gamble, Rachel asks, "What do you want Mommy to bring you when she comes home?" A bribe will help everyone save face. "A Mickey Mouse," she offers, "or a Donald Duck?"

She hears a faint gasp. The breathing stops for an instant before the distant, high-pitched voice squeals, "Oh, Daddy." Delighted, it says, "Pull my hair, Daddy! Fuck me up the ass!"

It's not April. It's the guests next door, a voice filtering through the wall.

"How about we use a solid-gold, thousand-pound bar of chocolate-covered Rocky Road ice cream?" Rachel deadpans, shouting away from the receiver. She pounds a fist against the wall and yells, "How about a pretty pony fucks you?"

Over the phone she hears the little robot vacuum humming around—a replacement—cleaning the floor and bumping into walls, like—what else?—a sightless animal. Ted sits on his ass half the day, but he still wants his laborsaving Sharper Image gadgets. It scares Rachel, the idea that April might accidentally stumble over the vacuum, but Ted insists she's smarter than a cheap machine.

In a flash Rachel knows. Even if she's a little tipsy, it all makes sense. Ted blames her for what had happened to Belinda Carlisle. He's not brilliant, but he's not stupid. Holding a grudge is something April inherited from her father. He's bided his time, and now he's getting his revenge.

A thin crack opens up in her voice, and now all of her panic rushes to escape. She asks, "April, baby, is your daddy hurting you?" She tries to not ask, to stop asking, but the effort is like trying to unpop a balloon.

—

By the time April had been born, they were settled in a cookie-cutter ranch house a few blocks away. Ted had wanted to bury the cat in the new backyard, but the fire marshal never surrendered the remains. The ranch house was less dramatic. It had no open fireplace and no bidet, but with a blind child that was just as well. How could Rachel not be affected, living pregnant for six months with smoldering cat turds? As the obstetrical put it the toxo parasite attacks the optic nerve, but Rachel knew there was more to it than that. It was retribution. Of course, Rachel swore she hadn't seen Belinda Carlisle before she'd flipped the switch. And Ted had accepted Rachel's statement at face value.

There were lies that married people more effectively than any wedding vows.

—

On Sunday, Rachel phones and insists Ted listen. "The next call I make is to the police," she swears. Unless April says something to change her mind, she's going to call Child Protective Services and request an intervention.

Her husband, Mr. Passive Aggressive, laughs a confused laugh. "What do you want me to do, pinch her?"

Pinch her, yes, Rachel says. Spank her. Pull her hair. Anything.

He asks, "Just to clarify . . . if I *don't* smack my kid, you'll report me for child abuse?"

Nodding, Rachel tells the phone, "Yes." She pictures him drinking coffee out of the black-glazed mug he'd salvaged from the fire's wreckage. The color and finish are so ugly the mug looks as good as new.

"How about I burn her with a cigarette?" he asks, his voice warped with sarcasm. "Would that make you happy?"

"Use a needle from my sewing box," Rachel instructs. "But

117

sterilize it with some rubbing alcohol, first. She's never had a tetanus shot."

Ted says, "I can't believe that you're serious."

"This has gone on long enough," she says. She knows she sounds crazy. Maybe it's too late. Maybe this was the toxoplasmosis, an infection in her brain talking, but she knows she's serious.

—

When their insurance settlement for the fire had failed to come through in a speedy fashion, by then the fire marshal was calling it arson. Their lab tests had found a residue in the cat's fur. Some incendiary chemical agent had kept Belinda Carlisle aflame during her panicked, agonizing final flight. It looked fishier yet, that a few weeks before the fire Rachel had doubled their homeowners coverage. Even with a baby clamped to one breast, she hadn't hesitated to lawyer up.

—

On the phone Sunday night, Rachel says she's not bluffing. Either Ted makes their daughter emit some words, some *sound,* or they'll have this battle in family court. It seems like a long time, but Ted responds.

His voice pointed elsewhere, he says, "April, honey. Do you remember what a flu shot is?" He says, "Do you remember when you had to get a shot so you could go play at Easter camp?" Silence answers. Rachel shuts her eyes in order to hear more. All she can detect is the hum of the fluorescent bulb in the bedside lamp. She stands up from the bed to shut off the air conditioner, but before she takes a step Ted's voice is back.

"Can you get Daddy the sewing basket?" Nothing seems to

happen, but now his voice comes full into Rachel's ear, "Are you happy? Does this make you happy?" His footsteps sound in the hallway. "I'm going to the bathroom." His delivery is singsong, like a lullaby. "I'm getting the rubbing alcohol to torture our daughter." He sings, "Rach, you can stop this at any time."

But Rachel knows this isn't true. Nobody can stop anything. The people will always be humping next door. The burning cat will always be rocketing like a comet around every house in which they'll ever live. Nothing will ever be resolved. Again, it crosses her mind that Ted might be tormenting her. April is upstairs in her room or playing in the backyard, and he's only pretending she's there. That's easier to swallow than the idea that her own child despises her.

"You don't understand," Rachel tells the phone. "I need you to hurt her to prove she's alive." She demands, "Hurt her as proof of how much you don't hate me."

Before the TV can sell another thousand diamond wristwatches, April screams.

Not a beat later, Ted asks, "Rach?" Breathless. The scream echoing in her head. It would echo in her head forever. A cater-wauling. The shriek of Belinda Carlisle. It's the same squeal April had made when she was born.

"You did it," she says.

Ted replies, "You screamed."

It wasn't Rachel's scream or April's. It was still another sex noise from the next room. It's another stalemate. The bag will always be half full, Ted will always be cheating.

Rachel asks him to put April on the phone. "Make sure she's got the phone to her ear," Rachel says, "and then I want you to leave the room."

"Your father doesn't understand." Into the phone, Rachel says, "He owed more on that house than it was worth. Someone had to make the ugly choices."

She explains to her daughter how the only problem with marrying a spineless, lazy, stupid man is that you could be stuck with him for the rest of your life. "I had to do something," Rachel says. "I didn't want you born dead *and* blind."

It doesn't matter who's listening, Ted or April. It's another mess that Rachel needs to clean up. She describes how she'd combed hair spray into the cat's fur, simple cheap hair spray, every day for weeks. She knew it was using the fireplace as a toilet, and she hoped the pilot light would be enough. Rachel overfed it so the cat would need to defecate more often. She crossed her fingers that an increase in intestinal gas might do the trick. She was no sadist. On the contrary, she didn't want Belinda Carlisle to suffer. Rachel had made certain the smoke detectors had fresh batteries, and she'd waited.

"Your father," she begins. "He thinks that if the dishes and the toilet are black to begin with they never get dirty."

Their last night in Ted's house, Rachel had stepped into the living room. She'd rushed inside from the cold. She'd intentionally turned down the thermostat, hoping to make the pilot light more attractive. To set her trap, she'd buried tuna fish in the crushed gravel. That night, she'd walked into the dark room, into the shadow cast by the Christmas tree, and seen two yellow eyes blinking at her from the fireplace. A little drunk, she'd said, "I'm sorry."

On the phone in Orlando, very drunk, she says, "I wasn't sorry."

Rachel had told the cat good-bye, and she'd flipped the switch. The click-click-click, like the tapping of a white cane.

The banshee scream. Flames raced up the living room curtains. Flames raced up the stairs. Eventually the insurance company couldn't prove definitively that any chemical residue wasn't the scorched remains of dry-cleaning plastic.

Saying this, she senses that April has become a stranger. Someone separate who must be respected and deserves to know the truth. April has split away to become another person. "Your daddy's stalling is the reason why you'll never see a sunset."

The silence could've been anyone or no one. If it's April she won't understand, not until she's older.

Rachel says, "I only chose your father because he's weak. I married him because I knew I could push him around." She says that the problem with passive people is that they force you to take action. After that, they hate you for it. They never forgive you. Only then, over the phone, clear and unmistakable, does Rachel hear Ted begin to weep. It's nothing she hasn't heard before, but this time his sobs build until, like blasts from a whistle, a child screams. Like a smoke alarm, a high-pitched frantic child's shriek erupts, sirening from the telephone.

Rachel's goading has worked. He'd bullied her, coerced, controlled, and steered her into hurting something innocent. Now they were even.

With her child's screams and her husband's weeping still loud in her ears, Rachel gazes at a gigantic revolving diamond, entranced, trying to divine the new future as she whispers, "Good night."

■

THE FACTS OF LIFE

Troy's father was determined to do better than his own father had. When his dad, Troy's granddad, had explained the birds and the bees, he'd told it like a joke, asking, "What's the difference between anal sex and a microwave oven?" Troy's dad had been six years old at the time, the age Troy was now. Troy's dad didn't know so his own dad had said, matter-of-factly, "A microwave won't brown your meat."

That was it: the facts of life. So when Troy climbed into the car after school one afternoon and announced the second graders were doing a module on Unsafe Sex, his dad recognized a teachable moment. The school hadn't even covered sex, and already they were telling kids what not to do. Nonetheless, Troy's dad knew what all politicians know: You don't answer the question you're asked, you answer the question you wish to be asked. When it came to Unsafe Sex, Troy's dad had written the book.

They were in the car, so that seemed as good a launching pad as any. They were driving home so Troy's dad had to watch where he was going. He told Troy that sometimes when mommies and daddies love each other very, very much, they want to be alone. He said how, when they're only high schoolers, sometimes the only place to be alone is in a car, even if it's a Dodge

Dart with sticky duct tape covering the rips in the vinyl upholstery, and even then they need to buy tickets to a drive-in movie—something almost impossible to explain to a kid these days, except to say it's like a television set so big it could cover one whole side of the building where Daddy works—even if the movie playing that week is *The Getaway* with Sally Struthers, which is almost beside the point because the only reason mommies and daddies go to drive-in theaters is to be alone, and when they're in high school, the urge to be alone together and kiss and touch and torch a little weed and wrestle around like two freshly skinned porn stars on a bed of hot salt, well mommies and daddies in that situation would buy tickets to watch paint dry if it guaranteed them a couple hours of being out-from-under everyone's thumb, even if what they have is a real, true eternal love that older mommies and daddies have forgotten is even possible, even then a Dodge Dart isn't the best set of hookup wheels because some dipshit previous owner had replaced the front bench seat with two bucket seats, and the backseat offers only room enough to do it front-to-back, pitcher-catcher-style, lying on their sides, not the best of positions because the mommy says it always, always puts too much air inside her, even now Troy's dad is watching the road and not seeing his kid's reaction, even when he says pitcher-catcher is the mommy's only position because if she tried cowgirl even once she'd be sitting up, bobbing up and down for everyone to see, her tits and hair flopping until the whole drive-in would flash on their headlights, high-low, high-low, and honk and yell rodeo giddyups until the story would be all over school, even then this daddy at the drive-in nominates they try a little sixty-nine to get the party started even as he's describing them stripping off their clothes and wrestling around the backseat, even then his little boy, Troy, asks what this has to do with where babies come from even if his dad has reached the moment where the mommy takes the daddy's danger zone between two fingers of one hand like she's picking up used trash off the floor of a public bathroom and she says he's not smelling as fresh as she'd like and she's having second thoughts even after he's explained and explained about how clean he is and the nature of foreskin, even so she's not buying it even when he throws out his old argument about "What makes it only genital mutilation when it happens to girls?" even then she's frosting over even when he says, "Genital mutilation is genital mutilation no matter how you slice it," even that doesn't make her laugh even when he winks to indicate he's just kidding, even then she's dug in her heels regarding the possibility of copping his junk so he climbs his top half into the front seat and pops open the glove compartment and digs around the old road maps even if that means explaining a road map to his kid, a generation of kids who have GPS everything so they'll never know the origami nightmare of trying to refold some old paper at night in the wind, even then he's searching for a condom and something, anything, to cover the smell, even if that smell is nothing but the way a healthy pre-mutilated danger zone is supposed to smell, even then all the daddy can locate is a big bottle of hand sanitizer left over from the last winter panic about Asian bird flu, and even though that was a decade before the kid was born, his boy wants to go off on a tangent about what-was-bird-flu? and what's-a-bucket-seat? even if none of that matters in the big picture, even now he's explaining how this daddy shows the hand sanitizer to the mommy in the backseat covered with duct tape and he offers to sanitizer his entire danger zone if that will make her happy, even her frosty heart can't not melt when exposed to that big of a romantic gesture, even so he's worried this is going to hurt because the bottle says it's a big percent alcohol, even then his danger zone is aching with a need so bad it overrides his common sense so he squeezes out a jumbo handful of this clear, cold, slimy gel and uses it to jack his danger zone, and even with almost a hundred germicidal ingredients listed on the label, not counting a trace amount of aloe vera, even then it doesn't hurt as much as he'd imagined, not as much as his zone is already aching, as if he might die from an impacted sperm, like a wisdom tooth but between his skinny teenage legs, the pain's not so much that his danger zone changes its mind even when the mommy still won't give him throat, even then his danger zone is still as rock hard as the nose on his face even when he face-plants dead center in mommy's danger zone and goes to town, playing this game they used to call "Flipper" which is based on a TV show so old that even Nickelodeon won't touch it, even then this mommy won't put her lips to work because now she's worried about being poisoned by chemical compounds, even then, instead of giving up, the daddy stays facedown, holding his breath, playing Flipper, treading her water with his tongue because he knows if she's hot enough she'll agree to anything, even now Troy's dad keeps his eyes on the road while he senses a tidal wave of questions building up from his kid, even then the drive-in daddy doesn't come up for air, only dog-paddles with his tongue until the moment she's so flooded he can flip his face back so fast a spray of her mommy juice will fly off the end of his nose in a sloppy arc of splash while he squeaks a fast Eee-Eee-Eee-Eee of dolphin laughs and claps his hands together like little dolphin flippers like every time they watched that show growing up on TV, even then his danger zone is full-to-bursting with about two thousand pounds per square inch of pressurized daddy juice when smell-or-not this mommy wants nothing more in the world than pitcher-catcher, front-to-back on the rear seat of his Dodge Dart, air or no air inside her, even then what's left unsaid is how her monthly mommy time is no fewer than eleven days past its normal ETA, even then she's telling herself it could be from throwing up one too many corndogs, even if she's done the math in her head and pictures her mistake already the size of a cell cluster, even then his kid, Troy, asks, "Was that the start of me?" still trying to steer the whole birds-and-the-bees routine, even then the daddy in the Dart is slamming danger zones with the mommy, such sweet perfect memories, with Sally Struthers saying something to Steve McQueen on the drive-in movie screen, even then he's got no idea he's already a daddy, no he's just slamming away with dried Flipper water making the skin tight across his face until he hears the mommy squeal like every Christmas morning rolled into one, and he lets himself go, and even then he wants to go again, but she says to first smoke a fatty she's got in her purse and crawls out from next to him and pinches out this blunt and sparks a lighter, paraquat and malathion be damned, and even then she's complaining about the air he's trapped inside her, even as she torches the blunt and they can hear it's not great stuff because even with Sally Struthers squawking about something they can both hear the seeds popping when she takes a long drag, even as they start swatting together their danger zones again, because in a daddy's high school years it never really goes all-the-way soft, even then the kid, his kid, Troy, wants to know why they'd smoke a fatty at the risk of giving him unborn brain damage, and isn't this just like a kid to ask a question and not wait for the answer and to be so self-involved, even with his kid lecturing about Unsafe Sex and the effects of THC on the first trimester, even then he's describing how this one seed pops, loud, pops and sparks like July Fourth and showers sparks down until these sparks land in the mommy's bush.

The next part is pretty. A pretty glow. Like a flickering blue Bananas Foster or a Crepe Suzette served tableside. Like a Spanish coffee when the bartender showers it with cinnamons that light up like fireflies so pretty the daddy and the mommy can only gaze down at this blue nimbus like from a black-and-white television showing old movies, this spellbinding blue light that dances down there in her lap hair which must be drenched in secondhand hand sanitizer because that stuff never fully evaporates and because her bush explodes like napalm in the morning behind Charlie Sheen in a second feature, even then the mommy and daddy don't think to stop-drop-and-roll, stop-drop-and-roll like Bill Cosby told them their whole growing up, instead they scream and even the mommy's danger zone screams with all the air the daddy's put inside her, until this blast of air blows fire like a fire-breathing dragon, like a Vietnam War flamethrower or Lieutenant Ellen Ripley chasing the Alien around in the dark, a total kick-ass feminist hero the likes of which nobody had ever seen before until she turned out to be just Sigourney Weaver, even then that fire shot across the backseat to set fire to the daddy's hand-sanitized danger zone, not just the hair but the skin parts, too, which are still stuck straight out under internal pressure, until having extra foreskin is the least of his worries, even then he's trying to do justice to how this looks, even if the expression on his kid's face, Troy's face, is abject horror, Troy's dad says it's like when they go camping and get their marshmallows too close to the flames and they're left holding this spitting, dripping blob of melting, sizzling mess nobody can extinguish, tons worse than just browning his meat, even then the mommy's monthly time decides to come, even when it's not her time, that's how the ladies do if something startles them, like a spider next to the kitchen sink or a scary Halloween mask, they contract all their muscles in a defensive maneuver, the way a squid will squirt ink to create a smokescreen so she can make her getaway, the mommy gushes out this volcano of blood encircled by a ring of fire. Even that doesn't help when the Dodge Dart's interior ignites making this a fiery fire within a fire like a fireplace inside a burning-down house located in a subdivision of Hell, even then the daddy's so close that when he's pulled out he still spits his spermatozoa only on fire from hand sanitizer, shooting pow, pow, pow like tracer bullets, like July Fourth, even then the mommy's not feeling this big rush of not-pregnant relief, even then the mommy and daddy just jump around the backseat of the Dodge Dart until every headlight behind them is flashing high-low, high-low, and everyone is making rodeo whoopees and shouting, "Let 'er buck!" not knowing it's a danger zone conflagration, not until the mommy tumbles out one back door of the Dodge and the daddy tumbles out the other back door and even then the idea of stop-drop-and-roll is the last thing that comes to mind, even when they're both running on fire, trailing burned bits of marshmallow, smoldering, dropping off Bananas Foster gobs that sputter in the drive-in movie gravel, setting fire to paper napkins dropped by litterbugs, even while they keep running to where the faces of Sally Struthers and Steve McQueen just keep kissing bigger and bigger, even then his kid's face, Troy's face is one big question mark, even then the kid asks, "Is that where I came from?"

By this point they're home, parked in the driveway where Troy's mom waves at them from the kitchen window. What's left of her. Even then Troy's father is so determined to outdo his own dad's lame performance that he says, "No, my son." He says, "That's why you're adopted."

■

COLD CALLING

The computer feeds me a Mrs. Wayne Timmons with a Battle Creek area code. It's the first week we're cold calling for the Wonder Wet Wiper, not just a mop but a whole entire floor-enhancement system, the only sure way for you to protect and preserve your fine-quality floor coverings, an inexpensive way to save you thousands of dollars in ruined hardwood or costly vinyl-laminate damage, all of that peace of mind for just three easy payments of . . .

And Mrs. Wayne Timmons says, "Hold up." She says, "Why should I buy anything from you?"

Policy says to jump back to the Level Two statements: because the Wonder Wet Wiper will save you far more than its cost, in time saved and eventual resale on your home.

And Mrs. Wayne Timmons says, "Do you even believe in God?"

It's not on the approved response script, but I answer. Dialogue outside the established flow charts, officially it's called a "jog." Officially we're not supposed to engage with off-track subject tangents, but I tell her, "Yes."

And Mrs. Wayne Timmons says, "Our one, true Christian God?"

Yes. Officially, I'm supposed to redirect the topic back to the Wonder Wet Wiper, saying how it's so easy that cleaning her kitchen floor will no longer count as servile work on the Sabbath . . .

And Mrs. Wayne Timmons says, "Not some smiling elephant god?" She says, "Are you sure you don't worship some naked woman with lots of wiggling arms?"

The basics of any outbound call are you start with Greet, the Grant, and the Pitch. First you say good evening or morning or whatever; that's the Greet part. You ask for permission to speak with the customer: the Grant part. Only then do you Pitch.

"What time is it there?" says Mrs. Wayne Timmons. "It's four in the afternoon, here."

It's three, here, same afternoon. Another jog. Enough jogs, and the training supervisor registers a demerit. Enough demerits, and you'll be looking for an even worse-paying job.

"Don't lie to me about the time," says Mrs. Wayne Timmons. She says, "Are you in Calcutta or New Delhi? India or Pakistan?"

Another jog. I'm in Walla Walla. I pray to her exact same God, the big man with the white beard.

"What's your name?"

Bill.

"Don't lie to me, Omar or Akbar," says Mrs. Wayne Timmons. "We Americans know how you're trained. It's been in the newspaper and on the TV. You're given regular names and they teach you to talk like a normal, real person." She says, "But we still know you're taking food out of the mouths of our own sweet babies . . ."

Across the networking floor, the training supervisor looks up from her desk. Meets my eyes, her eyebrows sprung up. She points one fingernail at the digital readout on the wall: the calls in progress, the total calls per shift, and how my jogs are dragging out the average length per call. The three-minute average is stretching to four-point-five. The training supervisor drags a fingernail sideways across her throat.

In my headset, Mrs. Wayne Timmons says, "You don't even eat hamburger. I've seen pictures," she says, "you let dirty cows block traffic . . ."

My eyes are watching the average call time stretch to five minutes, associates at other desks and other banks are looking at me, shaking their heads at how I'm wrecking their monthly bonus. The script says I should apologize and terminate, but I don't. I keep jogging, saying my name is William Bradley Henderson. I'm seventeen years old and go to Thomas Jefferson High School in Walla Walla, Washington. I work four nights each week doing telephone sales to save up for a car . . .

And Mrs. Wayne Timmons says, "You people don't miss a trick . . ."

And too loud, I say it. Into my mouthpiece, I say, "Trust me."

All around me, headsets pop up. Eyes spin around to pin me from a million directions. Black associates, Hispanic and Asian associates, Native Americans.

Into the phone I whisper, "Listen, lady . . ." I almost yell, "I'm just as white as you . . ."

My next night at work, a man with a Sioux Falls area code says, "You people hijack our jetliners and crash them into our skyscrapers, and I'm supposed to buy your crappy mop?" He says, "Well, no friggin' thanks, Haji . . ."

A man in the Tulsa area code says, "Towel head," and hangs up.

A man in the Fargo area code says, "Camel jockey," and hangs up.

In the Memphis area code, a man says, "Sand nigger," and the line goes dead.

Next in the phone queue, the computer feeds me a west Los Angeles area code, and the woman who answers says, "Tiananmen Square was a human rights tragedy, but you have to keep striving toward freedom." She says, "As a member of Amnesty International, I spend every extra penny in my fight to get a decent living wage and safe working conditions for your people." She says, "You need to rise up and throw off the shackles of your imperialist corporate overlords."

She says, "The peoples of the world are marching alongside with you."

But she doesn't buy the mop.

Next in the phone queue, the computer feeds me a Mr. and Mrs. Wells in Washington State, area code 509, and a girl picks up.

I say, "May I talk to you about a revolution in floor maintenance?"

And she says, "Sure." The girl says, "Talk."

The Greet, the Grant, the Pitch.

Interrupting, the girl says, "I envy you." She says, "I'm trapped in this dinky town called Walla Walla, a tankful of gas from anywhere good. I go to school with clone kids—the same clothes and hair and dreams—like we all came off the same assembly line. And I'm never getting out. Ever."

I say how the Wonder Wet Wiper constitutes a whole entire floor-enhancement system—

"Do you have an elephant?" she says. "I mean, do you drive to work on a real, alive elephant?"

The queue, the average call time, the floor supervisor. And I say, "Yes." Breaking script, I say, "A five-year-old Indian elephant."

She says, "How cool is that?"

I say, "Named 'Sinbad.'"

132

The girl says, "I love that!" She says, "I have a cat, really she's an ocelot. I mean she'll be an ocelot when she's full grown, but her name is 'Pepper.'"

The floor supervisor is looking, walking my way, close enough to overhear.

"My parents adopted me," the girl says, "when I was a baby in Zaire where my adopted dad was in the Peace Corps. They're nice and everything, but it's weird being the only African American girl in, like, a whole place." She says, "Do you know what an ocelot is?"

Writing her phone number on my scratch paper, I ask the girl if I can put her on our callback list for some other night. We can talk some more about the Wonder Wet Wiper.

"Yes, please," she says. "Samantha. I'm Samantha, but my birth name is Shamu-Rindi."

And I terminate the call.

That week at school, I walked up to a black girl during lunch and asked, "Are you from Zaire?" And she just looked at me. She tossed her shoulder at me, turned, and walked away.

Another day, I asked a black girl, did she have an ocelot?

And she said, "A *what*?"

"It's a little-sized wildcat," I said.

And she rolled her eyes, saying, "I *know* what an ocelot is!"

Another day, I walked up to the last black girl in Thomas Jefferson High School and asked, "Is your real name Shamu-Rindi?"

This girl blinked her eyes, slow, looking back, waiting.

So I asked, "Samantha Wells?"

And the girl lifted one hand, slow, and pointed a fingernail at a girl across the lunchroom. A white girl. With long blond hair. Wearing a cheerleader outfit.

On my callback, Samantha "Shamu-Rindi" says, ". . . no

133

one likes the music I like, that kind of tribal, global world-beat techno stuff. Or the organic, natural food that's the only kind I can eat. I mean, my taste is so beyond their limited experience . . ."

I don't say anything.

"A good example," she says, "is summertime, around here, the humid weather makes my hair all nappy . . ."

I don't say anything.

She says, "How's your elephant?"

Good, I say. He's fine.

"Sinbad?" she says. "Right?"

I ask if she wants to buy the Wonder Wet Wiper.

And Samantha says, "If I buy one, will you call me again, tomorrow?"

My next night at work, a man with a Yakima area code says, "Right this moment," he says, "what I want to know is how come our taxpayers keep feeding you billions in financial aid and you never get better? You're always getting AIDS or having a famine!"

The floor supervisor steps up beside my chair. Shaking her head, she draws a finger across her throat.

And I terminate the call.

On another callback, Samantha says, ". . . I love the fact you're East Indian." She says, "That's so sexy." She says, "Or are you Pakistani?"

I ask if she wants to buy a fifth Wonder Wet Wiper?

And she says, "Wait, while I sneak my dad's credit card."

That next week at Thomas Jefferson High School, I walked up to the blond cheerleader and said, "Hey." I said, "Are you Samantha Wells?"

And she said, "Who's asking?" Her voice, the same as over the telephone. The girl with almost a dozen Wonder Wet Wipers, but no ocelot.

Me, the make-believe elephant boy, I say, "Would you like to go out, sometime?"

And Samantha said, "I'm kind of involved right now." She said, "He doesn't go here." Fake whispering, leaning close, in her cheerleader sweater, her blond hair pony-tailed down her back, she says, "He's a Hindu." She says, "We have this romantic long-distance thing . . ."

I say, "What's his name?" I never told her my name.

And shaking her head, Samantha says, "You wouldn't know him."

So, I ask her . . .

I ask, how can you date somebody who doesn't believe in the one true Christian God?

Standing here, my hair and clothes and dreams, everything about me coming off the same assembly line as her, just another clone, I say, "All those Hindus . . ." I say, "Hindus are fags . . ."

And she says, "Sorry," and turns, her ponytail swinging, and starts to walk away.

And after her, I'm yelling that she's white. I'm yelling, she's a girl of the white race. She needs to be dating white Christian guys . . . Not hooking up with some colored homo, halfway around the world, making godless half-breed babies . . .

I yell after her, "I'm Bill." I yell, "My name is Bill Henderson."

Only by now Samantha Wells is all-the-way—gone.

■

THE TOAD PRINCE

Mona Gleason has a little tattoo of Mickey Mouse on her butt cheek so Ethan decides to start with that. He kisses it and says, "Imagine the first caveman," whispering the words against her skin.

Mona says, "Don't." She says, "No tickling." But she doesn't turn over.

Again, he kisses her mouse and says, "Imagine a caveman getting poked with a burned stick. The soot sticking under his skin, and the caveman realizing his black spot is never going away . . ."

This is after Ethan's already tagged first, second, and third base. Mona's in his room, the two of them on his bed with one long afternoon before his folks get off work. It's been a battle to keep his blue jeans on. Mona's clothes are all over. Her T-shirt and skirt. Covering his desk, covering everything but her. He's squeezed her titties and inched off her underpants. Her tattoo's someplace her folks will never know it's there. That's the idea. Mona's so wet to go all-the-way. She's whimpering and dripping on the sheets, but Ethan doesn't want to repeat his recent, past disasters.

Unlike the first tattooed caveman, he wants history to give him credit for his discovery.

He puckers his lips and sucks, giving Mickey Mouse a nasty purple face. He says, "Check it out: Hickey Mouse." Stretched out on her stomach, Mona twists around but still can't see, not without using a mirror.

Ethan asks, "Imagine that first caveman making his black spot bigger?" Ethan describes the soot and a sharp shard of bone and somebody jabbing himself until he's covered in blood. How crazy that must've looked to other cavemen. How what looks cool later on always looks crazy at first. He pinches the Mickey Mouse skin and says, "Imagine the first cave lady who poked an earring through her ear?" He says, "Whatever it was, a fish bone or a cactus thorn, she didn't even know it was an earring."

Mona giggles and rubs him through his pants.

"You ladies are bulletproof, anymore," says Ethan. "You're all vaccinated against HPV, and you've got a million ways to not get pregnant."

Her eyes twitch back and forth between his crotch and his face. Mona wets her lips.

Ethan describes the practice of "pearling," invented by natives of South Sea islands. A native, he makes a little cut in the skin along the top of his penis. He implants a pearl just under that top layer of skin and sews the cut closed. Probably he doesn't do this himself. It probably takes a football team of Tongans to hold him down while some witch doctor does it. But if it heals right, they do it again. They bury pearls, a line of pearls, all along the top of his dick. That way, when he's hard, those pearls, those hard little lumps, they bump just-right against a lady.

Hearing this, Mona's rubbing but not as hard. She looks at his pants and asks, "Is that what you're not telling me?"

"No," Ethan says. He lets her think it's nothing that bad.

The trick will be to get to the truth in baby steps. From the tattoos to body piercing, next: pearling. After that, he describes saline inflation. How people, guys mostly, will make a little nick in the skin near the top of their scrotums. He stresses the plural, saying "guys" and saying "scrotums," to make it sound less like the isolated pastime of perverted circus sideshow freaks. A guy inserts a sterile tube into the little nick and fills his scrotum with liters of saline. A guy's sack swells to the size of a basketball, and he tapes the incision to heal.

Listening to this makes Mona quit hunting for his zipper. She looks a little green, but that's part of the plan.

"Ladies do it, too," Ethan explains. To their breasts, from underneath, with a big needle like for giving blood. If it's breasts or a scrotum, it stays big for a couple days before the person's body absorbs the water. "I've seen pictures on the web," Ethan says. "It makes your titties all big and pushed together like a Victoria's Secret water bra, only without the bra."

The image makes Mona cross her arms over her chest.

Ethan chose her, not just because she's hot. He thought she'd be more open-minded. Not like Amber Reynolds or Wendy Finerman. He'd found Mona Gleason in Advanced Placement Microbiology. During a section on virology. He loves her because she loves viruses. Theirs is a match made in heaven. Something stirs in his crotch like a baby ready to be born.

"Body modification," he says. Every age embraces some fashion trend that looks ridiculous from any other point in history.

Now he can tell that Mona feels two ways about getting into his pants. She's revved up. But all his talk has taken the edge off her hot and horny.

"The way I see it," he continues, "a person has to sacrifice his life to something."

He notes that she's put some empty bed between the two of them.

Ethan asks, "Have you ever heard of Brothel Sprouts?"

Mona, she says, "Brussels sprouts?"

Ethan repeats, slower, "Brothel." He says, "Like in a whorehouse."

Now, Mona looks wary. Her forehead wrinkles like she doesn't really want to connect the dots.

He asks, "How about 'speed bumps'?"

The worry lines disappear off her forehead. She nods.

He asks, "You know 'corn-on-the-cob'?"

Mona rolls her eyes. Looking dopey with relief, she says, "Of course."

Ethan shakes his head. "You don't have a clue what I'm talking about." He looks to make sure the window is shut. The door is locked. He listens for the sound of anybody walking by within earshot. When he's sure the coast is clear, he continues, saying, "That's what the streetwalkers call them."

"Hookers?" Mona asks.

Ethan holds up a finger to correct her. He says, "Prostitutes."

"Corn-on-the-cob?" Mona asks.

"Just listen," Ethan tells her. He describes going to the east side of town. Sneaking out of the house and riding the bus over to the east side late at night. Other times, on weekends. It was for research. It didn't cost much.

Hearing this, Mona makes a face like she knows where he's going.

"I wore latex gloves," Ethan says, to defend his methods. His scientific protocol. He describes how he stole sterile cotton swabs from the nurse's office at school and petri dishes from the Chemistry lab. He cultured the samples right on the desk in his room.

Mona looks at the desk, cluttered with books. Textbooks on virology. No petri dishes. She asks, "You had sex with prostitutes?"

Ethan winces. "No," he says. "All I did was I swabbed them."

To judge from her expression Mona is picturing someone mopping. Sailors on a ship swabbing the deck with mops and buckets of soapy water.

To clarify, Ethan explains, "I asked each subject about the history of her infection. How long ago it first manifested. How fast it had spread. Questions about the discomfort and any negative symptoms."

The way Mona looks now, she's ready to find her clothes.

To stall for time, to calm her down, Ethan says, "It's not what you think." He says, reassuringly, "If you've been vaccinated, I promise you're not in any danger."

Mona starts to reach off the bed. She's reaching for her phone, but Ethan reaches it first. He holds the phone away from her at arm's length while he reiterates, "Remember how crazy the man with the first tattoo must've looked?"

Mona's eyes stare back at his.

Ethan's telling her this because he wants her to understand. He's not a lunatic. It's not that he's a prude, either; some things he just needs to keep under wraps. He wants her to know what to expect when he drops his pants. He's an artist. He's a groundbreaking pioneer. He's telling her so she won't scream when she sees.

He climbs to his feet, standing over her. He prompts, "Remember the first cave lady to put a bone through her nose?" Now, he's reaching for his belt. Reaching to undo the buckle. He tosses the phone over his shoulder. He flops open the belt.

He doesn't want her to scream the way Amber Reynolds screamed for help. Or to dial 9-1-1 the way Wendy Finerman tried.

Ethan's the missing link that doesn't want to go missing. He says, "I'm what comes between human beings and what comes next."

Mona's no longer revved up. But she's no coward. She's hooked by curiosity. She backs into a crouch on the bed, her knees tucked under her as Ethan stands there. She rakes the hair back from her face. Her titties, the nipples have gone flat. He pops open the top button of his jeans.

Ethan says, "I'm not the first scientist to serve as my own guinea pig." As he pulls down the tab of his zipper, he can read Mona's expression. This isn't going well. He's started so slow, made his case so gradually, but what she sees has wiped all scientific rationality from her face. Her eyes go round. Her mouth sags open. The only sound she makes is a tiny jerking spasm of gasp.

"My method," Ethan tries to explain, "was to make tiny pinpricks and to infect each with a different sample." He struggles to stay reasonable and not react to the look on her face. "Like in Biology," he says hopefully, "like Gregor Mendel with the peas?" He says. "I'm my own test garden."

This is how the first tattooed caveman must've felt. Or even Prince Albert, with everybody in his high school locker room staring, thinking he's a crazy freak, not knowing Prince Albert's a brilliant trendsetter and a few years from now everyone will want the same deal. No, every stupid football player probably gaped at Prince Albert the way Mona is gaping, with all the blood drained out of her cheeks.

Despite how carefully he's prepared her, Mona does nothing but stare between Ethan's legs. Mute. Her face freezes like a silent laugh as he tries to explain his scientific method. Like pearling, like so many forms of body modification, his aim has been to heighten sexual sensation. All the ladies are vaccinated so what does it matter if a guy is infected? He's planted his test rows and watched to see what would sprout. The pinpricks weren't much. They were easier than a tattoo. Less painful than a piercing.

When the first results had burst from his skin, they made a track of little buds. Cute, almost. Like Old MacDonald's Farm. Running the length of him was a delicate trail of tiny baby nubbins too small to see except with a magnifying glass. When those little buds had started to grow Ethan could see why they were called Brothel Sprouts. After all the rows were up and getting bigger, rows of bulbous little bulbs going all the way around his junk, then he understood why their other name was corn-on-the-cob.

Mona kneels at his feet, glancing at the window. At the locked door. Standing spread-legged, looming over her, Ethan says, "From a scientific standpoint you have to admit they're fascinating." Some were red. Others, pink. Bright pink drippings of flesh. Others looked darker, lavender eruptions bursting from purple eruptions. A few were pale white, growing larger, telescoping outward. In Microbiology, they'd studied how a virus was neither alive nor dead. Not technically. Science wasn't sure what a virus was, other than a particle of nucleic acid coated in protein.

It goes without saying that he has to sit now to take a leak.

It's another safe bet that Mona's lady parts have dried up.

More and more, his dad tells him he's too smart for his own good, but this time he knows that's not the case. Once he can perfect his process he'll patent it or copyright it or whatever, and it will make his family rich. Ethan has invented the one safe and effective way to grow and customize a guy's junk. The world will beat a path to his door.

The problem is Ethan's garden has kept growing. Even now the garden is still swelling. No longer is it corn-on-the-cob. It's a field of corn. It's not just a test garden, not anymore. It's a forest of nodes and nodules. Down there are clusters of warts so purple they look almost black. Fat skin tags spring from sprouts and

142

branch like tendrils until they form a jungle that hangs halfway to his knees.

These hanging gardens, dangling between Ethan's legs, they look shaggy, bristling with bumps that drip from the backs of larger lumps that dangle from shapeless mounds of lank flesh. They form a tapering cluster of stalactites, slack and flopping tissue that hangs like a heavy curtain. Out of this rich fringe of aberrant cellular growth slowly descend ropey strings of seminal drool, colorless as spider spit, which any motion or breath or thudding heartbeat set to gently pendulum from side to side.

And somehow this, this drooling jungle, it can sense Mona. It smells her titties, feels the heat of her bare skin. The way it had sensed Amber and Wendy. And it's growing, stealing the blood that normally would go to Ethan's cerebral cortex. It's usurping his nervous system. And growing, it's becoming a beast that continues to flop out fleshy stalks and feelers until the rest of Ethan, the original Ethan, begins to wither and shrink. The beast expands, nodules blooming from warts, puffing up, ballooning from renegade spurts of inflating flesh. It expands with blood and lymph until all that remains of Ethan is a wadded, shrunken vestige perched midway down the red-dappled, wart-pebbled back of the beast.

It rears up over Mona, foreign and mindless. Ethan, no more than a skin blemish sliding down to its ass. No more than the Hickey Mouse is to Mona.

The beast moves the way it's always moved. Without muscles. Without bones. The way a paramecium moves by expanding itself in one direction across the bed. The beast moves with a peristaltic pushing out of trembling nodes, a hydraulic flooding and alternate drainage of cellular walls. It needs no skeleton to give it shape. And doing so, it tumbles closer to her.

By this far along, Ethan is almost asleep. Neither alive nor dead. He can hardly speak because the beast has co-opted most of his blood. In a tiny voice, he says, "The worst thing you can do is panic." He reasons with her, wanting to explain sanely and logically about aesthetics. The cutting edge of culture and evolution.

Whispering, he says, "You ladies aren't the only ones who can bring new life into the world." He's proof of that. At first, he was just a kid trying to grow his dick and get rich, and the next thing he knows is he's the gateway to a new dominant species.

The problem is: He can't accomplish this alone.

He begs. If only Mona would reach out and touch it. Pet it. Maybe even kiss it like the ugly toad in a fairy tale. Popular culture is chock-full of monstrous things that grow out of ordinary, normal young men. To Ethan's way of thinking, this wasn't so different from what had happened to Spider-Man. Mona Gleason could be his co-inventor. She could befriend it and make the swelling go down. Between the two of them, they could tame it.

With just one . . . one kiss and he'll turn back into her Prince Charming.

The little bit that's left of Ethan is sucked dry, scrunched down to a pimple on the monster's ass, but he continues to listen for Mona's scream.

After the scream, he knows she'll try to escape. The same way Amber and Wendy tried. And after he recovers, he'll wake up to find Mona like Amber: suffocated and bruised and everything else, and he'll have to stash her body in his closet before his folks get home. Then he'll have to go to school the next day and sit next to her empty desk. In the afternoon, he'll have to rush home and bury her. He's almost certain the police and his parents would never understand. Once the hookers he's swabbed catch wind, they'll raise a ruckus and no one will get exclusive patent rights.

Then, to make matters worse, he'll have to start all over with a new girlfriend.

It's then Ethan feels something. A tickle. A tickling.

In that moment he feels something warm. It's the warm touch of fingers, as Mona reaches deep into the shuddering mess of tangled hairs and dangling flesh and her lovely, soft lips close around the small, wet part of what's left of him.

■

SMOKE

None of his words just came out anymore. Every syllable had to be weighed and measured. Each was calibrated to trigger laughter or to dominate or to earn him a dollar. He sat in the kitchen, drinking coffee while his wife looked at a magazine. She lowered it a smidgen and asked, "A penny for your thoughts?" He could see only her blue eyes above the binding. She said, "Cat got your tongue?" Anything he might say in response felt chewed over. To talk about . . . to create more words, would just worsen an already dismal situation. For too long, language had used him as its brood mare, and he resolved not to say anything until he had something important to say. He set aside the newspaper crossword puzzle he did every morning. The book he'd been reading, he used as a coaster for his coffee mug. Already, he could feel the words pent up inside him, the pressure building, expanding toward an explosion. He worried that language had come to the Earth and invented people in order to perpetuate itself. The Bible said as much: "In the beginning was the Word, and the Word was with God, and the Word was God." Language had arrived from outer space and mated together lizards and monkeys or whatever until it had customized a host which could sustain it. That first person had been introduced to the complicated

DNA sequence of proper nouns and compound verbs. Outside of language he didn't exist. There was no method to escape. To feel anything, anymore, required ever-increasing amounts of words. Great landfills and airlifts of words. It took a mountain of talk to achieve even the tiniest insight. Conversation was like one of those Rube Goldberg machines wherein a bird pecked a kernel of corn glued to a button, pressing the button which activated a diesel locomotive and sent it speeding down a hundred miles of polished track until it slammed into an atom bomb the explosion of which startled a mouse in New Zealand so that it dropped a crumb of blue cheese onto a scale and tipped the pans so that the empty pan rose and flipped a switch which jiggled a trip wire, unleashing a tiny hammer so that it swung down with just-sufficient force to crack the shell of a pistachio nut. His wife drew her breath as if about to say something. He looked back at her, expectantly, hoping for the nut. The large, yellow words on her magazine said "Elle Decor." She coughed. She went back to reading, lifting her coffee cup, tipping the brim against her mouth to make a white mask of it while telling him, "The French have a phrase for what you're thinking." Everyone, he knew for a fact, was populated by billions of microbes, and not simply the flora in their digestive tracts. People played host to mites and viruses that all wanted to reproduce and continue life elsewhere. They jumped ship with every handshake. It was folly to imagine we were anything more than vessels, carting around our bossy passengers. We were nothing. He sipped his coffee, sending everyone aboard more sugar and caffeine. To relieve the pressure, he pictured himself shoveling words into a furnace where they burned to power a colossal ocean liner wherein every stateroom was the size of a football field, and every ballroom ballooned too large to see the far walls. That ship was steaming across an ocean where it was always night. Every light on every

147

deck blazed bright as surgery while a waltz played, the smoke-stacks spewing out the trailing cinders of incinerated dialogue. He stood in the bunkers, sweating, with his feet planted wide apart for stability and stoked "Hello's" and "Happy birthday's" and "Have a nice day's" into the roaring flames. He shoved in a pile of "I love you's" and a heap of "Does that include sales tax?'s." He pictured a planet, blue and perfect, without words until this ship would someday arrive. Or, not even the ocean liner. Just a lifeboat would suffice. Just a dying sailor with a few viable words still incubating inside his mouth. With his last breath, the sailor would ask, "Who is he?" and that's all it would take to wreck a paradise.

■

TORCHER

The sandstorm didn't come in on little cat feet. It wasn't like a Dashiell Hammett fog creeping over San Francisco or a Raymond Chandler fog setting the stage in Los Angeles. This desert storm descended on the tent city like a scorching, brown blizzard. Overnight, campers hunkered down inside their billowing tents. They tied wet bandanas over nose and mouth. In lieu of hoop dancing and fire-eating, they torched bong hits and told muffled tales by flashlight. In hushed respect for the dead, they recalled burners who'd left the safety of their tribes. Fools had ventured out in a storm, like tonight's storm, trusting some drunken sense of direction. Their destination might be only a few feet away, but blinded, their eyes shut against the scouring grit, the travelers had sidestepped. Lashed by sand, they'd compounded the error. Stumbling forward on sheer faith, they'd been certain they'd grasp hold of something solid. Salvation always seemed to be within their reach . . .

At dawn, a walkie-talkie squawked. Static at first, followed by a voice. A female voice. Half buried, clotted with dirt, the walkie-talkie asked, "Rainbow Bright, do you read?" Another cough of static hung in the dusty air. "This is Strawberry Short-cake," the voice said. "I have a Code Spearmint. Do you copy?"

With sunrise, the dust had settled. Near the walkie-talkie, a long zipper descended. A hand reached from inside a damp sleeping bag. Each finger lined with curlicue henna designs. Black-painted fingernails. A mood ring, its stone turned onyx: anxious. The lowest state. It wasn't a young hand, it had been younger. It felt around on the dirt floor of the tent, rejecting dead light sticks and filth-coated candy necklaces and gummy, used condoms until it found the walkie-talkie and dragged it back inside the sleeping bag. Muffled, a man coughed. He answered, "Rainbow Bright, here."

"Thank the goddess," replied the female voice. Strawberry Shortcake.

Groggily, the man poked a finger deep into his navel. That was one perk of hitting middle age: He'd grown a gut. Life had given him the kind of hard, round belly that bore down and forced a girl to arch her back when he took her from behind. The bigger a guy's gut, the deeper his belly button; Rainbow Bright's was like a kangaroo's pouch. His fingertip felt a five-milligram Stelazine. A South African Mandrax. A fifteen-milligram Mellaril, stashed for just such emergencies. He pinched out a green, ten-milligram Mellaril and popped it between his chapped lips. He asked, "Are you for sure this is a Code Spearmint?" The sleeping bag folded back to reveal its occupant: a bearded, sunburned man. A tangle of beaded necklaces threatened to strangle him. They snagged in the hair on his bare chest. One beaded strand was looped through a silver ring that pierced his lower lip. Holding the walkie-talkie to his ear, he asked, "Where?" He could smell cat piss. With his free hand, he gathered a fistful of his dreadlocked hair and brought it to his nose.

Strawberry Shortcake's voice said, "I'm at the Mud People campsite."

The sleeping bag felt wet with more than sweat. Lying next

to Rainbow Bright was an empty bong, spilled. Its water had soaked into his braids. It wasn't even water. The previous night, he'd filled the bong with Jägermeister. Between the 'meister and skunkweed tar and THC, his head stunk.

Curled up even closer was some naked somebody. Some young, feminine seeker lay fast asleep. The comatose brand of asleep. Asleep like somebody under a fairy-tale curse. An unknown person had pasted stars all over her face and bare tits. Nipples as dark purple and big around as plums, or bigger. The foil stars teachers used to grade homework, red and gold and silver. Someone had used black laundry marker to write something across her forehead. Rainbow read the words and winced. In all caps, they said "Daddy's Grrrrl." He looked at the penmanship, hard. It didn't look like his handwriting.

The kid slept so sound that even the gang of flies working over her tits didn't wake her. Rainbow waved them away. An empty gesture of gallantry. They'd buzz in the air; the moment he left, they'd descend on her like vultures.

Strawberry asked if she should call the cops.

This brought him back to reality. Almost reality. Near enough. The Mellaril was performing its magic. "Negatory," he said. "We never bring in the heat." He waited for emphasis. "Do you copy?"

The voice over the walkie-talkie started to cry, she was begging. "Please come quick."

He waited for her to catch her breath. "Strawberry, do you copy?" He picked a crab lice the size of a lentil out of the sleeping kid's pubes and flicked it toward his dozing tent mates. "Don't call any outsiders. Got it?"

The Mud People Camp. It wasn't Rainbow Bright's favorite hangout. Not by a long shot. He'd rather spend a full-moon night watching fire-eaters and hoop dancers at the Sad Clown encampment, and he really despised those Sad Clown freaks. For now he crawled out of his purple Barney the Dinosaur sleep sack and found his phone in the dirt. He wiped a layer of fine desert dust off the screen. It wasn't eight, yet. Most of the tent city would still be asleep. The screen said it was already ninety-four degrees. He stretched his arms. Sunshine predicted all day. After he found his flip-flops and adjusted his loincloth, he set off for a cup of coffee at the Hospitality Pavilion. It was on the way to Mud Camp. He wasn't in any hurry. A corpse could wait.

As he skirted around an art installation, an erect penis sculpted of papier-mâché, Rainbow Bright texted a couple of potential deputies. The penis has been trucked here on a flatbed by some freaks all the way from East Lansing. It was the size of a church steeple, filled with illegal fireworks, ready to be set ablaze on this very night of the festival.

Build it. Burn it. Build it. Burn it. Worship and destroy. The festival was civilization on Fast-Forward. They embraced and celebrated the pointless lunacy of human endeavors.

His thumbs dancing over the keyboard, Rainbow reiterated that this was a Code Spearmint. He texted, "This is not a drill."

He paused between tents to take a leak. At most, maybe half his piss actually hit the ground. The morning air was already that scorching hot.

His phone rang. Someone calling from a blocked number. Either his wife or a redhead he'd seen broadcasting for some cable network. He took a gamble.

"Ludlow Roberts?" It was his wife. "Where are you?" For being a six-hundred-and-fourteen-dollar airplane ride away, excluding tax and baggage fees, she sounded amazingly clear.

Rainbow Bright considered hanging up.

"I called the hotel," she continued. "There's no Allied Free-lance Artists convention in Orlando."

He held his tongue. The tip of one index finger went fishing in his belly button, seeking the Luminal in case he'd need it.

His wife had her own demons. Working a state agency job, pushing paper for twenty-plus years. Computing accounts payable. Interest accrued. This is after attending high school with Bill Gates. Double pinkie swear. William Henry Gates III. Not in the same class, she was three years behind him, but she used to catch him watching her in a meaningful way. Significant long stares she did nothing about. Fate, everybody knew, didn't offer you that big a brass ring twice in one lifetime. She worked her job, these days, like it was the penance she deserved. Over the phone, she continued, "You're *there*, aren't you? You broke your promise." She sounded crushed. "With all those flower children."

Rainbow Bright hung up. He found the Mandrax and chewed it for faster results.

The crew at the Hospitality Pavilion knew how he liked his coffee. No soy anything. No LSD. No mescaline. Especially no decaf. Best of all, no coffee. They filled a hand-thrown stoneware mug and gave him a whole-grain bagel to go with it. He put the mug to his lips and drank deep: rum, sugary banana-flavored rum. Such were the perks of being a Fellowship Facilitator. Rainbow Bright watched the crew members for any signs they might know about the dead man. Every square inch of their skin that wasn't carpeted with hair, it was busy with tattoos. Nobody seemed agitated. Nobody wore the requisite hairnet. It seemed like business as usual.

Being a Fellowship Facilitator wasn't the worst position. It beat Sanitary Crew. His first three years at the arts festival, he'd pumped scalding crap water out of baking-hot fiberglass shit sheds. Nobody on that crew ever got laid, but a newbie had to start at the bottom. He'd been so young. A crew-cut high school graduate. By the time his hair had grown to shoulder length, he'd worked his way up to Hospitality. The festival lasted only three weeks, but it was the only three weeks of the year that counted. When his hair hung to his elbows, he'd made the Water Brigade. Following that, Yoga Crew. After a few more seasons, Fellowship Facilitation. These days he was the lead facilitator with the wristband and headaches to prove it. He was John Law, around these parts. That was a sight more than he was in the outside world.

For forty-eight weeks of the year, he designed video special effects for the medical industry. There was more to it than that. Rainbow Bright was a medical illustrator; at least that's what he listed on his tax returns. His accountant didn't need to know the finer details.

These days his dreads hung to his waist, but they were going gray and beginning to split and break off at the roots.

When he got to Mud Camp, his deputies were waiting for him. Tinky-Wink and Sun Baby. They were good kids. Not college material, but not total burners. Not yet. Without three chest hairs between them. Both looked shaken, pale under their layers of peeling skin and Nevada suntan. Both were naked except for various lanyards and feathers, those and their Fellowship Facilitator wristbands.

As if Rainbow Bright could feel any more ancient, both young men had foreskins. When had the whole world woken up to the fact that male circumcision was genital mutilation? Even the crew in Jew Camp had foreskins. Nothing made Rainbow Bright feel more like a dinosaur than his old-fashioned penis. The last girl he'd been with, she was a sprite from Fairy Tale Camp. Naked except for a pair of pink gauze wings strapped to her shoulders with elastic. She was so young, she'd asked if he'd been in an accident. Before going down, she'd marveled over his junk and said, "You're just like that guy in *The Sun Also Rises*."

That's why he always wore a loincloth. Plus it seemed in keeping with his position of authority to cover his private junk.

Tinky-Wink had a pink pacifier hanging from a cord around his neck. Sun Baby wore giant-sized sunglasses with rose-colored lenses, the frames paved with rhinestones that hurt to look at in strong daylight. Rainbow took both deputies to be surf bums. Trustafarians. Globetrotting in their restless quest for better waves and raves.

Rainbow asked if they'd seen Strawberry Shortcake. Tinky-Wink jerked his braids toward the rear of the Mud Camp tent. Most of the occupants were still unconscious, snoring away in the growing heat. The walls of the huge tent flapped in the dry breeze.

Out back, Strawberry Shortcake was standing with a Mud Person. It was their tribe's custom to spend the entire three weeks naked, coated in a dried crust of gray mud. They went barefoot and wore round helmets that enclosed their heads in gray spheres with only three holes. A mouth and two eyes. All of them looked identical, like gray bowling balls. And they danced around the tent city like aliens or aborigines. The one standing with Strawberry had taken off her head. She was crying so hard she'd washed most of the mud off her rack. Cleaned up, they were nice tits. College girl tits. Despite his role as John Law, Rainbow hoped she'd keep crying until she washed off some real estate below her waist. The girl was kneeling over a mud-smeared body. Her mud, cracked and flaking off.

It worried him, how, anymore, his only reaction to beauty, beauty and vulnerability, was to grow himself a boner.

A voice behind Rainbow offered, "I have this . . ." It was Sun

Baby. The deputies had followed him. Sun Baby held up a plastic knife from the Chow Tent and said, " . . . If you need to perform, you know, a postmortem."

The figure collapsed on the ground looked as gray as the flat, arid land that spread for a hundred miles in every direction. Despite his thick coating of dirt, flies had already found the holes of his bowling ball mask. His bladder had let loose, and flies hovered over the moisture of his mud-caked genitals. He lay on his side, curled slightly, with his belly sagging against the ground. There was no telling if he was white or black or Asian. Not without some soap and water. To Rainbow Bright, the deceased looked like a melted sand candle. Even the dead Mud Man had foreskin.

He handed his half-empty coffee mug to Strawberry. "Does anybody else know?" He waved his hand to indicate the people on the scene. "Except us, five?" He motioned for her to take a sip. To calm herself. Doing so, he noticed his mood rings were brighter, nearly brown.

Strawberry Shortcake had shaved her head. A smart-cookie move. Last year had been a banner one for lice, and this year she'd told everyone she wasn't going to spend the best part of her summer clawing at another raw, bloody scalp. She wore a shiny wig of long, shimmering strands the color of bubblegum. She shook her head, No.

As he spoke, Rainbow leveled his gaze at each of them, in turn. "If we notify the sheriff's office, they'll shut us down." He waited for his words to sink in. The only sound was the buzz of flies. "There will never be another Playa Rock Arts Festival, not here." He smirked. "Unless you want to spend your next vacation at Disney World . . ." he nodded sagely, " . . . we're going to have to deal with this by ourselves."

The blistering winds brought the distant beat of trance

music . . . hip-hop . . . drum and bass. Rainbow Bright would have to think fast. The campers were gradually coming awake. "You," he indicated Tink with a jerk of his head. "You issue an all points text, blast that we have an urgent Code Scabies in the Chill Tent." Nothing, not reports of scorpions nor rattlesnakes, cleared a tent faster than rumors of a bedbug infestation. Once the word got out, no one would venture near the Chill Tent. "Take the body there, stat. I'm going to need a stiff paintbrush and about ten thousand wet wipes."

At Sex Witch Camp, he tracked down the head of Member Registration. She'd have the entry records, the cards people had to fill out. The legal liability waivers. The Sex Witches were busy erecting a gigantic effigy of Sandra Bernhard. They'd built her in sections, her arms and legs, in places like Memphis and Brownsville, according to engineering diagrams they'd found on the Internet. The daunting task at hand was getting her stacked correctly.

The registrar, her name was Tinkerbelle. Rainbow Bright was ready to barter for the information.

The girl from Mud Camp, the one who'd found the victim, she'd said his name was Scooby-Doo, but she didn't know from where he'd come. She'd pointed out his sleeping bag. It contained nothing but fleas and a paperback copy of *Fight Club*. Rainbow Bright had picked around in his navel until he'd found some peyote and some Toquilone. She'd swallowed them without hesitation, and he'd convinced her that Scooby-Doo wasn't dead, the kid had only been overdosed. The girl had been quick to accept the story that some Narcan had set things back on the straight and narrow. Strawberry Shortcake had tucked her into bed with a lullaby and a hashish brownie.

At the Sex Witch tent, Tinkerbelle cupped a hand over her nose and mouth. "Your head smells like cat box." She wore nothing except a skeptic's raised eyebrow and a coat of coconut oil that made the hair look like faux wood grain painted between her legs.

Rainbow Bright offered, "You want rubbers? I can trade you some for a look at the records."

"You got Ritalin?" she countered.

He shook his head. "Sunblock?"

"SPF 54, then?" asked Tinkerbelle. She looked pointedly at his dreads. "I have stuff, can deodorize pet stains."

Rainbow Bright suggested, "You need Imodium? A200? Hand sanitizer?"

The arid plains around them teemed with characters. Like a planet someplace weird. Like a *Star Wars* cantina. Freaks walked past them on stilts. Freaks, perched high up on unicycles, wore sombreros and juggled plastic human skulls. A *Mad Max* future grafted onto a cowboy past. It had the mishmashed look of a Hollywood studio back lot from a hundred years before: a jumble of sets and characters, all of them looking for the thread of a grand narrative to unite them.

Tinkerbelle asked, "How's Thumbelina?" It was his wife's festival name. She and Tinkerbelle went way, way back. "Home with the kids, I suppose?" Her tone was baiting, like she knew something he didn't.

Rainbow Bright escalated to offering the big stuff. Twinkies. Kettle Korn. Hydrogenated tropical oils and bioengineered artificially Cajun-flavored snack chips. Here, after a few days of macrobiotic, whole-grain, soy everything, Oreos were as sought after as rubies.

Tinkerbelle leaned close to him. So close, he could smell her sage. Her eyes scanned for anyone within earshot, and she whispered, "Can you get your hands on some meat?"

"You want chicken? Pork?"

"Beef," she whispered.

"Hamburger okay?" They'd struck a deal. Anything to escape the regimen of tempeh and tofu. He'd find her two pounds of ground beef in exchange for a look at the camp registration records.

In the Chill Tent, they cleared the communal altar of sacred objects, setting aside quartz crystals and brass Hanuman ape statues, the framed Ram Dass photos and Yoda action figures, the Skeletors and Miss Piggy dolls and My Pretty Ponies, Malibu Barbies, Gumbies, and vanilla-scented votive candles. Cleared, the altar was waist high and covered with a bedsheet tie-dyed in swirls of red and orange. It gave them a practical place to examine the body. While Rainbow worked, Sun Baby documented every step of the procedure, snapping cell phone pictures and shooting video.

According to entry records, forty-eight campers had registered under the name Scooby-Doo. The air was rich with the aroma of barbecues. Here, it was always summer. Rainbow Bright weighed the likelihood that the dead Mud Man was not among the six Scooby-Doos who'd given their driver's license numbers at registration. Odds were better that he'd hitchhiked.

Working, Rainbow felt like an archeologist, brushing away the loose dirt, then swabbing with baby wipes to expose patches of clean skin. He was looking for track marks, injection sites, evidence of an overdose. Stab wounds. Bullet holes. Snakebite. The more he scrubbed, the more Rainbow Bright was certain he'd never seen the kid before. This was a frat boy. A lily-white homeboy, lured here by the music television footage of a zonked orgyfest and drugged desert nymphs. He had no tattoos. No piercings. Once Rainbow had examined the body, he asked Tinky-Wink to fetch him some chicken shears from the Chow Tent, and they cut away the papier-mâché of the bowling ball mask. Peeling away strips, the way a person would peel an orange, they released no fewer than a billion black flies.

A dyed-red Mohawk of spikes ran back from the peak of Scooby-Doo's forehead, back to the rear of his skull. The spikes stood up, stiff as iron. The row of points looked less like a rooster's comb than the crest of a scarlet cockatiel.

The phrase *natural causes* popped into his head, and he'd already begun to wonder where they could bury the kid's body, when Tinky-Wink turned away and doubled over at the waist. Out of his mouth hurled a long runny cascade. Half-digested tofu splattered a reclining Buddha. When Rainbow Bright looked again, the Mohawk wasn't a haircut. The hot air was instantly the smell of puke. The spikes sticking out of the dead kid were metal. Embedded in his shaved scalp was a ninja throwing star glazed red with dried blood.

Rainbow's phone rang. Another blocked number. It was a long shot, but it might be one of his kids calling so he picked up. "Hello?" What possible fingerprints the dust hadn't obliterated, the blood had.

"Mr. Bright?" the caller asked. It was a voice he knew from television. A girl voice gussied up with a Brit accent. Very King's Road. That brought to mind a halter top and a chirpy, freckled announcer broadcasting live from some Spring Break location on the Jersey Shore. It was the last person who needed to find out about a Code Spearmint. Regretfully, he hung up on her.

The last thing he needed was for some airbrushed, bunny podcaster to catch wind of a slumming college kid with a split-open skull.

At this moment, he needed a spliff and a piece of sunbaked nineteen-year-old squeeze. Over at Zombie Camp, a zombie cheerleader wearing a short pleated skirt and nothing underneath had given him a long once-over. On most days, he'd have a piece by two in the afternoon. Zombie pussy. Hobbit pussy. The girls who crowned him with silk flowers and sprinkled glitter in his beard, they all had serious daddy issues. God forbid his own daughter would grow up to tangle with a big-gutted, middle-aged, lowlife predator.

These three weeks were the only time of the year he got any respect. The only time he felt like a productive human being. Here, he was a person of some importance. He wasn't going to let some journalist bungle his one good deal.

Sun Baby bent low for a closer inspection. "I'd say, this star thing-y is your probable cause of death." He nodded, knowingly, and crossed his skinny arms across his bare chest like a conferring physician.

These weren't ideal conditions for postmortem. The increasing music of chimes indicated the desert wind was gaining strength. A thick dust storm would cover the tracks of a killer just as effectively as the pea soup fogs of London had masked Jack the Ripper. Always the doubting Thomas, Rainbow asked, "What makes you so certain?"

Sun Baby reached down to scratch his crotch with one hand. "I'm a paramedic."

Rainbow Bright wasn't sure he'd heard right.

"Outside of here, I mean," Sun Baby said, and he sniffed his fingers, "I'm a paramedic." He said, "Actually I'm in med school at Rutgers." A neon-pink baby pacifier hung from a cord around his neck. In another year it would be a stethoscope.

Rainbow Bright dismissed the statement with a derisive snort. He wasn't going to concede authority to some Doogie Howser with his first crop of pubic hair. "Well, if you're so smart, tell me how this went down?"

Sun Baby considered the dead man for a moment. "Angry Ninja Camp."

161

Tinky-Wink wiped the vomit from his lips. He spat to clear his mouth. "No doubt." His straight teeth gleamed, even in the candlelight and incense smoke. Some vomit clung to the rhinestone frames of his sunglasses.

Rainbow Bright shuddered. The Angry Ninja Camp was about his least-favorite place to pay a call. Especially on official business. Down to a tribesman, every Angry Ninja was a world-class joker with sharp weapons and an ax to grind.

"Scooby-Doo's copped to all he's going to fess." Rainbow Bright snapped his fingers and jerked a thumb backward over his shoulder. "Get him lost."

His two deputies stared back. Uncomprehending. Sun Baby lifted his pacifier to his mouth and started sucking it. Tinky-Wink ducked his head, sheepishly. "I might be out of line saying so, but wouldn't that be destroying evidence?"

Rainbow Bright smirked. "What? Are you a lawyer?"

The kid shrugged. He blushed and looked away. "Yeah, I specialize in entertainment copyright litigation."

Outside of the Playa Arts Festival, these three weeks of magic in the middle of nowhere, everyone was something different. The topless stoner chicks went home to be neurobiologists and software designers. The slack-jawed burner types were all district attorneys in real life. None of them wanted to lose this. Rainbow Bright waited for another objection. None came. "Plant him, deep. Someplace over the horizon. Put rocks on top to keep the scavengers from giving his bones a resurrection."

He watched them wrap the tie-dyed altar cloth around the body. As they hefted it, he assured them, "Things will get back on an even keel after we bring his killer to justice." In truth, Rainbow said it to convince himself.

He had an inside contact. The chief of the ninja tribe was a badass named Snidely Whiplash. Back in the Pleistocene Era, he and Rainbow had done shit-house duty together. Whiplash would never admit to being that old. He shaved his gray chest hair and talked a lot about getting his GED, trying to foster a youthful impression. Rainbow found him at the Media Pavilion, taping a podcast for some music video network. This season, camera teams from every nation in the world had found their way here to exploit the zany goings-on. They outnumbered the drum circles, and when their helicopters dipped too low, trying to film the topless limbo contest, their spinning blades churned the playa dust into choking funnel clouds.

What occurred here was a kind of collective Gestalt therapy for the world, and nobody could blame the world for wanting a peek. Monsters capered. Dreams slowly took shape. A full-sized replica of the New York Stock Exchange, complete with wide steps and fluted columns, rose from the barren, windswept hardpan. Nearly as tall, a bust of Chairman Mao was under construction. A Rhineland castle. An ocean liner, mired in the sunbaked caliche. The gargantuan penis. A Trojan horse. Everything built of balsawood and cork. Each of them, overnight products of lath and papier-mâché, chicken wire, stretched canvas, staples, and paint. All of them swarmed with tiny naked figures. A Dalí painting. Tiny arms swung and the sounds of miniature hammers followed a moment late. Everything distorted by scale and distance. In the avenues between these monuments, figures promenaded in towering peacock feather headdresses and carved African masks. Roman centurions marched alongside mincing geishas. Catholic popes and uniformed United States letter carriers. A constant throng of costumes and nudity. People parading, on leash, their willing slaves. People serenaded with tubas that glared blindingly bright, their brass hot in the midday sun.

Among this company mingled Rainbow Bright, accepting their greetings and accolades. To young people he was proof that age wouldn't end their fun. To older campers, he was a living link to their youth.

Here was the incubator, the test tube, the petri dish. And he was proud to play a part. The fringe was the future, and what happened next in the world, it happened here first. Fashion. Politics. Music and culture. The next world religion would take form, here. Of these experiments, almost all would fizzle, but some would take root and grow.

In contrast, there had only been one season for the Occupy event. Rainbow Bright reasoned that the Playa Rock Arts Festival had endured for decades because its premise was creation not complaint. Producing versus protest.

The outside world was a sewer of corruption and discord. It was irredeemable, and the only hope for a cure would come from this band of artists and freethinkers engaged in play.

This, their special, fragile world, wasn't going to end. Not on his watch.

First, he'd pay a visit to his own tent and dig around in his navel. He knew Snidely Whiplash was a pushover where mescaline was involved.

At the Media Pavilion, the interviewer was the Brit. A redhead with arresting hazel eyes and a shaved pussy. She sat cross-legged with Snidely in the shade of a blue-and-white-striped beach umbrella. Whiplash wore a loincloth of macramé hemp. That was smart of him. To a euro girl a cut dick would look like a birth defect. Whiplash and the girl kissed cheeks, and he stepped away. As the elderly ninja left the interview, Rainbow fell into step beside him. He flashed Whiplash a glimpse of his phone. A snapshot of the dead mud kid. Asking, "You ninjas missing any throwing stars?"

Whiplash gave the photo a glance and shook his head. The denial was clearly a lie.

Rainbow kept his voice innocent. Naïve. "You think I should go to the county sheriff with this?" The question gave Whiplash pause. He knew what all was at stake. If their killer was a ninja, his tribe wouldn't harbor him. Or her. With all of their twisted swords and scimitars and spiked cudgels, the ninjas would sacrifice a member before they'd let this messy business shut down the tent city.

Whiplash gave the photo another look. A longer look. "Forward me the picture," he grumbled. "I'm familiar with the weapon in question." He plucked a spliff from behind his ear and a cigarette lighter from deep in his loincloth. Putting flame to what smelled like Californian Skunk and good tobacco, he drew a chestful of smoke. Exhaling it, he said, "If the transgressor is one of ours, we'll settle the score."

He offered Rainbow a toke, and Rainbow accepted it. They parted company at the Furbie tent. A whole tribe slouching around in full-body animal costumes and plush masks. How anyone could wear fake fur in this heat, it was impossible to comprehend.

As he strolled, his phone rang. "Ludlow, I know I'm being a drag." His wife, again. She hadn't always been a drag. They'd met at the festival. In the days when she'd been a fire-walking, pill-popping, body-painted freak. She'd been beautiful, back then. Fearless. Now she shaved her armpits. Over the phone, she said, "Luddy, you've got two kids. You can't spend your whole vacation away from your family."

As before, Rainbow Bright let her say her piece. He didn't respond. He didn't defend himself. The clarity of the signal impressed him. He could even make out the grinding of her teeth.

"Part of me says I should leave," she baited him. "Should I leave you? Take the kids, change the locks, and move out?" Her voice clenched like a fist, she waited. "Is that what you want?"

He listened. Letting her blow off steam. His mood ring was going dark, darker, again, almost obsidian.

"Ludlow, are you there?"

He was there but didn't say so.

"Fine," she said. And hung up.

He doubled back to the Media Pavilion. The redhead was between interviews. She was drinking a diet cola when her hazel eyes caught sight of him. Sizing up her come-hither expression, Rainbow Bright was glad he'd worn his clean loincloth. He worried that his wife and kids might see the broadcast, but he prayed that his business associates would. The cameraman seated him under the striped umbrella, and the redhead checked herself with a mirror. After some fumbling, they finally clipped a tiny microphone to his beard.

"I tried to phone you." She offered him a freckled hand. "I'm Skipper." Turning to the camera, she asked, "You ready?" A man wearing a baseball cap and a headset gave her a double thumbs-up.

Rainbow Bright understood the camp's official stance on media. It was here to exploit and turn the festival into a commodity which could be leveraged to sell other commodities: beer, condoms, anything young partygoers sought. Nonetheless, the media gave the burners a means to share their message and vision with the world. The trick was to not get snared with a gotcha question. He answered, yes, his name was Rainbow Bright. No, he was not the head of security for the tent city. His job was to facilitate communication between tribes. She asked the standard line of questions about fights. About drugs. About sexual assaults.

Out of left field, the presenter, Skipper, asked, "What's a Code Spearmint?"

Rainbow wasn't sure he'd heard correctly. "A code . . . ?"

166

She nodded. "A sad clown told me to ask."

Rainbow shrugged. "We don't have that term."

"It signifies a serial killer, does it not?" The redhead didn't miss a beat. She pointed a finger toward the crowd that stood watching them. "That's the clown, if I'm not mistaken."

He followed to where her eyes focused in the audience, and there was a frowning clown. It looked familiar, but only because all clowns looked similar. Something about its eyes or the posture of its body.

Rainbow Bright flinched. "This isn't like the outside world." He flashed her an aw-shucks grin. "We don't have anything remotely like that, here."

"You're saying that even with the drugs and young people and extreme conditions"—her eyes were laughing, daring him to tell the truth—"you've never had a killing?"

He pretended to think. Cocking his head. Furrowing his brow. A pitcher's long windup before throwing a fastball. "No," he said. "Never have."

His phone chimed to signal a new text message. Live on camera. He'd been told to turn it off but was glad he hadn't. With Skipper glaring, he checked the text. It was from Strawberry Shortcake, she was reporting on shouts and the sounds of a violent scuffle at the Angry Ninja Camp. Despite the cameras, he started to text her back.

To provoke a response, Skipper asked, "Is that your Code Spearmint?"

Rainbow used the message as his excuse to bail. He looked straight into the camera—another action they'd specifically forbade him to do—and he said, "Time to go fight the bad guys."

By the time he left the makeshift stage the clown in question was gone. Absorbed into the milling masses of ballerinas and leather-clad bikers and drag queens.

Off camera, he called Strawberry. She'd found nil. Nothing to report. The Vampire tribe and some members of the Superhero tribe had heard a man screaming. Yelling for help. Before anyone could investigate, everything seemed to have returned to normal. As normal as it got for these parts. Rainbow Bright thought of Snidely Whiplash and wondered if some righteous ninja justice had been dished out.

At this point, each of Sandra Bernhard's legs was as tall as a telephone pole. Fully assembled, she'd tower as high as an old-growth redwood. The schedule called for her to be burned in two days' time. She'd hardly be finished before she'd be put to the torch. Rainbow Bright stood and watched as they hung the arms on her headless torso. The afternoon shadows stretched longer. By dusk, the shadows of everything went for miles, striping the vast flatness. Strings of Christmas lights were blinking on, and soon the great shadow of night snuffed out all the smaller ones. The clear desert air began to stink of diesel smoke from the generators. Somewhere, some idiot played the bagpipes.

On his phone, a text bulletin came through from the National Weather Service. High winds were predicted for midnight, and that meant another blinding dust storm. He hoped it would hold off. The gigantic papier-mâché penis was scheduled to burn at nine. A big crowd was expected. The evening consisted of the usual verbal altercations concerning love or drugs. A couple of cases of heat prostration. Tribes paid their respects as he ambled past their camps. Girls tossed candy necklaces over his head. People offered beer and chai. These were his people. Failed artists. Rejected musicians and writers. Part-time idealists and closet visionaries.

As a young man, he'd been an idealist in a corrupt world. It was no surprise that he'd turned out equally as corrupt, just a new and different form of corrupt. That might be the best any generation could achieve: to pioneer its own brand of corruption.

He'd attended art school, it was bunk. A stinking, lousy racket. They'd cashed his checks and told him he had Rembrandt potential. His advisors and professors, they'd painted a picture of his future prettier than any masterpiece they'd ever painted in real life. What a put-on. They'd told him he had talent. That word was heroin to the young. *Talent.* Four years, five years, six, and he'd kept buying the fix. His dream had been to do computer animation in movies, maybe video games. He'd spend his career bringing CG heroes and angels to life. Making the impossible possible.

Student debt and a string of service jobs—interrupted each year for this, where he'd met his wife, a woman who could stick to a boring pigeonhole—and finally he'd found his calling. A proctologist, of all people, had recruited him. Funny, but he used to trust doctors. Now he knew doctors were just like every other working stiff.

Rainbow Bright had suffered through his first sigmoidoscopy. Still high on the Demerol, he'd watched the video with his doctor. A guided tour of his healthy large intestine. They hadn't set out to hatch a con. Just two smart guys acting smarter. Rainbow Bright had asked for a copy of the video. It was digital. Everything was, anymore. And he'd taken it home and stayed high and uploaded the colon footage to his digital animator. He'd Photoshopped JPEGs of the gnarliest precancerous polyps to be found on the web. These he merged with images of Jesus Christ. It was the most creative work he'd done since his boy-genius days in art school. Lastly, he'd planted the polyp faces on his colon wall and downloaded the video back to his sawbones. Shocked the butt doc, he did. They both got a good laugh, but then the good doctor took the prank seriously.

They only worked it on people who could afford to pay, people with lavish insurance coverage. It was a scam, of course. When a sigmoidoscopy revealed no abnormalities, Rainbow worked his art school magic. One gander at the horrors Rainbow so meticulously detailed inside them and people begged to go under the knife. No cutting actually took place. Maybe some drugging and poking around, but nothing traumatic. The patients went home, stoned, energized with new life because they'd cheated death. Rainbow Bright and his doctor split the fee. Money rolled in.

As of late, he'd taken a couple of commissions from an oncologist, doctoring chest X-rays. Tumors mostly, some tuberculosis. Not that he needed the money. He just wanted to explore a new avenue for his artistic expression. It was a con, a dirty con and a scam, but no more so than art school had been. Besides, it proved one thing: Marcel Duchamp was right. Nobody could hoodwink the French. Context was everything. You could depict something lovely, a lovely sun setting over a lush rose garden, and no art lover would fork over a red cent. But if you executed a masterpiece, something misshapen and discolored, and you stuck it up some rich somebody's ass, they'd pay a king's ransom to have it gone.

By nightfall, the mammoth penis loomed over them. So tall it disappeared into the gloaming. It was of course uncircumcised.

As a crowd of thousands watched, a nude Sex Witch stood off at a distance and pulled back the string on a bow. With perfect aim, she shot a flaming arrow which traced a bright arch across several thousand retinas before lancing the glans. Every man present winced. The flames roamed in every direction, like some blazing herpes flare-up. Following that, firecrackers popped.

170

The brand that whistle, Piccolo Petes, were beginning to shriek. Other fireworks exploded, rocketing sparks into the night sky.

To his imagination . . . it had to be his imagination, but the Piccolo Petes sounded almost human. By then it was too late to listen. Everyone was shouting and wailing, dancing in circles around the fiery spectacle.

The screaming inside the penis prompted the crowd to scream. In the din, Rainbow Bright noticed Snidely Whiplash sidle up beside him.

His eyes on the fire, Whiplash said, "Dude picked a fight at Mud Camp. Said his stars and knives went AWOL."

The night air smelled like barbecue, but no more than it always did. Grilled meat and diesel smoke and gunpowder.

Snidely sounded self-righteous. "We took a vote. Dude lost." He continued to stare at the burning phallus. "Don't worry," he added, his focus never leaving a certain high-up spot on the pyre. "We gave him enough Rohypnol to knock out a horse. Dude won't feel a thing."

For a moment, to Rainbow Bright, the festival no longer looked like the future. It looked like demons smeared with blood and feces, dancing around a tower of flames, accompanied by the music of tortured screams. It was the weed, he told himself, it was the weed, until his vision went back to what he wanted to see. Until foremost among his worries was the question of where he'd be able to acquire two pounds of fresh ground beef.

The penis spent itself into the night sky. Slumped to one side. Collapsed sideways in slow motion. And the fire burned down to a hill of coals the Mystic tribe wasted no time in walking all over. As predicted, the winds were picking up. People started heading for shelter. It was going to be another pea soup dust storm.

Even the biggest raves, the Neverland Camp, and the Applied

Science of Kinetic Ritual Laboratory, they pulled the plug on account of hurricane-force gusts and blowing dirt. The air grew so thick Rainbow Bright couldn't see from his tent, down the path as far as the Sex Witch Camp. He couldn't make out the lights of the Chow Tent. The moon and stars were blotted out.

From the comfort of his sleeping bag, he dialed a number he knew by heart. "Thumbelina?" It was her festival name. In the outside world, she stuck to her birth name. Sloane. Mrs. Sloane Roberts. He asked, "Are you okay?"

She asked, "Are you okay?"

Exhausted, he replied, "We had an incident, but it's resolved."

"Ludlow?"

He hesitated. "Not to worry."

He heard her waiting. He listened to her deciding something. He could hear the roar of the sandstorm building outside the tent. Scouring the desert clean. Erasing from his memory the screams of a killer burned alive. Where his next words came from, he wasn't certain. When neither of them had spoken he waited for the silence to deepen. He waited longer. At last, he spoke. "A dog got into our school, this one time. I was in fourth grade. It ran around and licked everything. I was eight years old, and that dog made me aware of everything I was giving up forever." That's all that came to mind. He'd had his say.

Sloane or Thumbelina, she seemed to understand. His wife countered, "It made the children laugh and play, to see a lamb at school."

She understood. To stay at home was to doom his children to a future of the same. This was the cradle of a better civilization. She had to see that. This wasn't a midlife crisis or a stopgap measure, but an original option. Seekers had always trekked into the desert in pursuit of a big answer.

"I was thinking," he said hopefully, "maybe next year we'd all attend the festival as a family." He was drifting toward sleep.

Her voice stiff, soft but not-unsympathetic, his wife said, "There won't be a festival next year."

Rainbow Bright marveled at how close and clear she sounded despite the wind.

Her voice dropped to a purr. A teasing murmur. And she said, "Ludlow?" She said, "I'll make you a deal."

He echoed, "A deal," unsure he'd heard correctly.

"If you'll come home," she offered, "I'll stop killing your people."

Rainbow Bright was instantly wide awake. He hadn't told her. Strawberry Shortcake didn't have her number. Nobody but him had this number.

She whispered, "A throwing star to the back of a stupid Mud Man's head . . . does that ring any bells?"

Everyone here used fake names. So many wore masks. Was Sloane capable? Yes, once she'd been a savage, smeared in crud. When they'd first met, she'd been the throwing half of a knife-throwing act. But now she was a mommy who chauffeured kids to soccer practice.

The voice over the phone asked, "Who do you think told your television friend about 'Code Spearmint'?"

He asked, "Where are Lisa and Benny?"

"With their grandma Roberts."

Ludlow Roberts asked, "While Mommy slaughters burners?"

Today, she'd been the clown who'd given him the evil eye. The sad clown in the audience. Tonight, she'd allowed them to execute an innocent man, and she'd danced among the furbies and the zombies and sweating, disguised revelers. A real monster among the make-believe ones.

Listening, he felt heavier and heavier as if, instead of his purple sleeping bag, he lay in a bathtub as the warm water ran out from around him. No longer buoyant, he could feel the full weight of his bones and flesh. A burden suddenly too heavy to budge. The inert bulk of someone dead.

The voice on the phone dictated, "Tomorrow, you'll make up some excuse, and you'll come home before I go after another." She paused. "You decide." And she hung up.

The wind, the wind made people crazy. In the dense, blowing sand, she might be a few feet away. The tent city was filled with drunks and drugged-out kids, and if the dead ninja was to be believed, she'd stolen his arsenal of pointed, honed, and razor-bladed weaponry. She knew that if he called the police, the party was over. Finished forever because he'd neglected his husbandly duties. If he didn't fold his tent, more people would die.

At best, he'd go home to a ruthless killer.

His fingertip rooted around in his navel, searching, rummaging, and plucked out the hundred-milligram Luminal tablet. People took their leave of the tent city every day. Others arrived. There was no keeping track. At worst, every night would cost the life of another person. He pictured Strawberry Shortcake dead. Tinky-Wink. Sun Baby. He could call her bluff. Maybe, if he got the word out, they could catch her. Do damage control.

One burner per night, that penciled out to seventeen more dead. Every year a kid or two left a party, staggering into the windblown sand, and was never heard from again. The desert consumed them as a sacrifice. As tribute. Somewhere in the thousand square miles of wasteland, the storm buried each of them where they fell.

Build it. Burn it. Build it. Burn it. Worship and destroy.

He'd need the Luminal, tonight. Even as he fell asleep, he

felt the excitement growing in his chest. A worthy game was afoot. If he caught her, then what? Knowing the truth, could he drug her? Would he roast his wife, alive, within the head of a gargantuan Sandra Bernhard? Now that he knew how great and glorious-grand was his wife's devotion?

■

LITURGY

In light of recent property damage at 475 Battlinghamshire Court, the homeowners board would like to reiterate association policy on both dog ownership and the proper disposition of biohazardous organic materials. As per association regulations, all domestic dogs must be tethered or fenced within the property lines of the owner. At no time may a dog be allowed to roam unattended.

As for human remains, county health regulations require that they be relinquished to the acting authorities for sanitary disposal. Under no circumstances is burial at home permitted.

Compliance with either of the aforementioned regulations would have precluded the recent wide range of property damage. It is now possible, by creating a timeline of destruction, to chart the course of the medically hazardous material in question and to implicate the animals involved. The first reported incident took place on May 17, between the hours of 10:00 a.m. and 3:30 p.m. The partially decomposed remains were apparently disinterred from an unknown location by a dog. In this initial case, the apparent culprit was "Buttons." Once exhumed, the family beagle relocated the remains to the formerly white, shag-carpeted master bedroom at 475 Battlinghamshire Court, where they were cavorted upon for an unknown period before being interred in the backyard of that property.

By mapping the path of damage from 475 to 565, 785, 900, 1050, 1075, and 1100 Battlinghamshire Court, it's possible to trace the unhappy progress of the thoughtlessly discarded human viscera as it was discovered and relocated by a series of both domestic animals and indigenous vermin, namely rats or raccoons, all of whom lay claim to the increasingly decayed item, abused it, and interred it at a new location. Similar property damage to carpets, upholstered furniture, and bedding suggests the contraband found its way, next, to Surreydaledown Mews. Significant evidence of it follows in several households along Knightsbridgeton Close and Regentrosetudor Crescent. Owing to the increasingly unstable qualities typical of degrading tissue, each subsequent visitation created a more detrimental and lasting effect on the soft furnishings of each home.

A special assessment has been proposed to cover the expense of draining and cleaning area swimming pools. In addition, residents are encouraged to review their vaccination histories; most notably those bathers who encountered the item, failed to recognize its nature, and mistook it for a sad, purple, deflated beach ball. In at least once instance, flinging it at one another in oblivious delight.

This, this abomination was the waterlogged, alien horror that the youngest Sanchez daughter innocently retrieved from that household's swimming pool. Using a pair of barbecue tongs, she lobbed it over a hedge, landing it in the DiMarcos' pool. There it was discovered by that family's oldest son, Danny, who eschewed taking any noble and decent action. Instead, he pitched it up, onto the roof next door at 8871 Ivy High Street. There, it was feasted upon by crows, one of whom eventually carried the sodden carrion aloft, high into the blue summer sky, losing pur-

177

chase of it directly above the chaise lounge occupied by Ada Louise Cullen. At this point, the journey of the nuisance ceased abruptly.

Regrettably, several Internet news outlets have already carried the story, headlined "Recklessly Discarded Dead Flesh Brains Nude Sunbather." The story went viral after it became fodder for nationally syndicated talk radio pundits.

At the time of its recovery, the nuisance had lost much of its original volume. Law enforcement officials were summoned. After debate, paramedics on the scene attempted to determine the nature of the organic mass, estimating its final weight at twenty-two ounces. They treated Ms. Cullen for shock, nausea, a possible concussion, and soft-tissue trauma to her cervical disks.

After extensive discussion, the majority opinion held that the mass of flesh in question was not the result of any act of violence. It appeared to have been shed naturally. The first determination was that it was human in origin.

While many might beg to differ, such shed tissue structures do, indeed, legally qualify as medical waste and therefore constitute a threat to public health, not to mention the resale value of the homes to which said waste was exposed by subsequent domestic animals which it appears disinterred the mass and continually relocated it over the course of three long, highly temperatured days.

Under forensic examination, the matter in question proved to be the not-too-recently expelled uterine lining and associated blood-engorged tissue structures resultant from the delivery of a newborn. The superfluous leavings of the human birth process.

A number of households in Corningmarblerock Estates have celebrated the arrival of a new member, but this is not to say the medical waste in question might not have been transported from outside the subdivision, delivered here for a ritual tree planting or some similar celebration. A quick review of applications for permanent landscape alteration submitted over the past three months reveals permission to plant five rosebushes, a lilac, three mock oranges, a weeping cypress, fourteen boxwoods, and a pin oak. Any of these might have marked the original resting place of the expelled matter.

It is not beyond the realm of possibility that a far-ranging animal, say, a coyote, one of those four-legged vultures, might've acquired the nuisance remains from a community other than our own. Mockingbird Farms, for example. Or Belle Lakeside Villas, where the cavalier tossing aside of sloughed-off natal leftovers is, in all probability, a less frowned-upon practice.

Frankly, the board wouldn't put it past half the residents at Heron Cove to pull this kind of hippy-dippy stunt, but what can one do? Run a classified ad under Lost and Found? *Found: one bedraggled placenta, partially decomposed. Gnawed on by every curious animal within a two-mile radius. Call to claim.* Whatever action the board takes, there will be no satisfying some alternative-everything types who feel that Heaven and Earth should be moved in order to return the nuisance to its originator.

The board will not entertain debate over either the spiritual or ritual value of these dispositions of surplus reproductive tissue; however, this incident makes it clear that a policy is needed to address future occurrences.

Not only were furnishings soiled. No small number of domestic animals ingested portions of the nuisance. As a result, the Siamese belonging to Mr. and Mrs. Heywood Marshall-Simon regurgitated the same into Mrs. Marshall-Simon's lap. As did the Scotch terrier, Buttons, onto the heated leather backseat of Mr. Clayton Farmer's new Jaguar XJR LWB.

The homeowners board is not without empathy for our neighbors who have suffered. Save for Ms. Cullen, none are sans blame. From the party who so laxly interred the nuisance to the pet owners who blatantly disregarded off-leash protocols, everyone directly affected is implicated. Among those whose property was damaged, some advocate for genetic testing in order to determine ownership and pursue financial compensation to offset restoration costs. The board, however, maintains that such measures would be legally difficult both to justify and to execute.

It's not difficult to picture a new father finding a hole crudely pawed in his backyard, and knowing of the recent ruckus, not coming forward to claim responsibility. In lieu of an immediate solution which will satisfy all concerned, the board has elected to take a long-term stance on the episode. Namely, that such are the shared disasters that stitch neighbors together across time. In our current society, where homes are sold and families relocated on an average of once every seven years, this saga will serve as a more lasting remembrance of our fleeting time as friends and acquaintances.

The facts will warp in the retelling. People whose lives weren't directly involved will claim that they were. Those who might've suffered the loss of a rug will claim their entire homes had to be abandoned. The events of recent will expand to become the mythology of our community. Long after our pets are dead, we, ourselves, will resurrect the memory in order to savor it and carry it forth into the world. We will fling it at one another for laughs. Distort it. We will toss the story into the air at parties and howl over its ripeness. Degraded as it was, we will degrade it further. Make it more swollen. We shall render it impossibly awful, making of it the mythology of ourselves. A comfort. Proof of the trials we've survived.

Our continued prayers go out on behalf of Ms. Cullen, who reports repeated nightmares following the incident.

In light of no better options, the remains have been surrendered to the Shaysaw County medical examiner's office where they will be warehoused for two months after which time they will be respectfully incinerated.

■

WHY AARDVARK NEVER
LANDED ON THE MOON

Almost a lifetime ago, when Rooster was barely a cockerel, he was playing chess with his friends. They were all in the fifth grade, Rooster and Rabbit and Aardvark, sitting cross-legged around a chessboard in a quiet corner of the playground during recess period. Aardvark moved a rook to set an obvious trap, and Rooster took one of Aardvark's bishops, saying, "Check," when a huge shadow fell across their game. A shadow the size of everything. A foot stomped into the middle of the pawns, scattering the knights and crumpling the game board which Rooster had gotten for his tenth birthday and brought to school in its own latched carrying case with a handle because it looked like a briefcase, like the leather briefcase Rooster planned to carry when he was a lawyer. An intellectual property lawyer, ideally specializing in entertainment law. The carrying case even had Rooster's initials embossed in the fake leather—embossed in gold—a gift from his mom and dad. Aardvark had been on the cusp of winning, but now the board was creased down the middle and torn at the edges. His little black-plastic king and white pawns were routed, and standing in the middle of the disaster was Warthog, grinding Rooster's birthday gift into the dirt.

With a savage war whoop, Warthog fell forward, yelling and driving both knees, hard, into Rooster's chest.

Rabbit and Aardvark fell back, scrambling in the grass to escape, each glad that, for once, it wasn't him getting hit. Warthog's knotted fists hammered the eyeglasses off Rooster's face. Warthog's knees drove at Rooster's thin ribs, and flattened his nose. For Rooster's part, he fought back by bleeding copiously through his split lips and spouting nostrils. As he rolled across his own fallen chess pieces, the bishops stabbed him in the spine and the rooks bruised their castle shapes into his backside. Rooster was full-out sobbing like a little crybaby right from the get-go.

A shrill whistle blew in the distance, and Warthog retreated as suddenly as he'd attacked. Of Rooster's glasses, one lens was popped out and the hinge of one earpiece had snapped in half. The chess set was so filthy and broken that Rooster instantly felt ashamed for ever having loved it. Rooster had loved it so much that, now, with Aardvark and Rabbit watching, silent, he stomped what was left into the playground dirt. He kicked knights and queens in every direction, tears and blood streaming down his face. Rooster pounded his own gold-embossed initials into the mud of his humiliation, saying, "Fucking son of a bitch bullshit stupid little pussy game!"

Aardvark and Rabbit were embarrassed for their friend's embarrassment, but they understood completely. The three of them studied and did supplemental reading for extra credit. They each got top marks, and even in fifth grade they seemed destined for lofty futures. Rooster as a lawyer, Rabbit, a brain surgeon; and Aardvark, a rocket scientist. They were the runts among their peers. All of their teachers loved them for boosting the overall standardized-test scores. Their current fifth-grade teacher, Miss Scott, who was pretty and young and wore her long hair tied back with a ribbon, especially loved them, and they adored her. Rooster, Rabbit, and Aardvark came from clean homes and had parents who expressed love and respect for them. It goes without saying that they were beaten by bullies almost weekly.

To make matters worse their school practiced a no-tolerance policy regarding violence so if any hitting occurred everyone involved was punished with a mandatory suspension. For the bully, this amounted to a week's vacation, but to the victim it meant falling behind in coursework. So when Miss Scott rushed out to where Rooster was stomping his chessboard and swearing bloody oaths, he mopped his streaming eyes with the back of one bruised hand and told her, "We were playing tag. I ran into a tree."

When Rooster came back from the school nurse with his cuts washed and bandaged, the fifth-grade girls watched him and giggled behind their hands. Hummingbird pointed for Swallow to see his fat lip and chipped tooth, and they rolled their eyes. Rooster took his assigned seat at the reading table and told himself, "You test as a genius." Rabbit and Aardvark would not lift their eyes to meet his, but he leaned across the reading table and told them, "We must think of our own scheme to deliver ourselves."

Silent Reading was followed by Math Skills. Monday became Wednesday. Spelling and Vocabulary. Rooster's scrapes were healing but not his ego. Near the tail end of a spelling bee, Rooster realized hostile eyes were upon him. As he began to spell "receipt" he caught sight of Warthog in the back row of the classroom, glaring and grinding the fist of one hand into the palm of the other, his teeth bared in a silent snarl. Panicked, Rooster accidentally transposed his "i" and his "e" and threw the victory to Dolphin. That same afternoon, when Miss Scott went to the school office for more chalk, Warthog slammed Dolphin across the back of the head with a dictionary. Just the sound of book-hitting-skull hurt everyone within earshot.

For Rooster the moment was an inspiration.

Walking home from school, he told Rabbit and Aardvark, "Listen, my friends." He said, "I have a plan for our salvation."

The plan was simple. It seemed easy but brilliant. Rabbit and Aardvark agreed, it was sheer genius.

The next day, Miss Scott called Rooster to the blackboard and asked him to multiply 34 by 3, and to show his work. Rooster took the chalk and wrote for a long time, half filling the front chalkboard, and his answer was 97. Miss Scott again asked him to answer the problem, and his new solution was 91. She gave him a worried look and told him to take his seat. When she asked Rabbit to solve the problem, he got 204. Aardvark got 188. During a pop quiz in Social Studies, Rabbit put down Athens as the capital of Finland. Aardvark gave Denmark as the capital city. Rooster wrote down the Sea of Cortez.

She asked them to stay after class. She asked if they were happy at home and if their moms or dads ever yelled. Miss Scott's hair was so bouncy and her cheeks so bright that the three best friends could only adore her with full-moon eyes.

In the weeks that followed, Aardvark forgot how to spell his own name. Rabbit muffed the lyrics to "Twinkle, Twinkle, Little Star." When it was Rooster's turn to read aloud from *Little House on Plum Creek*, he stumbled over the word "hermaphrodite." Miss Scott handed back the History tests the class had taken the week before, and all three friends received F grades. F for Failed. They brought down the grading curve so far even Warthog got a C. During Recess period nobody beat them up.

F for Freedom.

With Math and Science and Reading and Geography forgotten, Rooster and his friends worked doubly hard. They came to school with dirty faces as proof they'd neglected Hygiene. They pushed past the crossing guard to prove they hadn't retained Citizenship. They slumped to fail Posture.

They were flunking every subject. Rooster's plan was working perfectly. As he'd proposed, all they needed to do was flunk fifth grade. And not just once, but three or four times. Let Warthog and Hummingbird and the rest of the bullying, giggling class, let them advance to sixth grade and seventh grade. In a few years, Rooster, Rabbit, and Aardvark would be physical giants towering among their fellow fifth graders. For the remainder of their schooling they'd be the class presidents, the team captains, and prom kings. And not just bigger, they'd be smart, smarter and more benevolent than any campus heroes, ever. Theirs would be muscle size and physical coordination and the wisdom of former underdogs. In the meantime, they'd relax and enjoy a beautiful four years of extra attention from solicitous Miss Scott.

They knew that flunking a grade was only an embarrassment if you were held back alone. Walking home the afternoon of that botched spelling bee—the sound of a dictionary smacking Dolphin's skull still echoing in their ears—the three had spit in their hands and made a triple swear to flunk together. They could eventually succeed, but only if all three failed as a team. Also, they would not tell a soul about the plan. It was Rabbit who dubbed them the "Flunk Klub."

"The first rule of Flunk Klub," Aardvark said, "is you don't talk about Flunk Klub."

The actuality of their plan was more difficult than they'd anticipated. First, they were forced to go cold-turkey on praise. The withdrawal symptoms were terrible, but if one friend felt tempted to experiment with his chemistry set or reread Plato's *Republic,* he had only to telephone the others for support until the negative impulse passed. Watching hours of television seemed to help, but it took brainpower to be so dumb. Thank goodness Aardvark found a shortcut. Walking to school one morning, Aardvark stepped into an alley and motioned for Rooster and Rabbit to follow him. Where no one could see them Aardvark looked both ways before reaching into his jacket pocket and producing a crumpled paper sack. When he unrolled the sack the only thing inside was a tube of model airplane glue.

Aardvark uncapped the tube and squeezed it flat, letting the viscous ribbon of milky glue dribble into the paper bag. He dropped the crushed tube into the bag—they wanted to be idiots, not litterbugs—and held the open bag over his nose and mouth. Aardvark's eyes were uncovered, watching Rabbit and Rooster while he drew breaths so big they inflated and deflated the bag like a brown-paper balloon. The only sound in the alley was paper crumbling and Aardvark's heavy inhaling and exhaling. His eyes glassed over, and Aardvark handed the bag to Rooster.

The glue smelled like soft bananas freckled with rot. The effect of breathing the fumes was brilliant! No longer were they merely acting stupid, the members of the Flunk Klub actually were stupid! The Glue Method, as they came to call it, didn't last forever; but under its spell Rabbit couldn't hold a pencil. Aardvark fell asleep at his desk and wet his pants. Rooster suggested stealing vodka from his parents' freezer and the magic combination of glue and vodka gave the three friends a greater ignorance than they'd ever hoped to achieve. By Christmas they were demoted to Remedial Reading. By Easter they couldn't tie their own shoes!

Miss Scott, pretty, solicitous Miss Scott, almost never left their sides. She petted them and praised them for so much as opening a comic book. Before Rooster's bruises faded she repeatedly asked, "Tell me, again, how did you hurt yourself?" She'd catch

Aardvark alone and ask, "How did Rooster get hurt?" None of them thought to synchronize their stories, and the glue didn't help. Rooster said he'd fallen off the top of the playground slide. Rabbit said he'd been tackled in a game of football. Eventually she walked Rooster to the school office where the nurse snapped three photographs of him and Miss Scott together, her arm around his shoulders. Despite how his split lips stung, Rooster grinned. He beamed into the camera, he was so much in love.

No one punched them anymore. Nobody laughed or pointed. Nobody even noticed them. Initially, it wasn't easy to be invisible. Soon it was. Rooster continued to dream of going to law school. He'd pass the bar exam with flying colors and argue passionately in courtrooms in defense of the downtrodden and the wronged. The school must've sent a warning letter to his parents—the opposite of a progress report—because Rooster's mom and dad kept him at the table after dinner one night. Rooster's father sighed deeply and asked, "Okay, what's up, mister?"

The telephone in the kitchen rang, and Rooster's mom left the dinner table to answer it. Through the kitchen doorway Rooster could see her lift the receiver and say, "Good evening," and her voice was suddenly serene. "Just a moment, please," she said, and pressed the mouthpiece to her breast as if covering her heart to give the Pledge of Allegiance. Calling to Rooster's dad, she said, "It's Hamster."

After Rooster's dad had listened a little, he told the phone, "As your chief legal counsel I have to advise you to immediately ditch that cheese . . ."

Back at the dinner table, Rooster's mother looked at him with red outlining her worried eyes and said, "We know this isn't about your grades." She bit her lower lip. "You know we love you regardless, don't you?"

In the kitchen, Rooster's father said, "Salmonella isn't worth the risk, and if our liability carrier gets wind of this they'll void our coverage on the basis of active neglect." He hung up the receiver and came back to the dining room. It took all the skill Rooster had acquired in being stupid to not understand his parents' concern, but his father said No Television until the grade situation improved. Beyond that came No Telephone Privileges. Then, No Anything Fun. Before the end of it, Rooster, Aardvark, and Rabbit were each sleeping in a bare room with no bright posters on the walls and not even A.M. radio music, nothing to distract them from their neglected studies.

Miss Scott kept Rooster after class one Friday and begged him to tell her what was wrong. Why had he drifted to the bottom of the class? She asked in a voice so heartbroken that Rooster started to cry. He cried as hard as when Warthog had beaten him. To see Miss Scott's suffering expression felt even worse than the kicks and slugs. Rooster cried until his nose started to bleed and his eyes looked bruised like Raccoon's. But even with Miss Scott's arms around him, hugging him as she also cried, even then all Rooster could say was, "I can't tell you. I promised that I'd never tell."

The following Monday a judge in family court issued a bench warrant, and Rooster was removed to foster care pending an investigation by social welfare agents. Wednesday, Aardvark and Rabbit were also placed in foster homes.

Rooster told himself, "These trials are merely for the short term." Rooster rallied his comrades, telling them, "The glory of our future will justify these present, temporary hardships." They had one another, he said. They had Miss Scott's lovely ministrations. In a few years they'd run the school; as the biggest, smartest kids they'd rule the hallways and the playground. The three suffered now so that their future runty classmates would not be bullied and humiliated.

One day Rooster would be a lawyer. Rabbit, a brain surgeon. Aardvark, a rocket scientist. And they'd each buy their respective parents a country club mansion and a private jet. They'd explain, finally, about the secret pact of Flunk Klub, and everyone would share a hardy guffaw. Their parents would love and admire them even more for the foresight and dedication the three friends had shown as fifth graders.

Sniffing glue also helped. If Rooster sniffed hard enough his mind sputtered and hissed like a lump of burning plastic. He buried his face in a paper bag and breathed until he could feel bugs crawling under his skin and he could hear strangers' thoughts. One Saturday afternoon Rooster made a game of following Aardvark. Rooster lingered a block or two behind, dodging behind hedges and crouching in the shadow of garbage cans so that he'd not be seen. By doing so he trailed Aardvark all the way to the public library. Watching his friend duck inside, Rooster's blood boiled with rage. He told himself, Aardvark is plotting to betray us. He is doing assignments for extra credit, and at year end he will move on to the sixth grade and abandon Rabbit and me to our shame!

Rooster went to inform Rabbit of this treason. Rooster looked everywhere: at the foster home, in the alleyway, behind the grade-school Dumpster, but Rabbit wasn't anywhere to be found. A horrible truth took shape in Rooster's burnt-plastic mind, but he rejected the idea. When his resignation outweighed his fear, Rooster went to the Natural History Museum. There, studying an exhibit about ancient Egypt, stood Rabbit. To make matters worse, Rabbit had a pad and pencil and was jotting notes.

Rooster, who had founded Flunk Klub, was bereft. He would be held back to repeat fifth grade, alone. His comrades who had shared so much abuse were traitors. Such treason! Their selfishness would doom future generations of ten-year-olds to the same cycle of harassment and misery. How quickly they had forgotten, but Rooster was resolved to remind them.

On Monday, leaning sideways from his desk, whispering, Rooster proposed, "Friends, let us share glue behind the Dumpster during lunch period."

Innocently, they both accepted. Once the trio was assembled and the paper bag was readied, Rooster graciously allowed his friends to breathe the fumes before him. When Rabbit and Aardvark were thoroughly wasted, their eyes dilated and their slack lips leaking drool, Rooster roundly confronted them. "I expose you!" shouted Rooster. He leapt upon the helpless pair, his knees battering Aardvark and his fists pummeling Rabbit. Rooster shouted, "The library? The museum?" He shouted, "Explain yourselves!" So totally were his friends incapacitated by the toxic fumes of glue that Rooster could slug and stomp them with no resistance.

After lunch period, when Miss Scott almost wept over the sight of Aardvark's broken nose and Rabbit's torn ears, the two took their seats at the Reading Table and told her not to fret. "I tumbled down some stairs," Aardvark said. "It is the price I paid for not thinking more of others."

Rabbit said, "It was my own clumsiness. My ears are a small loss in exchange for a brighter future."

So that he might better mentor his friends, Rooster went begging to Miss Scott, asking that they three be billeted in the same foster home. Miss Scott championed his request, and soon Rooster, Rabbit, and Aardvark were sharing the same bedroom, the same bathroom, the same brown paper bag. None was tempted to visit the library or museum. They hung a calendar on the wall of their room and crossed off the remaining days of the school year. They forgot the difference between Idaho, Iowa, and Ohio. They forgot the difference between "repugnant" and "repellant." By far, the most difficult goal to which they'd ever aspired was to not live up to their enormous potential, but they bravely met the challenge. It wasn't easy, but they flunked. In summer school they were forced to work extra hard to not make any effort.

On the final day of summer school, they watched Miss Scott open the drawers of her desk and extract photographs . . . keepsakes . . . mementos, these she collected in a cardboard box. When her desk was emptied and the box filled, she looked at the three of them in the otherwise deserted classroom, and Miss Scott said, "I'll miss you, next year."

"We've failed at failing," Rooster told himself. Despite all their worst efforts they were being sent on to sixth grade. They'd forfeited their prestige, their families, their time, and ultimately they were to be shunted to the next grade where they'd remain at the bottom of the insidious pecking order. Oh, such corruption! In that moment, Rooster's anger overwhelmed his love for his teacher. If she cared at all she'd never graduate them. To Rooster, it was obvious Miss Scott was merely passing her problems to another teacher. She was discarding them. His blood leapt to his face, his entire body clenched into a fist of rage, and Rooster shouted, "You bitch!"

Aardvark and Rabbit stared at him. Miss Scott stared at him.

"How can you send us to sixth grade?" Rooster demanded. "You call this an 'education'?" Only because he'd loved her so much, he ran to the front of the room and knocked the cardboard box from her desk. Scattering the photographs and keepsakes on the floor, Rooster ground them under his feet, tearing and spoiling them, and he shouted, "Fucking son-of-a-bitch bullshit stupid little pussy game!"

When everything was ruined, Rooster waited, panting, sweating, for an answer.

Miss Scott didn't cry. Nobody cried. It was progress, if you could call it that.

"You're not going to sixth grade," she said. Making no effort to retrieve her ruined things, Miss Scott took her coat from the back of her chair and slipped her arms into the sleeves. She fastened the buttons. She pulled open a drawer of her filing cabinet and took out her purse. "I've had three students fail regardless of my best efforts," she said, snapping open her purse and fishing out a ring of keys. "Therefore, I've lost my job." Leaving the mess beneath Rooster's feet, she walked to the door, opened it, stepped through it, and disappeared from their lives forever.

Instead of graduating to sixth grade, Rooster, Rabbit, and Aardvark graduated to marijuana. They'd acquired great skill at being stupid, and their second year came and went much easier. The three never even learned their new teacher's name. They returned to their respective parents. They persevered.

The next year, instead of graduating to sixth grade they graduated to prescription painkillers. They were twelve-year-old giants towering over ten-year-old runts. At this point they lumbered like great lummoxes among their fellow fifth graders. No one treated them like heroes; no one treated them with so much as an ounce of respect until one spelling bee when Rooster flubbed "receipt" and overheard Gnu giggle. When Recess period rolled around Rooster, Rabbit, and Aardvark stalked out to the playground where they took turns slamming their fists into Gnu's weeping face. It goes without saying that Gnu wouldn't tell, and if he did . . . what did it matter? Flunking fifth grade no longer held any terror for them, and to bolster their stupidity, the three friends sat in a quiet corner of dirt and rolled a joint. They smoked it and giggled over what they'd buy when they were rich. As Rooster sprawled on the ground something sharp jabbed into his spine. He reached around and found the object: a little statue, a figure wearing a crown . . . he almost recognized it but couldn't quite. Rooster showed the little figure to Rabbit and Aardvark, but they only shook their heads. No one could give it a name. Rabbit licked it with his tongue and bit it with his teeth and declared the figure was made of black plastic. Aardvark proposed they melt it, and to this end he produced a wooden kitchen match. When the little crown caught fire it burned with a guttering blue flame and gave off the odor of feces and burning hair. Whatever the thing was, it offered a spiral of acrid smoke that, without thinking, all three friends leaned forward to inhale.

■

FETCH

Hank stands with one foot planted a step in front of his other, all his weight balanced on that behind foot. He crouches down on his rear leg, squatting low on that behind leg, his knee bent, his torso, shoulders, and head all twisted and pulled back to the farthest point from the toe of his forward foot. At the moment he exhales, Hank's rear leg explodes straight, that hip flexing to throw his whole body forward. His torso twists to throw one shoulder forward. His shoulder throws his elbow. His elbow throws his wrist. All of that one arm swings in a curve, cracking fast as a bullwhip. His every muscle snaps that one hand forward, and at the point where Hank should fall onto his face, his hand releases the ball. A tennis ball, bright yellow, flying fast as a gunshot, the ball flies until almost disappearing into the blue sky, following a yellow arc as high as the sun.

Hank throws with his entire body, the way a man's supposed to throw. Jenny's Labrador retriever bounds after the tennis ball, a black smear shooting toward the horizon, dodging between the tombstones, then bounding back, tail wagging, and drops the ball at my feet.

How I throw a ball, I only use my fingers. Maybe my wrist, a little, I have skinny wrists. Nobody ever taught me any better

195

so my throw bounces off the first row of tombstones, ricocheting off a mausoleum, rolling through the grass, and disappears behind somebody's grave marker, while Hank grins at his feet and shakes his head from side to side, saying, "Good throw." From deep down in his chest, Hank hawks a wad and spits a fat throat oyster into the grass between my bare feet.

Jenny's dog only stands there, part black Lab, part stupid, looking at Jenny. Jenny looking at Hank. Hank looking at me and saying, "What're you waiting for, boy, go fetch." Hank jerks his head at where the tennis ball has vanished, lost among the headstones. Hank talks to me the same way Jenny talks to her dog.

Jenny twists a strand of her long hair between the fingers of one hand, looking behind us to where Hank's car sits in the empty parking lot. The sunlight shining through her skirt, no slip underneath, the light outlining her legs all the way up to her panties, she says, "We'll wait. I swear."

Written on the close-up tombstones, no dates come any newer than 1880-something. Just guessing, my throw landed around the 1930s. Hank's throw went all the way back to the stupid Pilgrims on the stupid *Mayflower*.

With my first step I feel wet against the underneath of my bare foot, some ooze, sticky and still warm. Hank's spit smears under my heel, webbed between my toes, so I drag my foot on the grass to wipe it. Behind me, Jenny laughs while I drag that foot up the slope toward the first row of graves. Bouquets of plastic roses stick in the ground. Little American flags twitch in the breeze. The black Lab runs ahead, sniffing at the dead, brown spots in the grass, then adding its piss. The tennis ball isn't behind the row of 1870s graves. Behind the 1860s, more nothing. Names of dead folks stretch away from me in every direction. Beloved husbands. Cherished wives. Adored mothers and fathers. The names stretch as far as I can see, getting pissed on by Jenny's dog, this army of folks lying dead just below us.

With my next step, the ground explodes, the mowed grass geysers with land mines of cold water, hosing my jeans and shirt. A booby trap of sheer, freezing cold. The underground lawn sprinklers drive sprays of water, blasting my eyes shut, washing my hair flat. Cold water hits from every direction. From behind me comes laughter, Hank and Jenny laughing so hard they fall into each other for support, their clothes, wet and sticking to Jenny's tits and molded over the shadow of her bush. They fall to the grass, still hugging, and their laughter stops as their wet mouths come together.

Here's the dead pissing back on us. The ice-cold way death can hit you in the noontime of a sunny day just when you'd never expect.

Jenny's stupid Labrador barks and snaps at a stream of water, biting the sprinkler head next to me. Just as fast, the automatic sprinklers drop back into the ground. My T-shirt drips. Water runs down my face from the soaked mop of my hair. Sopping wet, my jeans feel stiff and heavy as concrete.

Not two graves away, the ball sits at the base of a tombstone. A headstone not coated in dust or moss. Fresh-carved in granite, the words "Beloved Husband," the name "Cameron Hamish," and this year's date. Some poor dead bastard. Pointing my finger, I tell the dog, "Fetch," and he runs over, sniffs the tennis ball, growls at it, then runs back without it. Walking over, I pick up the wet yellow fuzz. I tell the tombstone, "Sorry to disturb you, Cameron. You can go back to feeding the worms, now." Stupid dog.

When I turn to throw the ball back to Jenny, the grass sloping down below me is empty. Beyond that, the parking lot spreads, empty. No Hank or Jenny. No car. All that's left is a puddle of black oil dripped out of Hank's engine pan, and two trails of their wet footprints walking out and stopping where the car was parked.

In one huge throw every skinny muscle the length of my arm whips, heaving the ball downhill to the spot where Hank spit. I tell the dog, "Fetch," and it only looks at me. Still dragging one foot, I start back downhill, until my toes feel warm, again. This time, dog piss. Where I stand, the grass feels coarse. Dead. When I look up, the ball sits next to me, as if it's rolled uphill. Where I can see, the cemetery looks empty except for thousands of names carved in stone.

Throwing the ball, again, down the long slope, I tell the dog, "Fetch." The dog just looks at me, but in the distance the ball rolls closer and closer. Returning to me. Rolling up the slope. Rolling uphill.

One of my feet is burning, the scratches and bunions of my bare foot stinging with dog piss. My other foot, the toes fused with Hank's foaming, gray spit. My shoes, in the backseat of his car. Gone. Me, dumped here to babysit her stupid pooch while Jenny's run off.

Walking back through the graves, I drag one foot to wipe it clean on the grass. With the next step, I drag the other foot. Dragging each foot, I leave a trail of flattened skid marks in the lawn all the way to the empty parking lot.

This tennis ball, now the dog won't go near it. In the parking lot, I stand next to the pool of dripped crankcase oil, and I throw the ball, again, chucking it hard as I'm able. The ball rolls back, spiraling around me on the hot, gray cement, forcing me to keep turning to watch it. The yellow ball circles me until my head's spinning, dizzy. When the ball stops at my foot, I throw it, again. Rolling back to me, this time the ball takes a detour, rolling against the grade, breaking that Law of Gravity. The ball circles in the pool of Hank's crankcase oil, soaking up the black muck. Stained black, the tennis ball rolls within kicking distance of my bare foot. Looping, jumping, doubling back on itself, the ball leaves a trail of black across the gray parking lot, then it stops. A black tennis ball, round as the period at the end of a sentence. A dot at the bottom of an exclamation point.

The stupid black Lab shakes, too close, spraying me with dog water from its sopping fur. The stink of wet dog and spatters of mud stick everywhere on my jeans and T-shirt.

The ball's oily, black trail forms letters. Cursive letters spell words across the concrete parking lot, writing the sentence: "Please help!"

The ball returns to the puddle of engine oil, soaking its fuzz with black, then rolling, writing in big, loopy handwriting: "Rescue her."

As I reach to pick it up, just squatting down to grab the tennis ball, it bounces a few steps away. I take a step, and the ball bounces, again, reaching the edge of the parking lot. As I follow, it bounces, coming to a complete stop as if glued to the road, leading me out of the cemetery. The blacktop burning hot and sharp under my bare feet, I follow, hopping from one foot to the other. The ball leads, bouncing a row of black dots down the road ahead of me like the twin tracks of Jenny and Hank's footprints leading nowhere. The black Lab follows. A sheriff's patrol car cruises past, not slowing. At the stop sign, where the cemetery road meets the county road, the ball stops, waiting for me to catch up. With each bounce, the ball leaves less oil. Me, not feeling much, I'm so pulled forward by this vision of the impossible. The ball stops bouncing, stuck in one spot. A car trails us, crawling along at the same speed. The horn honks, and I turn to see Hank behind the wheel, Jenny sits beside him in the front seat. Rolling down the shotgun window, Jenny leans her head out, her long hair hanging down the outside of the car door, and she says, "Are you crazy? Are you high?" With one arm, Jenny reaches into the backseat, then reaches out the car window, holding my shoes in her hand. She says, "For crying out loud, just look at your feet . . ."

With each step, my raw feet leave behind a little more red, blood, my footprints stamped in blood on the pavement, marking my path all the way from the cemetery parking lot. Stopped in this one spot, I'm standing in a puddle of my own red juice, not feeling the sharp gravel and broken glass on the roadside.

One bounce ahead of me, the tennis ball waits.

Sitting behind the steering wheel, Hank twists one shoulder backward, hooking his arm over the seat back and pinching the tab of the door lock between two fingers. Pulling up the tab, he reaches down and yanks the handle to throw open the door, saying, "Get in the car." He says, "Get in the fucking car, *now.*"

Jenny swings her hand, dropping my tennis shoes so they fly halfway to where I stand, flapping down in the roadside gravel. Their tongues and laces hang out, tangled.

Standing here, my feet dark as hooves or church shoes, so coated with dried blood and dust, all I can do is point at the dirty tennis ball . . . fat, black houseflies circling me . . . except the ball only sits there, not moving, not leading me anywhere, stopped along the edge of the blacktop where the pigweeds grow.

Hank punches the middle of his steering wheel, blasting me with a gigantic honk. A second honk comes so loud it echoes back from the nowhere over the horizon. All the flat sugar beet fields, the crops all around me and their car, filled with Hank's loud horn. Under the car hood the engine revs, the pushrods banging and cams knocking, and Jenny leans out her shotgun window, saying, "Don't make him pissed off." She says, "Just get in the car."

A flash of black jumps past my legs, and the stupid Labrador jumps in the door Hank holds open. With his twisted-around arm, Hank yanks the door shut and cranks the steering wheel hard to one side. Flipping a big U-turn, his beater car tears off, gravel rattling inside the wheel wells, Jenny's one hand still trailing out her open window. Behind them, Hank's tires leave twin smoking tracks of burned rubber.

Watching them go, I bend over to pick up my shoes. It's right then when—pock—something slams into the back of my head. Rubbing my scalp with one hand I turn to look at what hit me, and already the stupid tennis ball is on the move, bouncing down the road in a direction opposite that of Hank's car.

Kneeled down, knotting my shoes, I yell, "Wait." Only the ball keeps going.

Running after it, I yell, "Hold up." And the ball keeps bouncing, bouncing, big jumps right in line with the road. At the stop sign for Fisher Road, mid-jump, at the highest point in one bounce, the ball cuts to the right. Turning the corner in midair, and bouncing down Fisher, me still trucking along behind. Down Fisher, past the junkyard where it turns into Millers Road, there the ball turns left onto Turner Road and starts going upriver, parallel to the bank of Skinner Creek. Staying out of the trees, the oil-soaked, dust-packed tennis ball really flies along, puffing up a little cloud of dirt every time it smacks down.

Where two old wheel ruts leave the road and run through the weeds, the ball turns that way, rolling now. The ball tracks along the dried mud of one rut, swerving to go around the worst puddles and potholes. My shoelaces dangle and whip against my ankles. Me panting, shuffling along after it, losing sight of the ball in the tall grass. Catching sight of it when the ball bounces, bouncing in one place until I find it, there. I follow, and the houseflies follow me. Then, rolling along the rut, the ball leads me into the cottonwood trees that grow along the creek side.

Nobody's standing in line to give me any scholarship. Not after my three big, fat D grades Mr. Lockard handed me in Algebra, Geometry, and Physics. But I'm almost sure no ball should be able to roll uphill, not forever. No tennis ball can stop perfectly still in one place, then start up bouncing off by itself. Based on what little I've learned about inertia and momentum, it's an impossibility, how this ball comes flying out of nowhere, socking me in the forehead to grab my attention any time I even look away.

One step into the trees, I need to stop and let my eyes adjust. Just that one little wait, and—pow—I have dirty tennis ball stamped on my face. My forehead feeling greasy and smelling like motor oil. Both my hands raise up by reflex, swatting at air the way you'd fight off a hornet too fast to see. I'm waving away nothing, and the tennis ball is already jumping out ahead of me, the thumping, thudding sound going off through the woods.

Going all the way to the creek bank, the ball leaps out ahead, until it stops. In the mud between two forked roots of a cottonwood tree, the ball rolls to a standstill. As I catch up, it makes a little bounce, not knee high. It makes a second bounce, this time waist high. The ball bounces shoulder high, head high, always landing in the same exact spot, with every landing pushing itself deeper into the mud. Bouncing more high than I could reach, up around the leaves of the tree, the ball clears away a little hole, there, between the roots.

The sound of birds, the magpies, drop to silence. No mosquitoes or buzz of deerflies. Nothing makes any sound except this ball and my heartbeat in my chest. Both, thudding more and more fast.

Another bounce, and the ball clinks against metal. Not a

sharp sound, more a clank like hitting a home run off the gutter of old Mr. Lloyd's house, or skipping a rock off the roof of a car parked on Lovers Lane. The ball hits dirt, hard as if it's pulled with a magnet, stops, and rolls to one side. And deep in the hole it's dug, a little brass shines out. The metal of something buried. The brass lid of a canning jar, printed Mason, same as your mom would put up tomatoes inside for the winter.

No tennis ball has to tell me more. I dig, my hands clawing away the mud, my fingers slippery around the buried glass outsides of the jar. The ball waiting, I kneel there and pull this dirty jar out from the sucking mud, big around as a blue-ribbon turnip. The glass so smeared I can't see what feels so heavy inside.

Using spit, spit and my T-shirt still wet from the graveyard sprinklers and sweat, I wipe. The lid is stuck on, tight, swollen with rust and crud. I spit and wipe until something gold is looking back from inside the glass: gold coins, showing the heads of dead presidents and flying eagles. The same as you'd find if you followed a stupid leprechaun to the base of a rainbow—if you believed that crap here's a quart jar filled with gold coins packed so tight together they don't rattle. They don't roll. All they do is shine bright as the alloy wheels I'm going to buy to blow Hank's crap-burner car off the road. Bright as the diamond ring I'll take Jenny to buy at the Crossroad Mall. Right here in my two hands—and, pow.

The bright gold, replaced with shooting stars. The smell of motor oil.

The next smell, my own nose collapsed and filling with blood. Busted.

The tennis ball blasts against my face, bouncing angry as a hornet. Slugging me, the ball flies in my face while I fight it back with the heavy jar, shielding my eyes with my arm muscles burning from the gold weight. Blood runs down from my nose, sputtered out by my yelling. Twisting one foot in the slick mud, I launch over the creek bank. Same as Cub Scouts teaches you to do in a wasp attack, I splash into the water and wade out to over my head.

From underwater, between me and the sky, the ball floats on the surface of the creek. Waiting. The heavy jar of gold coins holds me tight to the rocks on the creek bed, but rolling it along, my chest full of my breath, I work my way upstream. The current carries the tennis ball downstream, while the gold anchors me, cut off from the sun and air. Working my way into the shallows, the moment my breath gives out and the ball's nowhere to be seen, I pop my head up for a gasp. One big breath, and I duck back under. The ball's floated, bobbing, maybe a half-mile downstream, hard to tell because it looks so oily black on the deep water, but the ball's following the trail of my nose blood, tracking me in the direction of the current.

When my new air gives out, I stand up, half out of the water, and wade to shore, hauling the gold and making as little splash noise as possible. Snorting the blood back up my busted nose. One look backward, over my shoulder, and I see that already the ball's swimming, slow as a paddling mallard, against the current, coming after me.

Another Sir Isaac Newton impossibility.

With both my arms wrapped around that jar full of gold, I scramble up the creek side, the water squishing in my shoes, and I take off running through the woods.

With my every running step, mud slides under my shoes. The jar swings me sideways, almost off balance, spinning me when I jerk too far the other way. My chest aches, my rib cage feeling caved in. With every footfall I just about face-plant, grabbing the jar so tight that, if I fell, the glass would bust and stab straight into my eyes and heart. I'd bleed right to death, slipped here, facedown in a puddle of mud and gold and broken glass. From behind, the tennis ball shoots through the leaves, snapping twigs and branches, whistling the same whiz-bang noise as a bullet ripping through the Vietnam jungle next to your head in some television war show.

Maybe one good bounce before the ball catches me, I duck low. There, the rotted trunk of a cottonwood has busted and fallen, and I stuff the heavy jar deep into the boggy center of the roots, the mud cave where the tree's pulled out from the ground on one side. The gold, my gold, hidden. The ball probably doesn't see because it keeps after me as I run faster, jumping and crashing my way through blackberry vines and saplings, stomping up sprays of muddy water until I hit the gravel of Turner Road. My shoes chew up the gravel, my every long jump shakes the water from my clothes. The cemetery sprinkler water replaced by dog piss replaced by Skinner Creek replaced by me sweating, the legs of my jeans rub me, the denim stiff with stuck-on dust. Me, panting so hard I'm ready to vomit both lungs out my mouth, turned inside out, my innards puked out like pink bubblegum bubbles.

Midway, between one running step and the next, the moment both my legs are stretched out, one in front and the other in back of me, in midair, something slams me in the back. Stumbling forward, I recover, but this something smacks me again, square in my backbone between my shoulder blades. Just as hard, arching my spine, something hits me, a third go-round. It hits the back of my head, hard as a foul ball or a fast pitch in softball. Fast as a line drive fresh off the sweet spot of a Louisville Slugger, slamming you dead-on, this something hits me another time. The stink of crankcase oil. Shooting stars and comets swimming in my eyes, I pitch forward still on my feet, running full tilt.

Winded, sucking air and blinded with sweat, my feet tangled together, the something wings me one more time, beaning the top of my skull, and I go down. The bare skin of my elbows plows the gravel. My knees and face dive into the dust of my landing. My teeth grit together with the dirt in my mouth, and my eyes squeeze shut. The mystery something punches my ribs, slugs my kidneys as I squirm on the road. This something bounces, hard, to break my arms. It keeps bouncing, pile driving its massive impact, drilling me in my gut, slugging my ears while I curl tight to protect my nuts.

Past the moment I could still walk back and show the ball where the gold's hidden, almost to the total black of being knocked out, I'm pounded. Beat on. Until a gigantic honk wakes me up. A second honk saves me, so loud it echoes back from the nowhere over the horizon, all the bottomland cottonwoods and tall weeds all around me, filled with Hank's loud car horn. Hank's whitewall tires skid to a stop.

Jenny's voice says, "Don't make him pissed off." She says, "Just get in the car."

I pop open my eyes, glued with blood and dust, and the ball just sits next to me in the road. Hank's pulled up, idling his engine. Under the car hood the engine revs, the pushrods clattering and lifters knocking.

Looking up at Jenny, I spit blood. Pink drool leaks out, running down my chin, and my tongue can feel my chipped teeth. One eye almost swelled shut, I say, "Jenny?" I say, "Will you marry me?"

The filthy tennis ball, waiting. Jenny's dog, panting in the backseat of the car. The jar filled with gold, hidden where only I can find it.

My ears glow hot and raw. My lips, split and bleeding, I say, "If I can beat Hank Richardson just one game in tennis, will you marry me?"

Spitting blood, I say, "If I lose, I'll buy you a car. I swear." I say, "Brand-new with electric windows, power steering, a stereo, the works . . ."

The tennis ball sits, nested in the gravel, listening. Behind his steering wheel, Hank shakes his head side to side. "Deal," Hank says. "Hell, yeah, she'll marry you."

Sitting shotgun, her face framed in the car window, Jenny says, "It's your funeral." She says, "Now climb in."

Getting to my feet, standing, I stoop over and grab the tennis ball. For now, just something rubber filled with air. Not alive, in my hand the ball just feels wet with the creek water, soft with a layer of gravel dust. We drive to the tennis courts behind the high school, where nobody plays, and the white lines look faded. The chain-link fences flake red rust, they were built so long ago. Weeds grow through the cracked concrete, and the tennis net sags in the middle.

Jenny flips a quarter-dollar, and Hank gets to serve, first.

His racquet whacks the ball, faster than I can see, into a corner where I could never reach, and Hank gets the first point. The same with his second point. The same with the whole first game.

When the serve comes to me, I hold the tennis ball close by my lips and whisper my deal. My bargain. If the ball helps me win the match—to win Jenny—I'll help with the gold. But if I lose to Hank, it can pound me dead and I'll never tell where the gold is hid.

"Serve, already," Hank yells. He says, "Stop kissing the damned ball . . ."

My first serve drills Hank, ka-pow, in his nuts. My second takes out his left eye. Hank returns my third serve, fast and low, but the tennis ball slows to almost stop and bounces smack-dab in front of me. With my every serve, the ball flies faster than I could ever hit it and knocks another tooth out of Hank's stupid mouth. Any returns, the ball swerves to me, slows, and bounces where I can hit it back.

No surprise, but I win.

Even crippled as I look, Hank looks worse, his eyes almost swollen shut. His knuckles puffed up and scabbed over. Hank's limping from so many drives straight to his crotch. Jenny helps him lie down in the backseat of his car so she can drive him home. Or to a hospital.

I tell her, "Even if I won, you don't have to go out with me . . ."

And Jenny says, "Good."

I ask if it would make any difference if I was rich. Really superrich.

And Jenny says, "Are you?"

Sitting, alone on the cracked tennis court, the ball looks red, stained with Hank's blood. It rolls, making looping blood-red handwriting that reads, "Forget her."

I wait and wait, then I shake my head, No. I'm not rich.

After they drive away, I pick up the tennis ball and head back toward Skinner Creek. From under the roots of the downed cottonwood tree, I lift out the Mason jar heavy with gold coins. Carrying the jar, I drop the ball. As it rolls away, I follow. Rolling uphill, violating every law Mr. Lockard tried to drill into me, the ball rolls all afternoon. Rolling through weeds and sand, the ball rolls into the twilight. All this time, I follow behind, lugging that jar of pirate treasure. Down Turner Road, down Millers Road, north along the old highway, then westbound along dirt roads with no name.

A bump rides the horizon, the sun setting behind it. As we get closer, the bump grows into a lump. A shack. From closer up, the shack is a house sitting in a nest of paint curls peeled off its wood by the weather and fallen to make a ring around its brick foundation. The same way dead skin peels off a sunburn. The bare, wood siding curves and warps. On the roof, the tarpaper shingles buckle and ripple. Stapled to the front door, a sheet of yellow-color paper says "Notice of Eviction."

The yellow paper, turned more yellow by the sunset. The gold in the Mason jar, shining even deeper gold in the yellow light.

The tennis ball rolls up the road, up the dirt driveway. It bounces up the brick steps, hitting the front door with a hollow sound. Bouncing off the porch, the ball beats the door, again. From inside the house come footsteps creaking and echoing on bare wood. From behind the closed door, the "Eviction" sign, a voice says, "Go away."

A witch voice, cracked and brittle as the warped wood siding. A voice faint as the faded colors of paint flaked on the ground.

I knock, saying, "I have a delivery, I think . . ."

The jar of gold, stretching my arm muscles into thin wire, into my bones almost breaking.

The tennis ball bounces off the door, again, beating one drumbeat.

The witch's voice says, "Go away, please."

The ball bounces against the wood door, only now the sound is metal. A clack of metal. A clank. Across the bottom of the door stretches a slot framed in gold-color metal, written with the word "Letters."

Crouching down, then kneeling, I unscrew the Mason jar. Twisting off the cap, I put the lip of the jar against the "Letters" slot and tip the jar, shaking it to loosen up the coins inside. Kneeling there, on the front porch, I pour the gold through the slot in the door. The coins rattle and ring, tumbling inside and rolling across the bare floor. A jackpot spilling out where I can't see. When the glass jar is empty, I leave it on the porch and start down the steps. Behind me, the doorknob pops, the snap of a lock turning, a dead bolt sliding open. The hinges creak, and a crack of inside darkness appears along one edge of the frame.

From that inner dark the witch voice says, "My husband's collection . . ."

The tennis ball, sticky with Hank's blood, coated with dirt, the ball rolls along at my heels, following me the way Jenny's dog follows her. Tagging along, the way I used to follow Jenny.

The witch voice says, "How did you find them?"

From the porch, the voice says, "Did you know my Cameron? Cameron Hamish."

The voice shouts, "Who are you?"

But me, I have nowhere I want to be more than bed. After that, I'm thinking this tennis ball owes me. I figure this Mr. Hamish is going to make me the number-one tennis hustler in the world.

■

EXPEDITION

*"In order to know virtue we must first acquaint ourselves
with vice."*

—Marquis de Sade

Even first-time visitors to Hamburg will notice a curious aspect
of the Hermann Strasse: A portion of the street in question is
blocked at both ends. Not just a single barricade, no, but two
layers of wooden fencing standing four meters tall run across
the thoroughfare from building to building, the inner barricade approximately six meters from the outer. Vehicular travel
is forbidden. Wooden doors allow only male pedestrians to pass
through, and those doors are spring-loaded, slamming shut the
instant they're released. Furthermore, the doors of the outer
barricade are offset from those of the inner, making it impossible to see clearly into or out of the blocked section of street.
Men are mentioned here intentionally because women are dis-
suaded from passing through the doors. By custom, only men
are encouraged to breach the barricades.

As a result, an array of fuming, furious, stoop-shouldered
women can always be found standing outside the cordoned-off
area. Her eyes downcast, each stands alone from the others,

knowing she's an object of public pity. In German, these women are called *Schandwartfreierweiber*. A rough translation of which means "women who wait in shame for their men."

Within those barricades is Hamburg's vice district, lined with female prostitutes, many of them amazingly lovely who call to the men strolling past, "Hast ein frage?" Or, "Haben sie ein fragen?" The barriers are to exclude the innocent and the judgmental, specifically respectable women. It's accepted that the presence of a woman not selling her body would shame those who were, and doesn't every person deserve some measure of respect? Perhaps no one more so than the women who have so little else.

It's an informal arrangement. No law prohibits respectable women from entering the district; however, the custom is that local children, the children of prostitutes, fill male prophylactics with urine. Male children, merely because of the physiology required to fill a sheath with urine. They knot the resulting balloons—warm, stinking, unstable, be they lambskin or rubber—leaving them in rows, placed in locations of strongest sunlight so that the contents will ferment to the peak of foulness. Throwing these noxious bombs, they drench any curious, voyeuristic, or no doubt impatient females who venture within seeking a husband or boyfriend who's taken leave for too long a time. Yet more interesting is the fact that it's the bastard male offspring who assume the role of defending the honor of their fallen mothers.

Awareness of these balloons, so fragile, so rank, so handy, and of the children so excited to throw them, this keeps the *Schandwartfreierweiber* outside when their men—foreign tourists, people from the countryside—insist on entering "Just for a peek" or "Just for a moment, my dear, I can't see not taking a look" and are gone for an hour. Two hours. As long as such visits take.

Every city has such a barrier, tangible or intangible. To preserve the respect of the fallen and the sensitivity of the others. In Amsterdam, the De Wallen. In Madrid, the Calle Montera off the Gran Vía. And it was into such a district of his own city that Felix M—— ventured more times than he'd care to admit, even to himself. Especially to himself. Especially since it was into a similar low haunt that his own father had vanished more than two decades before. And most especially since now Felix M—— had a son of his own, a boy now ten years old.

Having a child, a son, Felix M—— had thought would settle him and end his wandering habits: his endless circuitous perambulations penetrating certain dives and dens of depravity which are all but unknown and invisible to the general culture. For that which can't be spoken of does not exist. And these places go unmentioned in any newspaper of record and are therefore undocumented. Nonexistent. Perhaps that is their greatest appeal: the idea that in delving therein one vanishes.

It was scarcely a lie, the nights he absented himself from his marital bed, telling his wife he'd been summoned into work for an emergency. No, she hardly seemed to notice as he dressed himself in the dark and kissed her good-bye. To her credit, his wife was intelligent and charming. A personage very highly regarded among the circle of their peers. Unlike most women, she was more lovely unclothed than clothed for her body retained the proportions of youth and the sun had never mottled her skin, and for a long time, several years at least, that had been enough.

Tonight, as every night Felix ventured out, he had but a short commute to get from the world that existed to the one which did not. A carriage ride. Making his way through the dark city, he felt the speed exaggerated, the way one feels walking forward the full length of a train as it travels at fifty miles an hour. Superhuman. That hurtling recklessly forward.

Quickly was he among the haunts and low places, rubbing elbows with such denizens who did not exist in the comfort of daylight and human industry. Mishaps and history had condemned them, these crippled minds and mangled bodies, and Felix M—— sought as Krafft-Ebing had, to observe them and compile a taxonomy of the circumstances which had so irreparably sunk them so low. A compendium, he considered it, of human failure. An exposé of the despicable society which had robbed him of his father. To that end he equipped himself with a journal and a pen, both inconspicuous, the tools for recording the best bits his eavesdropping might detect. Otherwise, a paltry sum bought sufficient draughts of some stygian black lager to loosen the tongue of even the most-secretive lurker.

As engineers tested the ductile strength of steel elements, so did Felix strive to locate the breaking point in himself and others. Sought to collect through interviews the events which had landed each man upon the dust heap.

In the manner of Darwin or Audubon, he sojourned into that wilderness, those uninhabitable habitats, the dank taverns reserved for the occupations of drinking and smoking opium and consorting with those who, too, cultivated self-eradication. In the dim light, the shadowy walls shimmered with great, sparkling mosaics of motallaric cockroaches. Furred vermin of dimorphic sorts traversed the floor on claws, unseen beneath the tables and chairs, on occasion sepaciating themselves upon Felix's shoes.

Here he settled, opening his journal to a blank page, and he made ready to harvest the misfortunes of those present. If the perfect words didn't exist, Felix M—— crafted them. He invented words as if creating tools for entirely new purposes. Because the sounds he heard were not identical to what others heard, he needed something beyond the standardized language that tied every human to the past and reduced every new adventure to merely a slight variation on some earlier episode.

Bleak and daunting as the scene appeared, it stimulated his mind as did no other. Pressing him from every direction were tales more exciting than any the magazines dared publish, stories enervated with lunatic violence and blackguards brought to no lawful comeuppance. Here were tragedies of hearth and home more cathartic than the saddest work of Dickens or Shakespeare. Here, chaos did not lead to enlightenment. No lessons were learned by these nittoctic wastrels and volmaritary tosspots. More so, on a personal level, it gave Felix M—— great comfort to hear such tales. While his own life as a clerk and husband wasn't ideal, compared with these, he was a king.

The book he was penning, no, it was no mere diary. He expected it to attract a vast readership, for not only would it provide valuable lessons regarding perseverance and self-determination, but it would also serve as a balm. A vivid pornography of other people's misery. Such a tome, bound in Moroccan leather, the pages gilt-edged, it could be pored over by someone seated in a velvet armchair beside a snug parlor fire while sipping port. All those suburban pleasures would the unhappiness of this book render more glorious. The folly within those pages would validate the tedious, timorous lives of bank clerks and shopkeepers.

The well-off adored scrutinizing those in poverty. The moral craved stories of immorality, more so when those stories were couched in the spirit of social reform. Under a morally unassailable guise such as that, he'd publish the most titillating accounts of base goings-on in whoredom. Their prices and perversions. Although framed as a progressive tract, his chronicle would boast more freaks and aberrations than the combined circus sideshows the world over. The feebleminded. The malformed. Acts of beastly sadism and inhuman humiliation, he would parade brazenly before the reader.

Buried deeper was his real motive. A secret of which Felix himself was only vaguely aware.

Herr Nietzsche had only recently declared God to be dead. If Felix succeeded, his expedition would prove otherwise. Exploration, documentation (was he no less an explorer than Mr. Darwin had been?) would prove his theorem.

Not just a measly record of grim experience, he wanted this to be a proof. An undeniable proof of divinity. In the same manner mathematicians—those brilliant men who could distill all of time and space using a piece of chalk—could solve the riddles of existence with an equation, Felix felt that he might boil the mysteries of the eternal down to a single sentence.

If numbers could explain the physical world, words would explain the invisible one. Felix had staked his life on it. And if history remembered him as an idiot, well, he was only one among billions of people. History could spare one man. All men are doomed to spend most of their existence among the dead.

His expedition might be deemed wrongheaded, but so had the travels of so many. Mr. Darwin among them. Vasco da Gama or Ferdinand Magellan. To be a husband and father, employed as a day clerk in a bank, these circumstances would not prevent him from launching his own quest for discovery.

Empirically, inarguably—as Henry Stanley has so recently discovered the long-lost Dr. Livingstone—Felix would strike out to rescue God. In the coarse, in the profane, his expedition to find God would lead Felix into the darkest depth of the human heart.

To that end, his journal had become an encyclopedia of missteps and mistakes. A cookbook compiled of the recipes for getting lost forever. A primer of all that might befall one, Felix's would be a book to save people.

Where the horrors of actual human suffering fell short, his own imagination provided the more-extreme elements, transforming the merely shocking into the truly appalling. No depth had he not plumbed. From no horror had he averted his eyes. And in truth, his book was ready. Tonight was merely a lark, a victory lap. In a few weeks' time the creatures he regarded around him, these tipplers and dope fiends, the misbred, absent limbs or blessed with extras: with fins and webbed fingers, every literate person on the street could wonder over them and mutter their secret names: Sloe-Eyed Waltraud, Alligator Holger, Dent-Headed Bertina.

Felix longed to hear the stories only told in whispers, in tears after midnight. He yearned to see the something behind the curtain of everything visible. To this end he sponsored strangers' ale so he might siphon off their madness. And better was his side of the trade. For men cannot know each other's hearts, not while they're of sound mind. Standardized words are more handicap than help. Neither are gestures any use. It is only after the intellect collapses that any true communication exists.

In this would be his revenge, for among these misfits, Piss-Pot Manfred and Leper Fritz Marie and Bruno the Albino Hermaphrodite, included among their company was his father, unrecognizable still. The man had abandoned the bosom of his family for this crass world and in retribution, Felix M—— would shine a destroying light on everything here. When he'd been no older than his son was at present, Felix had been compelled to become his own guide through life, and he'd been cast as the sounding board for his mother's endless suffering and worries. This compendium would establish his fortune in the world, and with luck it would devastate his father's.

These were the thoughts agitating in his brain when a voice called across the littered tavern. Every sensate face, toothless mouths agape, eyes festering, glanced up in response, and the voice called, again. A male voice, so vibrant as to carry through the din, it said, "Who'll front me a glass, anon?" Someone laughed in dismissal.

"Prithee a drink," the voice called, "forsooth a drink and in trade mayhap shall I personally shew thee a most loathsome monster."

Piqued was Felix's interest. The slums, these wallows and sump holes of dissipation, might yet offer a fright he'd over-looked. Such would be a fine addition to his missive. He'd still no clear view of the caller, but Felix shouted back, "What monster?" While the crowd quieted out of curiosity—for even among the deformed and demented, there exists a curiosity for truer monsters—Felix placed a hand in his coat pocket and counted out the price of a draught.

The voice, in its attic faux-cabulary, called out, "The monster tis a wee 'un, but methinks 'tis not like any child thine eyne agone beheld." With this the speaker stepped forward, making himself known in the mass of swaying, salivating, sin-pitted sub-degenerates.

Presenting himself was a rapscallion of the most exuberate sort. The man who stepped forward showed no ill effects of having availed the vice surrounding him. His limbs appeared sound. His age and physicality were not dissimilar to Felix's own, and the latter guessed that here was a predator, one who took advantage of the weaker sorts and siphoned off their meager resources. More than a spark of orange mania gleamed in his eyes. To accompany this robust type into the empty night would be sheer folly. Any proposed excursion would doubtlessly end in Felix being robbed and drugged and his eventual corpse being sold to the instructor of anatomy at the local college of surgeons. Tomorrow would dawn with his viscera displayed upon a marble slab for the edification of a gallery filled with yawning first-year medical students.

Yet, and yet Felix waved for the man to join him and signaled for the barkeep to serve them. As the stranger took occupancy of a chair within whispering distance, Felix noted that he was not ill-formed. Albeit disheveled, his costume suggested a dissolute gentleman. The man's untidy, shoulder-length hair hinted at a desert prophet lifted from some verse of the Old Testament. Felix steeled himself for disappointment: He'd come to consider himself a connoisseur of the grotesque, and the stranger's promise would most likely amount to hyperbole. At best, the bargain would reveal something along lines similar to Barnum's Fiji Mermaid: the taxidermied torso of one unfortunate victim grafted onto the legs of another, with the talons of an emu drafted to serve as arms, and the ears of a fox sewn to the head of a long-expired chimpanzee.

Nevertheless, Felix M—— knew that his genius relied not so much on what was shown him but on his skill at depicting it. No matter how makeshift and mundane the actual horror, he could bring it to greater life on the page. He would provision this wag with ale and take the short walk to witness his so-called monster, but whatever was revealed would never surpass the Image already taking shape in Felix's imagination. There, the cast-aside product of a mentally deficient whore and her physically deformed attacker, the child of violence was merely a bolus of flesh with features scarcely recognizable as human. In the notes Felix jotted, the monster was already dragging its boneless self across a filthy basement floor. The abandoned creature survived by any means possible. It survived like a stray cur that fed on the feces of other animals. It supped on spilt acts of onanism, so much like curdled milk or viscous egg whites. For sustenance, it gummed rags saturated in stale menses, and when the sewers overflowed, that was the occasion for Felix's monster to feast.

Oh, as the stranger led him from the tavern, Felix vowed silently that he would make much of this monstrous child. It would serve him as the centerpiece of his taxonomy, and he would mount a cause célèbre for its redemption. Subjected to his account, no feeling heart would be left unscathed. To perpetrate such a coup, the possibility beguiled him. The public sympathy would be greatly aroused. A rescue campaign, mounted at his insistence. But no monster would ever be located, at least none to rival the monster put forth by Felix's mental faculties.

Leading him along passageways and mews flooded with puddles of corruption, the stranger said, "Avaunt, good sire." These low byways of the city were well known to Felix from his months of traipsing. He'd grown to be an authority on the tunnels and warrens which formed a city beneath the city.

A heavy snow was falling. The swirls of white turned each of the district's few streetlights into a tall bride draped in a long wedding veil. A sarcophagied quality characterized the dark. The trickaricious crumbling down of snowflakes. And as the pair trod along, a sepulchrious quiet jellied around them.

Felix M—— gave a warm thought to his wife, asleep, her body poured out of milk.

Advancing upon each gas lamp, their shadows fell behind them, and while taking leave of each their shadows fell before them. In this way, each measure of the journey marked a false day with the rising and setting of each flickering sun. Through this succession of seeming weeks did they continue to walk until arriving at the terminus of a blind alley. There a forbidding wall defaced with graffiti blocked their progress. Thick was the work of vandals: their painted opinions and signatures, opinions layered over opinions, filling the wall and succeeding one another with such vigor that the very stuff of the wall was obliterated. Whether it consisted of brick or wood, of mortared stone or troweled plaster, Felix could offer no guess. So thick was the application of paint, and so hectic the effort to obliterate the competing brushwork, that no clue remained as to the wall's purpose or belonging.

So dense were the painted outcries that none were legible. Were these words of warning? In runny scrawls were all the words obliterated in ruddy hues of blood and tar.

Even at this impasse, the stranger did not stop but reached forward toward the commingled curse words and profanities. His fingers found purchase around something invisible among the blasphemies whose paint censored earlier blasphemies. Felix watched the man's wrist twist and heard the clack and drag of a bolt being drawn aside. A dark crack opened in what had been a solid wall of words. The crack widened, as the stranger drew open a door. Yes, Felix marveled, before them stood a door so layered over with competing spatters that no one might ever discover it.

His body positioned so as to bar the entrance, the stranger spoke. "Prithee pay heed, the first-most rule regarding the monster is thee must nevermore speak of meeting the monster."

The stranger continued to speak thusly in the stilted, archaic parlance of his forebearers a century ere. "The second-most rule regarding the monster is thee must nevermore speak of meeting the monster." Then, only when Felix had agreed to those terms did the stranger move aside with a welcoming sweep of his arm, and Felix stepped into the void beyond the mysterious door. No more than a stride within, a narrow set of stairs descended into still a more-lightless realm.

Together, the two men descended stone steps in near-total

221

darkness. They navigated along branching shafts that ramped steadily downward, scented with the drippings from the cemeteries below which they passed. They stumbled along underworld galleries as dark as catacombs. Progressing below the seepage of cesspits, they passed through stenches so bilious that Felix feared his lungs might be poisoned. During these episodes he took to breathing through a sleeve of his coat.

Every age brought its specific terror. As a boy, Felix had lain awake, afraid the house would burn down. As a youth, he'd dreaded bullies. Later, it was conscription into the army. Or the fear of not learning a trade. Or never finding a wife. After school, his career. After his son was born, he feared everything. His secret dream was to face down such a horror that it would leave him inoculated. He'd never suffer fear of anything, ever again.

These tunnels proved older than he'd thought possible. To judge from the marks cleaved by primitive implements, these walls had been ancient when the cornerstone had been laid by Babylonian magi for the great Cheops of Lethe. Buried thusly, these rank pavements predated the sad jungle-engulfed dilapidation of the fabled Moon Temple of Larmos.

The mud, confirmed by the blatt and klosp of each mugrubrious footfall.

At this juncture Felix took note of a strange effect. A faint luminescence glowed from the stranger's lengthy hair. Likewise, an orange light seemed to emanate from the exposed skin of the man's hands and face, a pale shade of the same manic orange that distinguished his fevered eyes. This glow, another detail with which to embroider his future account.

Anxious of becoming lost, Felix had taken to tearing small bits from his notebook and dropping them to blaze a trail for his return. These were nothing vital, not at first, just blank pages. When those were exhausted, he tore out only single words. No word was so important, he reasoned, that its loss spoilt the entire book. Between fits of coughing, he asked, "Is it far?"

"Yon monster? 'Tis it nigh?" the stranger echoed, always a few steps ahead.

"Have we far to go?" asked Felix, ready to turn and retrace his steps. By now he had enough of a monster in his head to surpass anything he might be displayed.

As if reading his thoughts, the stranger asked, "Plan ye to tell the world of my monster?" The echo of their footsteps served as the only clue of more open tunnel ahead. His voice taunting, the stranger asked, "Plan ye to write of it in thine book?"

His sense of the way had failed Felix. Every step felt more foreign. In desperation, he felt in his coat pocket and found a box of matches. He struck one and in the moment of its burning saw that the stranger had outpaced him, and that tunnels shunted off to the side in every direction. The match died, and Felix scrambled to strike another. With it, he saw his guide had pulled even farther away and seemed at risk of outdistancing him forever. When Felix hurried to catch up, his increased speed snuffed the match prematurely. He sprinted a few strides before lighting the next only to see his luminous host almost gone in the narrowing distance. To extend the life of his match light, he put flame to a page of his notebook. It hardly mattered, one page. He could re-create the lost bit from memory. Put to the test, he was confident he could recount all of his excursions through the years into the morass of the underworld. Holding the small torch aloft, he called after the distant figure, "If I lose you, then how am I to find the monster?"

Once more, the flame failed and he was plunged into pitch dark. The stranger's orange glow was no more.

These stony ways, he recognized, had stood antique before the great Onus of Blatoy. Since even before the ante-Druidical, before pagans had erected the Altar of the Cymric Cleoples. In his astonishment, Felix put flame to still another page of his musings so as to catch one more glimpse of these aged, meso-esomerical surroundings.

Ahead of him, from ahead and behind and around, distorted by echoes, Felix heard the stranger laugh. Likewise, from every direction, the man's voice assured him, "Ye must not worry." A duration of silence went on, counted out by dripping sounds and nothing else. Felix struggled to strike another match.

To break the seeming infinity of waiting, the man's voice spoke, adding, "Methinks the monster will quickly find thee."

When a new match was successfully lighted and a new page of the notebook sacrificed, Felix lifted it and found himself alone. Fully, totally, and unmistakably abandoned. The light guttered and sputtered out, but he resolved not to waste another match on a page until he'd gathered his thoughts. Anger would serve him as a better ally than panic, and Felix pictured a scene in the not-so-distant future when he'd enter a bar to discover the man who'd led him on this fool's errand. This was hardly new territory for him: Once more, he'd been discarded, rejected, left behind. He'd survive. If need be, he'd retrace every footstep. Circumstances had forced him to blaze his own path through every lonely, difficult day of his life. Since childhood nothing had been given to him and nothing had been explained, and this empty bequest had built in him a great faith in his own ability. He'd never lost hope. If anything, adversity had only tempered his determination.

This miasmire.

The polystenchous vaporous streamings.

The lack of any sound was so weighty it seemed to press against his eardrums the way water would at a great depth. The silence began to smother him.

Felix M—— found his hands balled in fists. His breathing fast and shallow. A temper tantrum threatened to overwhelm him. The sensation seemed a third-generation echo of scurrying to keep pace with his own father, so long ago, this entire situation evoked a rage he hadn't suffered since becoming an adult.

"Go then," Felix shouted after the phantom. "Let me be rid of you!" He shook his notebook above his head in the dark. "You will suffer all the more in my retelling of this." The stranger's name remained a mystery, and he cursed himself for not having asked. "It's twenty years since I've sought my way without an advisor of any sort, as my own apprentice, with none but my own encouragement." He would not be defeated so easily. He was shouting now, his curses sounding the length of every tunnel contiguous with this. He railed about his father's departure. He ranted over the bullied years of his boyhood. Thrashed, he had none to teach him how best to conduct or defend himself.

Despite the grim diamonsity of predicament, he would not fall prey to nervous ideas. Fear stalked him, only an arm's length away in the dark, and panic lurked immediately behind that. Left with no point of reference in space, Felix focused on the comforting glulubrious flavor of his own tongue.

To be a boy without a father is to grow guns in place of arms and a loaded cannon for a mouth. Always, at all times to be under siege with no reinforcements. To sprint at full speed into the pitch dark with fury trumping your fear, not aware that what you actually want is to hit a brick wall, or stumble into a pit, to find some limits, some restrictions and discipline. A broken leg. A concussion. Punishment from a surrogate father, even if that father is merely physics, to slap you down and make you toe some ultimate line.

Since boyhood, fury had become his father. His older brother. His only protector. Fury gave him strength and courage and spurred him to always move forward despite always getting things wrong and always failing and no mentor there to help him or teach him and everyone always laughing. Anger delivered him from catastrophe. Rage kept him from going under. It had come to be his greatest asset and only strategy.

His life was powered by a battery with loneliness at one pole and rage at the opposite and Felix existed, suspended between the two, helpless. His father never knew the bitter raging woman Felix's mother had become. How, as a boy, she'd lectured him on the weakness of his papa. She'd drilled him to recite this catechism of venom. And as he'd grown to become a mirror of her missing husband, she'd begun to subject Felix to the fullness of her scorned fury. His impossible task, Felix's trial had been to make a life in this seething home where every slice of bread was buttered with disdain.

Felix hated his father for relinquishing him to her sole abusive custody. He hated them both, loved and despised them with a passion that dwarfed and colored all else in his life.

To escape, he'd married a woman who already counted her affections by the pfennig and dealt them out as a miser, as scant wages for those behaviors she wished to cultivate in husband and son. Even in the merriest circumstances, Felix's wife could surrender herself to an unhappy mood. These attributes he recognized, too late, she shared with his mother. Not impossible was the idea that he was acclimatized to finding comfort in such familiar discomfort.

If he failed to return, his son, that tiny model of his self, would bear the brunt of his wife's animosity.

Felix's own son, on the morrow that boy would discover the same fate. Felix's wife would awaken to find his portion of their marriage bed empty. Soon after, she'd learn he'd not been summoned into work. Worry would descend, followed by fear ripening into despair. Choosing his own wife, despite her virtues, Felix had been drawn to a submerged potential for vengeance. A trait of character not far removed from his mother's emotional frugality.

A train passed by in a tunnel somewhere far above. To describe how the ground shook, Felix vacillated between the words *abbeltomish* and *abbelhomish*. The skirling noise was everything, and then it was gone.

His fury spent, Felix paused to draw a breath and in the stillness heard the tread of distant footsteps coming toward him in the darkness. Not the stranger's, these were dragging, stumbling, heavy footfalls. The monster he imagined as every horror in his mind took shape in the tunnel ahead.

The glory of anger was how it left no margin for fear. Whether what approached in the lightless gloom was the trickster guide or his grotesque infant, Felix made ready to throttle it. To free both his hands, he tucked his journal into a pocket of his coat. Lest the advancing creature anticipate him, he quieted his ragged breathing, bracing his body from legs to neck, ready for the moment he and his adversary came into blind contact. Pitched forward, he ran full-out, pell-mell, throwing punches at thin air, fighting everything and hitting nothing.

His fists became bombs ready to explode on contact. When he sensed the being within arm's length, Felix threw himself upon it. Every hard joint he wielded as a weapon, his knees and elbows, his fists and the heels of his shoes. As cudgels and truncheons, this arsenal pounded the shape he couldn't see.

He felt his weight balanced atop and hammering down upon the crushed meat and mangled organs of his unseen foe, and the opponent made little effort to defend himself. Although larger than a child, the figure seemed nonetheless frail. Having rage on his side, Felix pounded away until the other offered no resistance.

The heaving mass beneath him issued a great sigh. In a voice rusted and dusty from disuse, it made a sound. The voice crushed with certainty, it said, "Sohnemann." In doomed tones, it sighed. "You've come."

In the darkness, the monster offered up a prayer, saying, "Please don't be my boy."

Struggling to strike a match, Felix traced the sound of the voice, back, to among his oldest memories. The match flared, and he put it to a page of the notebook.

In the guttering light, a face shut its eyes and twisted to look away from the brightness.

Felix froze in shock. It wasn't possible. What a cruel trick. The guide, the trickster ruffian had known something of his past and staged this false reunion. It was the prank itself that was monstrous.

Still pinned beneath Felix's knees, the apparition bade, "I've waited, always hoping you'd never arrive."

Here was merely some hired beggar, a gross imposter, and Felix sneered at the clever sadism of the stunt. He made ready to shove the corpse aside. "How dare you?" he snarled. So wounded was his heart, that he backhanded the frail old man, toppling him to the floor. Standing over him, unable to step away, frozen to the spot by both love and revulsion, he cried, "You are not my father!"

The old man inspected him. "He's fooled you, as well."

"No one's made a fool of me," Felix swore.

The monster said, "Tyler has."

In a desperate frenzy, Felix M—— shouted for the guide to return. Wrong-worded as that label had proven, for a guide's task was to lead one to a destination while this had only led him into confusion and disorientation. Choking back rage and despair, Felix bellowed, "Your fine prank is accomplished!" He

228

shouted, "You have wounded me far worse than any blade or blow might!" He looked down upon the figure on the floor and shouted, "Now make an end to this or I shall—on my word—I shall thrash your vile accomplice!"

The only answer was his own words: blade and blow, thrash and vile, echoing back from the darkness. To make good his threat, Felix lifted the frail figure and gripped him 'round the bony throat and felt his pulse beating like a hare's heart in the moment before its spine is broke.

At this, in a strangled, gargling voice, the imposter inquired, "My boy, do you still enjoy to invent words? From the first, you've always harbored your own secret language." Here was a detail from childhood that Felix himself had never confided to anyone except his father.

Hearing these words, Felix regarded his tormentor with a closer eye. The man's brow was the one depicted in a daguerreotype the family owned but disdained to display. The man's eyes were more-aged versions of the eyes Felix saw each morning in his own shaving mirror. His grip softened on the sagging throat. Felix could only ask, "How?"

The sad eyes met his. The voice, crushed to a whisper, said, "My boy, the same as you." The lips smiled with resignation. "Tyler will not return, not for many more years."

Felix asked, "Tyler?"

His father, this man, said, "Your guide."

Without him there might be no escaping this place. Clearly this man, if he was indeed Felix's father, clearly he would've discovered an exit after searching so long. Still, that was a possibility impossible to entertain. Too appalling for Felix's mind to accommodate.

Felix considered his own son. The child at home, still abed, asleep. How in an hour that boy's world would change course, and he would become his own guide. Another boy forced to invent himself from scratch. Another young man who'd grow up helpless in the face of any sullen or angry woman.

"You will see him again," his father assured him. "That is the sadness of it." The older man smiled wanly. "In perhaps twenty years. Then, your son will knock you to the floor, in anger and love, just as I struck my own father."

For here, in these gloomy halls, had Felix's father found his own father. And here had Felix's grandfather been reunited with his own sire. Here were his father and his grandfather as well as the bones of his great-grandfather and all who'd been before. Exceeding them, here were the fathers of countless sons.

"This Tyler," Felix asked, "what purpose does he serve?"

As if the old man could anticipate his son's growing panic, he smiled warmly. Already, purple bruises were blooming on his pale cheeks and forehead. "Do you forgive your papa?"

Tentatively, Felix said, "I do."

"Do you forgive God?"

Felix shook his head.

With that, his father swung one arm in a wide arc, slamming a fist into the side of his son's skull.

Fireworks exploded, sparks that only Felix could see. He rubbed the spot, whining, "You've smote me in the ear!"

"Our salvation lies in not only forgiving one another," his father intoned, "but in forgiving God as well."

Without apology, his father said, "I will search with you." He said, "We will search together."

With this Felix turned to retrace his homemade words: sarcophagied . . . trickaricious . . . sepulchrious . . . mesoesomerical . . . miasmire . . . polystenchous . . . diamonsity . . . glulubrious . . . abbeltomish or abbelhomish. He set alight another page of his journal, hoping to backtrack to the first word before

230

his light went out for good. As he sought the trail he'd blazed, Felix heard his father call out.

"Let's not be so quick to find our way back," the old man bade. "Let us go deeper." The words, sonorous against the stone. "Let us discover some worthwhile adventure before we return to the light and the air we already love so well."

The old man had turned and was progressing farther into the labyrinth, plying the darkness. Delving blindly into the dense unknown. After a moment's hesitation, Felix turned to follow him.

■

MISTER ELEGANT

Don't ask how I know this, but the next time you think you're fat, there's a whole lot worse you can look. Something to picture, when you're at the gym counting stomach crunches or hanging knee raises to flatten your ab muscles, just know that some people have a whole other person growing out of that spot on their body. That fleshy, jiggly area under the bottom of your rib cage, where to you is just a "muffin top," those other people have arms and legs, most of a whole other person hanging over their belt.

Doctors call this an "epigastric parasite."

Some doctors call that extra person a "heteradelphian," a fancy word for "different sibling." It means somebody who should've been your brother or sister only got born with their head still inside your stomach. That extra person, he's born with no brain. No heart. He's just a parasite, and you're the host.

You couldn't make this stuff up.

And, please, listen. If I'm telling you this and you do have another person growing out from underneath your arm right now, please don't get all bent out of shape.

The only reason I'm telling you is I kind of, used to have one, too.

And trust me, what's worlds worse than some jiggling subcutaneous fat is you popping out some heartless, brainless stranger. Sometimes that happens even years and years after you're already born.

Don't ask how I know this, either, but after you've done a hundred million stomach crunches, when you apply to be one of those Chippendales-type sexy dancers—just to get hired as a buff, naked exotic dancer—they ask you: "Do you suffer from epileptic seizures?"

The question's on the form they give you at the doctor's office for the physical exam right after your audition. The nurse hands you a clipboard full of forms and a pen and a Dixie cup she wants filled with piss. And the dance company, it's not even the real Chippendales, but you ask any has-been, washed-up male exotic dancer what troupe he was with, and just to shortcut a lot of explaining, he'll tell you Chippendales.

We all recognize those copyrighted white paper cuffs and the black bow tie.

Really, my audition was for the Savage Knights. That's "Knights" with a capital "K." The Savage Knights are your Chippendales-type of all-male, high-energy, feel-good touring exotic dance company that caters to a ladies' audience. Their home office ran this ad on the website Backpage. Under the category "Adult Jobs," their ad led with the headline: "Live Your Fantasy."

In the banquet room of the airport Holiday Inn, on that Sunday afternoon, my smile on my face was a lie. My tan was a lie. So was my hair being blond. On the job application, when I wrote one hundred eighty-five pounds, that was a lie. Under eye color, I wrote the color of my contact lenses. During the sit-down part of the interview, I said I wanted to be a Savage Knight because I enjoyed traveling to interesting places and meeting new people.

The truth was, really I just wanted a career where every night, hundreds of drunk young virgins, they would stuff cash money into my underpants with their teeth.

For my age, I lied away three years and wrote down twenty-four. Every one of my capped teeth, it was a shiny white lie.

I buzzed off my brown pubic hair, and the agent for Savage Knights said they had an opening for another Mister Elegant. At any moment, she told me, sixteen different companies of Savage Knights are crisscrossing the world, meeting the male-stripper needs of global billions. Each troupe includes a fireman, a police officer, a soldier, a construction worker in a yellow hard hat. Like a roving high school Career Day. Plus Mister Elegant, who makes his entrance in a breakaway tuxedo and gives roses to all the women in the ringside tables. All smooth and cosmopolitan. A cool James Bond.

Troupe Eleven, their last Mister Elegant had turned gun-shy and bailed after some coked-up birthday girl in Fairbanks yanked him a torsioned testicle.

That's when my own parasite started coming out.

In that Holiday Inn ballroom, I looked like nothing I'd ever seen in my bathroom mirror. Tanned and oiled. Blond and smiling.

And the agent shook my slippery hand, saying, "Good." She said, "From now on, you'll be Mister Elegant . . ."

The emergence of my new heartless, brainless different sibling. Life is nothing if not a baby-oiled slope.

What was true was, I figured if I made a relentless and ongoing effort I could pass for twenty-four, forever. For my dance part of my audition, the song "Bodyrock" by the artist Moby gives you your best 3:36 grabber. Call my taste a little retro, but you start with a song folks like and you've halfway won the game. Plus the dropout toward the end, when the track cuts to just lyrics, that gives you your perfect window to nail some stunt work.

Inside that frame, I pegged a standing flip, dropped to splits, and recovered with a kip-up. After all my tanning and shaving and smiling, the agent for Savage Knights, she gave me a sheet of paper printed with directions to a clinic. The nurse gave me a cup for piss. And the forms asked:

"Do you have a history of epileptic seizures?"

So after all that bullshit, it was easy to check the little box marked: NO. I just made sure and took my Clonazepam.

If you've seen the video people uploaded on the Internet, of the naked muscleman flopping like a fish, surrounded by women holding Rum Hurricanes and Blue Hawaiis, his pink balls popped out one side of his black G-string and slapping in a puddle of his own piss, then you know what kind of mistake that last lie turned out to be.

Everybody in the world's seen that video. Little bastard teenage kids, now they even do a dance they call the Mister Elegant where they keel over in the middle of the dance floor and wiggle like hyperactive spastics being electrified. Little shitheads.

People imagine it's so easy to be a Chippendales-type, high-energy exotic dancer. Male people, they imagine your worst problem is not sprouting a woodie.

Some other questions on that same medical examination form, they ask you: "Do you suffer from stress-related incontinence?" And, "Have you ever had an episode of narcolepsy?"

Just from those questions, I should've seen where this was headed. Lawyers don't just pull those questions out of a hat. Any big dance company from your Bolshoi Ballet to Chippendales, they've mapped out their doomsday scenario. Maybe smack in the middle of *Swan Lake*, some swan pitching a fit center stage, her eyes rolled up to only show the whites, drool gushering out from her long, yellow beak. Sweating. Pissing her lovely white feathers.

In the Savage Knights training brochure, they teach you to watch for anybody in the audience with a pad and pencil taking notes. Some deal called ASCAP—stands for American Society of Composers and Something-Something—if they catch you dancing to a song and not paying a royalty, they'll sue you and Savage Knights. Besides them, every state sends liquor commission spies to fine you for touching a patron inappropriately. Even just wearing white paper cuffs and a black bow tie, you risk a cease-and-desist letter from the real Chippendales for copyright infringement.

Don't even ask me about managing body hair. Really, the worst part of this job is paying to buy people a new tequila sunrise after you boogie off a pubic hair. Just a single good hip check can mean you buying the front two rows a fresh round of banana daiquiris.

Live Your Fantasy . . . Again, you couldn't make this stuff up.

Getting a drunk anybody to put money in your pants with their teeth, it's worlds harder than it sounds. So is staying twenty-four years old. One minute you're shaking your bag in the face of some bachelorette so shitfaced on Long Island Iced Teas you can smell your pube stubble curl from her lit cigarette. Her ugly bridesmaid is sticking a dollar bill up your ass with her tongue, and her mother's shooting video. That's how drunk virgins behave. Police officers or firemen—I mean real ones—they complain about job stress. They don't know real stress. Dancers I worked with, they used to soak their bag in salt water, the way a boxer will pickle his face to tough it up before a big fight. Every bit of your free time, you spend pickling your balls and managing body hair.

The only other most-important part of job training is telling time by songs. David Bowie's "I'm Afraid of Americans," that gives you an exact five minutes of fuzzed power chords. Keith

Sweat's "One on One" is a slow-grind song (5:01) perfect for choreographing an elephant. By that, I mean any dancer too bulked up to move except for hitting competition poses. Step, flex, step. The Double Bicep. The Crab.

How you keep from getting a hard-on is you're counting all the time to anticipate the end of each song. You name a song, and I can peg the time—and not just the minutes and seconds listed on the jewel box liner. I can tell you the actual time that shows on the deck in the booth. A good dancer knows the Digweed remix of Bryan Ferry's "Slave to Love," the liner says four minutes, thirty-one seconds, but in actuality it's twenty-four seconds. A lazy dancer will find himself still waist-deep in drunk women when the music stops.

You shaking your private junk to a pounding mix of Underworld's "Mo Move"—a relentless bass heartbeat for six minutes and fifty-two seconds—that's artistic. But if you don't make it backstage by when the music stops, even in just one moment of silence, you shaking your shaved parts at strange ladies—that's just harassment.

Again, another slippery slope. And do not ask me how I know.

Silence. Silence and the closing lights coming on, bright, that's Cinderella turning into a grinning, naked, greasy, and sweaty guy with his penis too close to your face and your watery ten-dollar White Russian.

As outlined in the Savage Knights training brochure, Mister Elegant makes his entrance, handing out roses to the front tables. He dances the Joey Negro club mix of Raven Maize doing "Fascinated." A three-minute, forty-two-second grabber song. Then he moves to the edge of the stage and dances one shorter high-energy song to bait out the folding money. He works the edge and the floor, humping laps and taking tips, and he's offstage just one beat before the Police Officer's grabber song.

The next night in Spokane, same deal. Then Wenatchee. Pendleton. Boise. A job so simple even a brainless, heartless parasite can do it.

Mister Elegant loved the dollar tips and the phone numbers. Phone numbers written on dollars. Phone numbers on scraps of paper towel, looped under the elastic leg straps of his black G-string. All the way up until Salt Lake City.

Don't ask how I know this, but there's people with Milroy disease, where their lymph nodes in their legs never develop and they end up with feet the size of suitcases on legs like tree trunks. Or cyclopia, where you're born with no nose and both eyes in the same socket.

Mister Elegant, his nipples looked too small and pale pink, so to make them swell, big and red, he learned to paint them with something called Lip Plumper. Comes in a bottle with a little brush, like nail polish, and when you paint it on your nipples and lips and the head of your dick, they all swell up, huge. Mister Elegant outlined his washboard abdominal muscles by drawing between them with a mascara. Then blending with a wad of tissue so his belly wouldn't look like Tic-Tac-Toe.

If he popped out one blue contact lens and looked at himself in the steamy mirror of a motel bathroom, yeah, he could still pass as twenty-four. But between Billings and Great Falls and Ashland and Bellingham, between the Fireman's giving everyone crab lice and the Army Soldier's snoring, Mister Elegant was feeling wore out. By Salt Lake City, his pickled balls were dragging.

Mister Elegant strutted out with his armful of red roses. Still in his breakaway tux, he gave out the roses, then started into the buttons on his pleated shirt. The only thing that makes Salt Lake City any different from Carson City or Reno or Sacramento is after the tux broke away, after Mister Elegant was counting into his second song, smiling and keeping his pubic hair out of

238

people's drinks, watching the dollar bills come out of purses and pocketbooks, the virgins writing their phone numbers on old bank machine receipts, between his dropping to full splits and bouncing back in a perfect kip-up, one deep breath before his handspring and a full midair flip, two minutes and thirty-six seconds into the N-Trance cover on "Stayin' Alive"—(4:02)—the faces and drinks and dollar bills started to blur. Mister Elegant thumbed up the elastic loop around each hip, high and tight for his handspring, crouched down, jumped—and that's all I remember.

In case you didn't notice, the music's stopped and here I am still shaking my dick in your face. Like after all this time I didn't learn any better.

What a spaz.

Early as I can remember, I used to have Simple Stare syndrome, a form of temporal lobe epilepsy. My mom or dad would be talking to me, and I'd freeze. My vision would blur and all my muscles would stop. I'd still hear my mom talking, telling me to pay attention, maybe snapping her fingers in my face, but I couldn't talk or move. Breathing is all I could do for a half minute, which seems like forever.

They took me in for MRIs and EKGs. I couldn't ride my bicycle except on deserted streets. I climbed trees and my vision would start to blur. I'd wake up on the ground, my friends asking if I was okay. One school play, the baby Jesus, Mary, Joseph, six shepherds, three camels, an angel, and two other kings waited what felt like a year while I stood frozen with a gift of frankincense, Mrs. Rogers leaning out from the wings, whispering, "Bless me, for I bring you this humble offering . . . I bring *this*!"

But after ten years of Clonazepam, I pretty much had that licked.

Trouble was my prescription ran out in Carson City. Being

tired makes it worse. Drinking and cigarette smoke, fatigue, loud noise, all risk factors. In Salt Lake City, I'd pitched what's called a tonic-clonic seizure, what people used to call a grand mal seizure. I woke up in the back of a screaming ambulance, just in time to see a med tech stuff a thick stack of piss-soaked singles into his wallet, saying, "Mister Elegant . . ." and shaking his head. A blanket wrapped with belts held me flat, and I could smell shit. I asked the med tech, What happened? And he stuffed his wallet in his back pocket, saying, "Buddy, you don't want to know . . ."

By the time the hospital released me, Troupe Eleven was already in Provo with a new Mister Elegant shipped out to meet them at the venue. The Motel 6 where we'd stayed the night before, they were holding my suitcase.

A social worker came and sat next to my hospital bed, saying how the human mind is nothing if not a constant cycle of electrical activity. She said a seizure is like a burst of static, a storm inside your head.

I said, Tell me something I don't know, lady.

And she told me about phocomelia, a condition where you're born with your hands emerging from your shoulders. No arms. The old-time term for this birth defect was in fact "seal arms." It's linked with the sedative thalidomide, but it's existed long before that. She told me about sirenomelia, where you're born with your legs fused together, to make what looks like a fish tail. Hence the name: sirenomelia, and possibly the original idea of mermaids. This social worker, she told me her name was Clovis, and she herself had been a dancer, an exotic dancer, trying to hide the fact she suffered from narcolepsy. She used to have long blond hair and blue eyes, long smooth legs and no tan lines. Next to my bed, her hair was curly and brown. Her eyes were

240

brown, and the thighs of her white pantsuit looked stretched too tight for her to cross her legs at the knee.

While dancing, she kept her condition under control with Provigil except she ran out and started skipping doses, breaking pills in half, your standard false economies. One night headlining in a biker bar in Rufus, New Mexico, Clovis made her big entrance, hit the brass pole high up and spinning from centrifugal force, her blond hair swinging, her tanned body spiraling toward the stage below.

Saying this, her brown eyes mist over. Clovis can't recall ever sliding to the bottom of that pole. She woke up backstage and pregnant by some thirty-two customers. Some twice.

I ask her, What song?

And misty-eyed, Clovis says, "Portishead doing 'Sour Times.'"

Ah, I agree. The sweet dark vocals of Beth Gibbons. Four minutes and eleven seconds.

"Four minutes and eight seconds," Clovis says. One eyebrow arched at me, she says, "Always check your deck time. Never trust liner notes."

I ask, What was her stage name?

And Clovis looked at her wristwatch, saying, "That was a long time ago." She says, "I'm almost thirty,"

Me too, I say.

And looking at some hospital form on her clipboard, Clovis says, "I kind of figured this age they put here, was a lie."

Before she could stand up and walk away, I asked Clovis to tell me what happened. What really went on.

The baby was born, she said, nine months after she woke up, a textbook delivery. A boy. It didn't look like anybody and immediately drove off in a limousine to live a gated lifestyle in the Malibu Colony with two gay millionaire movie studio executives. Clovis said, "Talk about popping out a brainless, heartless stranger."

She'd already told me about epigastric parasites.

And I said, No. I asked her, What happened to me?

And for a long minute of balls-out silence, Clovis just blinked her eyes at me. Finally, in the voice of a health care professional, she said, "There's a videotape of the . . . event."

Some bachelorette had smuggled a pocket camcorder into the nightclub and was filming me as I handed out long-stemmed red roses. I launched into my set, and she'd kept filming. They had to digitally fuzz the part where my nuts popped out, but the video had been aired on television. First just a Japanese funny-home-video program, but then in Europe. On the Internet, the four-minute, twenty-one-second segment went viral, down-loaded worldwide. The stuff of jokes on every late-night talk show.

ASCAP was suing websites and search engines over the un-authorized distribution of "Stayin' Alive." The Chippendales syndicate wasn't thrilled I had on white paper cuffs. Someone claiming to be a producer from the *Late Show* called the hospital switchboard, asking to be connected with my bedside.

I told Clovis, I wanted to see for myself.

And Clovis said, "No." She said, "You don't."

I asked, How bad could it be?

And Clovis said, "During the episode, you lost momentary control of your bowels."

The smell in the ambulance.

"A G-string," Clovis said, "doesn't leave much room for error."

I never did watch that video.

Utah was a good enough place to hide, so I stayed in Salt Lake City and let my pubic hair grow back. I dyed my blond hair brown. I scrubbed off my suntan, and ate all the food—fried chicken and Hostess fruit pies and barbecue potato chips—that Mister Elegant could never eat.

By the time you turn thirty, your life is about escaping the person you've become in order to escape the person you've become in order to escape the person you started as. So for a while there, I was becoming Mister Fat-Gutted-Pale-Bitter-Pig. I worked a fast-food job, and every few million cheeseburgers some customer would stare at me across the greasy counter, their eyes working fast to figure out how they knew my face.

And I'd snap my fingers, asking, "You want fries with that?"

I never took a single from anybody without washing my hands.

Maybe if I'd been wallowing in my own feces, maybe people would put two and two together, but then all those Chinese died on security videotape in that really goofy department store fire and the comedy world forgot all about me and my messy disaster.

But Clovis didn't. And I couldn't.

Clovis came to have lunch, cheeseburgers, bringing along a young client whose fingers were fused into two fleshy pincers and whose legs were withered and useless. Ectrodactyly syndrome, what people used to call "lobster-claw syndrome." She introduced me to a young woman with pygomelia, which means she had four legs, basically two pelvises side by side and four functioning legs which she hid under long skirts.

Me, I still told time by songs. Joe Jackson's "Steppin' Out" is four minutes and nineteen seconds, time enough to smoke a cigarette in the alley. Kim Wilde singing "You Keep Me Hanging On," that's four minutes and fifteen seconds, the time it takes me to change the carbonated gas cylinder for the soda machine. Everything you want to forget, you never can. Every moment you want to escape.

At last, Clovis asks me back to her apartment to meet some people. I tell her my entire day is nothing if not meeting people. And Clovis says this is different.

At her apartment, she's introducing me to a girl with two arms and legs, almost a whole other person sprouting from under the bottom hem of her tube top. My first real heteradelphian, her name is Mindy. Next, I meet a kid with a face huge and lumpy as a bed pillow. Neurofibromatosis, the Elephant Man disease. He's twenty-three and his name is Alex. I meet a cute redhead with no legs and only her feet growing out of her stomach. Osteogenesis imperfecta. Her name is Gwen, and she's twenty-five.

Clovis says to me, "You know music. You know the staging." She says, "It's their idea, but they hoped you could teach them exotic dancing . . ."

She meant stripping. A troupe of differently abled exotic dancers. They were all young and bored with Salt Lake City. Their thinking was: Anyone can bulk up some muscle, bleach their hair, and spray on a fake tan. Why not offer an audience something that wasn't based on a pile of lies? Why not serve up dancers not hiding behind fake smiles? That bunch of crazy, idealistic kids. Only in Utah.

I tell them, Sure, they're young and full of dreams. Sure, they're monstrously deformed. But can they *dance* . . . ?

And Clovis says, "I've taught them what I know about working a pole, but I was hoping . . ."

The millionaire studio executives had fronted seven figures in low-interest start-up financing. Hell, if I can teach some of those steroid elephants to dance, I can teach anybody.

Like it says on Backpage: Live Your Fantasy.

I wish I could say it's been easy. People will always misunderstand your intentions. People accuse me of exploitation.

That, and no small business is all beer and skittles. In Boulder, Glenda, our girl with both eyes in one socket, she eloped with a stockbroker millionaire. In Iowa City, Kevin, our dancer with parastremmatic dwarfism, he knocked up some bachelorette. It helps that Clovis tours with me and the troupe, as a kind of den mother. God only knows what we'll do come September, when we launch our escort service.

Me, personally, not a show starts without me sweating in the wings. Counting the seconds of every song. Watching for ASCAP people taking notes, and every muscle in my legs and arms twitching, reliving every handspring, cartwheel, midair flip, and kip-up I ever nailed onstage. Watching those crazy kids bait the folding money and lap dance for the tips, I catch myself still whispering.

Whispering, "Bless me, for I bring you this humble offering . . ."

Whispering, "I bring *this*!"

∎

TUNNEL OF LOVE

People say human hair keeps growing after death. They cite bodies dug out of graves, dead bodies, with long glamour-girl hair they didn't have at the funeral. These disinterred corpses have fingernails only women of leisure could ever grow so long. It's like in death, we all get a Glamour Shots makeover.

Myth or fact? My last appointment on Friday night, she says, "Let's find out."

She'd phoned a week before and asked for the latest appointment I could make. The woman has the wrong kind of muscles, she says, for sitting still.

In my studio, she pulls a candle from her purse. She says, "Burn this," and hands it to me. She asks if I have anything other than sitar music.

She showed up maybe a little unsteady on her feet. It was hard to tell because she was in a wheelchair. In this business a wheelchair doesn't raise an eyebrow. Lots of people pay for the hands-on nurturing. It's like submitting for a whole permanent wave when all you need is the nice sensation of someone washing your hair. Not that this woman needs grooming. She already has the hair, bleached Hollywood blond from root to tip. Her legs are smooth as bone. It's all part of the experiment. Eventually she's naked except for a wristband heat-sealed around her wrist, like a baby is born wearing, only this one says "Do NOT Resuscitate."

Half her hair she had waxed off, she says, the body half. The other half she had bleached Jean Harlow blond, Lana Turner blond. Before I lift her onto the massage table she says to do her legs last. She said that if I feel stubble, it will prove the myth is true. She says the best aspect of being in the end stage is that she'll never have to get her roots touched up.

The worst part of being in a wheelchair, she says, isn't that it makes your legs superfluous baggage. What's worse is that a wheelchair makes most of your furniture superfluous. This woman, she says she had exquisite furniture, Louis Seize armchairs with needlepoint upholstery, Louis Quinze settees. Once she was reduced to a wheelchair all her most-prized possessions—chairs, sofas, heart, brain—were nothing but obstacles.

Her purse, she says, is stuffed full of cash. "When we're done you can dig in like Halloween and treat yourself." The police don't have to know she had any cash. Or diamond wristwatch.

I could tell her drugs were working because she didn't laugh. The kind of drugs she'd used are legal in this state. They're so not-suicide that they were paid for under her prescription coverage. There was a ten-dollar co-pay, but it was still a huge cost savings when compared to hospice. Massage, ironically, wasn't covered.

In my experience, I told her that unless you're in a serious car accident, massage is never covered. In this profession, what she has in mind is the new definition of providing a "happy ending." That usually gets a laugh. People have to make some noise.

After a particularly long stretch of silence I ask if she's okay.

"Sorry," she says, "that's the phenylalanine *not* talking."

I tell her that this wouldn't be the first time someone made their final exit on my table. It's why massage therapists have begun demanding payment before the session begins. It's awkward to tell someone in her situation that she's not such an original thinker. It's like the final insult. After the first such incident, the responding police officer told me, "You might want to keep every voicemail just in case there's an inquest." Anything to prove that I'm not complicit.

I thank her for requesting my last time slot of the day. It would feel strange to do a swollen rotator cuff after this. Not to mention, nobody sitting in the waiting room wants to see the previous client leave the therapy room inside a zippered bag.

No one ever tells me up front what they have in mind. But once that cocktail of modern science, those hemlock substitutes, kicks in, their entire lifetime of secrets spills out.

I tell her, "The long strokes make the blood work faster." What I meant to say is "drugs."

To keep her talking, I ask about whom to call. I'm fishing for next-of-kin, someone more intimate than the medical examiner.

She tells me that when her first husband wanted to wrap things up, physicians weren't allowed to assist. In lieu of professional help he consulted with a Gillette double-edged. She found him in the bathtub.

She asks, "What's the worst massage you've ever gotten?"

I ask if she remembers a book called *Everything You Always Wanted to Know About Sex (But Were Afraid to Ask)*.

She nods and says, "1969."

In the chapter about pheromones, the book advised male readers to do the following: When you first wake up in the morning, before you get dressed, wipe your bare testicles with a clean linen handkerchief. Fold the handkerchief neatly and wear it as a pocket square in your jacket all day. The book promised that women would find the smell irresistible. Whether or not it worked, the advice made pocket handkerchiefs hugely popular.

The worst massage I ever got was in 1985, I tell her. I was a late bloomer.

The massage therapist was a girl. She must've had a head cold. Or she was allergic. Hay fever, maybe. Something sinus-related, because she kept sneezing. This wasn't what they call a "Jack Shack" where every massage ends with a "full release." But maybe she'd worked in one of those lowlife places where she'd been the one dodging one hot outburst after another. As if seeking revenge, she sneezed and sneezed, and even when I said "God bless you," she wouldn't cover her nose and mouth. I was facedown on the table, and the spray would mist down onto my back.

She did this without apology. She did it so easily I started to wonder if it wasn't a new kind of massage. She'd sneeze again. Without missing a beat she'd just rub the next sneeze into my skin. It must've saved her a fortune on oil.

When the session was up I got dressed and paid her. She was still sniffling so, like a gentleman, I whipped the handkerchief from my pocket and offered it to her. As she put it over her nose and mouth, she got a funny look on her face, like the book might be wrong about women. I told her to keep it. As my parting shot I told her to take care of herself. You never know what an infection can turn into.

The woman on the table laughs. I can feel it through my hands. At last, my money shot.

She'd found me on the Internet, she says, on Angie's List, which seems odd. Clients who see me for this kind of specialized bodywork don't usually refer their friends and family. "I never have what people call repeat business." Not for this type of session.

How she found out, she says, is she went to Zoom Care for a head cold that wouldn't go away. It was the Zoom Care next to the Westfield Outlet Mall, between Shoes-For-Less and Connecticut Candles where they sell factory seconds at a discount. Candles that sputter. Candles that won't stay lit. She says, "There was nothing 'Doctor Kildare' about the place." She was thinking strep throat and—blam. The nurse-practitioner at Zoom Care didn't say Stage Four, but that's probably not required at his pay scale. Without hesitating, she went next door and bought a pumpkin-colored candle formulated to smell like nutmeg.

By the time she was diagnosed, it was already too late to do the part where your hair falls out.

I ask if she's given any thought to the body. She tells me that it was an uphill climb, trying to find an aesthetician who would give her a Brazilian after this far along.

She says she told the mortician an open casket and a short skirt. By that she meant a negligee. "I want my ex-husbands to see what they're missing."

When I ask, "Why blond?" she asks if I read the newspapers. Incredulous, she says, "It's always more tragic when a blonde dies."

She mentioned husbands so I redirect. "How many?" I ask. She says the first was so long ago that a wedding license only cost ten dollars. A massage costs more. Even a car wash costs more if you factor in the sales tax. "Ten dollars to screw up the rest of my life," she says. "How could I pass up such a bargain?"

She asks if I won't do her feet last. "They're so ticklish that I don't want to be here by the time you get down there."

I switch to hard, percussive strokes between her shoulder blades, but not as hard as she'd like.

She says, "That's nice," but coaxes me to go harder. She assures me there's a handwritten note in her purse to explain everything, just in case the police ask why she's covered with bruises.

I pretend to hit harder. Not that she'd notice the difference, not this far advanced. The drugs, they're mixed to be an overdose a dozen times over. She's so far gone I could punch her with my fists and it wouldn't be enough.

She says, "You know what this reminds me of?" I don't.

I work her so hard it makes her voice jump like she's driving over the ruts in a rough road.

"When my first husband asked me to marry him," she says, "he took me to the car wash." She says the franchise name.

I'd been through that same car wash in a dozen different cities. The trickiest part is always aiming your tires straight to get them between the little rails. The pimply teenager who guides you, he or she waves his or her hands, pointing left or right like someone on a runway telling a jumbo jet where to taxi. You pay through the driver's window and they tell you to put the transmission in neutral and keep your engine running. Whatever happens, they tell you not to touch the brakes. A conveyor belt comes out of the floor and drags you along.

This car wash her first husband took her through, it was the same as others: a long narrow building with a few windows where it's always a typhoon on the inside.

"He called it the 'Tunnel of Love.'" She sighs.

That first fiancé, he'd told her, "Not to worry, baby. I'm smart enough for the both of us." He'd paid for the most expensive version, where the automatic scrubbers circle your car for what seems like forever while spinning brushes descend from the ceiling. It's steamy as a jungle and takes as long as an afternoon nap. His eight-track stereo was playing "We've Only Just Begun," sung by the Carpenters. His car had power windows and door locks.

She said, "I thought he was flirting."

She said, "I didn't know it was supposed to hurt."

A few feet into the car wash, she said, he used his controls to lower her window. By then it was too late to open her door and jump out. Even if she escaped there was no place to go. The robots had the car hemmed in, tight. A jet of scalding water raked the side of her head and she screamed. He must've been using the child-guard features because she couldn't get her window to raise. "He said to me, 'Sheilah.'" Screaming to be heard over the noise, he said, 'Before you marry me I want you should know what marriage is about.'" By now the boiling-hot suds were foaming at her, burning the sides of her neck. The heavy chamois straps descended to start flogging her.

Moving at a snail's pace, she says, "It was like cilia. Like I was food being digested."

She tried to unbuckle her seat belt and escape to the back, but a high-pressure squirt of detergent blinded her. Her eyes were stinging. When she opened her mouth to scream she was choked by more detergent. She couldn't even see what was hitting her, but it felt like wild animals clawing the skin from her face and neck. It felt like hydrochloric acid when the spinning brushes ground more soap into the open wounds.

This young man she planned to wed, he yelled, "You think marriage should be happily-ever-after. Well, this is more like it!"

The way his words sputtered, she could tell that his window was open, and he was planning to drown sitting next to her. She pictured the tunnel spitting them out at the end: two water-logged corpses. Coughing water, he shouted, "If you think I'm only being mean, the truth is I'm doing you a huge favor."

Recounting the pain, she said there was no arguing with how much it hurt. Some sense told her he'd taken this trip before, with other women, and that's why he was still a bachelor.

All the while, grabbing jaws snatched at her long hair and yanked it from her scalp by the roots. A deluge of freezing-cold rinse water drenched her. It was like torture. Like ducking a witch. It was like being water-boarded with no secret confession to offer. Blind and in agony, she felt him suffering beside her and that was her only comfort. The scrubbing brushes gave way to insensate robots blasting streams of melted Turtle Wax straight into her ears. She couldn't hear anything except the roar of gears. Clutching, scratching mindless machinery ripped at her favorite blouse.

Her fiancé, he kept shouting, "You and me." He shouted, "We'll never again have sex together for the first time!"

They kept rolling forward. There was no going faster. No stopping or going back.

He shouted, "When we're married, we'll say words to each other that make right now feel like a chocolate cake."

After the Turtle Wax, gigantic rollers scourged them. Thundering hurricanes of air pounded and stretched their faces. By then she felt like something cast up by a storm on the beach. They were both half bald. The hair they had left was gleaming white with soap and wax.

"That's what this massage makes me remember," she tells me. "No offense." She's drifting in and out. I can feel it in the way her breathing slows. It's no crime, but I'm already doctoring the version I'm going to tell the police. To keep her awake, I ask, "So what's your beef with sitar music?"

Her first fiancé, he never laid a finger on her, but after the car wash, there she was: bruised and scraped and burned. The hair she had left was tangled and matted. A trickle of hot Simoniz ran down between her breasts.

Blowers like high-powered fans at the exit hit her with scorching wind. The sound, it sounded like the end of the world. Like getting sneezed on by God.

She accepted his ring anyway, thinking the worst was over. She was correct, but only for about seventeen years.

I asked why she helped, when she found him in the bathtub, and she said she had to. To not help him, she said, "It would be like giving birth to only half a baby." By "helping" she meant she had to massage his arms. To keep the blood from clotting. She said it was like milking a cow. The idea was to keep things moving in the direction of the outside world. So he could be gone by the time the bathwater got cold.

She says this while I'm doing her arms.

She says what she did for her first husband, it was the real definition of what people talk about when they refer to "heroic measures." What's the difference, if it's what the person wants? It was exhausting, all that work to become a widow. In retrospect, she should've quit while she was ahead. The joys of widowhood only last until you get married again.

■

INCLINATIONS

There was this girl. She was named Mindy. Mindy Evelyn Taylor-Jackson. That's the name a bailiff would eventually read into the public record. You see, everything that comes next will ultimately end up in a court of law. Not to ruin the suspense, but justice will prevail.

There's a lot of ground to cover, but what you need to know first is that Mindy got knocked up. At thirteen, no less. She wanted a spot on the cheerleading squad and a career as a paralegal and a 911 Carrera 4S Cabriolet in Obsidian No. 2 with the Special Edition Stuttgart leather interior. The last thing Mindy wanted was a baby. Her parents, on the other hand, weren't inclined to agree. They were born-again Pro-Lifers. Life begins at conception, they told her; nonetheless, eventually they had to promise that if she carried full term and gave it up for adoption they'd buy her the Porsche.

At first she could only drive it around, the Porsche, after hours, in the big parking lot at their church. She cut black-rubber doughnuts and smoking figure eights like something pacing inside a cage. Around there, back then, Porsches weren't so easy to come by. They were like Social Security or getting to Heaven.

Grown-ups said to work hard and keep your nose clean. You'd get your turn.

Her mom and dad had wanted to teach her about the beauty and sanctity of life. But Mindy learned something else. Before her sixteenth birthday she had three Porsches. Three Porsches and the biggest boobs in the junior class. And no stretch marks. Those were just some of the perks of starting early. The gossip was that she got a cash kickback from the Porsche dealership in St. Cloud. That, and the rumor mill said she'd recently been back to the obstetrician, and if her parents' money held out—and her cervix—people said Mindy Taylor-Jackson was carrying twin Porsches. That meant she'd have five cars before she graduated high school.

—

What came next is Kevin Clayton saw Mindy with her 400-horsepower, driving on her deluxe, chromed wire–rimmed wheels. So for his sixteenth birthday Kevin Clayton asked for a subscription to *Elle Decor* magazine. In September, he asked for a gerbil. Days later, when it went missing, he asked for a replacement. He was going on his fourth gerbil by Homecoming. His sixth by Halloween. He went to his mom's grocery list stuck under a magnet on the fridge door, and he wrote, "We need more Vaseline." Using squares of Kleenex, he'd scooped out the jar in the bathroom and flushed most of its greasy contents down the toilet.

When his mom bought more, he noticed that she'd marked a line on the side of the jar in black felt-tipped pen. It recorded the level, the same way they marked the bottles of vodka and gin in the liquor cabinet. Right away Kevin scooped out a batch and flushed it. He went to his bedroom and opened the gerbil's cage. Reaching inside he caught the little fur ball by its tail.

Somebody knocked at the bedroom door. Kevin lifted out this, the most-recent gerbil. From the hallway, his father said, "We need to talk, mister."

Kevin carried the gerbil to the window. He slid the pane open, and carefully lowered the little rodent to within a few inches of the ground. "I'm coming in," Mr. Clayton said. There was the sound of keys. Kevin dropped the gerbil and watched it scamper away. It was autumn. Everything was going to seed. Everything was food. He closed the window and flopped on the bed and opened the latest issue of *Elle Decor* just as his dad came through the door. The first place his dad looked was the empty cage.

"Where's your hamster?" he asked.

Kevin shrugged. He tried to look like he was trying to not look guilty. He told his father, "Be honest." Indicating a photo in the design magazine, he asked, "Do you *really* think that vividly patterned foil wallpapers can rally for a comeback?" He yawned and smirked like a boa constrictor that had just swallowed a goat.

His father's eyes moved slowly from the cage to where Kevin sprawled on the bed. Mr. Clayton tried to smile, but his lips trembled with the effort and fell flat. When he spoke, his voice came out strained and high-pitched. "Another one got away?" He shuddered and wiped his face with the palm of one hand.

Someday, when Kevin was grown and wed and brought home his future kids for his folks to swoon over, he swore to himself he'd tell his dad the truth: He'd set all the gerbils free. By that point, there would be a gerbil population explosion. He and his dad would drink beer on the front porch and laugh about the terrible images that were at present filling Mr. Clayton's head.

Stretched on his bed, Kevin turned a page and grimaced, muttering darkly, "Enough with the glass tile, already." He looked everywhere except at his father. He farted. It irked him a little how easily his dad jumped to a gruesome conclusion.

Before they agreed to another gerbil, Kevin's parents asked if he'd see the family's GP. They didn't give a reason. He suspected they wanted to scout around his ass cheeks for tiny claw marks.

When issues of *Playgirl* started hitting their doorstep, his mom and dad were inconsolable.

Kevin didn't want a Porsche. Let's not pretend. No kid wanted a Porsche. This wasn't 1985. But what else was there to ask for? It couldn't be anything too easy. It had to be a challenge. Still, Mindy Taylor-Jackson had established the standard unit for measuring teenage power and parental love. One Porsche. Two Porsches. And so forth. Hers was the record to beat.

The next time the Vaseline ran out, both his folks confronted him in his room. Another gerbil had also come and gone. His mom and dad stood near the empty cage, where it rested on his bedside table, while Kevin lolled on his bed.

Kevin knew exactly what buttons to push. "Why would I want to be like the two of you?" He made a mean face. "So I can be miserable?" He thumped a fist dramatically against his skinny chest. "So I can raise a good-for-nothing freak of nature who'll just break my heart?" He threw the latest *Elle Decor* so that it slammed against his new poster of Lady Gaga and the combined paper of both crumpled and fell. He lashed out, knocking the empty cage to the floor, scattering cedar chips on the braided-rag rug. He chewed the scenery. It was easier for him to cry once he saw real tears running down Mrs. Clayton's cheeks.

It felt wonderful. He'd told jokes before. Any clown could make people laugh. But this was a terrible new ability. He had the power to make his mother cry. It wasn't much of a super-power, but it was a start.

"You're not a freak," wailed Mr. Clayton.

"I am!" Kevin said this with a ferocity that impressed himself. "I'm a sexual invert!" He ranted at his mom, "You should've aborted me!" The words, these words felt thrilling and self-indulgent. Self-loathing as they sounded, he was still the center of attention. The problem with being a teenager is that parents could be so calm. The prospect of a whole career occurred to him. This was acting. He could become a movie star.

As proof of Kevin's natural talent, his dad held his mom by the shoulders, restraining her as she struggled to step forward and throw her arms around her son. His dad's face was shut tight. At school, Kevin's friends would be so jealous. He couldn't wait to describe to them how anguished his mom looked. The way his dad was sniveling. Kevin had forced their hand. This was love. This was how much they loved him.

He was holding himself hostage. They'd have to meet his demands.

Mindy Taylor-Jackson, her parents had sent her to a place outside town. A big fenced-off building like a boarding school or a rehab clinic. Not too far away from that place was another building, but for boys. It consisted of a few gravel acres around a six-story, redbrick building. It only *looked* like a factory. According to scuttlebutt there was nothing to do inside except lift weights and get injections of testosterone. Residents got to play cards and surf porn. It was like a jail but without the constant threat of getting corn-holed. Plus, they brought in strippers and whores.

Kevin marveled at how his campaign tormented his folks. This was a gamble. And it was a trap, even Kevin saw that. He could never fess up. Not without forfeiting all the credibility he'd ever have. To watch them, trembling and distraught, it was like attending his own funeral. Nothing he'd ever done in his life had ever felt so satisfying. Kevin's father seemed to age, becoming a stooped old man right before his eyes. To witness them wilt and blubber this way, the depth of their pain was nothing less than astounding. A permanent shift had taken place, and they would never again be his masters.

Seeing them in such agony, Kevin had to throw them a bone. Rolling over on his bed, he pressed his face into his pillow to keep from laughing. Muffled, he said, "If only there was some cure . . ."

He wasn't relenting. He simply realized that the solution had to occur like their idea. They had to bring up the redbrick factory in the middle of nowhere.

—

Officially it wasn't called the "Fag Farm." It was built as someplace else—a hospital or a prison. But then the Commander came along with his theories about reorientation. The first thing he did was reorient the building by running fences around it. The place was red brick rising up six stories above corn fields. In the space between the redbrick walls and the fence, where there used to be green, mowed grass, the Commander put gravel and roaming, bloodthirsty, Stalag 13 dogs.

When his parents drove him, there was the usual mob blockading the gate. A crowd of Rock Hudsons waved protest signs and lay down in the road, thick as a carpet, trying to get themselves run over. Lady softball players wore too-tight T-shirts with pink triangles and no bras even though it was practically Christmas. The rainbow-colored balloons were printed with "=" signs. They carried bunches of these balloons and babies. Somehow they all had little babies.

Kevin's dad had to honk the horn while their car idled with the doors locked and the heater blasting. The Rock Hudsons rushed them from every direction. They waved to draw Kevin's attention, yelling that he didn't need to be ashamed. Some were dressed as nuns who had beards and wore too much eye makeup.

Kevin couldn't look at the Rock Hudson faces pressed against the car windows, so close he could see straight down their yelling throats. Instead he looked at the babies. He studied the babies, it was like looking in a mirror.

One Rock Hudson shouted, "It gets better!" Kevin wanted to yell, *Get lost!*

Cameras perched on the gateposts, swiveling to follow their progress. A figure stood on the roof, a rifle slung over his shoulder. "It's good security," Mr. Clayton said. "You can just imagine if these deviants ever overran this place." He jerked his head toward the gates. Again, he honked.

Even now, Kevin was tempted to explain about Mindy and the gerbils but there was too much at stake.

The fence had accordion rolls of razor wire running along the top. Inside that fence was another fence with signs that said "Danger High Voltage." When they were inside the first gate they waited. Only when it closed did the inner gate finally swing open. Even then, inside the second fence there were the German dogs barking and snapping at their car. The dogs sniffed at the windows until an old man came out the doors of the building. Leaning on a cane he stood at the top of the front steps. He lifted a chrome whistle that hung from a cord around his scrawny neck. He blew it until the veins stood out in his spotted forehead. Kevin heard nothing, but the dogs scattered in every direction.

The old man who met them was called the Commander except for behind his back. There, people called him Mr. Peanut because of his skin. It puckered into squares and looked yellow like a shell. He was bald as a peanut. The whiskers on his chin were yellow. Even the white parts of his eyes were yellow.

The Commander motioned for them to hurry. Once they were safely inside, he sat them at a desk and presented them with a pancake stack of documents. There wasn't time to read every page so he told them where to sign their names. Kevin could smell perfume. He smelled cafeteria food. His mother was snuffling into a handkerchief. His father was writing a check. Mrs. Clayton kissed Kevin on the cheek, and Mr. Clayton shook his hand.

———

The other boys assigned to Kevin Clayton's floor were: Jasper, Brainerd, Pig the Pirate, Tomas, Whale Jr., Troublemaker, and Kidney Bean. Those were the names written in felt-tipped pen on the paper tags stuck to their shirts. "Hello, My Name Is . . ." Kevin, Jasper, Brainerd, Pig the Pirate, Tomas, Whale Jr., Troublemaker, and Kidney Bean. For some of them, that was their given name. For some, that was only a name they went by.

Their floor, the sixth floor, the top floor, felt tornado-high surrounded by nothing but cornfields. If a person could see far enough, over the curve of the horizon a little, he might see the girls' camp where Mindy Taylor-Jackson had been sent to have induced childbirth and surrender her sin. From one window they could look down on the front gate. There, the crowd of Rock Hudsons was too far away for him to see faces, but Kevin could make out their pink triangle picket signs and rainbow flags. He could see the German dogs prowling the fence line. Watching them, he felt like the angel trapped within Lot's house in the Old Testament. Outside, the assembled sodomites laid siege to the building.

On Kevin's first afternoon, the boys were unpacking suitcases. The new inductees. The whole room was open like a barracks. A cot was assigned to each of them. Next to that was a tall, skinny metal locker like in high school. Nobody made overtures, not even to say "hello" or ask, "What about those Packers?" Nobody made himself acquainted. The floor supervisor assigned Kevin a bed between Brainerd and Whale Jr. Kidney Bean was assigned the next bed over, in a corner. They had until chow time to get settled in.

When the floor supervisor left, Troublemaker went to the corner bed and grabbed up Kidney Bean's clothes in one arm load and threw them across the room in the direction of his own assigned bed. He claimed the corner, and Troublemaker lifted his hands above his head. Clapping them together, he shouted, "Listen up, my fellow perverts!" Tattooed on the inside of one wrist, he boasted a vampire bat or, maybe, a long-handled ax.

He snapped his fingers and whistled until everyone was looking. Once he had them all watching, he said, "Just so you know . . ." His biceps flexed. They made the short sleeves of his black T-shirt bunch up to his armpits, exposing dense armpit hair. A dark-blue tattoo banded one side of his neck. In thorny letters it spelled out "Suede." He was a brute.

Troublemaker leveled his gaze on Kevin, his eyes twitching between Kevin's bed and his own bed not an arm's reach apart. Troublemaker waited until Kevin was turned all the way, listening with his eyes and ears. Talking slow, like a list of words instead of a sentence, Troublemaker said, "I—Am—Not—A—Homosexual." He raised his forehead in expectation and waited for his words to sink in.

Otherwise the floor had gone silent. Everyone looked frozen, posed like a photograph of kids unpacking.

Troublemaker made one hand into a gun and poked the muzzle into the middle of his own chest. Like a Tarzan, he said, "Me: Heterosexual." To the room in general, he said, "I'm only here to blackmail my folks into giving me a Yamaha Roadliner S." Troublemaker said, "Capisce?"

Kevin stared at him in amazement.

It only took one person to fess up before there was an epidemic of truth. Whale Jr. said he'd hoodwinked his entire church. Someplace in Montana there was a small town where the ladies were holding bake sales. The teenagers were holding car-wash-a-thons. Even the little kids were chipping in their Tooth Fairy pennies. Whale Jr. bragged that when he went home he'd be a local hero. The Rotary Club and the Kiwanis would ride him down Main Street in a big Welcome Home parade. He'd get to wave at everybody, riding up high on the boot of a Cadillac convertible.

Whale Jr.'s eyes misted over with the vision. He'd be living proof to everyone he knew that they could heal the corruption of this sick world. With the cakes and pies they baked . . . the turkeys they raffled off . . . they were saving a soul. Despite what godless liberal progressives preached, the good people of this nation could make a difference. Every cent they earned was going to help make Whale Jr. a raving pussy hound.

Of course, that was already the case. He'd never been a football star. He'd never taken home straight A's on a report card. But just by liking girls, Whale Jr. would soon be adored by everyone he knew. Everyone in his small town would be invested in keeping him a happy skirt chaser. Boasting about his scheme, Whale Jr. smirked. He polished his fingernails against the front of his starched, white shirt. To underscore his genius, he ducked his eyes with false aw-shucks modesty.

In response, Jasper said a parade was strictly small potatoes. Same with being a church hero. When Jasper graduated from the Farm, his grandparents had promised to pay for his college education.

Beaming, Pig the Pirate said he was getting flying lessons as his reward. Tomas had negotiated a season ticket to the Bruins.

Listening to them, Kevin hoped God graded on a curve. Someday, what kept him out of Hell wouldn't be his own goodness as much as it would be other people committing worse sins. Kevin had forced his parents' hand. He'd made them demonstrate how much they loved him. But other guys had whole towns praying for them. They'd go home as fake saints. As living proof of God's miracles on earth.

According to the bargain he'd struck with his folks, when he came home a recovered pervert, Kevin Clayton would get no less than twenty thousand dollars cash. It wasn't a Porsche, but that's what his parents were willing to pay.

—

That evening the boys of the sixth floor bowed their heads together over beef Stroganoff. Before the butter had melted on their green beans, they'd all confessed to running more or less the same scam. They were, each and every boy, fake inverts. As such, they all committed to toeing the line, here. Bowing and scraping, if need be. It felt good. To be around other kids, clever kids, felt like being pickpockets together in some book by Charles Dickens. It was better than organized crime, because their scheme made everyone happy. There wasn't a bona fide homo among them.

They were still joshing and slapping one another on the back, congratulating each other on their mutual brilliance, when the Commander entered through the back of the chow hall. He moved like a coffin through the center of the room, toward a lectern at the far end. The room was heavy with steam and sour milk smells. By the time he took his place, the boys had gone quiet. He shuffled a few pages. Without looking up, he began to read. "Gentlemen." He cleared his throat. "Gentlemen, welcome to the Healing Center. Please be assured that this institution has never failed in its mission. These doors have never, once, released a soul with troubled inclinations back into the world . . ."

He went on to describe how guests would be retained until the custodians declared them fully reoriented. To avoid temptations of the flesh they would shower separately. Dress in isolation. They'd never see each other unclothed. Once deemed ready, they would be integrated into the general population housed on the lower floors. The papers they and their parents had signed during the admitting process amounted to nothing less than a voluntary legal commitment to a residential treatment and recovery program.

"Please," the Commander read, "for your own safety, do not attempt to leave this building." He reminded them about the electric fence and the dogs. He explained that their contact with their families would be extremely restricted. "You may write letters, but know that those letters will be read by the staff, who have the option of censoring what they construe to be untrue or manipulative communications."

To Kevin, Mr. Peanut sounded tired, as if he'd delivered this speech too many times and his heart was no longer in it. Kevin's stomach was too full, and today had been a long one. As the Commander's voice droned on, Kevin exchanged bored looks with Pig the Pirate. Jasper yawned. Tomas sighed as if mooning over his future seat on the fifty-yard line. Brainerd looked at his wristwatch, smugly. The floor guards had confiscated everyone's phones. Nobody could text. Brainerd knew the time because only he wore an old-school watch.

Listening, Kevin fought off a feeling of cold dread. It wasn't the words the Commander said that spooked him. It was *how* he said them, as if he were reading those words off a stone tablet delivered to him atop Mount Sinai. Resigned and ominous, the Commander sounded like a judge decreeing a death sentence.

Jasper yawned behind his hands. Troublemaker shoved his dinner tray aside and leaned facedown on the table, cradling his head in his crossed arms. He'd barely begun to snore when the Commander looked up from his script. He surveyed the seven of them. He asked, "Any questions?"

No one replied. Kevin wasn't taking any chances. He sat straight with hands clasped primly in front of him. Fast-tracking to his twenty grand.

"Gentlemen," the Commander coaxed, "have you nothing you'd like to ask?"

Brainerd raised his hand as if they were in school. When called upon, he asked about their general studies. In reply, the Commander explained that they'd be tutored in History, English Literature, Latin, Mathematics, and Geometry. A library of devotional tracts was at their disposal. Under the table, somebody kicked Brainerd for being such a brownnoser.

Troublemaker whispered, "Disposal is right."

Kidney Bean asked, "What about sports?"

The Commander regarded him. His jaundiced eyes sought out a name tag. "Mr. Bean," he continued. "Time allowing, you'll be free to make use of the basketball court behind the building as well as the swimming pool located in the basement." He looked expectantly from boy to boy for another question.

"What about the steroids?" asked Pig the Pirate.

"And the weight lifting?" added Jasper. No one dared to ask about the promise of whores and strippers as part of their reconditioning.

The Commander cocked his head, confused. Despite whatever rumors they'd heard, there would be no anabolic steroids or bodybuilding. Kevin could tell by the stricken look on Whale Jr.'s face that muscles had been part of his Homecoming dream—to be a pumped-up, 100-percent-certified he-man riding past the adoring throngs. Whale Jr. looked crestfallen.

Kevin heard the sound of musical notes. Four distinct notes. It was someone pressing numbers on the keypad in the hallway. He watched as a floor guard entered from the back of the room. The guard caught the Commander's attention and jerked his thumb toward the exit. The Commander nodded and said, "If there are no more questions, then it's time for you to return—"

A voice interrupted. "One question." It was Troublemaker. Lifting his face from his arms crossed on the table, he asked, "When do we hook up with Betsey?"

Everyone looked at him with a new appreciation and respect. The name "Betsey" hung in the air. To judge from the Commander's face, the name had hit a chord. Troublemaker obviously had an inside track.

The Commander smiled. Not a happy smile, this was the smile of someone keeping a secret. "Tomorrow, you gentlemen have a treat in store for you." He lifted his discolored hands into the air. "Tomorrow, you will meet a lovely young woman." He closed his eyes as if swept away with happiness. "She is thoroughly . . ." To demonstrate what mere words couldn't convey, his hands molded a curvy, hourglass shape in the air. His palms came together, and he brought them to his chest. He pressed his clasped hands against his heart.

As if lost in a rapturous dream, he closed his eyes. He sighed. "And she will grant you access to all the erotic mysteries of the female body."

—

Breakfast was eggs and French toast. Afterward, the guard ushered them down a new stairway and through a couple security doors. With every step the air was tougher to breathe. More stale. Dense with humidity and heat. For a short stretch, Kevin could smell the chlorine of the swimming pool. That proved they were in the basement, but the guard led them down two, maybe three more flights. He halted the group like a traffic cop, with the palm of one hand. Holding each door open, he waved them through. These corridors were less like hallways than tunnels. Pipes ran along the ceiling, and the floor was scuffed concrete. Moisture condensed and dripped from the pipes. Puddles forced them to watch where they stepped.

They'd been awake most of the night, whispering the name between themselves. *Betsey.*

Now they acted like this was a big adventure, but every step felt like they were being buried alive. Jasper whispered, "I hope we get to wear a condom. My sperm could eat through steel."

Tomas agreed. "That would suck, getting a baby out of this." In whispers they griped about the prospect of becoming a teen father. They knew, firsthand, what monsters kids could be. Brainerd speculated that Betsey might be one of those expensive, incredibly lifelike, anatomically correct Real Dolls. Troublemaker alone kept silent.

At each new door, the guard punched a number into a keypad on the wall. Each keypad made a different series of musical tones. Each lock, it seemed, had a different four-digit code.

Betsey. The name rang in everyone's mind. All morning they'd repeated it while they ran their combs under steaming water and slicked back their hair. The Commander had said they should dress as if they were attending a formal dance. While they'd tied their neckties and shined their shoes, the girl's name had haunted them.

Now they crowded behind the guard. They tripped on their own feet and careened off the cinder block. Their whispers and giggles reverberated between the walls and floor. It was nerves, plain and simple. They acted like seven smart alecks, but in truth they were scared shitless. Seven teenagers on a blind date. To Kevin it felt like standardized testing in school. Whatever the conditions, he thought that if he could have sex with this stranger he'd be phoning his parents to come get him, tomorrow.

Once more, the dread haunted him. He was about to take part in a basement gang bang, sharing some girl he'd probably never again meet. Life was already too full of people you met only once. He was fairly sure Brainerd and Kidney Bean felt the same way, but he didn't want to say it aloud and risk spoiling everyone's fun.

To justify what was about to happen, Pig the Pirate kept saying the girl, Betsey, must be a whore. Not to be outdone, Whale Jr. insisted she was a nymphomaniac.

It filled Kevin with wonder. Every step took them farther down. Dungeon deep. Torture chamber deep. He was about to earn twenty G's from a single fuck. This had to make him one of the biggest whores in history. To launder the ill-gotten gains, his mind turned it into a wide-screen color television, a laptop computer, diapers.

They arrived at a door with no handle. The guard pressed a button on a call box mounted on the wall. He leaned close to it and said, "Sixth-floor residents." Static crackled from the box, and a voice said, "Stand clear." It was the Commander's voice.

The guard waved for them to step back, and the door swung outward. The room beyond it was dim compared to the hallway. The air that wafted out was cold as a vault. They shuffled through. Once the door shut them inside, it took a few blinks for their eyes to adjust. Kevin could hear a gurgle of running water. He could smell perfume mixed with chemicals that made his eyes sting. The only thing to see was the Commander. He stood under the room's one light, surrounded by darkness. Next to him was a long table. Whatever lay on the table, it was covered with a greasy sheet of milky plastic.

"Gentlemen," the Commander said. He stooped to grip an edge of the plastic. As he lifted it, he asked, "May I introduce you to Betsey?"

—

The Commander cast the sheet aside. On the tabletop lay a thing. Something. It stretched the full length of the stainless-steel work surface.

The thing's skin looked as white as soap. It wore a flowered dress that left its pallid arms and legs bare. The folds of the skirt draped its slender thighs as far as the knees. Its arms lay straight at its sides. Kevin prayed it was merely a life-sized dummy. He told himself it was just some statue molded out of soap or wax. If it were a person, he prayed she was only asleep.

That smell they'd noticed through a dozen locked doors— sweet and acrid—here was the smell's source.

Black flies circled it. They alighted on its skin, roving the back of each hand, wandering up and down its thin, bare limbs. They puckered their proboscises and kissed its arms like old-movie Romeos. A cloth bandage wrapped one wrist. Another bandage clung to the side of its neck.

A gold chain circled the other thin wrist. Little medals dangled from the links. A charm bracelet. A few of the charms, Kevin recognized. One was a tiny golden Bible. Another was two faces, the smiling and frowning masks of Drama Society. Hanging next to that was a gold baseball. Next to the baseball was the little flaming torch that symbolized high school Honor

Society. The collar of the dress was frilled with lace, but Kevin could see a gold cross sitting in the hollow at the base of its throat. The cross hung from a thin thread of gold beads that looped around its pale neck.

Kevin couldn't bring himself to look directly at its face. Not yet. In case its eyes might still be open. At the sight, his scalp prickled. Every hair on his head stood up so painfully it felt as if ghosts were tugging it out at the roots.

The thing laid out on the table, it had long auburn curls. They cascaded around its ashen, heart-shaped face and rested against the shoulders of its flowered dress. Some curls fanned out. They hung over the edge of the tabletop like a lank fringe. Clearly, Kevin and his crew weren't the first kids to mess with the Betsey thing. The more his eyes adjusted, the more Kevin could see black stitches like the seams on a baseball, only sewn with black string. They showed where the thing's pale skin had been sliced open and sutured back together. Some cuts looked fresh. Some didn't. It looked as if the Betsey thing had been taken apart too many times to count. Butchered by too many boys to keep track of.

The Commander fixed them with compassionate eyes. "My young gentlemen," he assured them, "you need not be terrified of women."

Tomas whispered that the stitches looked like tiny railroad tracks. To Whale Jr. they looked like zippers, as if they wouldn't need to cut anything. You could just pull one thread and the thing would come unraveled.

The Commander looked down at the Betsey thing. He cocked his head as if listening. He asked, "What's that, my dear?" He put a finger to his wrinkled lips as if to shush the boys. Bowing low, he turned his face sideways so that his yellow ear hovered over the painted mouth. Its lips sparkled with pink gloss. He closed his eyes for a moment and nodded. He said, "Yes, of course, my darling." He lifted his hand and curled a finger, beckoning them to come closer.

None of them moved.

The Commander planted his fists against his hip bones and stomped one foot in a huff. Indignant, he said, "May I remind you gentlemen that your families are sponsoring you in this program to the tune of one thousand dollars each week? Many of them have mortgaged their homes and farms." The Commander fixed them with a reproachful eye. "The sooner you engage with the curriculum, the less of a crippling financial burden you'll impose . . ."

A thousand dollars a week. Kevin knew that no health insurance in the world would pay this claim. The brutal size of the money stuck in his head. He stepped closer to the door. He felt behind his back, but his fingers couldn't find the knob. There was no knob on the inside.

In the glare from the one overhead light, he could recognize more charms hanging from the thing's bracelet. There were minuscule golden ballet slippers. A musical note, representing Choir. Future Farmers of America. The air in the room was so motionless that none of the charms moved.

The Betsey thing, her waxy eyes were open. Dull as blue paint, they stared straight up at the blazing, bare lightbulb, unblinking.

Troublemaker whispered, "This is her parents' revenge, sending her here." He meant the false eyelashes and the sparkle-pink-painted fake fingernails glued on top of her ragged real nails.

Mr. Peanut's finger flopped forward, a knobby wand of bone, pointing at the group of them. The brittle fingertip roamed from one boy to the next as the Halloween voice recited, "He loves me . . . he loves me not . . . he loves me . . . he loves me not . . ."

That night, none of them slept. After dinner, they'd each drunk a glass of chocolate milk shake spiked with syrup of ipecac. The Commander made no secret of it. They'd each choked down a whole glass of doctored milk, and they'd been left to watch a copy of *Steel Magnolias* on television in the sixth-floor lounge. This was yet another therapy. Before Julia Roberts was even hitched, Pig the Pirate was yakking out his guts on the linoleum. By the end of her wedding reception, Troublemaker had hurled. Big foamy waves of chocolate hurl. They couldn't even hear Olympia Dukakis cussing out Shirley MacLaine, the barfing was so loud. Big syrup of ipecac gushers. By the time Sally Field was standing at her daughter's grave, the TV lounge was awash in vomit.

Now they were all back in the dorm, tucked into bed. The room, pitch-dark. Unable to sleep, Kevin was still trembling. The toxic smell of the basement hung in his sinuses. Not even the acrid stink of barf could displace it. He could hear Kidney Bean, two beds over, sobbing into his pillow.

Kevin's head hurt. He slipped out of bed and crawled to the window. It was so cold the glass was frosted over on the inside. Kneeling there, he rested his headache against it. In the dark Kevin knew they were going down another wrong road. It had been wrong to force his parents' hand. To make them prove their love, he'd done something terrible. He dreaded the possibility that he might have to do something worse to prove he was normal. Still, he held on to the hope that another lie, a bigger lie, could fix everything.

To block out the memory, Kevin muttered, "Damn." The word hung in the silence and the dark. Tomorrow was going to be another day in the therapy room. Their second date with the Betsey thing.

Tonight, somebody said something. Brainerd. Moaning in his bed, his voice heavy with doom, he said, "We are in the hands of an elderly lunatic." He waited, but no one took the bait. "And I don't mean just God. I mean a *real lunatic.*"

From another bed, Jasper said, "All we need to do is tell our folks what happened."

"How?" Kevin shot back.

Pig the Pirate insisted, "The Commander will tell them we're just lying to get out of treatment."

Gazing out the window, Kevin griped, "I'm never getting my twenty grand . . ."

Whale Jr. wailed, "I'm never getting my parade."

Spitting mad, Brainerd countered, "Screw your parade. We've got to do everything that madman says, or my parents will go into debt for the rest of their lives."

Kidney Bean went back to sobbing. "I'm not screwing dead snatch."

"Screw all of you crybabies," a voice shouted from the dark. It was Troublemaker. He didn't talk like a sixteen-year-old kid sharing a room with a bunch of bedwetters. His voice sounded determined. Not frightened. He spoke with a hero's voice. Like a leader rallying his troops, he said, "We've got somebody more important to rescue."

———

A series of long letters arrived from Kevin's mother. She wrote that his father was killing himself with the effort to pay the weekly clinic charges. She scribbled her notes in "Get Well" cards, describing how his father had collapsed from overwork. She referred to it as a *cardiac episode,* but implied that it was akin to a broken heart. In closing, she urged him to obey the Commander and complete the program as quickly as possible.

Mr. Clayton wrote less often, but his letters were filled with details about how Mrs. Clayton had taken two part-time jobs. One, waiting tables, the other as a hotel maid. He confided that she fell into a chair, every night, and wept over her swollen, bleeding feet.

For his part, Kevin couldn't write anything that wouldn't be reviewed by the Commander's staff. It was easy to imagine the progress reports that old man was giving them. That nut-job was going to bleed everyone dry.

There were other boys in the building. To judge from the sound of their footsteps, there were mobs imprisoned here. At mealtimes and outdoors, the sixth-floor boys were segregated from them. In dry weather Kevin could see them on the basketball court outside the big window beside his bed. They looked broken-down. Their ankles showed below the frayed hems of their pant legs. A big stretch of bare wrist showed between their hands and the cuffs of their shirts. It looked as if they'd outgrown their clothes. As if these too-tight T-shirts and jeans worn out at the knees were clothes they'd brought here at least a year before.

One afternoon Whale Jr. claimed a headache and the floor guard escorted him to the infirmary. When he came back his eyes were glazed with shock. "Don't pound me," he said. "I'm just the messenger, okay?"

The way the nurse had told it, each new batch of boys started on the top floor. In a few weeks, once they'd learned the ropes, they'd be integrated into the general population of the clinic. The nurse hadn't cared. She'd dispensed two aspirin into his outstretched palm and told him to settle in. Nobody was ever discharged from the clinic. Not for years and years. It was only when a boy turned eighteen that he might be declared officially redeemed.

Those boys they saw shooting hoops, some of them had been admitted here when they were thirteen, even twelve years old.

To Kevin, things started to make sense. The Fag Farm was a cash cow. It made a fortune for everyone who worked there. Ultimately it made families happy, but not before pushing them to the verge of poverty. Church congregations throughout the country sponsored deviants the way they'd once financed missionaries overseas. The Commander and nurses and floor supervisors, they were all complicit.

Kevin supposed that a boy could sue. Set free, a boy could take his story to the media. Upon his release, he could charge the clinic with kidnapping or holding him against his will, but that would require admitting he'd faked his perversion and catalyzed the situation by taunting his folks. Chances were good that his parents would be furious. Besides, a judge or jury could always be convinced that such a boy was merely a vengeful, incurable Rock Hudson making scurrilous charges. It would be one admitted teenage liar's word pitted against the Commander's noble authority. Besides, there were all those legal forms he'd so eagerly signed.

No, a boy would do better to bide his time and emerge a hero. His victory might be delayed, but it would be intact. In the meantime there was nothing to do except study. Trigonometry. Calculus. Rhetoric. Physics. The tough stuff. As if to soften the blow, the nurse had told Whale Jr. that boys in the program almost always scored above 1400 on their SATs.

—

Beyond each door the next segment of corridor was dark. When they stepped through, automatic motion detectors switched on the lights. It was so quiet Kevin could hear the microscopic

277

ping-pinging sounds as the fluorescent bulbs flickered, before they came on steady.

The group was bunched up, following the floor guard down yet another corridor. Troublemaker lagged behind them, whispering to Kevin. Pig the Pirate walked too close behind Tomas and gave him a flat tire, and Tomas swore at him in Spanish. Tomas fell back a few paces and fixed the back of his shoe.

Whale Jr. whispered, "I wonder how she died."

Troublemaker said, "Her name isn't Betsey."

Brainerd asked, "Did you know her?"

Troublemaker whispered that she raced motorcycles. That's how she got the scar on her leg. She ditched during the final lap of a motocross race. Instead of winning, she died taking the turn too fast for the track conditions. Massive internal injuries. Troublemaker tells this with a wistful smile. His eyes shimmering with admiration.

Pig the Pirate asked, "Was she your girlfriend?"

"She was a badass," responded Troublemaker.

Kevin was examining his own hand. As he walked he recognized how his whole life showed in his hand. Through his fingernails he could see the pink, fresh skin he'd been covered with, all over, as a baby. Each fingernail was a little window onto who he'd been born. Conversely, the calluses on his palm showed how he'd look when he died. After he was dead his entire body would be covered with this same hoary, yellow skin. Here was proof that time passed. Looking at the difference between his baby skin and his dead skin made Kevin not want to waste a moment.

—

Urged by the Commander, they crowded around the steel table. While he folded back the greasy plastic and lifted the thing's skirt and began to snip a few stitches, Kevin pretended to help. Kevin

278

peeled back the cloth bandage that wrapped the wrist. The calluses on her palm were impressive. As were the muscles of her arms. Where Kevin had expected to find a slashed wrist, her skin was intact. Discolored but intact. There was a dark-blue bruise that more peeling revealed to be a tattoo. Inked on the inside of her wrist was a butterfly. On second consideration, it was a weird cross. At last, Kevin saw it as a double-bladed ax.

The Commander dimmed the basement lights. He took something from his pants pocket. Cigar-shaped it was, only shorter. He clicked a button on it. The device threw a red spot on the floor: a laser pointer. He directed its tiny red dot over Betsey's dull, colorless insides. "Behold the glory of the ovary!" The little spotlight pinpointed an unremarkable lump.

Kevin and Troublemaker watched as Brainerd peeled the bandage from the side of the neck. Anyone could see the hair was a wig with no real hair underneath. Just a shaved head. Under the neck bandage Kevin recognized another tattoo. It began with a dark-blue "T." Followed by an "R." Then an "O." Fully revealed, it said "Troublemaker," spelled out in thorny letters.

That's when Troublemaker dropped. Troublemaker of all people, the tough guy, his knees buckled, and he spiraled to the concrete floor.

The Commander set down the pointer so he could assist. After Troublemaker was propped in a chair and given a glass of water, the Commander turned his attention back to the ovaries, but the laser pointer was gone. He searched all through the thoracic cavity, checking behind the spleen and lungs but couldn't find it.

—

The same as every night, Kevin crawled out of bed. After Lights Out, he waited for the swing-shift supervisor to put the floor on lockdown. The jangle of keys and the squeak of tennis shoes receded down the hallway. Around that place a person needed a key to turn on the lights. A person needed a different key to monkey with the thermostat. To keep everyone in bed and under the covers, the guard turned off the heat. Within an hour, the old building was like a meat locker. The ward was just shadows too dark for the video cameras to work. Kevin saw nothing but nighttime outside the glass. He breathed against the cold window and used his fingers to wipe a hole in the frost.

He propped his elbows on the sill and brought his hands together in front of his face. In the event he was caught he could say he was praying. His prayers consisted of a click and a double-click, a triple-click, a repeated click-click-clicking. At the same time, a tiny red light flashed, and he pointed it into the darkness where he hoped the Rock Hudsons would be lurking. He flashed them long and short strobes of red laser light. Dot, dash, double-dot, triple-dash, dibble, drabble, dribble, dot, dash, dot, double-dash.

Troublemaker snuck out of bed and came to his side, whispering, "Good job."

Somewhere in the unknown, their little message was landing like the laser sight of a rifle. As if the question didn't mean anything . . . as if it didn't mean everything, Kevin asked, "Were you her boyfriend?"

Troublemaker squinted to see. His breath fogged the glass and he wiped it with his hand. "Not exactly."

Kevin was still clicking away. Flashing SOS. Flashing drumrolls of fast dashes and stuttering dots. Hoping the batteries would hold out, he said, "Cub Scouts is good for more than just getting your asshole stretched."

In a way it was a little prayer session, Kevin kneeling alongside Troublemaker. Brainerd came to kneel on Kevin's other side.

Whale Jr. snuck over and knelt beside Troublemaker until every pervert was lined up, elbows propped on the windowsill.

Tomas knelt beside Brainerd, whispering, "Troublemaker, that was the fakest faint I've ever seen."

Troublemaker whispered, "It worked, didn't it?"

Kevin whisper-shouted, "Both of you shut up." He made what they hoped would get attention. A bright-red fairy dancing around on the gravel road. He clicked fast-then-slow, blink-dash-blanks, strobes, and blazing-red winks he hoped at least one of the Rock Hudsons could read.

Kneeling there, fogging the glass, Pig the Pirate whisper-asked, "What are you telling them?"

Jasper whisper-ordered, "Tell them you're a power bottom."

Kevin ignored him.

Undeterred, Jasper insisted, "Tell them you have a smoking-hot man-gina."

Kevin gave him a cross look.

Tomas whispered, "Promise that if they break us out, we'll stick our hands up their butts."

None of them knew what to look for. They looked for anything. Kevin shut off the light and waited. He pointed it at a slightly different angle and flashed the same blink-double-blink coded message.

"We're going to get caught," whispered Brainerd. They all held their breath and listened for the rattle of keys. The squeak of footsteps on the stairs.

Whale Jr. whisper-threatened. He swore he'd pull the fire alarm before he allowed them to screw up his big homecoming.

—

The next day, Kevin could hardly stay awake as the Commander used two latex-gloved fingers to show how their penises would enter Betsey during intercourse. In theory, at least. Extracting the fingers, he produced a pair of shears, regular kitchen shears the cooks used to cut up chickens. He snipped the stitches up the front of her, careful to veer around one side of her clitoris. There was no blood. Kevin looked at Troublemaker who stood a step back, his arms crossed over his chest. Troublemaker lifted a hand and raked his fingers through his greasy hair. When he caught Kevin watching him he scowled.

It had to suck, Kevin figured, watching bored teenage jerk-offs hack apart someone you used to love. Even if she was dead. He wasn't without empathy, but he was still young, and the pain of other people embarrassed him. He was at an age when only his own pain seemed real so he was ashamed for Troublemaker. After that, Kevin resolved not to look at the brute. He'd been around enough bullies to know that rage and pain needed to vent, and he was careful not to make himself a target.

The Commander had to squeeze the shears with both hands to snip through the urogenital diaphragm. He flayed the vaginal cavity and laid it open as high as the cervix. He explained how sperm would collect at the upper end. Even now there was a small amount of viscous, cloudy fluid pooled there. He said just one word, "Formalin," and used a folded paper towel to sponge it up. He referred to the formaldehyde concoction Betsey was steeped in to keep her from rotting. Even Kevin knew that. But the nasty spunk the Commander was dabbing at, every boy present recognized what it actually was.

—

Of course these details would come to light during the eventual trial. Jump forward half a year and cable television would devote twenty-four-hour coverage to showing Kevin sitting in court, testifying about the laser pointer and the mysterious spunk. He'd spill the beans about the gerbils and the dead girl butchered in the basement. Next to him would be his girlfriend. More or less his girlfriend. That could be debated. What would be obvious and undeniable is the fact she would be so very pregnant.

———

A week went by and Kevin's dot-triple-dot-dashes got no answer. Nobody except Troublemaker knelt with him as he sent out his plea.

Kevin floated a trial idea. To him the protesters at the front gate were the equivalent of the protesters outside abortion clinics. The Rock Hudsons tried to stop people coming here the same way do-gooders tried to block people going to murder their unborn kids. The irony was in how those same rescued babies got adopted by Rock Hudsons.

Kevin said, "Between church people raising babies who would grow up to be homo and gay guys raising babies who would end up as breeders, I can't understand the fuss." He snorted in disdain. "To me it all looks like a wash."

Troublemaker squinted in the direction of the gate. He rubbed a bigger hole to see through the frost. He said, "Nobody called her 'Betsey,' only her mom and dad."

Talking at cross-purposes, Kevin ventured, "Imagine what Sex Ed was like for them." Sneering his words, incredulous, he said, "Absolutely no useful information. *None.*" As punctuation at the end of his sentence, he slugged Troublemaker in the shoulder. "For them, Sex Education was a pointless exercise, kind of like Black History Month is for white kids."

"Her real name," Troublemaker said, "was 'Suede.'"

Kevin listened. He didn't know why they were having this

conversation. He couldn't guess where it was headed. Putting a sharp edge on his every word, Kevin complained. Jabbing his finger at the window, in the direction of the front gate, he crowed, "For the first hundred years of American history it was illegal to teach blacks how to read. These days, people still ridicule them for being ignorant." Exasperated, he added, "Now we deny homos the right to get married, and at the same time we criticize them for whoring around." Kevin continued to flash-dash-dash-triple-dot-dash-dot into the unknown.

An unknown amount of night passed before either of them spoke. It was Troublemaker, his voice strained with his righteous speculation, "Imagine . . . imagine if everything you know about intimacy . . . you learned not from your folks or your teachers, but from strangers in the public toilet of a Greyhound bus station?"

—

On another day the Commander deconstructed the breasts. In the dank basement, while the sixth-floor boys watched, he snipped the stitches and peeled them like baseballs. He laid bare the fat deposits and glands. Skinned, they looked like someone had knocked the horse hide off a pitch and socked a home run out of the ballpark. Along the way he pointed out the milk-producing alveolus . . . the myoepithelial cells . . . the lactiferous ducts . . . his words defusing anything mysterious and erotic that Kevin had ever dreamt about bodacious, motorboat tah-tahs.

Troublemaker stood as far from the action as the room's size allowed, averting his eyes. Occasionally, he lifted one hand to smooth back his greasy hair. The gesture caught Kevin's eye, and he could see how the ax tattooed on the inside of Troublemaker's wrist matched the one on the dead girl. Suede.

284

Regardless, everyone else was in high spirits. The rumor was they were having pizza for dinner. In the overall giddiness, Jasper mistook the sigmoid colon for the fundus. When the Commander wasn't watching, Kidney Bean took out the fornix and smacked it across Whale Jr.'s cheek. Only Troublemaker didn't laugh.

——

That night, alone with Troublemaker, Kevin tried to explain his theory about parents in general. He started by asking, "You know what a manic-depressive is?"

Troublemaker didn't answer so Kevin kept going. "My idea is my mom and dad pushed me into fooling them." His hand knew its job by heart. The constant stream of dot-dash-dribble-dash-dot-dot never let up as Kevin built his case.

As a baby, he said, all he had to do was use the toilet and his parents showered him with praise. If he bumped his head or had a nightmare they were all over him with sympathy and attention. But the older he grew, the harder it became to get noticed. It wasn't enough to bring home a test with an A grade. Or a failed one. The best and worst events in his life barely warranted a response from them.

He wasn't alone. Among his friends he'd noticed a trend. As they received less attention they'd begun to escalate their highs and lows. No triumph was good enough. No defeat, too low. All the kids he knew, they'd devolved into gross caricatures of themselves. Kids who'd been funny grew to become ridiculous clowns. Girls who'd been pretty morphed, overnight, into beauty queens.

His folks were so dull. They always forced him to blow up every trouble, crisis-big, disaster-big, before they'd acknowledge it. Every triumph Kevin had to pump up, gigantic, before they'd notice. His parents had driven him to turn his whole life into

285

a cartoon. To his folks, in-between didn't exist. Good-enough didn't exist. He'd become a freak.

Troublemaker still didn't respond. The room was so dark Kevin couldn't tell if he'd fallen asleep. Not that it mattered. Whether or not anyone was listening, Kevin still needed to say what he was saying.

He rambled on. "I figured, for the first time in my life, I'd get straight A's. I'd break the curve . . . ace cunnilingus . . . screw a bunch of girls for extra credit . . ."

Finally, when he didn't know what else to talk about, Kevin ventured, "You see those babies they have out at the gate?" He told about Mindy Taylor-Jackson. He explained about the Porsches. Finally, he blurted out, "One of those babies is mine."

He waited for a reaction. Testing the silence. He hoped Troublemaker would interrupt him and change the subject.

"At least one," continued Kevin. "If you had binoculars or a telescope those babies look just like me." He explained how he'd been with Mindy. They were in love, he said. He'd been heartbroken each time she'd been shipped off to some maternity home to give birth. Now he expected Mindy was missing him. His mom's letters said as much. His mom described how Mindy was racing around like hell on her chromed wire–rimmed wheels. In secret, he and Mindy had decided twenty grand would buy them a new life together.

Troublemaker stared back, dumbfounded. "You're a dad?"

Kevin nodded. His laser hand, dash-dashing, nonstop. He explained about his twins being due in a few months. "That's how come I can't stick around here until I turn eighteen."

Dismissively, Troublemaker chuckled. "I've got that beat, hands down."

Kevin waited. He was simply happy that Troublemaker was awake.

Troublemaker whisper-laughed. A helpless, trapped laugh. "Believe it or not . . . I'm a homo." He scratched his head. "You can see my dilemma." Again, like a list of words instead of a sentence, he said, "And—I'm—A   Girl."

—

According to the Commander, Suede was a lesbian. He still called her "Betsey." He railed, saying she'd sinned in too many ways for God to want her anymore. Her parents had donated her body to the clinic because they'd wanted to redeem her deviant soul. Kevin suspected there was more to the story than that. He suspected some revenge was involved. Even in the dim light of the basement he could see Suede was dimpled, her ears and tongue, nipples and labia, with the holes for piercings no longer in evidence.

The Commander looked down at the table, his yellow eyes filled with pity for something so far from redemption.

According to Troublemaker, she and Suede had lived the steamiest romance since Eleanor Roosevelt and Lorena Hickok. They'd been regulars at the protest party outside the Fag Farm gates. They'd hiked the Pacific Crest Trail. The tattoo on his wrist . . . her wrist . . . Troublemaker's wrist, she explained that it was a Labrys. A double-bladed ax, from Minoan Crete. It represented matriarchal cultures.

After Suede died, Troublemaker had persuaded an older man and woman to pose as her parents and pretend she was their son. With their help, Troublemaker had come here to retrieve the body of her lost lover. Like some quest out of Greek mythology.

The whole project took Kevin Clayton's breath away, it seemed so heroic. In his mind he struggled to retrieve Mindy. But she was like a forgotten joke: something that had once possessed the power to make him instantly and reliably giddy but now escaped him.

———

By the fifth week they'd all but given up hope. Even the laser light had dimmed. Kevin maintained his vigil. Only Troublemaker kept him company. While everyone else slept in their warm beds, Kevin's knees ached from the floor. His arms shook with the cold as he continued to petition the unknown, flashing dash-double-dash-dot-triple-dot, biting his tongue to stay awake. His body exhausted, but his faith unwavering.

As they sat in the dark sending out code, Kevin told Troublemaker how he'd planned to use his twenty thousand dollars. He'd graduate this place and elope with Mindy. They'd drive into the sunset, and find someplace perfect to live. Their first goal was to have those twins they could keep.

When Troublemaker didn't respond, Kevin stopped talking. These nights, just the two of them sitting in the dark, talking, their situation reminded Kevin of something. A school thing. Some book. It was about a runaway kid and an escaped slave in olden times. They were floating down the Mississippi River on a raft. That book took boredom to a whole new level. Everything the slave had said didn't make sense. To Kevin, the slave sounded like an illiterate idiot.

For a laugh, he explained to Troublemaker about his trick with the gerbils. Of all people Troublemaker should laugh.

Troublemaker only stared back at him. One end of her top lip curled in contempt. She shook her head as if to dismiss Kevin's ignorance.

Kevin screwed up his courage. Without meeting Troublemaker's eyes, he asked, "Aren't you afraid of going to Hell?" He kept Morse coding into the unknown. Afloat in that ocean of night.

Troublemaker yawned. "Don't take this the wrong way, okay?" She chuckled grimly. "My idea of Hell would be going to Heaven and being forced to pretend I'm like you for the rest of eternity."

———

Afternoons, they picked through Betsey's insides. Suede's insides. That made it more difficult, at least for Kevin, knowing she used to be somebody real. Almost all her stitches were open at this point. Her carcass looked flattened and more spread out, except for her head. She looked like a tiger-skin rug. Having just the head intact, circled by houseflies, the scene reminded Kevin of another book they had to read for a class. Something about school kids stranded on a desert island after an airplane crash, it was nothing you'd bother to read if you had any choice in the matter. Once they'd been tested on it, the only details Kevin could recall were black flies and a pair of busted eyeglasses. To date, he was the only inmate who knew about Suede and Troublemaker and their star-crossed travails.

Suede was in ruins. Her organs and whatnot, leathery and preserved. The heart and stomach, they were all jumbled together. At the end of this anatomy unit the Commander was going to quiz them. Whoever had been here before, they'd written crib notes on several organs. The liver was a breeze, but someone had used indelible felt-tipped pen to write "spleen" on one slippery chunk. In different handwriting, the word "pancreas" was written on another.

Some unseen hand had scribbled "Raymond Was Here" and a date two months earlier on the anterior wall of Suede's abdominal cavity.

Enigmatically, there were four-digit numbers jotted in hard-to-reach nooks and crannies. The number 4-1-7-9 was on the rear of her bladder. The number 2-8-2-6 was penned behind her heart. Kevin didn't know what they meant, but he noticed Troublemaker repeating each number under her breath.

———

One night, sometime in their sixth week, Kevin's batteries gave out.

Troublemaker didn't hesitate. She shook Brainerd awake and demanded the batteries from his wristwatch. Brainerd asked why, and Troublemaker whisper-yelled, "To get us sprung from here."

They fought the quietest fistfight on human record. Silent and brutal, they slugged and choked one another, wrestling quietly and violently around the floor, their knuckles muffled by their flannel pajamas. Their noses bled without making a sound. Twice, Brainerd's body went limp, and he seemed beaten. Each time, Troublemaker started to unbuckle the wristband of the watch. But both times Brainerd rallied, rose to his stocking feet, and fought her off. The two combatants hammered with elbows and knees. When Troublemaker landed a bloody head-butt to Brainerd, the latter didn't get up.

The victor stripped the watch from his wrist and pried open the back. Her eyes glaring, daring anyone to stop her, she dumped out the batteries as if she were unloading bullets from a revolver. She reloaded the laser pointer and stoically took it back to Kevin at the window. Three nights later Troublemaker shook Pig the Pirate awake and demanded the batteries from his Game Boy. Seeing how Brainerd still had two black eyes, Pig the Pirate gave it up without a fuss.

Everybody told him he was crazy, but Kevin was steadfast. Without pausing in his dot-double-polka-dot-dashing he whisper-lectured them that doing something crazy was better than doing nothing at all. He whisper-preached that taking what seemed like a useless action was better than accepting that they were helpless.

Kevin knelt there on the edge of nothingness, his elbows propped on the sill. He clasped both hands together near his chin. Muttering words under his breath, he sent out his message. It was a coded distress signal to a total stranger who probably didn't even exist. He was trying to make contact with some mysterious somebody whom nobody could see or hear.

After seven weeks of no sleep, Kevin was half dead, but he held his ground. Not a glimmer of a response had come back from the dark. He looked like a fool, but his determination didn't waver. Just before dawn, Kevin slumped to the floor, too tired to stay at his post. Still clutching his laser pointer, his fingers swollen and raw, in crippled frustration he began to whisper-sob.

The sound woke Troublemaker who crept from her warm bed, dragging her blanket. She draped it over the fallen sentry and pried the laser pointer from his stiff hands.

"Tell me what to say," Troublemaker whispered.

"Dot," whispered Kevin. Like an incantation, he recited, "Dash-dash, triple-dot . . ." He whisper-dictated the message, again and again until Troublemaker knew it by heart.

The next night Kevin slept while Troublemaker took up the task. The night after, Jasper relieved Troublemaker. On the third night, Pig the Pirate relieved Jasper. On the fourth night, Tomas woke everybody up with his whisper-screaming . . .

Without a break in his flash-flashing-tap-double-click-dash-dashing, Tomas whispered, "Battle stations!" He whispered, "Calling all cars!" Whisper-yelling, "All hands on deck!"

Those who woke first rousted their fellows. Every bed emptied. Barefoot, they rushed the window.

—

Never taking his eyes off the blinking red light in the distance, Brainerd said something. Nobody heard. Nobody was listening, at least nobody took the bait. "It's like the green light." Brainerd waited, but nobody cared. By now he was just talking to himself, spouting bullshit from some homework assignment.

Somebody brought Kevin a pad and pencil, and he started to jot down each dot . . . dash . . . dippity-dash-ding-dot-dot-dash as it happened. He didn't look at what he was writing, just kept his eyes peeled. His pencil hand twitched, leaving marks across the paper. His fingers moved as if they belong to somebody else.

Whale Jr. watched the pencil marks fill up the paper. "What are they saying?"

Kevin didn't answer.

Tomas leaned his lips close to Pig the Pirate's ear. "They're saying they got AIDS," he whispered.

Pig the Pirate marveled, "Imagine getting AIDS and *not* dying . . ." His voice sounded hushed by the horror of the idea. "For the rest of your life, you couldn't mess around."

Brainerd seconded the idea, saying, "I'd rather die than not screw around."

Everybody mumbled in agreement.

Whale Jr. said, "Don't be stupid." He shook his head, appalled by the general level of ignorance. Everybody looked at him, waiting for his magic answer. Everybody except Kevin who kept watching the light blink.

"Having AIDS doesn't mean you can't fuck," explained Whale Jr. The voice of common sense, he said, "Having AIDS means you can only fuck the girls you hate."

Except for Troublemaker, the others nodded in somber agreement. Relieved. They were amazed how Whale Jr. could see the bright side. His glass would always be half full.

Not wanting to miss a flicker, Kevin didn't blink. His eyes watered with the effort it took to stare. On its own, his hand scribbled gibberish. The point of his pencil whispered across the page.

—

That night, they drew straws. As a sign of good faith, Brainerd advocated that someone among their ranks should show his dick at the window. It had been decided that whoever got the short straw should have to drop his pajama bottoms. To curry favor with the Rock Hudsons.

Troublemaker shook her head in disbelief, clearly panicked about getting the short straw.

Kevin pocketed his straw and waited until everyone except he and Troublemaker had displayed long ones. Kevin's was long, too, so to save Troublemaker from being found out or looking like a coward, he reached into his pocket and snapped his in half. He brought out the half straw.

Troublemaker looked like she'd weep with relief. She mouthed the words *Thank you.*

That was some consolation as Kevin stepped up, onto the windowsill. His thumbs hooked in the waistband of his pajama bottoms, he shoved them down. He swiveled his skinny hips from side to side. The frigid air didn't make him any more impressive.

Nobody said anything. Somebody coughed.

They heard a sound from the hallway outside the ward. Footsteps were coming. Keys jangled.

In a heartbeat, they were all tucked back in their beds. All except for Kevin.

Tomas hissed, "Someone's here!"

Kevin squirmed against the window. He tried to stoop and

pull up his pajama bottoms, but he couldn't. "I'm stuck," he whisper-wailed. "I think my dick's froze!"

The same way a person's tongue will freeze to a cold metal flagpole, the fleshy parts of him were welded to the frosty glass and steel window frame. To struggle tore his skin and threatened to break the window into razor-sharp shards. As the footsteps drew closer, he wept and begged for help. He appealed to their sense of comradeship and loyalty.

Troublemaker goaded the others, shouting, "We don't leave anyone behind!"

When the floor supervisor walked in they were all on their knees around Kevin. Nobody on staff would believe they were just blowing on the glass.

—

Kevin checked and double-checked his translation of the code. It didn't make sense.

Kidney Bean speculated that there existed an underground railroad of homos hiding homos in secret Anne Frank–type attics or in fake haystacks, by day, and smuggling them like illegal aliens, coyote-style, north to Canada at night. It was a long shot, but not out of the question.

The dots and dashes translated to *Catch the midnight balloon.*

Brainerd complained, "Like in Jules Verne or *The Wizard of Oz*?"

Troublemaker nodded, knowingly, and it dawned on Kevin that she wasn't without an exit strategy.

In the past a balloon would occasionally break free from the Rock Hudsons' perpetual party outside the gates. Mylar balloons shaped like little rainbows. Pink triangle-shaped ones trailing a little string of pink ribbon. And sometimes the prevailing winds carried the escaped balloon into the side of their building. It might skid along the sixth-floor windows, bumping against the glass, but eventually the wind carried it away. Even if the Rock Hudsons let loose their entire batch of the balloons it wouldn't have enough lift capacity to carry one person.

Everyone agreed it would be suicide. Kevin flashed to communicate their skepticism. In response the Rock Hudsons dot-double-dashed just one word: *Tomorrow.*

—

That day, Kevin stood close to Troublemaker while the others worked on Suede. Someone had written "Whale Jr. Is A Stud" inside the uterine cavity.

Out of the blue, Troublemaker spat the word "gerbils." She said it so only Kevin could hear. "Could you perpetuate a more-gross stereotype?"

"Sorry," Kevin whispered, skeptical. Embarrassed. He liked Troublemaker too much to start hating her now.

Troublemaker whispered back, "The key to a fertile imagination is filling your mind with bullshit."

Flattered but wary, Kevin whisper-asked, "So you're a lez? Why tell me?"

Troublemaker looked at the chopped-up mess that Suede had become. "Because you told me about your babies, I guess." She looked at the Commander standing to one side. She looked at the sheet of plastic they covered the body with every afternoon when they were done. The plastic was jumbled on the floor. Lowering her voice, Troublemaker said, "Because in every movie I've ever seen the queer is either the chickenshit victim, or she's the psycho super villain. I want you to know that the hero of this story is going to be a dyke."

295

The next night Kevin and his fellow pervs kept watch. It was freezing outside, but they opened the window to see better. Something loomed out of the darkness: a single yellow balloon. "You've got to be kidding," whispered Whale Jr. The balloon butted against the window frame and bounced away. It hovered just beyond reach.

"Hurry," Troublemaker said, "before the wind gets it." Before anyone could stop her, she stepped up onto the sill. Gripping the jamb with one hand she stepped through and stood on the outside ledge, leaning into the void. Hanging there, suspended over nothing, she grabbed at the air. She cried, "I can't get it." Her voice sounded shrill with frustration.

Kevin didn't think. He just acted. He stepped up on the sill and gripped the back of Troublemaker's pajama bottoms with one hand. With his other he grabbed the heaviest thing he could find—Whale Jr. As Troublemaker let go of the building and hung out over certain death Kevin held her. Whale Jr. held Kevin, and everyone else held Whale Jr.

With a wild grab, Troublemaker caught the balloon and her fellow perverts pulled her back to safety so fast that they all fell in a heap. Mashed among them, the balloon popped.

Pig the Pirate contemplated the busted skin of yellow latex and looked as if he might cry. Tomas scowled and asked, "Now what?"

In frustration Kevin grabbed the torn shred of yellow. "Maybe they put a message inside. Or heroin." Brainerd tried to grab it away, but Jasper grabbed at it, also. There was nothing inside. They were all tangled in the balloon's pink ribbon before they noticed it was so long. The ribbon still trailed out the window. It didn't merely droop down the side of the building, it looped off into the darkness in the direction of the gates. It seemed to stretch on forever.

Somewhere in the blackness it was attached to something. Or someone. All of their eyes tried to follow it. Troublemaker was the first to speak. "Don't break it," she said.

Slowly, carefully, they pulled it, taking up the slack. The ribbon gradually went tight.

"Don't let it sag," warned Brainerd, "or it might touch the fence." He meant the high-voltage fence. None of them knew if a ribbon could conduct electricity, but no one wanted to find out.

To Kevin, pulling the ribbon felt like pulling the string that held Suede's skin shut. They pulled, carefully reeling in what felt like an impossible amount of ribbon. It collected on the floor in a heap around them. They pulled until a knot appeared. Beyond the knot there was a thin nylon cord, like a clothesline. They pulled at the cord until another knot connected it to a thick nylon rope. The rope was so long and heavy that it took all of them pulling like a team, like those horses pulling beer on television. Troublemaker dragged a length of the rope into the room and said, "We need to tie this up high." She told Kevin to signal when it was knotted and the Rock Hudsons would pull it taut from their end.

Kevin gaped out the window. To no one in particular he said, "We're supposed to climb down this?"

Jasper shook his head, silently, at the prospect. It was too dangerous. Even if their hands didn't give out the rope might sag and drop them to the attack dogs or the fence.

By then Troublemaker's eyes had already found a thick sewer pipe near the ceiling, on the far side of the room. She was stacking one bed atop another, balancing a chair on them. Climbing the heap, she was hauling the rope up to the pipe. The rope spanned the room, stretching from the ceiling, slanting downward at a slight angle until it disappeared out the window. Looping it and lashing it in knots, she ordered, "Signal them."

They were still wearing pajamas. Lost in the excitement, none felt the cold.

Troublemaker went to her locker and retrieved a belt. She climbed the stack of furniture and looped the leather around the rope. She buckled it to make a hoop. A harness. She put her head and arms through the harness and lifted her feet to test its strength. It held. With her feet suspended above the floor, she bounced a few times. The rope didn't sag or stretch.

Before anyone could stop her, she stepped off the chair. Like a suicide, she hung there for an instant kicking her feet in midair, her head and one arm caught in the belt. The loop slid along the rope. The others stepped aside as it zipped the length of the room. At the window Troublemaker slipped free and nimbly dropped to the floor while the belt jetted away, following the rope into the free world.

Troublemaker got up from the floor and made a big show of slapping the dust from her pajamas. She went to the door. "I'll be back in less than an hour." She punched four numbers into the keypad. Four notes sounded, and the door unlocked. "The code was written on her gallbladder."

Kevin realized that all the codes for all the doors were recorded inside Suede's guts. Her insides served as the collective memory of every boy who'd passed through her. Kevin warned Troublemaker, "You'll never make it out that way. You'll never make it past the front doors." But Troublemaker was gone.

———

Troublemaker wasn't back in an hour. Two hours passed. It was almost sunrise.

Whale Jr. grumbled, "We should untie the rope. You guys are going to wreck my parade."

None of them had so much as gotten out their belts. For a while the Rock Hudsons had signaled from the dark, but even those flashes had tapered off. The sun would be up in half an hour. Brainerd voted that they untie the rope and toss it out. It was Kevin and Tomas in favor of keeping the lifeline. Everyone else, against. They heard a noise in the stairwell.

In another moment four musical notes sounded from the keypad in the hallway. The door creaked open, and there stood Troublemaker. She stooped, something flung over her shoulder. Panting with the effort, she walked into the room. Her burden was wrapped in a dingy plastic sheet. Nobody asked what it was. They could tell from the smell.

Something slipped out of the sheet and flopped onto the floor. It sparkled in the dim light. Everyone studiously ignored it until Troublemaker thrust her chin toward it. "Would one of you pervs pick that up?"

Kevin pulled the sleeve of his pajamas down so that it covered his hand like a mitt. He reached to get whatever had fallen. It was the charm bracelet. His pajamas didn't have any pockets so he knelt and fastened the chain around Troublemaker's ankle.

—

It wasn't lost on Kevin that something was happening, an event that he'd never need to exaggerate. He'd only have to tell the story and people would be impressed. He only needed to not die and he'd have a life worth more than $20,000.

Troublemaker decided to go last. Since she'd carry Suede she'd weigh double. Nobody wanted to go first so Kevin volunteered. He'd take the laser pointer and flash a code if he arrived safe and the coast was clear. He climbed the beds and chair and looped a belt around the rope. The window being open so long, the room was unbelievably cold, but his pajamas were soaked with nervous sweat. He looped his head and shoulders through, but couldn't bear to step off. He kept half remembering some book where kids thought happy junk and flew out a bedroom window. Some fairy-tale bullshit. In London.

At times like this Kevin felt as if he'd lived only through books or television. His best memories were a mash-up of different stories and movies. He was sixteen years old, and he'd wasted his entire life.

At the rate of one thousand dollars a week, every minute counted.

In the next moment the room was blazing with lights, and the building was shrieking with bells. Whale Jr. was standing next to the fire alarm. His hand wrapped around the handle, he was shouting against the bells, "I warned you guys!"

Kevin must've flinched. The chair under his feet shifted and toppled over. Before Kevin could untangle himself from his belt he was already sliding toward the window. Before he was free, he was outside, dangling in the dark, like live bait over invisible attack dogs. The alarm had woken them, and Kevin could hear their barking, their teeth snapping below him. Mindful of the electric fence, he lifted his feet and pulled his knees to his chest. He was sliding through darkness, soaking wet, suspended halfway between where he wanted to escape and a new future he couldn't begin to imagine. Behind him were the bright lights and the blaring noise, before him were the faceless shapes of silent people waiting to arrest his fall. A long howl escaped his lips, and the Stalag 13 dogs howled along with him.

—

Of course they got caught. Only Suede escaped, and that was only because Kevin, Tomas, and Jasper had carried her away. Pig the Pirate and Brainerd dug the hole, and they'd all buried her. So far none of them had confessed the exact location. The Commander had brought in search dogs, but they'd only wandered around tracking circles in the snow. Kevin and his fellow pervs had lugged the body in confusion, crashing through acres of cornfields, crossing and backtracking their own footprints for miles in panic. Wherever Suede's grave was, no one would ever find it.

Troublemaker was another story.

She'd come out the window, last, leaving behind only Whale Jr. Just as they suspected, her weight had made the line sag dangerously. She had hardly cleared the dogs. She could've dropped Suede to save herself, but she didn't.

They were all waiting to catch her. Nobody could see anything until a bright flash lit up the night. A supernova of blue sparks like a giant bug zapper. Troublemaker had *almost* cleared the electric fence. The blast of fireworks exploded as the charm bracelet around her ankle brushed the top wire. Kevin smelled smoke, and when they caught Troublemaker her fingers wouldn't let loose of the looped belt. Her pajamas were smoking, her pajamas and her hair, and they had to beat out the little flames with their bare hands. Kevin could see uniformed figures running around behind the windows of the sixth floor.

Suede's wig was scorched from the electric shock. Between her frizzed hair and her stitches she looked like the bride of some mad scientist's homemade monster. Troublemaker wasn't dead, but she wasn't waking up, either. Her eyes were half closed, the pupils weren't the same size. She looked like the monster.

The Rock Hudsons promised to keep the gates blockaded.

For the first time they would keep people inside rather than out. This would give the boys a head start. Kevin grabbed Suede around the waist. They all grabbed her. They were freezing cold, but now her skin was warm, warmer than alive. It felt good to hold her. And they took off running barefoot through the rows and rows of dead cornstalks.

———

Troublemaker never uttered another word. Days, they propped her among themselves. In the television lounge or the cafeteria, she was always the center of their group. And they told the story about how she'd memorized the security codes written on a dead girl's organs. They regaled each other with accounts of how Troublemaker leaned out above six stories of certain death and caught the yellow balloon. Pig the Pirate recounted how Troublemaker had looked, leaping from that window with a damsel flung over her shoulder. In that way, they spoke her into a legend. They took her out to sit on the basketball court, sunny days. They included her in everything.

They didn't include Whale Jr. Nobody spoke another word to Whale Jr. One day after basketball they came back to the sixth floor to find that he'd piled two beds together and balanced a chair atop them. He'd looped a belt around the pipe where Troublemaker had tied the rope. Whale Jr. had put his neck through the belt and stepped off the chair. He hadn't gone anywhere. Leastwise his body hadn't. His body got the homecoming parade he'd always craved, a long, slow, stately drive down Main Street, but nobody cheered and he wasn't riding in a convertible.

Troublemaker was still with them, but she was no longer Troublemaker. She stared into space, trembling, like she'd sat in an electric chair that had only executed her courage. To preserve her secret, Kevin had to take her to the bathroom. Kevin had to

302

feed her. If the staff of the Fag Farm had discovered her secret identity, they didn't let on. Maybe someone was still paying the bills for her. Maybe they were afraid of an investigation.

The sixth-floor inmates made halfhearted plans for another breakout. Jasper carved a bar of soap into a pistol and painted it black with shoe polish. Kidney Bean sat by the window at night, on the lookout for another balloon. In truth, none of them longed to reenter the outside world.

Kevin didn't see the point, not anymore. Who wanted to return to a world that was so corrupt? Who wanted to be celebrated by such despicable people? He might go back as a hero, but who wanted to be king in a world of assholes? None of the boys wanted to serve as living proof that this bogus system worked. If they went back, now, their natural desire for girls would vindicate people they'd grown to despise. The Commander would be a hero. Confined here, they had the comfort of knowing they'd be a drain. Their families and their communities would be crippled by the cost of warehousing them. Theirs would be a generation on strike.

Kevin sensed that, for the rest of his life, he would be rushing and striving. For now he could relax. It was okay to be trapped here. He didn't need to be in a Porsche driving two hundred miles an hour. It felt great just to sit still. These days Troublemaker didn't seem any more alive than Suede had been, and Kevin resolved to protect her.

He dressed Troublemaker and walked her to the classrooms. In trying to teach Troublemaker physics, Kevin learned it himself. Seldom did Kevin look at the calendar, he was so content. He didn't wish time away, nor did he long to be someplace else. His life was no longer a race into the future.

Something told Kevin that this was good practice. This was how it would feel to be a dad. Thus his idea of happily-ever-after

303

evolved, slowly. For the time being, the irony wasn't lost on him. His parents had sent him here to save his soul. As a prisoner he'd found it. His life, such as it was, was good enough. He didn't need to distort himself into a cartoon freak.

Hovering here above the endless cornfields, this prison had come to feel like a cloister. Heavenly, almost.

———

The same as most afternoons, Kevin sat Troublemaker on the toilet and waited. It was better to be on the safe side after a big lunch. The lavatory was so quiet he could hear the drumming of the basketball on the concrete, outside. Awkward, he stood to one side of the cramped stall, crowded by Troublemaker's hairy knees. Perverse as it sounded the smell of piss had come to fill Kevin's heart with joy. It would mean Troublemaker was doing her business, and the two of them could go.

No one was in earshot as Kevin Clayton made his confession in one-sided dialogues. "The only answer I know is running away." He patted Troublemaker's hair flat where the high voltage had turned it spiky. A black fly landed on his friend's cheek, and Kevin waved it away. "I escaped from my family," he continued. "I could've escaped this place and kept going." He listened for the sound of Troublemaker making water. "Time will rescue us." Troublemaker farted. That was a promising sign. "Time rescues everybody."

Absently, Kevin inspected a snag on the front of the black T-shirt. He poked a finger through to measure the size of the hole. "We'll have to get this mended."

Seated on the toilet, Troublemaker's shoulders were still heaped with muscle, her anatomy piling up around her thick neck. The "Suede" tattoo. Her arms still strained the sleeves of her black T-shirt, but Kevin babied her. "No offense," Kevin offered, "but the problem with homosexuals is they never grow up." In Kevin's opinion, homos never earned the dignity that ultimately won people's respect. Fags never brought the cattle rustlers to justice or slew the dragon with a gleaming sword.

He sighed. He tore off a few squares of toilet paper. Kevin pressed one hand on the back of Troublemaker's bulky shoulder and leaned her forward. Using the paper, Kevin reached down in back of her. When he checked the paper it was spotted with yellow. He dropped the first handful and tore off another wad of paper. This time when he wiped there was piss but something more. The paper gleamed, not white, but iridescent. Kevin knew Vaseline when he saw it. And there was more. Kevin wiped again and the paper collected a cloudy gunk. It was the same murky, viscous spunk they'd found inside Suede.

Whether it was the Commander's work or it came from the floor guard, someone else had discovered that Troublemaker wasn't a boy.

———

That spring, in her latest letter his mom complained that her garden was being destroyed. She was haunted by the ghosts of gerbils she knew Kevin had murdered. Kevin had brought this curse down upon their house. Ghost gerbils appeared at night, she claimed, and ate the strawberries. They decimated the early lettuce. It was a plague of vengeful gerbil spirits that had returned to starve them. The words she wrote, they trembled on the cusp of a truth she could never accept. She clung to the reality she knew: The gerbils were dead, her son was a pervert, the Commander would fix everything.

Rumors filtered from the floor guards that an investigation was pending. A possible lawsuit was in the works. Still, nothing actually got rolling.

Kevin pictured his mom weeping over her swollen, bloody feet. Despite the gossip about investigations, Kevin didn't expect one. Everybody was too invested in this awful system.

Before anything could happen the Commander announced that they would recommence their studies. Betsey was gone. He wasn't happy about that. But the bereft parents of a new girl had donated her physical vessel. She'd been killed in a car accident.

—

It took some time, but every detail would eventually come out in court—their predawn zip down a tightrope in the pitch dark, the way snow had started to fall as they dug Suede's grave with their bare hands. Much later, when the TV cameras would ask him about what happened, Kevin would say that those few weeks had been the happiest of his life. With one hand on the Bible, Kevin would say the impossible. To a judge and jury, he'd say that the nature of happiness is that we only recognize it after the fact. No one would believe him.

Seated beside him would be Troublemaker. Her hair grown out to girl hair. Her eyes vacant. Her belly two trimesters big.

The defense attorney would ask if Kevin had been afraid for his own safety. To that Kevin would answer, No. His worst fear was that true love only existed in retrospect.

In the future, when the prosecuting attorney asked who'd killed the Commander, Kevin would swear under oath, "I did."

When the defense attorney would call Kidney Bean to the witness stand and ask who'd murdered the Commander, Kidney Bean wouldn't hesitate. He'd say, "I did."

The medical examiner would testify that the Commander died from a single deep stab wound to the throat. It was impossible to determine who had administered it. When the guard had arrived at the Therapy Room to collect the boys, he'd found them all splashed with the victim's blood. Dead on the concrete floor was Mr. Peanut in a puddle of gore.

What none of them would say is what drove them. In a world where Troublemaker was hated, Kevin wanted to be hated, too. If the world despised Troublemaker, Kidney Bean only wanted to be despicable. Until the world welcomed Troublemaker, none of them—not Tomas or Jasper, Pig the Pirate or Brainerd—wanted to be accepted. Under oath to tell the truth, the whole truth, and nothing but the truth, one by one, each would say that he'd killed the Commander. As juveniles they'd still go to jail, everyone except for Troublemaker.

———

What none of them said is what really happened. Pig the Pirate would always say that he had the knife. Brainerd would insist that he, himself, had it. And so on, dot-dotting-dash-dippity-spot-spot. One Porsche. Two Porsches. And so forth.

On their last day at the Healing Center an ambulance had arrived at the gates but without any flashing lights or siren. Seeing it, the protesters had stepped aside. The babies the Rock Hudsons cradled, like magic even they'd fallen silent. The new girl was here.

That afternoon, the Commander sent a guard to escort the boys downstairs. Kevin walked alongside Troublemaker, holding her hand to lead her in the right direction. The charm bracelet still rattled around her ankle. The high voltage had fused the clasp. In the concrete hallways, the bracelet sounded terrible. The chain and the little medals clanked like leg irons in a prison movie. Troublemaker was a living, breathing legend, but that's all she was doing.

When they got to the Therapy Room and Kevin saw the shape shrouded by the grimy plastic sheet, his heart filled with dread. It had huge tits. Bigger than any high schooler he'd ever seen except for one. The new girl's belly was a mountain swelling up underneath the sheet. In St. Cloud, Kevin pictured two orphaned Porsches, fresh off the assembly line with no one to take them home. As before, he felt ghosts pulling his hair. He dropped Troublemaker's hand and crossed his fingers.

The Commander held a scalpel. "Our new girl was a reckless driver. She was promiscuous and sunk her beloved family deeply into debt . . ."

Before the Commander lifted the plastic sheet, Kevin knew this story would have no happy ending. The dead thing stretched across the table would have skin coarse and yellowed like the calluses on his palms. There would be no more babies with skin the same flawless pink as the skin under his fingernails. No one was pining for him to come home. It took no real effort to accept this traffic accident. It seemed so horrible but so perfect, and there was a perfect shape to fate. It was as inevitable as the shape of an egg. He couldn't deny it or argue it away. It had the perfection of truth.

"Gentlemen," announced the Commander. "Today will be your final exam."

The Commander cast aside the plastic sheet, and there was Mindy Evelyn Taylor-Jackson. Unlike Suede, she was unmarked. No one had explored her with knives.

She wore a regular, plaid dress Kevin remembered. She'd worn it on their third date, but it hadn't fit this tight. That night Kevin had lost his cherry. Now the Commander called him by name and bid him step forward and undo the buttons, and by reflex he did. They felt the same as the buttons he'd opened the time before. Mindy lay still, holding her breath. They'd both been too afraid to breathe.

The Commander offered him the scalpel and said, "Would you expose the inferior hypogastric plexus."

Kevin shook his head. He wouldn't accept the knife.

The Commander pressed the scalpel on the other boys, but no one would take it. Tomas, Pig the Pirate, Brainerd, and Jasper, they only needed to see Kevin's face to know something was wrong. They held back, wallflowers. A reluctant stag line.

At last, the Commander guided Troublemaker to the table and placed the knife in her hand. The blade gleamed. "Remove the left breast, please."

Troublemaker's eyes appeared as dull and unblinking as Mindy's.

"Don't," Kevin warned. "Or I'll tell everyone your secret."

Nothing showed in Troublemaker's face. Her arm rose, straight forward from the shoulder, like a puppet or a zombie. She lifted the scalpel toward the skin exposed between Mindy's buttons.

Kevin said the only thing left to say. Like a list of words, not like a sentence, he said, "You—Are—A—Queer."

Kevin didn't intend it as a taunt. Anymore, he wasn't sure what the word meant, but he declared it like an affirmation. A reminder that Troublemaker could still be the hero of this story.

■

HOW A JEW SAVED CHRISTMAS

It's a classic. A holiday tale the sales associates still love to tell.

As soon as the decorations start to go up, the new hires beg to hear it. They plead—Oh, please, oh, tell it—until on Christmas Eve, the senior store manager calls the staff together in the break room.

"You understand," the manager starts out, "this actually happened, but it was many, many shopping seasons ago . . ."

Working retail after Thanksgiving has always been the pits. The seasonal music, especially. An endless loop of carols blares from speakers in the ceiling. "After eight hours of hearing those songs," the manager says, knowingly, nodding, "Miley Burke used to wish that Jesus and Bing Crosby had never been born."

Long ago, Miley used to work here, weekdays, in housewares. Weekends, in bed and bath. Sometimes she went to costume jewelry if they needed an extra associate. Otherwise, Miley killed her time in the staff break room because it was the only place she could escape the music.

On the day in question, she got to work a little early. She'd brought a salted nut roll, boxed, and wrapped in shiny paper printed with snowflakes by sweatshop slave laborers in some country where they'd never heard of winter, let alone Christmas.

In block letters, Miley wrote "To Clara" on a Post-it. "From Your Secret Santa." She stuck the Post-it on the wrapped box and tucked it into the cubbyhole assigned to Clara.

"Clara used to work in infant wear," the manager explains, "selling onesies."

After all these years, that same grid of cubbyholes still lines one wall of the staff break room. One cubby per sales associate, with one cubby leftover as the Lost and Found. A long table and chairs take up most of the space. Lining the wall opposite the cubbyholes is a counter with a sink and microwave. The time clock and the time card slots fill another side of the room. The last wall is the door with, standing next to it, the staff refrigerator.

As Miley checked her own cubbyhole, already people were coming in. Punching their time cards. She could see that something was slid all the way to the back of the cubby. A glossy red bow glinted in the dark. She reached toward it and felt something soft. Slippery. Heavy. As she pulled it out, its weight shifted in her hands. A glittery card was Scotch-taped to it. Written on the card in block letters was "To Miley. From Your Secret Santa."

Somebody stepped up next to her. A voice asked, "What'd you get?" A male voice. It was Devon, an associate from Stock Shrinkage Prevention.

Miley held the gift in both hands and said, "I don't know." It was clearly homemade. Something stacked on a flimsy paper plate and covered with red-tinted plastic wrap. The red bow was pasted on top. She peeled back the plastic.

It was brown. Cubes of brown. Dark yellow flecked the brown. It didn't smell good.

More associates had arrived. A line had formed at the time clock. Miley didn't want to sound unkind in case the giver might be among them. She said, "Lucky me!" Peeling off the plastic wrap, she squealed, "It's homemade fudge!"

Devon didn't look impressed. He gave her a pitiful smirk and asked, "You're not going to eat that, are you?"

Devon could be such a dick. The previous year, he'd stolen items from the Lost and Found. A soiled muffler, for example, or a pair of scratched sunglasses. And he'd given them as his Secret Santa gifts. His job consisted of watching monitors all day and expecting people to be dishonest assholes. He said the work was very validating.

The fudge looked clean. Clean enough. The smell came from the dark-yellow flecks suspended in the brown. Miley's best guess was that they were butterscotch chips folded in as the mixture had cooled. She lifted the plate toward Devon, saying, "Help yourself."

His eyelids narrowed to wary slits. Devon twisted his face away and cut his eyes sideways to look at the fudge with suspicion. It wasn't lost on Miley how Devon and people like him, really everyone she knew, would gobble down meat by-product snacks processed on some grimy assembly line by Third World lepers who never bothered to wash their hands.

At the same time, those friends turned up their noses at fudge that had obviously been cooked by someone they saw every day. Miley studied their faces for a twitching lip, a wrinkled nose, any sign that might betray disgust. Deborah declined, asking if it was kosher. LaTrey shook his head, claiming to be borderline diabetic. Taylor, the only guy who worked in the cosmetics area, told her, "Thanks anyway, girlfriend, but that doesn't look worth getting fat over."

There were other people in the room, almost the entire second shift was there. But Miley had started to feel self-conscious about offering fudge that no one wanted. Oscar from the stock room put on a brave face and accepted a piece. So did Barry, one of the cashiers. And Clara. The plate was still full when Miley left it in the middle of the break room table. By the end of the shift, eight and one-half hours later, no one else had touched it.

That afternoon, Deborah found a bottle of perfume from her Secret Santa. Good perfume, better than anything the store sold. So good that Miley suspected that Deborah had bought it for herself.

Sitting out all day at room temperature, uncovered, didn't make the fudge look any more appetizing. Nonetheless, Miley took it home. How rude it would look to dump it into the break room trash can.

Other people got jars of macadamia nuts from their Santas. They got goofy knee socks patterned with reindeer. Deborah wasn't fooling anyone when she found a diamond tennis bracelet in her cubby. Only Deborah liked Deborah that much. It didn't help Miley's peace of mind when Devon sent her a text message. He sent her the link to a Mexican website where you could order tapeworm eggs. They came in an envelope, like an invisible powder, and fat people mixed them into food to lose weight.

Mixed them in food, Miley thought, like the butterscotch chips had been folded in. After the fudge was too cool to kill anything.

Devon sent her the link to a hospital where they X-rayed Halloween candy for free. Devon advised her to keep the leftover fudge just in case someone who'd eaten a piece died.

The next day Miley found a shoebox inside her cubbyhole. Inside the box was a hand-knit cap. Wide stripes of pink alternated with stripes of tangerine orange and black. Hideous, in a word. It reminded her of something old-fashioned. It reminded her of a dunce cap, and when Miley put it on the hat swallowed her head down to her shoulders. Devon was there to say, "Santa must think you have a big 'ol melon head."

That night he showed up at her door and asked if she still had the fudge. He'd brought a microscope and glass slides. Also, a forensics textbook. This was stuff he had to buy for a community college course. As he pulled on latex gloves and used a scalpel to cut razor-thin slices of the fudge, he talked about his most-likely suspects. Deborah, obviously. Jews always got so prickly around Christmas. If you believed half of what you could read on the Internet, Jews spent most of their time poisoning gentiles.

As for LaTrey? LaTrey didn't seem thrilled by white people in general. Third under suspicion was Taylor. Cosmetics department Taylor. He only pretended to not despise girls. Miley being a female, with a female's natural charms, made her a prime candidate for Taylor's ire.

Each year as they retold the story, the store manager explained, "Her Santa was a mystery." Then as now, all the team members would put their names on slips of paper. The papers would go into a hat. Everyone would draw a name and keep it secret. No one knew the identity of anyone's Secret Santa. Worse still, there was no security camera in the break room because sometimes associates were forced to change clothes there.

Devon smelled Miley's fudge and shook his head. It wasn't her imagination, he said. The fudge smelled questionable. Beyond questionable, it smelled like ass. The butterscotch chips were just a ploy to cover up the overall ass-y-ness of the candy. The humiliating knitted hat, he said, was a second salvo meant to publicly degrade her. Devon had watched enough *CSI* television to know about exposing crime scene evidence to fluoroscopic light. He took a fudge sample into the lab at the college. He took another sample to the emergency room and asked to have it X-rayed. When that turned up nothing, he asked for a CAT scan. Miley's health plan didn't cover diagnostic tests on candy so this was costing her a fortune.

It was worth it. The candy was covered in fingerprints. Most of the prints were hers, hers and Devon's, but there were some partials, characterized by more whorls than arcs. A possible signpost, Devon explained, that someone of African heritage had tampered with the candy. Bits of fudge, he cultured in petri dishes. He hadn't ruled out boogers. Or urine. The first thing they taught him in criminology was that people were all deviants.

No one but Devon had seen her unwrap the knitted dunce cap so Miley resealed the package and regifted it. The next day Taylor got a gift certificate to Just For Feet. Somebody else got a stuffed bear that giggled when you squeezed its belly. In Miley's cubby was another wrapped gift. She called Devon before she went anywhere near it. He wore latex gloves and touched the package with bomb squad carefulness. Using only his fingertips, he carried it to Miley's car. After work, after the parking lot was otherwise deserted, they set the wrapped gift on the ground and gingerly picked at the taped seams with a razor blade. The paper came loose, opening like a flower to reveal—something.

In the parking lot floodlights, it looked like a tray of insects. Maggots, specifically. A layer of little worms seemed packed together in a silver-rimmed, rectangular tray.

Devon was first to speak. "It's you."

Miley squatted for a closer look. The December wind across the asphalt was freezing.

Devon pointed with one gloved finger, tracing a shape but not touching the mystery gift. "There's your nose. This here's your mouth."

Miley continued to shake her head, dumbfounded.

Finally, Devon explained, "It's macaroni."

It was. Someone had spent hours, even days, of their free time painting bits of dried elbow macaroni and gluing them together to create a picture. What she'd thought was a tray was the picture frame. Someone had created this mosaic portrait of her.

"Obviously someone who hates you," Devon added.

Macaroni wasn't the most flattering medium, still the picture appeared too ugly to be anything but an intentional insult. It had taken extra effort to make Miley's eyes so small and misaligned. The macaroni meant to be her teeth were crooked and painted yellow. It might as well have been a voodoo doll. Just looking at the portrait made Miley feel cursed.

When Devon spoke again, his voice was resolute. "This is criminal harassment." Cryptically, he announced, "The next move is ours."

It was time to try and flush the guilty party out of hiding, he said. The Secret Santa exchange worked both ways. The next day, Miley wrapped the macaroni picture for regifting.

They were all present, all of the second-shift staff, waiting to punch in. Deborah seemed puzzled to find a large wrapped package in her cubby. Looking around, she said, "Whoever you are, Secret Santa, you shouldn't have." Deborah's voice sounded flat, like she wasn't kidding.

Watching her, Devon leaned close to Miley and whispered, "Get ready." He whispered, "She's going to explode."

The way Deborah lifted the gift, using both hands, and heaved it onto the break room table, it looked heavy. It landed with a solid clunk, like a cinder block. Or a frozen turkey. Written in block letters on the card, it said "Merry Christmas, Shylock. Eat Me!" Inside the wrappings was a canned ham.

At the same time, LaTrey was tearing open an envelope. Inside was a gift certificate to Kentucky Fried Chicken. He looked up, his eyes coolly assessing everyone present. His jaw, clenched.

By then Taylor had found the package in his own cubby. It was hard to overlook. It could've been a baseball bat swaddled in Christmas paper. But it wasn't. It was a beef stick summer sausage, one of the bargain-priced monsters sold alongside cheese logs and smoked jerky at Ye Olde Hickory Barrel in the mall. The card read "To Taylor—Santa's Sure You've Choked Down Bigger Meat Than This!"

Devon was ready. Only the guilty party would know whom to lash out at. Everyone looked either sheepish or bereft. Clara began to sob. Unnoticed, she'd opened the regifted macaroni portrait and held it in trembling hands. She raised her tearful face to look at Miley. Her voice broken with sobs, Clara said, "I know what you're doing. I know what you're doing with the gifts. You're wrecking Christmas!"

All eyes swiveled to focus on Miley.

Miley's response sounded huge. Inflated with indignation, hers was the voice of someone teased and taunted to the brink. "I'm wrecking Christmas? *I'm wrecking Christmas!?*" Her lips quivered with outrage. She lifted a shaky arm, straight out from her shoulder, to indicate Deborah, LaTrey, and Taylor. "I'm trying to *save Christmas*. It's one of them who's sending dirty fudge to people."

In truth, all Devon's testing—for fecal bacteria, for HIV, for semen, chlamydia, and a host of other gonococci infectious agents—had turned up only negative or inconclusive results, but Miley was on a defensive roll. She shouted, "One of them has been harassing me . . . sending me crude, insulting, disgusting . . . crap."

The three suspects looked at each other with new confusion. Everyone in the room looked at the trio with loathing. Miley Burke was redeemed. Hers was the moral high ground. Standing beside her, Devon beamed.

The break room was quiet like it was seldom quiet. It was so quiet they could hear the Christmas carols playing in the store beyond the door. Even Clara had stopped crying. She gazed down on the macaroni mosaic in her hands. "Two weeks," she whispered. She lifted it to show the room. She said, "I didn't mean to harass anyone. I did my best. I knitted the hat you gave back to me. I made the fudge."

People still talk about that moment. Telling the story, the manager always hesitates here. So people can hear the faraway music. The same music now as all those holidays ago. A dead Bing Crosby wails about peace on earth and goodwill to men. Behind him, a choir sings like angels. The manager throws a look at the wall above the microwave, and all eyes follow. There, like a religious icon, the eyes too small and misaligned, the teeth like a mouthful of yellow maggots, it still hangs. All that's left of Miley Burke: that mosaic portrait.

After all these years, the associates still love this tale. The whole shaggy-dog saga. About the fudge and Miley Burke, Devon and the canned ham. It's important to remember every detail and to get them perfect, right up to the last moment.

Because that's the moment Deborah undid her diamond bracelet and handed it to Clara.

■